# The Controversial Jesus

## and the Critics

ARTHUR PATERSON LEE

CLEMENTS PUBLISHING
*Toronto*

The Controversial Jesus and the Critics
Copyright © 2002 by Arthur Paterson Lee

Published 2002 by Clements Publishing
6021 Yonge Street, Box 213, Toronto, Ontario M2M 3W2 Canada
www.clementspublishing.com

*All Rights Reserved. No part of this publication may be reproduced, stored in a retrieval system or transmitted in any form or by any means – electronic, mechanical, photocopy, recording or any other – except for brief quotations in printed reviews, without the prior permission of the author.*

Scriptures are from *The Holy Bible, Revised Standard Version*, copyright 1973, by the Division of Christian Education of the National Council of the Churches of Christ in the United States of America.

National Library of Canada Cataloguing in Publication Data

Lee, Arthur Paterson
    The controversial Jesus and the critics

    Rev. ed.
    Includes index
    Includes bibliographical references.
    ISBN 1-894667-07-7

    1. Jesus Christ—Historicity. I. Title.

BT303.3.L44 2002        232.9'08        C2002-902946-2

*This book is dedicated to all faithful pastors, teachers and students of the Word who are set for the defence of the Gospel in an era of awesome scepticism and abounding misinformation.*

# Contents

*Preface* . . . . . . . . . . . . . . . . . . . . . . . . . . . . . . . . . . . . . . . 7
1. A Profusion of Opinions . . . . . . . . . . . . . . . . . . . . . . . 11
2. Facts of History. . . . . . . . . . . . . . . . . . . . . . . . . . . . . 25
3. The Dead Sea Scrolls. . . . . . . . . . . . . . . . . . . . . . . . . 43
4. The Controversial Jesus . . . . . . . . . . . . . . . . . . . . . . . 81
5. The Founder of the Faith. . . . . . . . . . . . . . . . . . . . . 113
6. The Cross and the Kingdom . . . . . . . . . . . . . . . . . . 139
7. The Grand Affirmation . . . . . . . . . . . . . . . . . . . . . . 169
8. Men, Myths and Morality . . . . . . . . . . . . . . . . . . . . 185
9. The Proof of Experience . . . . . . . . . . . . . . . . . . . . . 203
10. The Controversy Continues. . . . . . . . . . . . . . . . . . . 211
*Postscript*. . . . . . . . . . . . . . . . . . . . . . . . . . . . . . . . . . . 285
*Bibliography* . . . . . . . . . . . . . . . . . . . . . . . . . . . . . . . . 291
*Index* . . . . . . . . . . . . . . . . . . . . . . . . . . . . . . . . . . . . . 303

# Preface

Though J. B. Phillips is probably best remembered for his Living Bible paraphrases of the 1960s, he was also the author of lesser known but significant book entitled *Ring of Truth*, in which he set out to defend the historical accuracy of the Bible. The incident which prompted Phillips to write his *Ring of Truth* was the suicide of an elderly retired clergyman who had watched a series of televised programmes which alleged that the New Testament was no more than "a bundle of myths." It was too much for the old gentleman who was being told that his life's work had been based on a deception. He was also in a state of ill-health and was overcome with depression. He had been a man of conscience and he decided that he just could not live with himself. Phillips' reaction was well expressed: "I do not care a rap what the 'avant garde' scholars say; I very much care what God says and does. I have therefore felt compelled to write this book. It is my testimony to the historicity and reliability of the New Testament."[1]

The wheel has turned full circle and an epidemic of scepticism seems again to be infecting writers, religion editors of our newspapers, film-makers and some television programmes over the past decade and in this new millennium. Certainly an attack is being mounted against today's

Christian pastors on the grounds that they are failing to communicate to their congregations the latest findings of contemporary theology and biblical research. For example, the authors of *The Messianic Legacy* make the allegation that seminarians are well acquainted with the more controversial statements of theologians and historians "*Yet this knowledge has not been passed on to the laity.* In consequence, a gulf has opened between ecclesiastics and their congregations.... The flock receives virtually no historical background from its shepherd—who is believed to be the definitive authority on such matters." [2] They go on to refer to a "conspiracy of silence". [3]

Two of the three writers produced a later book entitled *The Dead Sea Scrolls Deception,* in which they suggested that another ecclesiastical conspiracy had been devised by the Vatican and certain members of the international team which first investigated the Qumran manuscripts—a theory which has since been completely debunked.

My concern is twofold. First, it is time for an honest and eloquent plea on behalf of faithful pastors who are engulfed today by social and moral problems, and who are genuinely seeking to bring comfort, care and spiritual restoration to society's casualties, many of whom are drop-out kids from school and family.

Our traditional moral values of marriage and the family seem so often to be denigrated by secular thinkers who have already rejected the Christian faith as something authentic for today's world. Ethics are being undermined, and criminal behaviour is reaching unsettling proportions. Civilisation, as we have known it, could be breaking apart. The Psalmist had something to say to this kind of situation: "If the foundations are destroyed, what can the righteous do?" (Psalm 11:3). Those who seek to shake the foundations should not complain when the structures collapse around them. Nor should they berate those who exercise themselves in the art of damage control, be they pastors, counsellors, or social workers.

My second, and equally urgent concern is that people in the church pews will be made aware of the often conflicting and contradictory views of scholars, and of the ding-dong battle of intellectuals that goes on behind the scenes in the world of academia. I think it needs to be said that any minister who would use his pulpit merely to demonstrate his agility in theological acrobatics will surely fall short of his mandate

# Preface

to equip his people out of the Word of God to face the realities of life. The ring of truth remains, and the bell of biblical teaching must be tolled loudly in these times of Babel confusion and moral decay.

## Notes

1 Phillips, J.B. *Ring of Truth* New York: Macmillan, 1967, p.9.

2 Baigent, M., Leigh, R., Lincoln, H., *The Messianic Legacy* London: Transworld, 1987, pp22,23, and 33.

3 Ibid., p.23.

or woman in history; 60,000 were written in the nineteenth century alone.[1]

Jesus remains a highly controversial figure, and many of his followers rightly believe that he will remain a contemporary of every age. He himself made the remarkable statement that though heaven and earth would pass away, his words never would (Mark 13:31).

In our sceptical era there are those who derive personal satisfaction by cutting others down to size. This is not always a bad thing, and scrutinizing journalists render a public service by exposing imposters and hypocrites. Mind you, our media often shoots off in other directions by elevating popular performers, sports personalities, politicians, far-out musicians, and even high-flying druggies, many of whom turn out to be notoriously unworthy of the accolades that have been strewn at their feet.

It must be obvious to many book readers that the 'downgrading process' is being vigorously applied these days to the person of Jesus Christ. It is this writer's intention to ascertain whether these revisionist theories have validity, or whether the traditional views of Jesus continue to stand the test of time. It can be said that a reading of some current literature might even suggest a demeaning effort is afoot to diminish the significance of Jesus, and even to discredit the entire Christian faith. Yet we must avoid any unjustified paranoia. We have a reassuring word from three such authors, Michael Baigent, Richard Leigh and Henry Lincoln, who claim:

> And we ourselves will instinctively be perceived as 'anti-Christian', as writers engaged in a fully fledged crusade which pits us, as militant adversaries, against the ecclesiastical establishment—as if we were personally bent on toppling the edifice of Christendom.[2]

They insist that such an expectation on their part would be quite naive. All the same, the theme re-emerges in a later production, authored by Baigent and Leigh, *The Dead Sea Scrolls Deception*, which reads:

> One should not, of course, expect a disclosure of such magnitude as to 'topple the Church'. or anything as apocalyptic as that.... But some people, at any rate, may be prompted to

## A Profusion of Opinions

wonder whether the Church—an institution so demonstrably lax, biased and unreliable in its own scholarship, its own version of history and origins—should necessarily be deemed reliable and authoritative in its approach to such urgent contemporary matters as overpopulation, birth control, the status of women and the celibacy of the clergy.[3]

Some of this criticism, if not all, is likely directed at the Roman Catholic church because of its firmness on such matters as birth control, ordination of women and celibacy of the clergy. Not all Christian bodies subscribe to these positions, but neither should any Christians consider themselves exempt from this attack on 'the church'. The same writers proceed to dismiss the Gospels as unreliable accounts of the life and teachings of Jesus, besides viewing Paul's theology as a corruption of the early Christian faith. In the vocabulary of naval artillery, these are broadsides indeed!

It needs to be stated that their opinions, generally speaking, are not new and have been expressed by others before them. Originality, it has been said, is the art of forgetting where you first heard it; but in fairness to Baigent and Leigh they do offer appropriate acknowledgment of their sources. It is certainly incumbent on all who hold to the traditional view of Jesus and the Scriptures, to respond to contrary arguments in such a way as to truly assess their scholarly value or otherwise. And this we will do.

For the lay reader it must be difficult to sort out which claims to scholarship are truly authentic, as over against those that are either false or flimsy. Quite opposite opinions are being debated these days both in regard to the person of Jesus and in the controversial subject of the Dead Sea Scrolls. A case in point is the claim by the same writers that "an ever increasing phalanx of supporters is gathered around Robert Eisenman, and his cause is being espoused by more and more scholars of influence and prominence"[4] Professor Eisenman occupies the chair of Religious Studies Department at California State University. He has advanced views out of his studies of the Dead Sea Scrolls which elevate the importance of James, the brother of Jesus, whom he considers to have been the 'Teacher of Righteousness' and leader of the

Qumran community. Thus he identifies the early Jewish Christians with the Qumran community, and sees them to be a warlike body bent on extirpating the Romans from their land.

It ought to be pointed out in the early stages of our enquiry that neither the name of Jesus nor that of James appears in the Scrolls. In complete contrast to the tribute given to Dr. Eisenman, as above, an eminent scholar, Dr. Hershel Shanks, founder and editor of *The Biblical Archaeology Review*, states that he does not know "of a single scholar who has expressed agreement in print with Eisenman's scenario."[5] James C. Vanderkam, professor of Old Testament at the University of Notre Dame, adds his comment: "Few, if any, scholars have been convinced by the arguments adduced by Eisenman, Thiering or Teicher,* but the popular press has sometimes given their sensational views widespread coverage."[6] Obviously this kind of situation creates either confusion or distrust in the minds of interested and innocent readers. More than that, it seems to betray the fact that the intensity of much current theological debate is characterised by emotionally charged efforts to win adherents rather than to carefully study and correctly assess the subject matter under discussion.

We will see that major disagreements have occurred in the past forty years relative to the translation, rights of publication and, more recently, in the area of theological interpretation of the Dead Sea Scrolls. Sometimes the professional contentiousness between scholars has been unbelievable. On February 1, 1993, a quarter of a million dollar civil action suit was launched by Elisha Qimron for alleged copyright infringement, and for vindication of injured personal honour. The defendants were Hershel Shanks, Robert Eisenman, James Robinson, and the Biblical Archaeology Society. The issues of the case are well summarised for us in Neil Asher Silberman's book *The Hidden Scrolls*,[7] along with the results which favoured the plaintiff, though not in the amount he had claimed.

---

*Barbara Thiering, of the University of Sydney, identifies Jesus with the 'Wicked Priest' in the Dead Sea Scrolls, while J.L. Teicher, of Cambridge University believes this figure to be the apostle Paul. (See also Chapter 3).

# A Profusion of Opinions

Another example of scholarly dissension are the claims and counter-claims relative to the so-called *Jesus Seminar* which is sponsored by the California-based Westar Institute, a private research and study centre founded by the New Testament scholar, Dr. Robert Funk. It is asserted that "the scholarship represented by the Fellows of the Jesus Seminar is the kind that has come to prevail in all the great universities of the world." [8] Yet another New Testament scholar, Richard B. Hays, reminds us that not one member of the New Testament faculty from Yale, Harvard, Princeton, Duke, University of Chicago, or Union Theological Seminary is involved in the project. Nor has he observed any major scholars from England or the Continent among the leaders of the Jesus Seminar movement.[9] The issue here is whether the actual research conducted by this body is any more trustworthy than the somewhat excessive claims to its own importance. This particular form of research is, to say the least, an over-indulgence in scepticism, and its results may prove to be as unreliable as its guesswork.

The Seminar has produced *The Five Gospels\**, a red-letter edition of the four canonical gospels plus the non-canonical Gospel of Thomas. This work is the product of the Jesus Seminar scholars who followed the technique of a colour code to indicate the likelihood, or otherwise, that Jesus actually spoke the words attributed to him. Thus red would indicate a strong positive, pink for possibly authentic, gray for probably inauthentic, and black for certain rejection. The participants would drop in coloured beads and this would constitute their vote. From this 'opinion poll' taken from among like-minded scholars, it turns out that most of the pages are in black, and the staggering finding of this research is that 82 percent of alleged Jesus' words are judged inauthentic, or not original to him.

Not surprisingly, this publication sent shock waves across the world of New Testament studies, though the turbulence may only reflect the confusion of those who compiled *The Five Gospels*. As the English New Testament scholar, N. T. Wright, has commented, this game of 'de-construction' is "like finding yourself in the middle of a

---

\*Eds. Robert W. Funk & Roy W. Hoover. New York: Poleridge/Macmillan, 1993.

rugby field with five teams and ten balls. There is all kinds of excitement: everybody is tackling everybody, and everyone thinks he's on the winning team."[10] Jacob Neusner, professor of Religious Studies at the University of South Florida, calls the Jesus Seminar "either the greatest scholarly hoax since the Piltdown Man or the utter bankruptcy of New Testament studies—I hope the former."[11] A wise word of caution against pin-ball type of analysis is given by E.P. Sanders and Margaret Davies in their masterly work, *Studying the Synoptic Gospels:* "Thus the student should not think that it is possible to go through the gospels marking Jesus-material in red and redactional material in green, thereby successfully assigning what is left in black to the intermediate church. The categories are seldom so clear that one can say 'this verse is pure Jesus-material, this one is entirely Matthew's composition.'"[12] Conservative scholars hold to the view that there is a necessary continuum between the words spoken by Jesus and the records written by the four evangelists, yet allowing for some latitude on the part of the writers who wanted to ensure that the meaning of his message would be accurately conveyed to their respective audiences. For example, we find that Matthew prefers the phrase *Kingdom of Heaven*, thus avoiding a repetitive mention of God, the sacred name. This custom remains even to the present where a Jew will write G-d even in personal correspondence. Luke, the Gentile, feels no such restraint in his gospel to a Gentile audience and freely writes of the *Kingdom of God*, an expression which would more clearly convey Jesus' message to his readers.

Elucidation, however, is very different from invention, and the Jesus Seminar all too often attributes many of the recorded words of Jesus to other sources without identifying who or what these are. Certainly Matthew, Mark and Luke make no claims of originality to material which in fact often appears in all three gospels. Are we then to suppose that some ghost writer, who chose to remain completely anonymous, was active between the days of Jesus and the compilation of the Gospels? And in doing so are we deliberately implying the inability of Jesus to have said what is recorded of him? This is the kind of untenable extremism to which the Jesus Seminar commits itself. That there was the utmost care on the part of the early church to preserve and faithfully transmit what Jesus really taught is stressed in the words of 1 Timothy 6:3-5:

## A Profusion of Opinions

If any one teaches otherwise and does not agree with the sound words of our Lord Jesus Christ and the teaching which accords with godliness, he is puffed up with conceit, ... and has a morbid craving for controversy, and for disputes about words, which produce envy, dissension, slander and base suspicions (1 Timothy 6:3-5).

That Christ's words are again causing widespread controversy should be of no surprise to us, since after all he was crucified in his day for whatever he had said then. His message was both comforting and provocative; strict in ethical standards—especially of marriage, yet critical of excessive legalism. He was firm but forgiving; was both loved and hated.

For many years, and particularly during the eighteenth and nineteenth centuries, it was the person of Jesus which was the subject of debate. The search was for the actual Jesus of history, as well exemplified in the work of Albert Schweitzer. Since the advent of what is called Form Criticism, however, and later the redactionary method, the focus has moved to a scrutinizing critique of the Scriptures themselves. For a current and comprehensive survey of these textual studies, the reader is referred to *New Testament Criticism & Interpretation*,[13] a work which merits the following statement by I. Howard Marshall, of Aberdeen University:

> This is a remarkably comprehensive overview of current methods of study of the New Testament. This book will do much to help students to see that so-called 'critical methods', freed from unsound presuppositions, can be used to help them to understand the divine message in the New Testament more fully (Book Cover).

This quote brings into focus the *issue of presuppositions*, and correctly infers that many of the results of biblical scholarship will depend on the initial ideas, or mindsets, held by the particular researchers. Back in 1971, in an article *Beyond Criticism in Quest of Literacy*, (*Interpretation 25*, p. 151) Robert Funk himself said that methodology is not an indifferent net. It catches what it intends to catch. We know that a wide net is designed to catch big fish, but it will miss all the small ones. The arbitrariness of this method is self-evident, and particularly in the meticulous area of textual research it must be suspect.

Nor will it be in the least surprising if some theologians who bring a purely rationalistic mindset to their studies will find it difficult or impossible to accommodate any story of a miraculous event in the Gospels. Such, of course, was Rudolf Bultmann who conducted his crusade for the demythologizing' of the Gospels. So extreme did his position become, it had to be assumed by his students that no historical Jesus could be retrieved from our Scriptures. Bultmann himself wrote:

> I do indeed think that we can now know almost nothing concerning the life and personality of Jesus, since the early Christian sources show no interest in either, are moreover fragmentary and often legendary; and other sources about Jesus do not exist [14]

In sharp contrast to this nihilistic pessimism of Bultmann, which was tantamount to declaring an everlasting moratorium on New Testament research, E. P. Sanders, the Dean Ireland's Professor of Exegesis of Holy Scripture at the University of Oxford, wrote in 1985:

> The dominant view today seems to be that we can know pretty well what Jesus was out to accomplish, that we can know a lot about what he said, and that those two things make sense within the world of first century Judaism.[15]

Fortunately, this sane and up-to-date assessment of New Testament research is also supported, with qualification, by the distinguished Semitic scholar, Geza Vermes, who has rejected what he called Rudolf Bultmann's "historical agnosticism."[16] *

Less radical than Bultmann, but more subtle is the school of thought represented by Burton L. Mack (see p. 88), and others of the Jesus Seminar, who will reject whole sections of the Gospels' sayings on the pretext that a non-judgmental Jesus would never have uttered some of the harsh sayings attributed to him. Obviously this kind of

---

*An illuminating work by a former Bultmannian student turned evangelical, Eta Linnemann, is entitled *Historical Criticism of the Bible - Methodology or Ideology?*, published by Baker Bookhouse in 1990.

# A Profusion of Opinions

revisionism leaves us with a Gospel according to one's own personal opinion. Perhaps it is time to post a danger signal, "Beware! Theological Termites at Work."

## ANALYSIS OF AN OPINION
### How you see it depends on where you are coming from!

It has been said that there are as many opinions as there are people in the world. True, and it is one of the distinctives of *homo sapiens*. We have a special capacity to conceptualize our thinking and to communicate our ideas with the greatest of precision. Yet not every opinion is valid. The value of any good opinion rests a great deal on the comprehensive sweep of its subject matter, and the keen perceptiveness of the analyst. It is also true to say that some opinions are more reflective of the person than they are of the subject under discussion. There are subjective elements to be considered even among members of the academic community. Are they entirely exempt from 'chips on their shoulders' or 'axes to grind'? Do they ever bend their data to fit some hidden agenda? And what about religious, political or racial prejudices?

Attitude, too, plays a major part in the forming of our opinions. Wendell Phillips declared that truth is always an absolute, "but opinion is truth filtered through the moods, the blood, the disposition of the spectator."* When the Wright brothers were conducting their elementary aeronautic experiments, many wagged their heads in sceptical unbelief that man would ever fly. Faith, in terms of an optimistic attitude, opens up vistas of possibility. Interestingly, such a definition exists in our New Testament to the effect that faith is the assurance of things hoped for, and the conviction of things not yet seen (Hebrews 11:1).

In the disciplines of science open-mindedness is a must. Otherwise theories once held to be sufficient to explain certain physical phenomena would not be open to revision. In his book entitled *Belief in God in an Age of Science,* John Polkinghorne, an Anglican clergyman, carefully traces the development of our understanding of light from Newton through Christian Huyghens, James Clerk Maxwell, and on to Paul

---
**Idols,* October 4, 1859

Dirac who, in 1927, gave a quantum mechanical account of light. This was suspected by Einstein to be incomplete, and in our time the relationship of matter to anti-matter has produced the principle called the CPT theorem. Polkinghorne comments: "The new wine of chaos theory bursts the mathematical wine skins of continuous function theory. The world is indeed stranger and more exciting than Newton imagined, even at the level of his own splendid achievements" (p. 66).

In contrast, some rationalistic theologians rule out the supernatural by their rejection of miracles, and of such ideas as divine intervention, angelic visitations, prophecy and resurrection. They consider these concepts to be completely unsupported by science, even though the true spirit of science refuses to rush to premature verdicts in areas of uncertainty. Some of us can claim to be intellectually athletic, but are found to be jumping to wrong conclusions. And, we might add, there are those writers who haste to their publishers just to propagate their limited conceptions and misconceptions.

A specific case in point would be Stephen Mitchell's *The Gospel According to Jesus*, in which he admittedly reflects his own psychological history. Thus Jesus' teaching on the Kingdom of God is seen to be simply a feeling like "floating in the womb of the Universe, that we are being taken care of at every moment" (p. 12)—an almost trivial view of a major theme.

Just how flatly contradictory the conclusions of Jesus Seminar critics can be is well illustrated by John Dominic Crossan, on one hand, and Robert Eisenman on another. The former does not question the historicity of Jesus but reduces him to an illiterate peasant-prophet of Galilee, while the latter seriously challenges his very existence, and prefers to regard him and his recorded teaching as the inventive reconstruction of later writers. In between these we can place Marcus Borg who sees Jesus as a "Galilean Hasid", as portrayed by Geza Vermes in *Jesus the Jew*, and Burton Mack who postulates Jesus to have been something akin to a Greek Cynic. To other classical scholars Judaism and Hellenism are irreconcilable opposites, as well attested in the Maccabean Revolt against Antiochus Epiphanes.

Much farther out on left field, as we shall see, Barbara Thiering presents Jesus as a married man, and the father of Mary Magdalene's

# A Profusion of Opinions

children. For her, Jesus was drugged and crucified, not in Jerusalem but at Qumran. Buried in a cave there, another crucified victim, Simon Magus by name, helped him to revive! Timothy Luke Johnson in his *The Real Jesus* appropriately asks what can account for the production of such books, and concludes that both controversy and sheer novelty are good for the publishing business (pp.31,32). At this point we can justifiably respond to the charge cited in our Preface, namely that our Christian congregations are being ill-informed, or even misinformed. Instead we would offer the complaint that our secular public is being subjected to a vast array of incredibly contradictory images of Jesus. Thus the founder of a faith which has impacted the world with a message of integrity, love and compassion, is himself made the plaything of imaginative and enterprising speculators. To the average book browser, when it comes to books on Jesus, he must surely be asking himself, "What's new?" and "So what!"

However, far from relegating the Christian message to well protected archives duly secured by a narrow-minded censorship, we must recognize the challenge of controversy. As the apostle Paul testified in his day, he was set for the defence of the Gospel. It was a righteous cause worth fighting for, and one for which many faithful people have given their lives. The apostle Peter added his own powerful exhortation:

> Now who is there to harm you if you are zealous for what is right? But even if you do suffer for righteousness' sake, you will be blessed. Have no fear of them, nor be troubled, but in your hearts reverence Christ as Lord. *Always be prepared to make a defense to any one who calls you to account for the hope that is in you,* yet do it with gentleness and reverence; and keep your conscience clear (1 Peter 3:13-15).

Opinions, too, need to be judged by their consequences. The person who believes in God will have a cosmological picture of creation and the place of humankind in that environment. He or she will be convinced that there is design and purpose at the various levels of nature, and will be open to the idea of accountability to the Creator. In contrast the atheist, who essentially believes that man is the accidental product of a biological evolutionary process, views humankind as the apex of that movement. As such, man is accountable only to himself and to such systems of law which his fellow human beings have promulgated. Even so, the temptation will be deep within him to play God if he can gain military or economic power, or similar advantage, over his fellows. This is the history of humanity.

In no way dare we imply that religious people are the only good people who do good things. We are painfully aware that hypocrisy can be one of the glaring sins of many churchgoers. Besides, a good humanist may desire the very best for all his fellow humans. However, believing in the survival of the fittest, his definition of the quality of life might be highly selective and dangerously elitist. Such was the diabolical motivation of the Nazis. Opinions in their outworking can be as diverse as life and death.

To bring this discussion back into our context we have to affirm that there are areas of human knowledge and experience which are factual and are not merely matters of opinion. When our history books tell us that World War I began on August 4, 1914, and World War II was declared on September 3, 1939, they are factual and not theoretical. There are thinkers who would like to remove Jesus Christ from the pages of history, while others are persuaded that he is woven inextricably into the very fabric of history and of our humanity. Opinions must always be welcomed, but on the basis of our foregoing discussion it will be recognized that factual evidence must never be diluted, distorted or denied simply to sustain an ill-informed and erroneous idea. A twentieth century secular historian who applies the critical method to his study of the New Testament has nevertheless paid this tribute to the Jesus of history:

> The most potent figure, not only in the history of religion, but in world history as a whole, is Jesus Christ: the maker of one of the few revolutions which have lasted. Millions of men and women for century after century have found his life and teaching overwhelmingly significant and moving (Michael Grant, *Jesus: An Historian's Review of the Gospels*, p. 1).

## Notes

[1] Grant, Michael. *Jesus—An Historian's View of the Gospels.* New York: Scribners, 1977, p. 197.

[2] Baigent, R., Leigh, R., Lincoln, H. *The Messianic Legacy.* London: Transworld, 1987, p. 25.

[3] Baigent, M., and Leigh, R. *The Dead Sea Scrolls Deception* New York: Simon and Schuster, 1991, pp. 234-235.

[4] Shanks, Hershel, ed. *Understanding the Dead Sea Scrolls.* New York: Random, 1992, p.286.

[5] Ibid., p. 286.

[6] Ibid., p. 185.

[7] Silberman, Neil Asher. *The Hidden Scrolls.* New York: Grosset/Putnam, 1994. pp. 246-252.

[8] Hays, Richard B. *The Corrected Jesus.* Review essay in Journal *First Things*, No. 43: May 1994, p. 47. See also Chapter 4, p.83.

[9] Ibid., p. 47

[10] *TIME* article by Richard N. Ostling. January 10, 1994, p.35.

[11] Ibid., p. 35.

[12] Sanders, E. P. and Davies, M. *Studying the Synoptic Gospels.* London: SCM., 1989, p. 190.

[13] Black, D. A. and Dockery, D. S., eds. *New Testament Criticism & Interpretation.* Grand Rapids: Zondervan, 1991.

[14] Bultmann, R. *Jesus.* Berlin, translated by L. P. Smith and E .H. Lantern, *Jesus and the Word.* London: 1958, p. 14.

[15] Sanders, E. P., *Jesus and Judaism.* Philadelphia: 1985, P.2.

[16] Geza Vermes writes in *Jesus the Jew, A Historian's Reading of the Gospels*: "My guarded optimism concerning a possible recovery of the genuine features of Jesus is in sharp contrast with Rudolf Bultmann's historical agnosticism." p. 235.

CHAPTER TWO

# Facts of History

Attempts have been made to treat Jesus as the figment of someone's imagination, a mere invention, a kind of phantom, or the hero in a fairy tale. James Frazer in his classic *The Golden Bough*, affirmed his credo when he wrote "The doubts which have been cast on the historical reality of Jesus are, in my judgment, unworthy of serious attention."[1] Intensely interested in the humanity of Jesus, Albert Schweitzer published *The Quest of the Historical Jesus* in 1906, and throughout our century an incredible sequence of books has tried to piece together the essentials of this Galilean's personality. In his fine book, *What do we know about Jesus?*, Otto Betz declares "no serious scholar has ventured to postulate the non-historicity of Jesus."[2]

It is often asked if there are any non-Christian sources which confirm his place in history, that is besides the four Gospels—a not unreasonable question. There are several, and each of these is highly significant, not only as historical proof but by way of gaining a knowledge of how the early Christians were perceived in terms of their beliefs and behaviour.

Joseph ben Matthias (born 37/38 C.E.), more commonly known as Josephus, was a Jewish aristocrat, politician, soldier, and turncoat in the Jewish War of 66-70 C.E. For his defection to the Romans he was rewarded with a pension and became a courtier of Emperors Vespasian, Titus and Domitian. This is what he writes in his *Jewish Antiquities*, to be found in a portion entitled *Testimonium Flavianum* (Antiquities: Book 18.3.3):

> At this time there appeared Jesus, a wise man. For he was a doer of startling deeds, a teacher of people who received the truth with pleasure. And he gained a following both among many Jews and among many of Greek origin. He was the Messiah. And when Pilate, because of an accusation made by leading men among us, condemned him to the cross, those who had loved him previously did not cease to do so. And up until this very day the tribe of Christians named after him has not died out.

Arguments have persisted over the centuries that this testimony could have been altered by Christians seeking to embellish the historian's mention of Jesus. The statement that he was the Messiah would be a case in point, but a thorough discussion of the subject is given in John P. Meier's outstanding book "A Marginal Jew—rethinking the Historical Jesus."[3] He points out that the phrase "Jesus who is called Messiah" also occurs later in Josephus' *Antiquities:* Book 20.9.1 when he makes a passing reference to the death of James the Just in Jerusalem. Describing the turmoil of those terrible times prior to the fall of Jerusalem to the Romans, Josephus wrote:

> (T)hese things happened to the Jews in requital for James the Righteous, who was a brother of Jesus who is called Messiah, for though he was the most righteous of men, the Jews put him to death.

We can be very sure that here we have the honest reflections of a Jewish historian who had recognized the futility of his people's stubborn opposition to Rome. There is therefore no reason to doubt that he could have written critically of his fellow Jews for their treatment of Jesus, as certainly he did in the case of James and his ignominious death at the instigation of Ananus, the High Priest in Jerusalem (ca. 62 C.E.). Incidentally, the reference to "the tribe" of Christians does not necessarily show disdain of the movement on Josephus' part, but

## Facts of History

it would not have been so phrased by a Christian. Christians were not high on the favours' list of the Caesars at this time nor for many years to come. The statement is Josephus' way of acknowledging their ongoing existence in the empire however the emperors might choose to deal with them. As a historian, Josephus knew that he could not ignore Jesus and his followers. They belonged to the history of his times.

We turn now to the notable Roman historian, Tacitus, who makes clear reference to the Christians who suffered great persecution under the Emperor Nero, and specifically to "Christus" who was put to death by Pontius Pilate. The text reads:

> Consequently, to get rid of the report (that he had given the order to set afire to Rome), Nero fastened the guilt and inflicted the most exquisite tortures on a class hated for their abominations, called Christians by the populace. **Christus, from whom the name had its origin suffered the extreme penalty during the reign of Tiberius at the hands of one of our procurators, Pontius Pilate,** and a deadly superstition, thus checked for the moment, again broke out not only in Judaea, the first source of the evil, but also in the City (Rome), where all things hideous and shameful from every part of the world meet and become popular. Accordingly, an arrest was first made of all who confessed; then, upon their information, an immense multitude was convicted, not so much of the crime of arson, as of hatred of the human race.[4]

Even prior to this, Emperor Claudius, as reported by the later historian Suetonius, had decreed an expulsion of Jews from Rome (ca. 49-51 C.E.), because it was alleged they had "constantly made disturbances at the instigation of Chrestus," an apparent reference to the spread of the Gospel as far as the Roman capital. This event is also mentioned in Acts 18:2.

Another secular source of information is Pliny the Younger's letter to Trajan. He was the governor of the province in 110 C.E. when he received an order from the Emperor Trajan to investigate the beliefs and behaviour of Christians.

Pliny's reply read in part:

(T)hey maintained ... that the amount of their fault or error had been this, that it was their habit on a fixed day to assemble before daylight and recite by turns a form of words to Christ as a god; and that they bound themselves with an oath, not for any crime, but not to commit theft or robbery or adultery, not to break their word, and not to deny deposit when demanded. After this was done, their custom was to depart, and to meet again to take food, but ordinary and harmless food.

And yet another pagan testimony to the person of Jesus comes from the satirist, Lucian of Samosata (ca.115—200 C.E.) who wrote a mocking life of one who had converted to, and then defected from Christianity. It was called "The Passing of Peregrinus." The Christians, he said, were so enamoured with Peregrinus that they revered him as a god "... next after that other, to be sure, whom they still worship, **the man who was crucified in Palestine** because he introduced this new cult into the world."

Much earlier, and well before the end of the first century, two very significant documents came from Jewish sources. These are generally accepted as having reference to Jesus of Nazareth and the Christian communities and, as such, are negative and condemning in their approach to the situation.

1. The Pharisee-dominated Sanhedrin meeting at Jamnia (or Jabney), a town to the east of Jerusalem, formulated the following synagogue prayer, as it is preserved in the version found in the Cairo Genizah.

> For the renegades let there be no hope, and may the arrogant kingdom soon be rooted out in our days, and the *nozrim* and the *minim* perish as in a moment and be blotted out from the book of life and with the righteous may they not be inscribed. Blessed art thou, O Lord, who humblest the arrogant.*[5]

---

*The term *ha-nozrim* is assumed to mean the Nazarenes, i.e. Jewish Christians, whereas *ha-minim* described heretics in general and definitely included Christians. See Donald A. Hagner, *The Jewish Reclamation of Jesus*, pp. 42-45.

2. Rabbi Eliezer is said to have preached a sermon against Jesus based on Numbers 23:19, which reads:

> Balaam looked forth and saw that there was a man, born of a woman who should rise up and seek to make himself God, and to cause the whole world to go astray. Therefore God gave power to the voice of Balaam that all the peoples of the world might hear, and thus he spake, Give heed that ye go not astray after that man; for it is written, God is not man that he should lie. And if he says that he is God he is a liar, and he will deceive and say that he departeth and cometh again at the end. He saith and he shall not perform.[6]

Most fascinatingly, Graham Stanton in his book *Gospel Truth: New Light on Jesus and the Gospels*, provides us with an insight into what he describes as "a fairly widespread rabbinic assessment of Jesus"(128). Here we read in Baraitha Sanh. 43a of the Babylonian Talmud:

> On the eve of Passover Yeshu was hanged. For forty days before the execution took place, a herald went forth and cried, 'He is going forth to be stoned because *he has practised sorcery and enticed and led Israel astray.* Anyone who can say anything let him come forward and plead on his behalf.' But since nothing was brought forward in his favour, he was hanged on the eve of Passover. Ulla retorted: 'Do you suppose that he was one for whom a defence could be made? Was he not a *deceiver,* concerning whom Scripture says (Deuteronomy 13:8), 'Neither shalt thou spare neither shalt thou conceal him?' With Yeshu however, it was different, for he was connected with the government.'

That Jesus and the early church met with incredulity and even fierce opposition is undeniable. The church's claim to his being the long promised Messiah would be hotly disputed by those Jews who had failed to see what they considered to be the essential signs of messiahship. A crucified Messiah, instead of a national hero, was a stumbling block. On the other side, the claim to any kind of a kingship on the part of Jesus would be a matter of ridicule for the Romans, or else, and more likely, a cause of serious concern and drastic action. Humanly speaking, it seemed like a 'no-win' situation (cf. 1 Corinthians 1:23).

This very scenario is clearly portrayed for us in the Acts of the Apostles, which though a canonical book alongside of the four Gospels, is also a work of history and should be respected as such. It is noteworthy that a number of contemporary historians, though not necessarily of Christian persuasion, acknowledge the value of the Acts as a reliable resource. Robin Lane Fox in his book *The Unauthorized Version: Truth and Fiction in the Bible*, pays this compliment: "As for Luke's Gospel, its companion volume, Acts, breaks intermittently into the first person plural during Paul's journeys, and, despite attempts by scholars to deny the obvious, it stands out as the work of a companion of Paul. The two books were written in a more educated Greek style and addressed to an eminent Gentile, Theophilus."[7] Recognition is thus given to the Acts as reliable, with many eye-witnessed events which occurred within the first twenty years following Christ's death and resurrection. Michael Grant, author of *Jesus: An Historian's view of the Gospel*, draws freely from Acts as a source book. Of particular significance is the comment of Baigent and Leigh, who regard the Gospels as historically unreliable, as earlier noted: "But it is Acts, much more than the Gospels, which has hitherto constituted the apparently definitive account of the first years of 'early Christianity'.[8] Certainly Acts would appear to contain much basic information not readily to be found elsewhere."

Quite obviously, in drawing from non-Christian writers, and finding the Acts of the Apostles also to be in the undoubted category of the historical, we know that we are not dealing with a mere mythology. For instance, the outcry against the Christians in Thessalonica, duly recorded in Acts 17:6-7, conforms exactly to attitudes which are described for us in non-Christian writings. It reads: "These men ... have turned the world upside down ... and they are all acting against the decrees of Caesar, saying that there is another king, Jesus." As this record shows, the movement was seen to be causing unacceptable upheaval both in Jewish and Gentile quarters.

Before turning to the Gospels, it needs to be stated that Paul's own letters constitute historically genuine memorabilia of the first half of the first century. Whether or not scholars agree with the theology of the apostle, the existence of these epistles and relevant contents must not be discounted as valuable sources of information. As a matter of interest, a discovery at Delphi in 1905 of an inscription confirms that a Roman proconsul of Achaea named Gallio, was in office after Claudius' twenty sixth acclamation as "imperator", a title originally conferred by soldiers on victorious generals. "This enables us," writes Schuyler Brown, in *The Origins of Christianity—A Historical Introduction to the New Testament*, "to determine the approximate date (50-51 C.E.) of Paul's first visit to Corinth, during which, according to Acts 18:12-17, he was brought before Gallio's tribunal." [9]

## The Witness of the Four Gospels

However, it is when we turn to the four Gospels that we face an avalanche of doubt. Unbelief goes on a rampage, rejecting the miracles, disputing the actual words of Jesus and questioning the resurrection. The assumption of many critics is that the Gospel writers simply created myths about Jesus and the works he did to attract converts to the new faith. Such novel writing, if we are so to view the Gospels, must have been a hazardous occupation and not one which was likely to reward the ingenious writers with a Pulitzer prize, but, more likely, with prison or death. It must be kept in mind that in contrast to some of the later fanciful Gnostic writings, the four Gospels are faithful to the teaching of Jesus as one who was preaching a kingdom—a concept potentially offensive to the Romans. Nor did these authors produce works which they thought would be *midrashic* or regarded at the time as either fictional or only parabolic.

It is remarkable indeed that recognition can be extended by some scholars to the Acts of the Apostles as true history, but not to the third Gospel which was written by the same person. So much for their logic and claim to impartial scholarship! The essential continuity between these two books is alluded to by Michael Grant: "Nor is it a coincidence that the author of Luke's Gospel is generally considered to have written Acts as well: it all seemed to him the same story, so that he projects the later period into the earlier one." [10]

This statement on a first reading would seem to be affirmative of both books, but the suggestion is that Luke's account of Jesus, his person and his ministry, was really coloured by the later events in the life of the early church. Other critics have adopted the view that each of the Gospel writers had become subject to Pauline influence, which made much more of Jesus of Nazareth than he ever claimed to be. Such discussion, of course, shifts the issue from facts to the realm of the interpretive and the dialectical. Arguments of this kind, as we shall see, can become circular and interminable, but let it suffice now to show that Luke is not in any way conscious of having 'cooked' either of his books. Let's read his honest and humble prologues to his Gospel and to his history of the early church, viz. the Acts of the Apostles:

> Inasmuch as many have undertaken to compile a narrative of the things which have been accomplished among us, just as they were delivered to us by those who from the beginning were eye-witnesses and ministers of the word, it seemed good to me also, having followed all things closely for some time past, to write an orderly account for you, most excellent Theophilus, that you may know the truth concerning the things of which you have been informed (Luke 1:1-4).

> In the first book, O Theophilus, I have dealt with all that Jesus began to do and teach, until the day when he was taken up after he had given commandment through the Holy Spirit to the apostles whom he had chosen. To them he presented himself alive after his passion by many proofs, appearing to them forty days, and speaking of the kingdom of God (Acts 1:1-3).

Luke makes no claim to supernatural inspiration but writes as a good editor who acknowledges his indebtedness to other sources. These he has carefully examined, and goes on to assure his reader of his own personal acquaintance with the sequence of events.

It has to be said that the patent arbitrariness of some contemporary scholars who accept the Acts but reject Luke's Gospel, simply pits their competence and integrity against that of Luke, who was chronologically close to the events. It boils down to whether the Gospel writers or their critics are more deserving of our trust. Whatever else, the case for the historicity of the life, teaching and crucifixion of Jesus is well established, and we have every reason to trust the Gospel writers to tell us the whole story as far as that is possible. Of course, as John wrote in the fourth Gospel, "But there are also many other things which Jesus did; were every one of them to be written, I suppose that the world itself could not contain the books that would be written" (21:25).

## The Dating of the Gospels

This is another area of controversy, for if it can be demonstrated that the biographies of Jesus were written long, long after his days on earth, then their accuracy may be more easily contested.

After all, with the passage of time memory can fade, especially in details. Yet, in our own generation evidence against war criminals is considered valid forty years after the Nazi Holocaust. The brutalities of those years in the forties cannot be erased from the minds of the survivors, nor the names and characteristics of those persons who executed such appalling atrocities in the concentration camps.

In the case of the Gospels, however, it is generally believed (even as Luke himself indicated, as above), that earlier proto-documents existed, which had recorded the sayings of Jesus. These could have been in circulation within twenty years of the events. Scholars speak freely of 'Q' (German 'Quelle', or source), an assumed document from which the Gospel writers draw some of their information. Of course there is material which is entirely unique to Matthew and other portions which are peculiar to Luke, while it is evident that both of these also derived material from Mark. This last point serves to prove an earlier date for Mark.

Newspaper readers, unacquainted with these intricacies, are often subjected to one-sided editorials. In 1992 Culver Nelson, adjunct professor at the Pacific School of Religion and a prominent member of the Jesus Seminar, was quoted in the Toronto Star as follows: "The oldest extant scrap of any Gospel is a tiny fragment of the Gospel of John that can be dated to about 125 C.E.—almost 100 years after Jesus' death."[11] Later in the same newspaper (December 21, 1995), a columnist by the name of Frank Jones insisted that the Gospels were all written "at least 100 years after the birth of Jesus." That the fourth Gospel was a late production is not contested here, but in neither of the above articles was there even mention of the general concensus among reliable scholars that the original writings of many of our gospel materials occurred between 60 and 85 C.E., or even sooner. It is most likely that Mark composed his work before the Neronian persecution of Christians in the mid '60s.* Mark is said to have been Peter's companion on the apostle's missionary tours, committing to writing what he had heard from Peter's sermons, or oral testimony.[12]

It is generally accepted that the gospels of Matthew and Luke (and certainly John) were composed after the fall of Jerusalem in 70 C.E., but a verse in Mark 13:14 strongly suggests a date well prior to this when in fact the Temple remained in place. Even Dr. Paula Fredriksen, the William Goodwin Aurelio Professor of Scripture at Boston University's Department of Religion, who leans towards later dating of the Gospels, agrees that this Markan reference to "the desolating sacrilege set up where it ought not to be" i.e. in the Temple, or the holy place, might in fact be describing the blasphemous act of Caligula placing a statue of himself in 40-41 C.E.[13] The further warning to those "who are in Judaea" (present tense), that they should flee to the mountains, would also indicate that Jerusalem had not yet fallen at the time of the writing of this Gospel (See Mark 13:14-18).

The collective facts really do postulate an early date for the composition of the second Gospel, yet Fredriksen states her position that Mark was "a Gentile, of the second Christian generation", and thus presumably removed from both the actual life of Jesus and the beginnings of the early church.[14] The name of John Mark does appear in Acts of the Apostles, at chapter 12, where his mother's home in Jerusalem was an important meeting place for Peter and the early Christians. Mark himself accompanied Paul and Barnabas on one of their missionary journeys, and over whom they actually had a serious dispute (Acts 15:38-39).

It must be noted that Fredriksen's thesis maintains that over the years 33-70 C.E. and later, the Jesus of history had become the Christ of faith, a metamorphosis induced by a developing church, and that Mark's Gospel was composed to fit that situation. "He (Mark) is not a

---

*The abrupt and inexplicable ending of Mark's gospel at 16:8, with an edited reconstruction of the events which followed the discovery of the empty tomb (vs.9-20), could have been due to the outburst of the great persecution. Tradition places the deaths of Peter and Paul at this time.

# Facts of History

historian in either the ancient or the modern sense; nor does his *spare sketch* of Jesus' career pretend to be a full picture of his life."[15] In the same paragraph she goes on to say that Mark "does offer a story, set in the past, whose *ostensible* subject is the earthly Jesus" (my italics in both cases). There are times when one is made to wonder if theological presuppositions are allowed to take precedence over actual historical data.

John Shelby Spong similarly stresses late dates for the Gospels, and strongly argues that the accounts in the Gospels of the empty tomb (in Mark), the earthquake and the angel (in Matthew), Peter's viewing of the linen clothes (in Luke), and Jesus' confrontation with doubting Thomas and Simon Peter at the lake (in John), are simply creations of the post-70 C.E. church. Such stories, he alleges, may have been concocted to impress the new generation of Christians. Most of this post-resurrection material he views as midrashic or legendary. Yet well before the writing of the Gospels, Paul had given solid witness to the resurrection of Jesus and his many appearances (1 Corinthians 15:5-7). This was pivotal to the apostle who insisted that if Christ had not risen then the faith was in vain (15:17). Without the resurrection there would have been no church. Nor was the resurrection of Jesus a mere theological afterthought of the later church; it was indeed the catalyst which moved the early church into action. The serious inadequacies of Bishop Spong's etherealized view of the resurrection, and his own mistaken concept of *midrash* will be fully explored in Chapter Seven.

In wrapping up our assessment of Dr. Frederiksen's thesis, there is little to support her assumption that the preaching of Jesus as the Christ represented a gradual transition both in time and thought from the early disciples' experience of Jesus. As in the case of the resurrection, the title of Christ as applied to Jesus was current in the earliest stages of the church's development. It was included in Peter's sermon on the day of Pentecost (Acts 2:14-36), and certainly it was standard in the earliest of Paul's epistles. There is absolutely no justification for postponing the origin of these central facets of the Gospel to sometime in the '70s.

In finalizing our argument in favour of Mark as a contemporary of the apostles, likely to have written his Gospel between the time of Caligula and Nero, and well before the fall of Jerusalem, we must refer the reader also to a strange but likely editorial comment in Mark's Gospel at 14:51:

> And there followed him (Jesus) a certain young man, having a linen cloth wrapped around his naked body; and the young men laid hold on him; and he left the linen cloth, and fled from them naked.

This verse has no theological value, unless possibly this person had hoped to be baptized by Jesus before his betrayal and arrest. That the statement is in fact auto-biographical of Mark himself has been suggested by eminent scholars like William Barclay and James S. Stewart. Barclay comments that neither Matthew nor Luke picks this up, and that "the most probable answer is that the young man was Mark himself, and that this is his way of saying, 'I was there,' without mentioning his own name at all." Barclay additionally speculates that the Last Supper may well have been celebrated in John Mark's mother's home.[16] Too young to be a disciple, Mark's curiosity may have propelled him to the scene of arrest.

In striking contrast to the meticulous attempts to establish the precise dating of the Gospels, and to ascertain how close or distant they are to the actual earthly life-span of Jesus, it might be mentioned that Arrian, the historian, who recorded the exploits of Alexander the Great (died 323 B.C.E.) did so around 130 C.E., or more than four hundred years later! Yet the major outlines of Alexander's career are not doubted. Tiberias was emperor at the time of Jesus' crucifixion, but whose major historical sources were Tacitus about 110 C.E., Suetonius about 120, and Dio Cassius about 220. [17]

Our New Testament Scriptures have been subjected to extraordinary scrutiny, sometimes unfairly and far beyond what many secular works have had to endure. C.L. Blomberg writes in *The Dictionary of Jesus and the Gospels:* "Notwithstanding all of the evidence in favor of the general trustworthiness of the Gospels, many critics find little they can confidently endorse because they adopt a skeptical stance on the issue of the burden of proof. That is to say, they assume that each portion of the Gospels is suspect, and reverse that verdict only when overwhelming

# Facts of History

evidence points to historical reliability. But this method inverts standard procedures of historical investigation; it applies more rigorous criteria to the biblical material than students of ancient history ever apply elsewhere."[18] When it comes to research of the documents of the faith, it seems that there is a predilection to doubt on the part of some scholars. Yet in terms of extant ancient manuscripts there are 5,400 such New Testament pieces "by far the broadest textual basis for any body of ancient writing." So writes Rhea Schoenthal in *Time* magazine of January 23, 1995 (p.47).

## The Fourth Gospel

This Gospel is characteristically different from Matthew, Mark and Luke. It preserves for us lengthy accounts of intimate conversations and prayer times of Jesus with his disciples. It is very much a close-up of the Master. There is no reason to doubt the declaration at the end of this work that the fourth Gospel was composed by "the disciple whom Jesus loved". This is attested to by a community of writers, since we read in the plural "This is the disciple who is bearing witness to these things, and who has written these things; *and we know that his testimony is true*" (21:24) John, as is commonly acknowledged, did not become a victim of the earlier martyrdoms under Nero and others, but lived to a ripe old age, residing in Ephesus. We know that he was banished to the Isle of Patmos during the reign of another of the persecuting emperors, Domitian (81-96 CE).[19]

For a long time it was considered scholastically correct to view this Gospel as a strongly Hellenized version of the story of Jesus, with such Greek thought patterns as Logos—the Word, light and darkness, and by its deifying of Jesus. It was felt that its advanced Christology resulted from the thinking of the church late in the first century, possibly in the 90s.

In this case, we need not be concerned about a late date, though it is interesting to note Bishop J.A.T. Robinson's change of mind in favour of a date as early as pre-70 C.E. [20] What is essential here, is whether the author was in fact an eye witness. Was he indeed one of the three 'inner circle' disciples, Peter, James and John? If this is so, we should not be surprised when we find statements by Jesus which are not recorded in the Synoptic Gospels, e.g. the significant "I am" portions.* Yet it is precisely at this level that redaction critics will attack the fourth Gospel and suggest that some of the 'far-out' statements of Jesus are merely the imaginative reconstruction of John himself, or whoever wrote this gospel. Perhaps this situation was anticipated by John when he reminded his readers that Jesus had promised the Holy Spirit who would bring to the remembrance of his listeners those things that he had shared with his company of disciples. (14:26).

The basic question must be: Does the Fourth Gospel have real historical value? The following attestations come from eminent scholars. Irving Zeitlin who recognizes the Jewishness of Jesus comments on John 5:17ff. where Jesus claims his equality with God: "One should not dismiss this as a later Christological insertion. The author of John's Gospel seems to be stating a fact here; and scholars are increasingly turning away from the older assumption that where Jesus' biography is concerned, nothing reliable can be learned from the Fourth Gospel."[21] James H. Charlesworth offers this comment: "It is unwise to continue to brand the Gospel of John as only a theological work devoid of historical facts. John may well preserve reliable historical information on Jesus' actions in the Temple."[22] A. M. Hunter, who had disputed the authorship of John, nevertheless conceded that the book is definitely a Palestinian document, and adds, "To put the matter in one sentence, the Scrolls have established its essential Jewishness....The trend of recent studies has been to make the Evangelist's links with Palestine much stronger than many of us have allowed."[23] Again we observe the tendency of the theological pendulum to swing from one position to another.

John's acquaintance with Jewish customs and Palestinian practices is recognized by two other authors, one a Christian and the other an agnostic. The first of these is Kevin Quast, who writes: "There are

---

*Matthew had his equivalent record of Jesus' self-proclamation sayings, e.g. "Come to me, all who labour . . . Take my yoke upon you and learn from me; for I am gentle and lowly in heart, and you will find rest for your souls." Cf. also 10:40. Hints of the divinity of Jesus are not confined to John's Gospel.

striking theological and terminological affinities between the Gospel of John and the Dead Sea Scrolls of the Qumran sect.... The Fourth Gospel, then has a fundamentally Palestinian Jewish origin, though it is evident that its final form is directed toward a Greek readership removed from Palestine."[24] The second is A. N. Wilson, writer of the controversial book *Jesus*. "Like the other three Gospels in the New Testament, the Fourth Gospel presents us with a number of historical statements which appear to be verifiable by means of modern historical analysis."[25] Thus "in the Fourth Gospels' account of the Feeding of the Five Thousand, for example, we find that the fish eaten at that miraculous meal is not *ichthus*, the normal Greek word for fish, and used by the other evangelists, but *opsarion*"—the term most likely to be used by the Galilean fishermen themselves.*[26]

An important quote comes from a classical scholar, R. H. Lightfoot, who stressed that John "plants the roots of his gospel most firmly in history and historical facts ... There can be no doubt that the evangelist believed himself to be giving the true interpretation not only of the Christian revelation, but of the historical Lord Himself."[27]

Finally, a historical tribute to John comes to us via Irenaeus, born around 115 C.E. He testified to having heard Polycarp (the martyred Bishop of Smyrna, 110-117), telling his friends what he had heard from John of Jesus' own words, his miracles and his teachings: "I listened to this then, carefully, copying it down, not on paper, but in my heart. And I repeat it constantly in genuine form by the grace of God" [28] In God's providence, one of Jesus' own very close disciples had lived on towards the end of the first century. Apart from anything else, John represented a precious source of verification of whatever had been written about Jesus, or was being written at the time.

It is important for us to remember that the early church enjoyed several tributaries of information—Matthew and Mark, Luke as the author both of the Gospel which bears his name, and of the Acts of the

---

\* Wilson draws this from J.A.T. Robinson's *The Priority of John* (1985), p.117. For a critical evaluation of A. N. Wilson's book *Jesus*, see N. T. Wright's *Who was Jesus?* Grand Rapids: Eerdmans, 1993.

Apostles; John's Gospel and what we call the Pauline, Petrine and Johannine traditions in the epistles, besides James, Jude and the writer to the Hebrews. This will be helpful not only to demonstrate the historicity of our faith, planted and rooted in Jewish, Greek and Roman cultures, but attesting also to the commonality of the early church's beliefs. These are the things, writes Luke, which "are most surely believed among us." (Acts 1:1 KJV).

## Notes

[1] Frazer, James. *The Golden Bough*, vol. ix. London: Macmillan, 1913, p.412n.

[2] Betz, Otto. *What do we know about Jesus?* E.T. London: SCM, 1968, p.9.

[3] Meier, John P. *A Marginal Jew: rethinking the Historical Jesus.* New York: Doubleday, 1991, pp. 56-88.

[4] Tacitus. *Annals* xi.44

[5] From the so-called Eighteen Benedictions (Shemoneh Esreh). According to Berakoth 28b Rabban Gamaliel II requested this addition although it was opposed by Samuel the Lesser.

[6] This and other unfavourable Jewish references to Jesus are candidly provided in J. Klausner's study *Jesus of Nazareth: His Life, Times and Teaching.* E.T. by H. Danby, 1925; reprinted, Boston: Beacon, 1964.

[7] Fox, Robin Lane. *The Unauthorised Version: Truth and Fiction in the Bible.* New York: Knopf, 1992, p. 129.

[8] Baigent, M., and Leigh, R. *The Dead Sea Scrolls Deception.* New York: Simon and Schuster, 1991, p. 175.

[9] Brown, Schuyler. *The Origins of Christianity: A Historical Introduction to the New Testament.* Oxford: University Press, 1984, p.26.

[10] Grant, Michael. *Jesus: An Historian's Review of the Gospels.* New York: Scribners, 1977, p.202.

[11] *The Toronto Star,* January 4, 1992, p. J9.

[12] The Papias testimony as recorded in Eusebius' *Ecclesiastical History* III, 39.15 It has been suggested that the abrupt end to Mark's Gospel was

due to the outbreak of Nero's persecution. For this discussion see William Barclay: *The Gospel of Mark* in The Daily Study Bible, Toronto: G. R. Welch, 1975, p.5

13 Fredriksen, Paula. *From Jesus to Christ.* New Haven: Yale, 1988, pp. 78, 80, 185.

14 Ibid., p.177.

15 Ibid., p.178.

16 Barclay, William. *The Gospel of Mark* in The Daily Study Bible. Toronto: G. R. Welch, 1975, pp. 347-348.

17 Barnett, P. *Is the New Testament Reliable?* Downers Grove, Ill., p. 41

18 Blomberg, C. L. *The Dictionary of Jesus and the Gospels,* eds ... Joel B. Green, Scot McKnight. Downers Grove, Ill.: InterVarsity Press, 1992, p.297.

19 Eusebius. *Ecclesiastical History,* 3.23.

20 Robinson, J. A. T. *The Priority of John.* London: SCM., 1976, p.308. Here Robinson refers to F.L. Cribbs' view that the Fourth Gospel may well have been composed by a cultured Jew of Judaea against a Palestinian background of the '50s or early '60s C.E.

21 Zeitlin, Irving, M. *Jesus and Judaism of His Time.* Cambridge: Polity, 1988, p.61.

22 Charlesworth, James H. *Jesus Within Judaism.* New York: Doubleday, 1988, p. 118.

23 Hunter, A .M. *The Expository Times,* LXXXI, 1959—60. pp. 166, 222.

24 Quast, Kevin. *Reading the Gospel of John.* New York: Paulist Press, 1991, p.4.

25 Wilson, A. N. *Jesus.* London: Harper Collins, 1993, p. 49.

26 Ibid., p.59.

27 *Saint John and the Synoptic Gospels* (1938), cited in R. M. Lightfoot, *St. John's Gospel.* Oxford: Clarendon Press, 1956, pp. 4-5, 30.

28 Eusebius. *Ecclesiastical History,* v.20

CHAPTER THREE

# The Dead Sea Scrolls
*Living Issue or Dead End?*

Of great significance to Jewish and Christian scholars alike was the discovery in 1947 of scrolls found by a Bedouin shepherd in a cave of the Wadi Qumran. Thereafter searches were conducted in ten other caves and on various sites in the Dead Sea and Jericho areas. Over eight hundred manuscripts, some only fragments or even scraps, have been categorized as biblical texts and non-biblical texts. Every book of the Hebrew Bible is represented, except the book of Esther, while the non-biblical literature includes hymns and psalms, commentaries, wisdom literature, legal texts, a letter, pseudepigrapha, and a designation of hidden treasure.

It was indeed an exciting discovery which scholars recognized would provide us with valuable details of the intertestamental period of Jewish history. With the disastrous fall of Jerusalem in 70 C.E., the destruction of the Temple and the loss of relics and scrolls, etc., Judaism had suffered a serious though temporary break in its historical continuity. Coincidentally, this was also the very time that the Christian faith had arisen in Judaea, rapidly spreading throughout the Mediterranean world. An almost fanatical expectation developed as to what the Scrolls would reveal about Jesus and the origins of

Christianity. The big question was whether the New Testament accounts would be confirmed or discredited. Would twentieth century Christianity be faced with an embarrassing denial of what it had believed so long about its first century roots? Would these Scrolls favour the traditionalists or the sceptics?

The Dead Sea Scrolls are thought to have been written between 250 B.C.E. and 68 C.E.* Professor Godfrey R. Driver, of Oxford, believed it possible that the scrolls were deposited there between this time frame and the rebellion of Simeon bar Kokhba (132-135 C.E.), a view which is at variance with the concensus of most other scholars. Coins found on the site can be dated from between 135 B.C.E. to 136 C.E. with the greater number around 103-76 B.C.E. and between 6 and 41 C.E.

The origin of the Qumran community is thought to go back to the times of the Hasmonean dynasty which, thanks to the Maccabean revolt against Antiochus IV Epiphanes (175-163 B.C.E.), sought to rid Judaea of the Hellenistic influence. Antiochus had terminated the succession of the Zadokite priesthood, opening the office of the chief priest to the highest bidder. The Hasmonean line of Jewish kings, consisting of Judas Maccabeus and his brothers Jonathan and Simon did not restore the priesthood to the Zadokites, but instead Jonathan usurped the priestly position to himself, followed likewise by Simon. When on a visit to Jericho, Simon and his two sons, Judas and Mattathias, were assassinated by Ptolemy, son of Abubos, while the three were drunk. This happened in February, 134 B.C.E. and Frank Moore Cross, of Harvard, believes that these events "comport well with certain historical allusions found in the so-called List of Testimonia from Cave 4 at Qumran."[1] One of the Testimonia (the fourth) refers to a 'Cursed One', predicted in Joshua 6:26 which describes the death of an elder and a younger son as the price to be paid by the man who seeks to rebuild Jericho. Such an event had indeed taken place in the ninth century B.C., when one by the name of Hiel also lost two sons (1 Kings 16:34), but the Qumran sect chose this particular text, once fulfilled, and reapplied it to its own time.

Many attempts are being made to identify the strange figure of

---

*Carbon 14 tests were applied to confirm the estimated time frames.

## The Dead Sea Scrolls

the Scrolls called 'the wicked priest'. Cross significantly adds: "I have not dealt, of course, with a large number of texts relating to the Wicked Priest and his relations with the Righteous Teacher and the exiled community (Qumran). Most fit equally well with Jonathan or Simon, or indeed with a number of other priests. In this era one cannot complain of a shortage of wicked priests." The great unpopularity of the Hasmonean king-high priest combination can be judged from the booing, hissing and pelting that Alexander Janneus received from pilgrims as he tried to officiate at the ceremonies of the Festival of Tabernacles. The Qumran community had nothing but disdain for what it must have regarded as a pretentious priesthood, and it looked forward to a restored and purified Temple worship.

Other interpretations of the Scrolls and their mystery figures, the 'Teacher of Righteousness', the 'Wicked Priest' and 'The Liar' will be considered later in this chapter, and it will become obvious just how much scholars are at variance. The plain fact of the matter is that all three figures are entirely anonymous in the Scrolls. It is the custom of the scroll writers to freely name kings, priests and prophets of the Old Testament, e.g. David, Solomon, Aaron, Kohath, Amram, Uzziah, Abiathar, Jehoniah and Simeon, but the names of John the Baptist, Jesus, his disciples, or James the Just, brother of Jesus, do not appear anywhere. Quite obviously some of the Scrolls are of a cryptic nature, but it is acknowledged that one of the characteristics of the earliest Judaean Christians was their free use of the name of Jesus. Indeed it was their custom to exchange the greeting "Peace unto you from God and our Lord Jesus Christ" so much so that the Sages began to encourage their Jewish people to use the name of Adonai (Lord), or even Yahweh, in any corresponding greeting, though such had been previously avoided.* The reverent and constant use of the name of Jesus in the Gospels and in the Acts of the Apostles is self evident.

In a cursory reading of the index of Robert Eisenman and Michael Wise's *The Dead Sea Scrolls Uncovered* it might be noted that the name of Jesus occurs fifteen times. The writers, of course, are referring to teachings

---

*See Solomon Zeitlin, *The Rise and Fall of the Judaean State*, Vol. 3, p. 359. Cf. N.T. James 1:1; 2:1.

in the Scrolls which might bear some similarity to the words of Jesus or *vice versa*. On page 180, for example, the authors remind us of Jesus remonstrating with the Pharisees that they would rescue a sheep on the sabbath, yet they would object to a man being healed. There is such a reference in the Scrolls, but the author of *A Pleasing Fragrance* (Halakah A) took the different view that the sabbath was so holy that no animal in difficulty should be rescued.[2] This quote, however, does not serve to establish a connection between Jesus and the Scrolls, but rather the opposite.

Eisenman and Wise believe that the frequent occurrence of the Hebrew word *Yesha* "salvation" in the scrolls is, as they put it, *underrated*, and they proceed to suggest that the Gospel writers may well have personified it (pp. 243-244) and hence the name of Jesus. Naturally the topic of salvation, as such, appears in many books of the Old Testament as it does in the Qumran Scroll 4Q416/418 entitled *The Children of Salvation* and *The Mystery of Existence*. Neil Asher Silberman, however, picks up on Eisenman's idea and writes: "Now as any of the Jews for Jesus can tell you, the Hebrew name of Jesus is usually rendered as *Yeshua*. The implication here—implicit and unspoken—was that Jesus was merely an abstract theme that was later given a specific earthly incarnation by Paul and his followers."[3]

If this play on words is an attempt either to read the name of Jesus into the Scrolls, or else to suggest that as a derivation of the word for salvation it was conveniently coined by Paul as a proper name, we must loudly protest. The fact is that the name of Jesus (Gk. *Iesous*) had been used as early as the second century B.C.E. by the translators of the Septuagint as the Greek equivalent of the Hebrew word for the Old Testament Joshua (*Yehoshua*, "Yahweh, my salvation" or "Yahweh is deliverance"). Josephus observed the same practice, and in his *Antiquities* and *War of the Jews* he makes mention of several persons by the name of Jesus.\* Similarly in the New Testament itself, as at Acts 7:45 and Hebrews 4:8, the name *Iesous* is selected as the Greek equivalent for Joshua. The simple point is that the name Jesus was already in current use, and in no way did it need to be invented (see below). All this strongly indicates that Jesus of Nazareth was never a member of Qumran and cannot be found in the Scrolls. Any arguments to the contrary, as above, are as untrustworthy as they are ingenious. Similarly the charge that Jesus was nothing more than an idea or a legend must receive the same verdict.

**Suspicions and Serious Charges.**
The delays in having the Scrolls made available became the catalyst for a crusade of criticism against the early translators. Edmund Wilson, author of *The Scrolls from the Dead Sea* (1955), John Allegro at that time a doctoral student under Professor G. R. Driver, and the eminent Semitic scholar, Dr. Geza Vermes, all censured the international team which had been appointed to unravel, examine and translate the Scrolls. More time passed, years in fact, and even those scholars who recognized the time consuming intricacies of translating ancient manuscripts lost patience with the International Team. In the summer of 1989 Hershel Shanks scoffed at the setting of a proposed accelerated timetable for the Team by the Israel Department of Antiquities, and wrote in the *The Biblical Archaeological Review* "They will never do it because they cannot do it. They have failed utterly and completely. The time for equivocation, explanation, and apology has passed."5

Long before this outburst, it had been felt that the team, under the leadership of Father Roland de Vaux, of the Ecole Biblique, who had been in on the earliest excavations, was dominated by Vatican influence. Long delays in the publication of the Scrolls, or some of them, helped to create a justifiable paranoia among scholars in general. Michael

---

*Josephus records several persons as having the name of Jesus, including one Jewish high priest, and a well known robber of the time. Indeed he relates how another Jesus, son of Ananias, was questioned by both Roman and Jewish authorities in 62 C.E., then beaten and released because he was said to be mad.4 **The shorter version of Yehoshua, i.e. Yeshua, (LXX Gk. Iesous) was also in early use among the Jews themselves:** see 1 Chronicles 24:11 and Ezra 2:36. Consult *A Hebrew & English Lexicon of the Old Testament* by Francis Brown with the co-operation of S .R. Driver and Charles A. Briggs. Oxford: Clarendon Press, 1907, reprinted 1966, p.221; also *A Greek-English Lexicon of the New Testament and Other Early Christian Literature* by William F. Arndt and F. Wilbur Gingrich, The University of Chicago Press (Fourth Revised & Augmented Edition), 1952, p. 374

Baigent and Richard Leigh, in their highly provocative book *The Dead Sea Scrolls Deception* (1991), could withhold no longer and charged that there had been a deliberate Vatican conspiracy to suppress vital information, most probably of a kind that could revolutionize our understanding of the origins of Christianity. They suggested that de Vaux was very likely aware of the fact that he might be handling "the spiritual and religious equivalent of dynamite—something that might just conceivably demolish the entire edifice of Christian teaching and belief." [6]

However, the highly informative and responsible work, *Understanding the Dead Sea Scrolls,* which combined the research of more than a dozen notable scholars, Jewish and Christian—Catholic and Protestant, was published the following year, In an important chapter (22, pages 275-290), Hershel Shanks, the presiding editor, positively dismissed the idea of a Vatican conspiracy as "hogwash", and proceeded to remind his readers of a previous scandal when John Allegro's *The Sacred Mushroom and the Cross* had to be denounced by fourteen prominent British scholars as grievously irresponsible.

As early as 1955 Millar Burrows, of Yale, wrote:

> There is no danger, however, that our understanding of the New Testament will be so revolutionized by the Dead Sea Scrolls as to require a revision of any basic article of Christian faith. All scholars who have worked on the texts will agree that this has not happened and will not happen. [7]

James C. Vanderkam, writing in *Understanding the Dead Sea Scrolls*, adds: "As matters developed, this viewpoint has largely set the general framework within which the relationship between Qumran and Christianity is still understood today."[8]

## Why All the Fuss?

We may well ask how reactions among academics could be of the proportions of a volcanic eruption, where molten lava can destroy a long standing town or village, sending ash across the sky to darken even the sunlight. It seems that there was a strong predisposition on the part of some thinkers to becloud, or even to bedevil, the beginnings of the Christian faith. John Allegro, it may be recalled, had alleged a purely

## The Dead Sea Scrolls

inventive making up of the story of Jesus and his resurrection. This he attributed to the use of a hallucinating drug, psilocybin, the active ingredient in hallucinogenic mushrooms. Allegro made no secret of his bias against the Christian faith. That he himself committed scholastic suicide is admitted by most colleagues in the field. Yet, as we are about to consider some of more recent discussions around the Dead Sea Scrolls, we might be tempted to think that other writers on the subject have also embarked on some fanciful flights of the imagination.

Barbara Thiering, of the University of Sydney, has claimed in her research of the Scrolls that John the Baptist is the Teacher of Righteousness while Jesus is the Wicked Priest. In her book, *Jesus and the Riddle of the Dead Sea Scrolls*, she goes on to spell out her theory that Jesus did not perform miracles, did not die on the cross but was revived by his disciples, and died of natural causes decades later just outside of Rome, survived by a widow (Mary Magdalene) and three children. She derives her extraordinary idea from a solitary and silly Gnostic reference to Jesus being asked by his disciples why he kissed Mary Magdalene on the mouth. The piece is known to have been written by some romanticist more than a century after the time of Jesus, and without any connection to the Scrolls (see my page 104).

With respect to Thiering, though many may feel reluctant to accord such a doubtful writer, her identifying the Teacher of Righteousness with John the Baptist is a view shared by the reliable scholar Otto Betz. Thiering's naming of Jesus, however, as the Wicked Priest will be considered unacceptable, and by some even heretical and blasphemous. Yet her reason for this opinion is that she contrasts John the Baptist with Jesus, the one whom she sees teaching a very different religion and "one of tolerance, love and compassion, concepts alien to the stroppy Essenes."9

J. L. Teicher, of Cambridge University, identifies the apostle Paul as the Wicked Priest, while Robert Eisenman, whose position is generally adopted by Baigent and Leigh, declares James, the brother of Jesus, to be the Teacher of Righteousness and the apostle Paul to be the Liar.

If, as Eisenman maintains, the Teacher of Righteousness is none other than James the brother of Jesus, three clarifications are essential. (1) Why does the historian Josephus, as already noted, feel it necessary to identify James as the brother of Jesus, if Jesus is less significant than

James? (2) If James believed Jesus to be the Messiah, why isn't the name of Jesus contained somewhere in those portions of the Scrolls which hint at a Messiah, and in fact two messiahs—one Davidic and one Aaronic? This would be particularly important if, as Eisenman further indicates, there is an obscure reference in the Scrolls to the possibility of a dying messiah.[10] (3) Has Professor Eisenman taken into account the profoundly reverent way James relates himself to Jesus in his own New Testament letter which reads: "James, a servant of God and of the Lord Jesus Christ" (1:1), and in the following paragraph:

> My brethren, show no partiality as you hold **the faith of our Lord Jesus Christ, the Lord of glory** (or, our glorious Lord Jesus Christ, NRSV). For if a man with gold rings and in fine clothing comes into your assembly, and a poor man in shabby clothing also come in, and you pay attention (only) to the one who wears the fine clothing ... have you not made distinctions among yourselves, and become judges with evil thoughts? (James 1:1; 2:1-4).

Not surprisingly, the two references to Jesus here have been questioned as possible later interpolations, but the textual evidence is overwhelmingly in favour of their early authenticity. Besides, the context in the second case is very natural. James, not unlike Paul in his letter to the Philippians (2:1-11), is calling his people to humility, mercy and non-discrimination on the basis of the one who descended from his glory to share our humanity.

James Adamson, a Cambridge scholar, writing in the The International Commentary of the New Testament, *The Epistle of James*; (Grand Rapids, Eerdmans, 1976), deals with the accuracy of the text and adds the helpful interpretive comment: "Do not try to combine faith in Christ with worship of social status" (p. 102).

## Are the Scrolls pre-Christian, Christian or non-Christian?

Assuming that the writing of the various scrolls took place between 250 B.C.E. and 68 C.E., many of these writings are unquestionably pre-Christian. But since a considerable body of the Scrolls consists of copies of Old Testament Scriptures, along with commentaries, there are bound to be resemblances to those New Testament passages which also draw from Old Testament prophetic and messianic teachings. Major differences in thought, theology and practice, however, outweigh the similarities; and these compel the verdict that the Scrolls are essentially Jewish. Norman Golb writes: "... the Dead Sea Scrolls are the remnants, miraculously recovered, of a hoard of spiritual treasures of the Jewish people of Second Commonwealth times. They are the heritage of the Palestinian Jews of that time as a whole." [11] Similarly Lawrence B. Schiffman's *Reclaiming the Dead Sea Scrolls* is a call for "a new hermeneutic in which Judaism is the issue at stake, not Christianity."[12] Nevertheless, a comparison of the Scrolls with early Christian thought and practice is still in order.

## a. Similarities

1. Of great interest to us as Christians is the occurrence in the Scrolls of such expressions as 'righteousness of God', 'works of the law', the 'church of God' and 'Sons of Light'. Joseph Fitzmyer, of Catholic University of America in Washington, D.C., has identified these parallels between the Scrolls and Paul's epistles. There is much use in the Scrolls of the contrasts between light and darkness, as there is both in the Pauline and Johannine writings of the New Testament[13] At one time it was thought that both Paul and John had been unduly influenced by hellenistic thought and vocabulary, but here we see the use of such terms by an essentially Jewish community. Peter's confession of faith which reads. "You are the Christ, the Son of the living God", followed by the promise, "I will build my church" (Matthew 16:16-18), were regarded by some scholars to have been later additions, and theologically quite un-Jewish in character. Word usage in the Scrolls is compelling a revision of those opinions which placed the origin of the Gospels in a Graeco-Roman milieu and late in the first century. This change is of great importance.

2. One of the most recently translated scrolls 4Q246 describes a coming figure who will be 'the King of the people of God'. "He will be called [son of the Gr]eat God ... He will be called the son of God; they will call him son of the Most High ... Like the shooting stars that you saw, thus will be their Kingdom ... His Kingdom will be an Eternal

Kingdom" [14] This translation is offered by Robert Eisenman (in co-operation with Michael Wise), who had earlier forecast that the unfolding of the still untranslated scrolls could be of sensational value. Indeed it is, for we have here the use of terminology within a Jewish sect which believed that a king would arise bearing a divine title. Just as the Book of Daniel had introduced the phrase *Son of Man* in the messianic sense, so it might be claimed that the Scrolls advanced the further concept of *Son of God*. Eisenman notes that Luke, in recording the words of the angel Gabriel, assigns the title *Son of the Most High* to the Christ child (1:32).

John Fitzmeyer links the Son of God with the line of David (cf. Psalm 2:7), but J. T. Milik and David Flusser prefer to identify the *Son of God* figure in the Scroll as an evil ruler who will demand worship as a deity. Any Jewish scholar will tell you that the title Messiah did not imply divinity. Cyrus of Persia is described as God's anointed in Isaiah 45:1. In the trial of Jesus, where Caiaphas put to him the two-fold question, "Are you the Christ, the son of the Blessed One?", it has been suggested that Jesus' claim to being the Messiah would not have invoked the charge of blasphemy, but the claim to being the Son of God did so. The sole point to be made here is that the phrase *Son of God* was already in circulation among the Jews, and probably was a matter of controversy.

That there was an intense messianic anticipation among the members of the Qumran community is self-evident, as well as elsewhere in Judaea, about the time of Jesus' advent. This of itself, however, would not mean that the Qumran community and the early church were at all identical.

3. Notable similarities do exist between the Scrolls and the Gospels. These include the phrases "the poor in spirit" and "turning the other cheek". Some students might think that such parallels rob Jesus' words of their uniqueness. On the contrary, these similarities serve to further establish the historical realities of Jesus and his times. Nor did Jesus avoid quotations from the Old Testament, believing, as he did, that many Scriptures were bearing witness to him. A beautiful example of how Jesus honored the Torah, yet proceeded to go beyond its requirements, was his encounter with the lawyer who asked what was the first and greatest commandment. To this Jesus answered out of the

Jewish Shema in Deuteronomy chapter six. His reply was in keeping with the Law, but, as we well know, his ethic further demanded that we should love not only God and our neighbour (extending the latter to include the despised Samaritan), but ought to include our enemy. This would be in keeping with our Lord's persistent emphasis on universal reconciliation. Interestingly, the intertestamental Ben Sira (Ecclesiasticus), fragments of which were found at Masada, counselled "Forgive your *neighbor* the hurt he has done you...." (28.2), but the calling down of God's wrath on the Gentiles, as the Sons of Darkness, characterized all too many of the Qumran materials.

4. A very important meal ritual of the Qumran community reveals a closeness to the Last Supper celebration instituted by Jesus on the night of his betrayal by Judas. The Manual of Discipline reads "And when the table has been prepared for eating, and the new wine for drinking, the Priest shall be the first to stretch out his hand to bless the first-fruits of the bread and new wine." (6:4-6). This text also mentions a "pure meal" that only those who have passed through a year-long probationary period were permitted to eat, nor were they allowed to partake of the "drink of the congregation" until a second year had passed (6:16-21). In this Qumran meal, however, two messiahs, one Aaronic and the other Davidic, are said to preside, and this seems to conflict with the eschatological expectation of only one Messiah as alluded to in Fragment 4Q521, which reads:

> [ ... The Hea]vens and the earth will obey His Messiah, [ ... and all th]at is in them. He will not turn aside from the Commandments of the Holy Ones.... For the Lord will visit the Pious Ones (Hassidim) and the Righteous (Zaddikim) will He call by name. Over the Meek will His Spirit hover, and the Faithful will he restore by His power. He shall glorify the Pious Ones (Hassidim) on the Throne of the Eternal Kingdom. He shall release the captives, make the blind see, raise up the downtrodden (Eisenman/Wise p.29).

It must be noted that these descriptions of God's Messiah are futuristic, thus corresponding to numerous similar passages in the Old Testament. As over against the New Testament meal, there is no hint of the Qumran meal being symbolic of an already sacrificed Messiah, nor is there any mention of atonement and forgiveness in the same context. These are fundamental differences. The Christian meal, however, is both messianic and futuristic since it is to be observed "until Christ comes" (1 Corinthians 11:26). One should not dismiss the possibility that this Qumran meal, acted out regularly by the sect, presented a prototype ritual in advance of what later became the Christian communion. This, however, does not mean that the Qumran people as a community had become followers of Jesus, or at the time of writing had even heard of him.

5. They also engaged in regular baptisms for purification. Again it has to be said that this resemblance to the Christian practice did not make it the same, any more than John's baptism which, in the New Testament, is recognized as but a prelude to baptism in the name of Jesus along with the promise of the Holy Spirit.* The repetitiveness of the Qumran baptism would in fact distinguish it from both John's baptism and that of Jesus. Adolf von Harnack once said of the Essenes that they never managed to get out of the bathtub day or night.[15] Judging by the extensive water fonts in Qumran the same could be said of Dead Sea community, whether or not it consisted of Essenes. It is altogether obvious that the Qumran community stressed personal cleansing and outer purity as of great importance, in rather striking contrast to Jesus' condemnation of the Pharisees for their over-concern about the cleansing of the outside of the cup (Matthew 23:25-26).

6. Another similarity between the Qumran community and the

---

*Mention is made of the Holy Spirit in the Scrolls and it has been argued that this is a further identification between Qumran and the Church. However, the Holy Spirit was no stranger to Judaism of the O.T. Indeed the 'pouring out' of the Spirit is predicted in Joel 3:1-5. It is interesting to note from our Gospels that John's baptism of repentance was recognized as preparatory to a baptism of the Holy Spirit, later to come with the advent of the Messiah. (Matthew 3:11; Mark 1:8; Luke 3:16; and John 1:31-33. Cf. Acts 19: 3-7) See further discussion of the subject in Chapter 10, pp. 261-264.

early Church is deserving of mention. This is the surrender of personal property to the community. The Manual of Discipline indicates that a novice will not "have any share of the property of the Congregation" (6:17), but when he has completed a full year within the group, and wishes to remain, "his property and earnings shall be handed over to the Bursar of the Congregation who shall register it to his account [but] shall not spend it for the Congregation" (6:19-20). However, after an additional year of probation it was stipulated that "his property shall be merged" with the community's possessions (6:22). Although much less stringent, Acts 2:44-47 describes the members of the early Church as holding all things in common, having sold their possessions and goods to distribute to the needs of others. Whether the Qumran practice was closer to a kind of cult-type collectivism, than to the voluntary self-sacrifice to which church members were exhorted, must be left to the consideration of the reader.

## The Case for a Crucified Messiah

7. When Eisenman and Wise finally obtained many of the then as-yet-unpublished scrolls, they announced to the world in late 1991 that they had found a fragment (4Q285) which described the foretelling of a "Branch of David" Messiah who would suffer wounds or piercings and be put to death.[16] This, said Eisenman, would prove that the Qumran community was operating in the same scriptural and messianic framework as early Christianity. Such a discovery, of course, would be no threat to the Christian position which recognizes such passages as Isaiah 53, the Suffering Servant, and Zechariah 12:10, the latter of which reads:

> And I will pour out on the house of David and the inhabitants of Jerusalem a spirit of compassion and supplication, so that, when they look on him whom they have pierced, they shall mourn for him, as one mourns for an only child, and weep bitterly over him, as one weeps over a first-born.

No doubt Eisenman viewed this find, which consisted of a tiny, six-line fragment and not much bigger than a special issue postage stamp, as a confirming seal on his theory that the Qumran community was in fact the beginning of the early church. Difficulties arose, however, when Professor Geza Vermes, who was already in possession of the fragment, arranged a consultation in Oxford with a body of twenty Qumran scholars. Their concensus was that the phrase (with the word *hmytw* transliterated on line 4) should read: "the Prince of the Congregation killed him"- presumably an enemy, rather than that he himself was killed. In whichever case the context is clearly that of a death in battle.

Certainly the prevailing idea of the Messiah where it occurs in the Scrolls, is one of the triumphant conqueror who leads Israel to a final victory over her enemies. This was the kind of military deliverer that all Judaea was surely hoping for in the dreadful days of the 66-70 C.E. Jewish War against the Romans, but this was not the New Testament concept of an atoning sacrifice, as we shall see along the way. Robert Eisenman has since pulled back from his earlier attempt to identify the 4Q285 fragment with the crucifixion of Jesus. It should give us real concern when an opinion has been dogmatically stated, then enthusiastically released to leading newspapers, only to be retracted soon afterwards. It is said that Robert Eisenman attributed this 'mis-identification' to his colleague Michael Wise.*

## The Concept of Resurrection

Both these scholars, later joined by James Tabor, further scrutinized the Fragment 4Q521, and noted the astonishing resemblance to the words of Jesus when he responded to John the Baptist's question, "Are you he who is to come, or shall we look for another?" (Matthew 11:5; Luke 7:19ff):

> Go and tell John what you have seen and heard: the blind receive their sight, the lame walk, lepers are cleansed, and the deaf hear, the dead are raised up, the poor have good news preached to them.

---

*For an informative summary of the various positions held by current scholars relative to the *Messianic, Son of God, Crucifixion and Resurrection* portions in the Scrolls (4Q175, 4Q246, 4Q252, 4Q285, 4Q375 and 4Q521) see *Solving the Mysteries of the Dead Sea Scrolls* by Edward M. Cook; Grand Rapids: Zondervan, 1994, pp. 152-181.

Again to quote from Fragment 4Q521, a revised translation:

> He releases the captives, opens the eyes of the blind, lifts up ... he will heal the slain, and will resurrect the dead, and will announce good news to the humble....

Intriguing as this verse is, it cannot be taken as solid proof that Jesus and his followers had been been members of the Qumran community any more than for us to claim that Jesus lived in the days of Isaiah simply because he quoted from the same prophet when he entered the synagogue in Nazareth.

> The Spirit of the Lord is upon me, because he has anointed me to preach good news to the poor, he has sent me to proclaim release to the captives and recovering of sight to the blind, to set at liberty those who are oppressed, to proclaim the acceptable year of the Lord (Luke 4:18-19).

It is unquestionable, however, that a concept was coming into focus which truly characterised the story of Jesus, namely that of resurrection. Of course, while the Sadducees, as over against the Pharisees, rejected the idea, the teaching is clear in the Book of Daniel which tells us that "many who sleep in the dust of the earth shall awake, some to everlasting life, and some to shame and everlasting contempt" (12:2). Both in Daniel and in this Dead Sea Scroll text the tense is future, whereas for Jesus the bringing of persons back from the dead was a present reality as in the cases of the daughter of Jairus, the son of the widow of Nain, and Lazarus of Bethany, all of which were but a prelude to his own victory over death. This was the miracle, *per se,* that gave birth to the Church. Words, phrases and titles, such as we have here in 4Q521, were in circulation in Jewish circles before the times of Jesus, and it is not without significance that in the Scrolls these messianic-type descriptions are not linked to any given *named* leader, priest or prophet. In striking contrast, the early church never concealed the name of Jesus, but was indeed prepared to face martyrdom for the honour of that name. Christians believe that concepts which were already forming in Jewish minds were made concrete with the coming of *the* Son of God, even Jesus.

## b. Differences

Was the Qumran community really identical with the early Church—in fact one and the same—as Eisenman and some others are insisting? The full implications of this theory will occupy our attention later, but a definitive examination of the beliefs and practices of the Qumran people will enable us at this stage to determine several basic differences. Initially we must recognize that the origins of Qumran definitely preceded the times of Jesus, and that a substantial portion of their writings would have occupied a longer time slot than the short period of history contemporary with Jesus and the fall of Jerusalem (30-70 C.E.).

In considering the following contrasts between the Scrolls and Christian doctrines of the early church, one must ask if they are substantial enough to suggest a mutual exclusiveness of the two movements in terms of their respective destinies. It is the view of this writer that such is the case, and that the Qumran community, by its own radical preparations for war against the Romans had in fact pre-determined its own destruction. That the two entitities, Judaism and the Christian faith, had much in common—the Old Testament Scriptures, messianic expectations and similar eschatologies, is not in dispute, but in their respective interpretations and outworking of these beliefs there were major divergences.

In our own times we have witnessed the phenomena of cults which so often seem to bear the hallmarks of Christian authenticity, quoting the Bible and having the strictest of rules, with an attitude of militancy toward the outside world, yet sadly self-destroying. These have not enjoyed the approval of the main body of Christians. They are seen to be the very opposite of the ethos of the Church and totally catastrophic in their consequences. Such debacles as Jimmy Jones and his Jonestown and David Koresh in Waco, Texas, are successful only in turning people away from the true biblical faith and from Christian love. Is it possible that Qumran, like suicidal Masada, was of this ilk? Can we say that in every religion there lies the fanatical fringe, and did the Zealots fall into this category? Or would they be better classified as the terrorist element in a society which longed for emancipation from the Roman subjugators? The basic question to face is whether the Qumran community was in fact the early church, as proposed by Dr. Robert Eisenman.

It is for the reader to weigh the evidences, *pro* and *con*.

## 1. A Militant Nationalism

The War Scroll, as its title suggests, is a manual for military strategy, troop formations, manoevres and action in battle. There are precise details of weaponry. What is most scary, however, is the delineation of the enemies, described as Sons of Darkness, and including Edom, Moab, the sons of Ammon, the children of Seth, Philistia and the Kittim of Asshur. Their fate will be in the form of tortured screams and hacked bodies. Silberman is convinced that the Qumran community believed the great pending battle was to be the turning point in the history of all humankind. They visualized the downfall of Rome and the conquest of territories far to the east of Israel. They anticipated a tremendous conflagration at which time the Protector Angel of Israel, Michael, (as already portrayed in the book of Daniel), would bring with him the hosts of heaven to achieve the final victory.

Michael Grant writes: "At a time when Judaism, under imperialistic oppression, was as nationalistic as it had ever been before, the Qumran community, for example, left no hesitation in relegating all non-Jews to destruction."[17] As one can see, the forces being assembled in Judaea to do battle against the hated Romans was no 'Salvation Army.' Contrast this, if you will, with the words of Jesus, "For all who take the sword will perish by the sword." (Matthew 26:52). We believe that on occasions Jesus metaphorically used sword symbolism to convey his message as in Matthew 10:34 and Luke 22:36-38, but in no way did he set about raising an army for military conquest. Here we have a startling contrast between Jesus and the teaching of Qumran. Compare also Paul's use of analogy in 2 Corinthians 10:3-4; where he writes "For though we live in the world, we are not carrying on a worldly war, for the weapons of our warfare are not worldly but have divine power to destroy (evil) strongholds."

## 2. Excessive Legalism

In the Scroll known as the Damascus Document an entire section is given to the strict observance of the Sabbath. There were proscriptions against drinking water unless it is within the camp, travelling more than

2,000 cubits for a beast pastured outside the town, using the fist as a hammer, opening a sealed vessel, picking up a stone or dust in the house or assisting a beast in birth.[18] This last reads "even if she drops [the newborn] into a cistern or pit, let him not keep it alive on the Sabbath."[19] These prohibitions seem out of keeping with the spirit of Jesus who, many times, was in conflict with the Pharisees on similar issues.

In the Manual of Discipline, which observes the principles of rank and promotion according to one's obedience to the Law and to the practices of the community, we read: "In whatever place the ten are, there shall not cease to be a man who expounds the Torah night and day."[20] Further it was stipulated that a third of the community should remain awake, presumably by way of a three-watch system to read the Torah. We find nothing to correspond with these practices in the teachings of Jesus nor in the habits of the early church.

## 3. Emphasis on External Cleanliness

In community life of this kind we should not be surprised to find laws of hygiene. Beyond this, however, there was strict adherence to Levitical laws declaring impurities among mourners who have been close to a dead body, and similarly the setting apart of a woman in menstruation. Baptism, unlike the Christian custom, was repeatable and apparently regular. While in no way denying the devotional nature of the members of Qumran, there was an inevitable externalizing of their piety which Jesus had condemned in the hypocrisy of the Pharisees who were known to have paraded their righteousness in public. One cannot but recall also the warning of Jesus about those who put such great stress on the cleansing of the outside of the cup while overlooking the heart of a man from which come adulteries, murders and all kinds of sin (cf. Matthew 15:19 and Luke 11:39).

## 4. A Strong Clericalism

The movement claimed to be part of the Zadokite priesthood which had been displaced by the Hasmoneans. The Sadducees, as successors to the priesthood, were not favoured by the Qumran movement, which proclaimed its own priestly status and allowed only the priests certain privileges in the worship practices of the community. Again in marked contrast, the Gospels, and indeed the rest of the New Testament, avoid anything of a 'priestly caste', other than to declare the priesthood of *all* believers.

The parable of the Good Samaritan did much to level the priests of Jesus day, and the Levites also, when he talked of their passing by the victim "on the other side." Interestingly, the Scrolls speak of the Zadokites and the Levites, the first of whom had charge of the work of the priesthood, whereas the Levites had the task of pronouncing curses. [21]

## 5. Relationship to Temple Worship

Because of their grievances against the 'usurper' high priesthood in Jerusalem, members of the Qumran community deliberately distanced themselves from Temple worship, hoping in the end for a restoration of the Zadokite line of priests. Jesus also recognized the need for a cleansing of the Temple, which in his words had become 'a den of thieves' instead of 'a house of prayer.' He also foresaw the inevitability of the destruction of the Temple with the fall of Jerusalem. Nevertheless he made it his practice to enter the Temple during the course of his ministry (John 7:14-28; 10:22), and encouraged his disciples to do the same (John 7:8). Not only so, but after Jesus' death and resurrection, the disciples kept up the practice of observing the prayer times in the Temple (Acts 3:1; 21:26). Qumran, it would seem, was a separatist entity, and therefore assumed many of the characteristics of the cults, whereas the Jesus movement was highly visible and active in the towns, villages and among the common folk. This was a major difference, and it is unlikely that the Qumran community would have approved of the friendly fraternising of Jesus with publicans and sinners.

## 6. Disciplines of Membership

We have already alluded to the strict procedures in becoming a member of the group, and it should be pointed out that a form of excommunication also existed. Discipline among Christians was also practiced, yet with restraint, as outlined in Paul's letter to the Galatians: "Brethren, if a man is overtaken in any trespass, you who are spiritual should restore him in a spirit of gentleness. Look to yourself, lest you too be tempted" (6:1).

The same apostle, however, pronounced anathema on any one who preached "another gospel which is not the gospel" (Galatians 1:8-9). In the Damascus Document (xii 2-6) we read "Everyone possessed by the spirits of Belial so that he preaches apostasy shall be judged according to the law concerning false prophets. If, however, someone desecrates the Sabbath or the festivals by accident, he shall not be executed but shall be placed under surveillance. Once he has been cured and has been under surveillance for seven years, he may again be readmitted into the community." The severity of Old Testament penalties, including death it seems, were being ridgidly maintained by the Qumran community. Jesus exhortation to forgive one another even "seventy times seven" must have sounded absurd in the ears of the puritanical Qumranites.

## Comparisons between John the Baptist and Jesus

Otto Betz holds to the view that John the Baptist may well have been the Teacher of Righteousness in the Qumran community. There are indeed many resemblances, and these, it has to be admitted, contrast with several aspects of Jesus' way of life. In an unforgettable speech to the crowds who wanted to know what he thought of his predecessor, John, he likened them to children playing in the market place. Some wanted to dance and others wanted to play funerals (Matthew 11:1-19). He drew a graphic picture of contrast between John, who came neither eating nor drinking and his own life-style, which had been dubbed gluttonous and drunkardly. Obviously Jesus is employing some hyperbole, or the technique of exaggeration to make his point, but, all the same, there were very significant differences between him and John. This, we might suggest, was a time of transition in the life, thought and destiny of Israel.

Paul is frequently blamed for having sidetracked the early church, taking it out of the mainstream of Torah obeying Judaism, but it is beyond argument that Jesus himself is seen to be the one who is ready to put new wine into old bottles. Consistently he stresses forgiveness for the sinner, even as Paul preached his gospel of redeeming grace. Yet, on the other hand, both pay respect to the Law, not as a means of salvation *per se*, but as a guide to the good life (cf. Luke 10:25-37) or, as Paul puts it, our schoolmaster (Galatians 3:25).

John the Baptist's awesome and prophetic preaching called for repentance in the light of God's uncompromising judgments. Jesus also called for repentance but offered pardon on the basis of God's love for the sinner. Here we can see the relationship between law and grace, between righteousness and mercy. The coupling of *tsedeq* and *chesed* in Hebrew thought (cf. Psalm 85:10-11) is the key to an understanding of God's nature, combining, as it does, these apparent opposites—God's *righteousness* on one hand, and his *mercy* to the undeserving on the other. For Christians this key actually takes the form of a cross, since we believe that God's judgment on sin and his mercy for the sinner were perfectly satisfied in the death of Christ.

Returning to John the Baptist and his possible connection with Qumran, Otto Betz points out several parallels between the two.[22] We have selected some of these, with additional comments:

1. Geography: Between the location where the Scrolls were recovered and Pliny the Elder's description of the location of an Essene settlement overlooking the Wadi Qumran it is thought that John, having come from "the wilderness of Judaea" as the Gospel of Matthew indicates, may have been taught in this very community over a number of years. According to Josephus, it was a habit of the Essenes to receive the children of other people when they were "still young and capable of instruction."[23] And Luke significantly adds in his account of John, "And the child grew and became strong in spirit, and he was in the wilderness till the day of his manifestation to Israel." It is also Luke (1:80) who tells us that John's mother, Elizabeth, conceived in her old age, so there may have been a pressing reason for the boy to be placed in someone else's care, all in keeping with God's will for the one who would be known throughout Judaea as the Baptist and a prophet of God.

2. Baptisms: The well known association of John with a baptism for the repentance of sins, is a strong indication of his possible relationship to Qumran. The Qumran community also taught that their ritual washings would be superseded with a purification by the Holy Spirit at the end of time, exactly as John also connects the coming of the Holy Spirit with someone "mightier than I" (Mark 1:7).

3. The Ascetic Life. John is described as eating locusts and wild

honey, while his cloak was made of camel's hair, and the girdle around his waist was leather, all well suited to his aim of strict purity and perhaps as a protest against the pollution of civilisation. Whether this would be the attire of all the members of the community is unlikely. On the other hand, if John had become a leader in the movement, even possibly the Teacher of Righteousness himself, it is not impossible that he would have been marked out by his appearance.

4. John's disciples were known to fast (Mark 2:18), and to recite their special prayers (Luke 11:1). These two acts of piety also appear in the Qumran texts. Infraction of even minor rules was punished by a reduction in the food ration, which meant severe fasting (Manual of Discipline 7:2-15). Cave 11 yielded a scroll of psalms in which new prayers were inserted into a series of Psalms of David.

5. John was a priest, the son of the priest Zacharias (Luke 1:5), and the Qumran community recognized its Teacher of Righteousness to be a priest to lead the repentant to the way of His heart (Commentary of Habakkuk 2:8, Cairo Damascus Document 1:11). Yet his teaching, too, was to be like that of a prophet.

6. John scolded the hypocrites who came to him in forms of rebuke similar to the vocabulary of Qumran. He calls them "a brood of vipers" (Matthew 3:7), which Betz believes to be the Hebrew equivalent of ma'ase 'eph'eh or "creatures of the Snake"—that is, Sons of the Devil. This same phrase occurs in the Thanksgiving Hymns from Qumran (1QH 3:17).

7. Very significantly we read in Matthew 21:32 that Jesus himself said that "John came to you in *the way* of righteousness and you did not believe him", and in Luke 7:28 "I tell you, among those born of women none is greater than John" The man who came from the wilderness to "prepare *the way* of the Lord" is marked out as an extraordinary person. *The way* was a common expression among the community of Qumran.*

---

*Derived from Isaiah 40:3, "In the wilderness prepare the way of the Lord." It was also used of the Christian movement as in Acts 19:9, where reference is made to "the way". Interestingly, this context includes mention of the conversion of certain disciples of John the Baptist.

# The Dead Sea Scrolls

These apparent coincidences between John the Baptist and the Qumran community—their locations, their knowledge and use of the Scriptures, their strict morality, with warnings of judgment to come are convincing arguments in favour of John the Baptist as the possible Teacher of Righteousness. Additionally, mention of the Holy Spirit in the writings of the Scrolls plus John's emphasis on the Holy Spirit in relation to the one whom he said would follow him, certainly indicated an expectation on his part that a major transition was imminent. Many of the writings of Qumran showed that same keen anticipation of God's intervention in the affairs of Israel. And we know the change was to be more radical and quite different from anything that anyone had conceived at the time.

As over against Eisenman's hypothesis that James, the brother of Jesus, was the Teacher of Righteousness, John's priority in time fits in with the yet-to-be arrival of the Messiah. Besides, Herod, who in a moment of passion ordered the imprisoned John to be beheaded no doubt enjoyed the favour, or at least the token support, of the pro-Roman Sadducean priesthood. Since there appears to have been no public denunciation of Herod, we can only surmise that the silence of the Chief Priest would be viewed by John's disciples, and by the Qumran community, as guilty acquiescence. Could this account for the condemnation of a wicked priest in the writings of the Scrolls? Was there fear on the part of the chronicler that Herod might retaliate against all the members of John's movement?

Would this explain the anonymity of the three figures? Or are we to prefer Eisenman's opinion that James' death (ca. 62.C.E.) at the command of another wicked high priest, Ananus, solidly establishes his identity as the Teacher of Righteousness? Or should we return to the view which commenced this chapter, namely that of Frank Moore Cross, of Harvard, which places these events along with the three figures around 134 B.C.E., in the aftermath of the forcible replacement of the Zadokite priesthood?

How shall we answer the question we posed earlier? Are the Scrolls pre-Christian, Christian or non-Christian? They could easily represent a time just prior to the coming of Jesus if indeed their Teacher of Righteousness was John the Baptist. If they were contemporary with Jesus, however, there are too many differences between their teaching and his to set them firmly within a Christian context. If, of course, James as leader of the Jerusalem church was stressing adherence to the Law, he might well have been respected or even adopted by the Qumran community. But with his sudden death, one would surely expect to find some evidence of a continuing Christian presence, viz., a recognizable following of Jesus in Qumran, or even in Masada, but we are not aware of any.

Instead the evidence is overwhelming that the Qumran community remained essentially Jewish with an intensely devotional way of life which finally centred on the need to cleanse the nation of the Romans and their hated imperialism. Despite some early victories over the Roman army, the tide of fortune turned against the Jews, and their hopes were tragically dashed, the Holy City was retaken by the Romans, and the Temple destroyed. Qumran fell to Vespasian as early as 68 B.C.E., Jerusalem to Titus in 70 C.E., while Masada held out until its mass suicide in 72 C.E. Of the last, Paul Johnson, the historian, writes of the archaeological discoveries obtained by Yigael Yadin during the years 1963-5, and offers the sad observation: "Among the ostraca found are what appear to be the lots cast by the last ten survivors to determine who was to kill the other nine and then himself. Abundant evidence of services in the fort's synagogue and parts of fourteen scrolls of Biblical, sectarian and apocryphal books indicate that this was a God-fearing garrison of militants, profoundly influenced by the terrible power of Jewish literature" [24]

## Some Re-assessments

Our progress, such as it is, forces us to explore much larger issues than the history, contents and interpretations of the Dead Sea Scrolls, as we shall do presently. The summation of most research on the Scrolls, is that for Jews and Christians alike, there is nothing which alters our understanding of our origins and the nature of our respective faiths. Neil Asher Silberman writes: "Looking back on the long, twisting course of the Dead Sea Scrolls story, we've come to a situation where access to the documents is open, but the acceptability of new ideas is strictly limited."[25] In point of fact opinions about Qumran and the Scrolls have been freely floated over the years and, after all, in our free society no restrictions are imposed on reliable writers who seek the publication of their ideas.

## The Dead Sea Scrolls

Most recently Norman Golb, who holds the Rosenberger Chair in Jewish History and Civilization at the University of Chicago, has blown open an entirely new vista of possibility in his book *Who Wrote the Dead Sea Scrolls?*. He challenges what is called the Qumran-Essene hypothesis by insisting that Khirbet Qumran was not at all the celibate community described by Pliny the Elder, but rather a Judaean fort dating back to the fourth or fifth century B.C.E., and restored from time to time then taken by the Romans in the late 60s C.E. The all too close proximity of many graves of men, women and children to the site is a strong argument against the supposed celibacy. His hypothesis regarding the Scrolls is that they were not composed in Qumran but were brought there from Jerusalem, Judaea and other places in Israel, to be safely preserved during the Jewish Revolt of 66 C.E. This view could explain the varieties of literary style, theological differences and other inconsistencies which are evident between one scroll and another.

In returning to Silberman's reference to the emergence of new ideas, we can only hope that these will not be a repeat of earlier mistaken assumptions that the Dead Sea Scroll discoveries would utterly demolish the traditional views of Christian origins. For over forty years various writers have needlessly led their readers into dark canyons of doubt. Thankfully we are returning to the daylight of scholastic honesty.

The one incontrovertible idea which does come out of Silberman's summation of the Dead Sea Scroll research is basically what has always been understood by historians. Essentially and correctly this was the fact that a subjugated people, goaded by its militants, rose up against a hated empire to regain their religious and political freedoms, also their national identity. Silberman bows to the tragic fact when he views the scene from the standpoint of the conquerors: "Fate had favored the empire. The Jews' God was defeated and humbled by the Romans' skill and might."[26]

Excitedly he then proceeds to show that the ideals of freedom and justice are common both to Judaism and Christianity, and indeed to all religions.[27] This for him is what makes the Scrolls a living issue for our times. They have been providentially preserved and now fortuitously retrieved for this crucial juncture in our world's history. However, his argument seems to lead to a condoning of militantly religious extremists. He writes:

Who can deny the resemblance between the rage-filled visions of the War of the Sons of Light Against the Sons of Darkness and the fervent calls for jihad among the scattered cells of Radical Islam? Who can deny the messianic and eschatological fervor that led David Koresh and his followers to create their own fiery apocalypse at Mount Carmel in Waco, Texas, as a final act of defiance toward the Sons of Darkness who had surrounded their community? (*The Hidden Scrolls*, p.254).

For those who have been wistfully awaiting some startlingly new disclosure from the intensive research on the Dead Sea Scrolls there must be disappointment, except for the valuable light it sheds on the inter- testamental period of Judaism. Silberman suddenly switches his attention to the debacle of 70 C.E. and its aftermath, complaining that Jewish and Christian communities settled for compromise with the Romans, both abandoning their earlier exciting apocalypticism. This occurred, he claims, with the Jews at Yavne (or Jabney) revising their positions, and the Christians by transforming their 'national saviour' Jesus into 'a transcendent being' with faith replacing the Law—thanks to the apostle Paul.

These conclusions on Silberman's part constitute a leapfrog jump away from the immediate subject of the Scrolls, and a political comment here is not out of place. Obviously he is taking an anti-assimilationist position, and one can appreciate his insistence on the freedom of a people to be what it wants to be. He is in the good company of Patrick Henry whose soul-statement "Give me liberty or give me death" sounded forth as a trumpet for battle, and rightly so. Still we must distinguish between fanaticism and love of freedom. Silberman seems to applaud the war of 66-70 C.E., which cost a million Jewish lives. He endorses freedom fighters, even if they settle for a needless fiery holocaust of women and children as in the Koresh case. He claims that the Christians abandoned their apocalyptic expectations of a Messiah to adopt Paul's presumably milder theology of a divine 'out of this world' kind of Saviour. This statement suggesting, as it does, that Christians deliberately altered their message to suit a changing political situation does not square with the known theological and historical facts.

Firstly, Paul's preaching of faith in a crucified and resurrected

# The Dead Sea Scrolls

Christ was primary and not reactionary. His epistles to the churches were written and circulated long before the fall of Jerusalem. His theology was not some kind of afterthought. The life, death and resurrection of Jesus was the core of the original message preached by the Jerusalem church. As we shall see in Chapter 5, Paul adhered faithfully to the teachings which he himself had received from others before him, adding to these his own experience of Christ (1 Corinthians 15:3).

The nature of Jesus, human and divine, was not a divisive issue in the primitive church. The Gospels, while clearly portraying the humanity of Jesus, also alluded to his divinity. He was seen to control the wind and the waves, to forgive sins, to cleanse the Temple, while claiming to speak with an authority above that of the religious authorities. In putting the question to his disciples "Who do men say that I am?", and "Who do you say that I am?" Peter answered "You are the Christ." (Mark 9:27-29). For Paul, Jesus is the exalted Lord (Philippians 2:9-11), but he does not deny the humanity of Jesus, declaring him to be "born of a woman, born under the law" (Galatians 4:4). Here is unity of the faith. Here is a continuing faith which did not find itself abruptly revised after 70 C.E.

Secondly, the Synoptic Gospel writers prior to and following 70 C.E. did not abandon their apocalyptic teaching as will be clearly seen from Matthew 24, Mark 13 and Luke 21. Even John in his Gospel, though developing what C. H. Dodd defined as realised eschatology, held firmly to the view that Jesus would return (21:23). The teaching of the Lord's return at the end of the age was an essential and unchanged facet of the Christian message (cf. 1 Corinthians 15:20-26; 1 Thessalonians 4:13-18; James 5:7-8; 1 Peter 1:3-9; 1 John 3:1-3; and Jude 21-25). Silberman's argument that early Christianity deliberately adapted itself to fit with the political status quo completely overlooks its commitment to the lordship of Christ. It was indeed this very issue along with the refusal of Christians to make sacrifice to Caesar which brought them under severe persecution.

Thirdly, Silberman fails to provide proof that the Qumran community was in fact the early church, as Robert Eisenman would have us to believe. Norman Golb notes: "These commentaries reflected Eisenman's own thesis—not shared by Wise—(his co-author of *The*

*Dead Sea Scrolls Uncovered*) that the scrolls represented an early stage of Jewish Christianity"[28] Indeed he rejects both Eisenman's theory and the traditional Qumran-Essene hypothesis on the grounds that they both represent sweeping interpretations of Scroll origins with insufficient regard for the literary and theological differences, even contradictions, apparent within them, i.e. the Scrolls. As we have seen, Golb firmly maintains that the Scrolls were essentially Jewish and that they came to be stored in Qumran from a variety of Jewish sources and from different periods of time. This particular view distances the Scrolls even more from the origins of the early church.

So much then for Silberman's misconceptions—theological and otherwise, but in terms of factual history he also fails to present a clear and precise picture of the internal conflicts between competing Jewish groups which characterised the warfare of the years 66-70 C.E., the names of whose leaders are well delineated in ancient chronicles. Christians are conspicuous by their absence from these records.

He is correct, however, in his statement that "Up to now, most Dead Sea scholars have had no time or no interest in universal religious behaviours" and that "they have prided themselves, first and foremost, on being specialists in paleography and textual analysis."[29] Well, of course, the thorough scrutiny of the Scrolls was their mandate, to which their expertise has been conscientiously applied. If their findings do not happen to coincide with the opinions of the more speculative among us, then perhaps the speculations need to be revised.

## Basic Questions with No Easy Answers

If we are to philosophize over the fall of Jerusalem in 70 C.E., it seems reasonable to ask why a similar tragedy befell the Jewish people in 586 B.C.E. when Jerusalem was captured by Nebuchadnezzar and the glorious temple of Solomon was destroyed. Similarly the attempts of Simeon bar Kokhba to restore Israel as a nation in 132 C.E. ended in abysmal failure with the loss of hundreds of thousands of Jewish lives. Was it that the God of Abraham saw a greater purpose in the scattering of his people, rather than sustaining the pillars of their narrow nationalism? Jesus caught sight of this when he forecast the destruction of the Holy City and of Herod's great temple within his generation.

## The Dead Sea Scrolls

The opinion of the sceptic, of course, could be that God does not care about his chosen people, any more than he did when Auschwitz opened the doors of its gas chambers to consume countless innocent Jews.* Likewise, it can be asked that if God is a caring God why would he allow his beloved Son to be subjected to the humiliating and excruciatingly painful death of crucifixion on a Roman gibbet. Jews and Christians alike have endured political and social rejection, persecution and unspeakable suffering.

Are then the arguments of the aetheist to be preferred, that there is no God and we should not expect any supernatural interventions in human history? Does this also mean that the moral ideals of Jewish and Christian philosophies are to be discarded; and, if so, what will replace them? Are we to cave in pessimistically to the idea that the Cross, Qumran and the fall of Jerusalem, events which followed each other in quick succession, are just dead ends of the past, and that no benefits emanate from any of these for us today?

Christians affirm that the message of the Cross has brought salvation to peoples of all nations, besides enormous benefits of compassion to our civilization, to which the founding of the Red Cross Society is but one living testimony. Equally there is validity to the undying view, shared by both Old and New Testaments alike, and very much accentuated in our own century, that Israel will return as a nation to the world scene. The prophet Ezekiel foresaw this event when there will be one King and one Shepherd over the nations, and Jerusalem will be a glorious centre of worship (37:21-28). The corresponding and most significant New Testament Scriptures are to be found in the Book of Revelation 7:1-8 and 21:10-27. Jerusalem is also referred to as 'the beloved city' (20:9), but the final descriptions are of the New Jerusalem which comes down from heaven, not unlike the apocalyptic vision of the new Temple described for us by Ezekiel in very large dimensions (chapters 40-45).

This is the cherished hope and long time expectation of both Jew

---

*It is not surprising that some Jewish thinkers as Richard L. Rubenstein have abandoned the idea of Jahweh as their God of history, opting instead for atheism or else a naturalistic and non-interventionist view of a Creator. See *Approaches to Auschwitz* Chapter 10, ( p.311).

and Christian. Yet we dare not overlook the painful fact, that Judaism and Christianity have been at serious odds over the centuries, often to the point of inflicting persecution and humiliation on one another. At the most it should have been only a lover's quarrel as between two members of the same household, but religious resentments can become extremely hostile. Even within each of these faiths there have been strains, stresses and open conflict, where fellow-Jews and fellow-Christians have been ostracized, or excommunicated, and made to suffer by their own religious kinsfolk. So often a hardening of attitude has manifested itself by those who felt they were defending the doctrines of their faith and thereby protecting almighty God from the assaults of heretics!

## How Jews and Jewish Christians Parted Ways

I am always impressed by the words of Gamaliel, the Pharisee, 'a teacher of the law, held in honor by all the people' (Acts 5:34) who was asked to give his judgment on the new Jewish sect which represented the beginning of the church:

> Men of Israel, take care what you do with these men.... So in the present case I tell you, keep away from these men and let them alone; for if this plan or this undertaking is of men, it will fail; but if it is of God, you will not be able to overthrow them. You might even be found opposing God! (Acts 5:33-39).

His counsel prevailed and they released the apostles who had been arrested and put in jail by the high priest and those of the Sadducean party (5:17-18). Along the way, however, the Jews of the Diaspora came to be unsettled by the preaching of Paul in Gentile areas probably for any one of three reasons. Paula Fredriksen deals with this development in her chapter entitled "Responses to the Resurrection".[30] In short, the Jews living abroad had already opened their synagogues to 'God-fearing' Gentiles, and a gospel which reduced the obligations of the Law for Gentiles was seen to be both competitive and compromising. Secondly, the preaching of a crucified Messiah, emphasizing the cross, would hardly be attractive in Roman dominated Gentile cities. Thirdly, whereas an apocalyptic messianic message would be familiar and acceptable to the Jews

## The Dead Sea Scrolls

in Jerusalem, it would be unwelcome among Jews who were assimilating well into Roman society elsewhere in the empire.

Indeed Judaism enjoyed the status of a *religio licita*, and it is clear that some Jews consulted with the local authorities to demonstrate their disassociation from Paul, thus exposing him and other Christian missionaries to the possibility of arrest. They knew, too, as had happened in Jerusalem, the claim of Jesus to be a king would always arouse instant reaction from Roman procurators, prefects and city mayors. It might be noted in Acts 21:27 that it was Jews from Asia Minor visiting in Jerusalem who called for Paul's arrest in contrast to the support he received there from many of the Jerusalem Pharisees (23:1-10), whose theology of the resurrection was more akin to Paul than to the Sadducees.

Of course the final separation of church and synagogue can be dated to the Eighteen Benedictions of the eighties, C.E., one of which effectively excommunicated the Nazarenes, or Judaistic Christians from worship in the synagogue. After all, the Christian sect was increasingly seen to be a menace to traditional Judaism and Rabban Gamaliel II felt it necessary to act in this way.[31] Sad to say, there was no "Father, forgive them" prayer on the lips of the Christians, and within fifty years of this event, the church fathers began to pour ridicule on the Jews. The rupture had taken place and no one sought for a reconciliation. The Christians, of course, were still a disadvantaged people politically, and their persecution by Rome continued on into the early fourth century; but with the conversion of Constantine the establishment of Christianity in the empire hardened the concrete wall between Jew and Christian.

Richard L. Rubenstein and John K. Roth, in their *Approaches to Auschwitz* [32] see major significance in the fall of Jerusalem and the ascendancy to power of Christianity almost as though these events were exactly simultaneous. It was in fact while Christians continued to be persecuted that a favourable agreement had been reached between the Jews and the Romans thanks to the diplomacy of the famous Rabbi Yochanan ben Zakkai, which secured an ongoing recognition of Jewish communities despite the calamity of 70 C.E. Both Yochanan and Josephus had been regarded by the Jewish Zealots as turncoats, but in point of fact it was they who exercised great foresight on behalf of their people. Similarly, Paul's inclusivistic teaching which emphasized the removal of 'the middle wall of partition' prepared the Christians for their adjustment and outreach to the Gentile world. This he did, however, without compromising on the lordship of Christ. In the eyes of Robert Eisenman this made him a traitor to Judaism, the 'Man of the Lie' in the Scrolls, and most likely an informer to the Romans. Paradoxically, then, Paul himself was eventually put to death by command of Nero.

In contrast to his attitude towards James the Just, Josephus had only contempt for the militant elements that made for the continuation of the war, namely the Zealots and the Sicarii about whom he writes: "imposters and brigands ... slaves, the dregs of society and the bastard scum of the nation."[33] This surely disposes of Eisenman's theory that the early church was the body that pressed hard for war against Rome. So persistent is he in this idea that he seeks also to implicate the Christians in Simeon bar Kokhba's renewed attempt to wrest Jerusalem from the Romans around 132 C.E. He believes that "there may well have been close links between Simeon's family and the descendants of Jesus—if, indeed, they were not one and the same." [34] Baigent, Leigh and Lincoln go on to say that Simeon was angered by what must have seemed a monstrous betrayal, or a display of contemptible cowardice, so "turned upon them and persecuted them as traitors." [35] History tells us that bar Kokhba did indeed conduct a campaign of terror on the Christians because they had declined to be conscripted (see p. 144). The outlandish suggestion of a family relationship between Jesus and Kokhba one hundred years later savours of a counterfeited Will.

On top of all this, Rubenstein and Roth want to identify the early church as portraying itself to be anti-Jewish in order to gain the favour of the Romans. Well do we know that the Christian message of a crucified malefactor would be no drawing card for patriotic Romans, and that the church, beginning with the murderous Neronian persecution was destined to be a despised and grossly abused minority for long after the fall of Jerusalem in 70, and on into the first quarter of the fourth century.*

The Rubenstein-Roth thesis then associates the catastrophic fall of

---

*It is estimated that over 750,000 Christians were buried in the catacombs of Rome. This figure, of course, does not represent all the victims of the successive persecutions.

## The Dead Sea Scrolls

Jerusalem and the rise of Christianity, as though these events were simultaneous, with the Nazi Holocaust of the 1940s. Adolf Hitler is seen to play the role of the all-powerful Caesar, unopposed by a submissive non-protesting church. In giving balance to their argument, however, they admit "Nevertheless, at no time in the two-thousand year history of the encounter between the church and the synagogue did the church ever have the extermination of the Jews as its objective."[36] However much the church in Germany failed to halt the incredible rise to power of the Nazis, there can be no gainsaying of the fact that this ruthless militant totalitarianism was of Orwellian proportions. It corresponded to what Nicolas Berdyaev called the 'demonic element' in history.

Between 1933 and 1938 the Nazis had orchestrated the Gestapo, a Hitler Youth Movement with young people trained to betray any dissident parent, and a military machine designed to take on the world if necessary. Germany was to be the master race. The awesome night known as Kristallnacht, when Jewish properties were smashed, synagogues burned and people brutally attacked, took place on November 9-10, 1938. It was a clear signal to the world of the barbaric anti-Semitic policies of Hitler.

It has been loudly protested that the world ought to have declared war on Hitler instead of waiting until 1939. Those of us who lived through those years know full well the absurd inferiority of military preparedness of the western Allies. An earlier entrance of Britain and France into war could have meant the fall of both. France at the time was considered the stronger of the two, yet she succumbed quickly to the German *blitzkrieg*. Nor should it be overlooked that Nazi Germany and Communist Russia had united in a non-aggression pact at the time.

The critics in our generation often have a naive view of the complexities of another era, and little is said about the courage of many within Germany itself who raised their voices in protest against Nazism. We ought to salute Martin Niemoller, Bernard Lichtenberg, Karl Barth, Alfred Delp and Dean Heinrich Gruber, besides the clergymen who courageously subscribed to the Council of Barmen, as well as numerous unnamed Germans and other nationals, clergy and laity, who were incarcerated for religious or political reasons, many suffering execution. Not least, we must admire Dietrich Bonhoeffer who broadcast a lecture on the Berlin radio (1933) warning the German public for its hankering after a leader (fuhrer), who would inevitably become a 'misleader'. The broadcast was cut off before he had finished. This German pastor was executed three weeks before the end of the war.

## The Hazards of Historical Revisionism

The kind of dialectic we have witnessed in some of the writings of Baigent, Eisenman, Leigh, Lincoln, Roth and Rubenstein, scholarly as it may be for the most part, does not always respect the total reality of a situation and the specifics of a given time, be it in the first or the twentieth century. Fifty years after the Holocaust, there is a noticeable tendency in some quarters to insinuate blame on Christians for the tragedy. Yet, without the intervention of western and nominally Christian nations, Hitler would have progressed unhindered towards his final goals, encouraged by the active alliance of Japan.

There is no denying of the tragic fact, however, that Hitler used to his own advantage Martin Luther's bitter denunciation of the Jews in the sixteenth century. Yet neither must it ever be obscured that John Calvin and the Reformed churches in Switzerland, Holland and Scotland, as well as Oliver Cromwell in England took a very different position. Even in the Middle Ages, there were Catholic voices which spoke out against the excesses of the Crusades. The saintly Bernard of Clairvaux, author of the hymn "Jesus, Thou Joy of Loving Hearts", gave this solemn counsel to those who were engaging in the wars against the Muslims:

> 'Go to Zion,' he urged, 'protect the grave of Christ your Lord, but do not harm the sons of Israel ... for they are the flesh and bone of the Messiah, and if you molest them you run the risk of injuring the apple of God's eye.' [37]

It fell on deaf ears, hardened hearts and men bent on war. Peter Abelard in his day articulated his convictions when he wrote, "We would declare God to be cruel if we thought the steadfastness of the Jews under tribulation could remain without reward. No nation has suffered so much for God." [38]

In the post-Reformation years, strong movements towards religious liberty sprang up in England and in America. As already mentioned, Oliver Cromwell (1599-1658), an ardent Christian reformer, saw to the return of Jews to England, a country which respected and greatly benefitted from the Disraeli and Rothschild families. In 1917 Great Britain signed the famous Balfour Agreement for the establishing of a national home for the Jews in Palestine. At the risk of repetition, I would endorse the adamant opposition of Winston Churchill and the vigorous war effort he waged against the anti-Semitic Nazis. This was done before the entry of the United States into the conflict of World War II, without whom victory would have been impossible. Such was the colossal military, naval and air power of Nazi Germany.

Across the Atlantic in the seventeenth century the seeds of true democracy were being sown, and this would ultimately make the United States a true home for the Jew and for everyone. Roger Williams, a wise and devout Christian non-conformist and founder of the Rhode Island community, wrote his famous Letter to the Town of Providence in 1655 which reads:

> There goes many a ship to sea, with many hundred souls in one ship, whose weal and woe is common, and is a true picture of a commonwealth or a human combination or society. It hath fallen out sometimes that both papists and Protestants, Jews and Turks may be embarked in one ship, upon which supposal I affirm that all the liberty of conscience that ever I pleaded for turns upon these two hinges—that none of the papists, Protestants, Jews or Turks be forced to come to the ship's prayers or worship, nor compelled from their own particular prayers or worship, if they practice any. I further add that I never denied that, notwithstanding this liberty, the commander of this ship ought to command the ship's course, yea, and also command that justice, peace, and sobriety be kept and practiced, both among the seamen and all the passengers. (Taken from *Familiar Quotations*, John Bartlett; Little, Brown & Co. Canada, 1968.)

Even prior to the drawing up of the Declaration of Rights, there is on record, in 1774, a written memorial by Isaac Backus, a Baptist of the New Light Movement, the first article of which is most significant:

> All men are born free and equal, and have certain natural, essential, and unalienable rights.

Finally, we must give due respect to the whole stratum of evangelical Christianity which has consistently acknowledged the priority of the Jew in the preaching of the Gospel (Romans 1:16), the privileged place of the Chosen People in the covenants of God, and the eventual restoration of the Jew to the land of Israel, from where God's righteous judgments will be mediated through his Messiah to all the nations of the world.

Secular histories are not always cognizant of the vital part played by the non-established 'free churches' in the struggle for separation of church and state, freedom of conscience and personal liberty. This long struggle witnessed widespread killings as in the case of the Hugenots in France and the Wyclifites in England, followed by the emergence of Mennonites, Baptists, Quakers, Congregationalists, Methodist and Brethren movements, etc. As religious minorities, like the Jews, they also suffered political, educational and social discrimination in Russia, in Europe and in Britain. A panoramic view is always essential to an understanding of real history as it has evolved through a great diversity of situations.

## Notes

1 Frank Moore Cross in *Understanding the Dead Sea Scrolls*, ed. Hershel Shanks. New York: Random House, 1992, p, 29.

2 Eisenman, R. and Wise, M. *The Dead Sea Scrolls Uncovered*. New York: Penguin, 1992, p.180.

3 Silberman, Neil A. *The Hidden Scrolls*. New York: Grosset/Putnam, 1994, pp. 243-244.

4 Vermes, Geza. *Jesus and the World of Judaism*. Philadelphia: Fortress, 1983, pp. viii-ix.

5 *The Biblical Archaeology Review*, Summer, 1989, quoted in The Hidden Scrolls, ibid., 218.

6 Baigent, M. and Leigh, R. *The Dead Sea Scrolls Deception*. New York: Simon and Schuster, 1991, p.137.

7 Burrows, Millar. *The Dead Sea Scrolls*. New York: Viking, 1955, p.327.

# The Dead Sea Scrolls

8 James C. Vanderkam in *Understanding the Dead Sea Scrolls*. Ibid., p.183.

9 Thiering, B. *Jesus and the Riddle of the Dead Sea Scrolls*. New York: Doubleday, 1992.

10 Eisenman, R. and Wise, M. *The Dead Sea Scrolls Uncovered*. New York: Penguin. 1992, p.24.-26.

11 Golb, Norman. *Who Wrote the Dead Sea Scrolls?* New York & Toronto: Scribner, 1995, p.383.

12 Schiffman, Lawrence B. *Reclaiming the Dead Sea Scrolls*. Books in Brief, March/April, 1995, and quoted in *Biblical Archaeology Review*, July/August, 1995; Vol. 21, No. 4, pp. 20-21.

13 Fitzmyer, J. *The Qumran Scrolls and the New Testament after Forty Years*, Revue de Qumran 13, 1988, pp.613-615

14 Eisenman, R. and Wise, M. *The Dead Sea Scrolls Uncovered*. Ibid., p.70.

15 Quoted by Ethelbert Stauffer in *Jesus and the Wilderness Community at Qumran*. Philadelphia: Fortress, 1964, p.13.

16 Eisenman, R. and Wise, M. *The Dead Sea Scrolls Uncovered*. Ibid., p.26.

17 Grant, M. Jesus: *An Historian's Review of the Gospels*. New York, Scribners, 1977, p.121

18 LaSor, W. Sanford. *The Dead Sea Scrolls and the Christian Faith*. Chicago: Moody Press, reprint 1972, p.127.

19 Ibid., p.127.

20 Ibid., p.81

21 Ibid., p.72

22 Otto Betz in *Understanding the Dead Sea Scrolls*. ed. Hershel Shanks. New York: Random House, 1992, pp.205-224.

23 Josephus: *Antiquities*, 18:117

24 Johnson, Paul. *A History of the Jews*. London: Weidenfeld and Nicolson, 1987, p.140.

25 Silberman, N. A. Ibid., p.253

26 Ibid., p.260.

27 Ibid., p.254.

28 Golb, Norman *Who Wrote the Dead Sea Scrolls?* New York & Toronto: Scribners, 1995, p.310

29 Silberman, Ibid., p.254

30 Fredriksen, Paula. *From Jesus to Christ.* Newhaven: Yale, 1988, pp.133-176.

31 See Solomon Zeitlin. *The Rise and Fall of the Judaean State,* vol.3, p.359.

32 Rubenstein, R.L and Roth, J. K. *Approaches to Auschwitz.* Atlanta: John Knox, 1987, pp.34-35.

33 Josephus, *War* 2:228, 431, and 441.

34 Baigent, M., Leigh, R., and Lincoln H. *The Messianic Legacy.* London: Transworld (Corgi). 1987, p.132.

35 Ibid., p.133

36 Rubenstein, R. L. and Roth, J. K. Ibid., p.44

37 Bernard of Clairvaux (1090-1153 C.E.) See *A History of the Christian Church.* Williston Walker. Edinburgh: T. & T. Clark, 1949, pp. 242-247.

38 Abelard, Peter (1079-1142) Migne, P.L., 178, p.1609

Chapter Four

# The Controversial Jesus

Do you remember the book which bore the pompous title *God Is An Englishman*? Well, with much more historical and geographical precision we can say that Jesus was a Jew. We might add that if he had been only a mythical figure, his creators would have done better to have given him another nationality more pleasing to the Graeco-Roman world. But God's ways are not our ways. Like so many of his fellow countrymen, Jesus had his full share of rejection and of being despised. Geza Vermes writes, "Zealot or not, Jesus was certainly charged, prosecuted and sentenced as one, and that this was due to his country of origin, and that of his disciples is more than likely."[1] *

As Christians we acknowledge with great respect the fact that God chose the Jews as his covenant people, through whom all the nations of the earth would be blessed. Neither should it surprise us if the one whom we honour as the express image of God is Jewish. Claude G. Montefiore described Jesus as "one of the greatest and most original of our Jewish prophets and teachers."[2] He also complimented the teaching of Jesus to love one's enemies as "among the noblest specimens of

---

\* Vermes' basic view of Jesus is that he was not a Zealot (See p. 94).

human ethics, among the finest of human ideals and commands."3

It is refreshing to sense the strong desire which is evident in areas of contemporary Judaism to reclaim Jesus of Nazareth as a Jewish figure and leader. Professor Pinchas Lapide, in his book, *Is This Not Joseph's Son?*, refers to no less than twenty nine Hebrew books on Jesus which have been published in recent years.4 Gerald Friedlander claims that "four-fifths of the Sermon on the Mount is exclusively Jewish."5 David Flusser, of the Hebrew University in Jerusalem, expresses his confidence in the historicity of Jesus and assures us that it is possible to write the story of Jesus' life directly from the Gospels which he considers are more trustworthy as historical sources than was commonly thought.6

Understandably, there is a wide variety of views within Jewish circles as to the person of Jesus. Joseph Klausner expressed his appreciation of Jesus as a Pharisaic rabbi, but his remark drew fire from A. Kaminka. He characterized Klausner's book on Jesus as "a truckling and kow-towing to the Christian religion, and an assertion of great affection for the foggy figure of its founder, a denial of the healthy sense of our saintly fathers."7 Pinchas Lapide rejects Jesus as the Jewish messiah in *Jesus in Two Perspectives*,8 but he surprised many by his sensational statement "I accept the resurrection of Easter Sunday, not as an invention of the community of disciples but as a historical event.... I believe that the Christ event leads to a way of salvation which God has opened up in order to bring the Gentile world into community of God's Israel." In the same article of *Time* magazine (May 7, 1979), Rabbi Peter Levinson from Germany snapped back, "If I believed in Jesus' resurrection I would be baptized tomorrow!" In the current reclamation of Jesus, we find several streams of thought.

## Jesus, a Pharisee?

The impression we receive from our four Gospels is that Jesus seemed always to be in conflict with the Pharisees. There are Jewish scholars who suggest that the Gospels are not fair to the Pharisees who were favourably described by Josephus as good teachers of the Law who had the greatest influence on the ordinary people. (*Antiq.* 18:17) He does hint at those certain regulations handed down by former generations which are not recorded in the Laws of Moses (*Antiq* 13:297), and this

## The Controversial Jesus

is our key to understanding both the criticism of Jesus on occasions, and the opposition of the Qumran Community to the Pharisees. Were it not for the Dead Sea Scrolls, however, the enigma of the situation might have remained unsolved.

Lawrence Schiffman writes: "Most of the Qumran material that sheds light on the Pharisees is in the form of polemics against their views. The Qumran sect virulently disagreed with Pharisaic teachings on a wide variety of theological and halakhic matters."[9] He goes on to tell us that the Pharisees were alluded to as "builders of the wall", apparently an adaptation of the concept known from the Mishnah (Avot 1:1), which teaches, "build a fence around the Torah". According to this rabbinic maxim, laws not found in the Bible could be created in order to make certain that the Torah was not violated. In alluding to the practice Josephus indicates that the Sadducees rejected the Pharisees on the grounds that only those regulations which were written down should be considered valid. Schiffman summarizes the case which Qumran had against the Pharisees when he writes, "The entire corpus of the Pharisaic laws thus consitutes, in the view of the sectarians, "annulment" of the Torah, because it replaces Biblical laws with the Pharisees'own rulings."[10]

The multiplication of laws, and the Pharisees claim to the right of interpretation could have had either one or both effects: first, by adding to the legal burdens of the people—a state of affairs which may account for Jesus' statement in Matthew 11:28-30; or, second, a casuistry which could provide convenient circumlocutions of the Law. This latter is probably what is meant by the Qumran complaint that these wall builders were also "seekers after smooth things" (*dorshe halaqot*). The phrase draws on the biblical usage of *halaqot* as meaning lies or falsehoods (cf. Psalm 12:3-4).

From Cave 4 of Qumran we have the Pesher Nahum, a commentary on the prophet's message, which includes the statement "whose falseness is in their teaching, and whose lying tongue and dishonest lip(s) lead many astray (4QpNah 3-4 II,8). Obviously the Qumran sect had little, if any respect for the Pharisees, and a further denunciation of them bears some resemblance to Jesus' words: "All these things the builders of the wall and the plasterers of nothingness did not understand" (CD 8:12-13, Damascus Document; cf. Matthew 23:27ff., e.g., "You are whitewashed tombs.")

How then is it possible to identify Jesus as a Pharisee? Donald A. Hagner provides us with a list of Jewish scholars who support this view.[11] Abraham Geiger described Jesus as a Pharisee "with Galilean coloring."[12] Daniel Chwolsohn believed that Jesus conducted himself as a Pharisee.[13] Modern scholars like Martin Buber, Paul Winter and Ben Chorin have identified Jesus with the Pharisees. Ben-Chorin argues that Jesus was a Pharisee since he was called rabbi, and those who called Jesus a prophet were only the uneducated common folk.[14]

Hyam Maccoby is forceful in his argument in favour of Jesus' identity as a Pharisee. He writes: "Jesus was not only educated as a Pharisee; he remained a Pharisee all his life.... As a Rabbi, Jesus was a typical Pharisee teacher. Both in style and context, his religious teachings show an unmistakable affinity to Pharisaism, and especially to the teachings of the great apostle of Pharisaism, Hillel."[15] As we shall see later, Maccoby's rigidity in this viewpoint, may have a strong bearing on his equally aggressive repudiation of Paul's claim to being a Pharisee.

In contrast to the Sadducees of his day, Jesus certainly would be seen as standing closer to the Pharisees in matters of providence, resurrection and belief in angels and spirits. Irving M. Zeitlin's comments are of value in establishing further connections. He writes: "Their aims were religious not political. So long as the Torah, the twofold Law, was rigorously observed, they could live with any government—and here too we may observe that this appears to have been Jesus' attitude when he said, 'Render unto Caesar the things that are Caesar's, and to God the things that are God's' "[16] Nor must we forget that Jesus commended the Pharisees in Matthew 23:2-3, and exhorted the people to respect those "who sit on Moses' seat." Note, also, Luke's mention of an incident when certain of the Pharisees warned Jesus of impending danger (13:31), and it must be gratefully acknowledged that Gamaliel showed an impartiality with leniency towards the new Christians (Acts 5:34). Indeed Pharisees were among those who professed the new faith and who actually formed a party within the church (Acts 15:5). The Pharisaic party was also known to be divided within itself, the conservatives following Rabbi Shammai; and the more liberal in their interpretations of the Law, particularly in the issues of marriage and divorce, adhering to Rabbi Hillel.

Perhaps the key to some of the apparent contradictions between Jesus and the Pharisees is to be found in the words of Ben Chorin who felt that Jesus was "a revolutionary of the heart."[17] No doubt many of the Pharisees were truly seeking the holy life which, as they would discover, was not to be found in external rituals but in "a clean heart and in the renewing of a right spirit" (Psalm 51:10). Jesus' message struck that chord many times.

However, it would be naive and misleading to minimize the contentions which Jesus had with the Pharisees, and they with him. The indictment that they preach but do not practice, spoken by Jesus at Matthew 23:3, finds an interesting parallel in the Scrolls. In the Damascus Document there is a statement, 'They shall surely preach', which, Schiffman says, is to be understood in terms of Micah 2:6 rendered:

> 'Stop preaching' they preach.
> 'That's no way to preach.' [18]

Presumably God is telling a false preacher to quit, yet he proceeds, and does so contrary to God's will. Here is hypocrisy at its height when religious leaders are themselves acting contrary to the spirit of the Law, seeking prestige and lacking in humility, even bearing down mercilessly in their demands on their people. This, it would seem, is exactly how Jesus saw the Pharisaic movement. So inconsistent was their behaviour towards others that he remonstrated with them that they could strain out a gnat yet swallow a camel. They advertised their piety in public.

> They do all their deeds to be seen by men; for they make their phylacteries broad and their fringes long, and they love the place of honor at feasts and the best seats in the synagogues, and salutations in the market places, and being called rabbi by men (Matthew 23:5-7).

Josh McDowell and Bill Wilson, co-authors of *He Walked Among Us*, point out that among the archaeological finds at Qumran are leather phylactery cases containing not just single compartments for the minute rolls to be inserted, but indeed sets of four. They add,

"Again, Jesus' words 'they broaden their phylacteries' fit comfortably into the Jewish cultural context."[19]

For a long time it was conjectured that the woes pronounced against the Pharisees, particularly in Matthew 23 and Luke 11, were not the actual words of Jesus, but were inserted by the Gospel writers by reason of growing hositility between the church and the synagogue. It is true that Rabban Gamaliel II asked his colleagues to compose a prayer against apostates and informers for inclusion in the Shemoneh Esreh. Solomon Zeitlin tells us that this prayer referred to Judaeans who had joined the sect known as Judaean-Christians. They had been propagating their view that Jesus of Nazareth had been the Messiah. Their missionary activities were perceived to be a threat to the unity of the Judaeans following the fall of Jerusalem in 70 C.E. [20] The forcible ejection of Christians from the synagogues that resulted may well have heightened tensions to the point that they, in turn, responded with their denunciations of the Jewish religious establishment.

Without ruling out this possibility, the cumulative evidence is that the pre-destruction (i.e. pre-70 C.E.) Pharisee movement already had come in for very serious condemnation by the Qumran community, which means that there is no reason to doubt that the 'woes' were indeed the words of Jesus himself. We also must ask that if Jesus had been a recognized Pharisee, why wasn't some concerted effort made to defend their colleague from death? After all, there had been a time that Pharisees stood together in their opposition to Alexander Janneus and eight hundred of them were crucified.

We must not underestimate the Jewishness of Jesus, but to identify him as a Pharisee does not seem feasible. Geza Vermes concludes: "It would be a gross overstatement to portray him as a Pharisee himself"[21]

## Jesus, an Essene?

In the middle of the nineteenth century Heinrich Graetz argued that the "unworldly" perspective of Christianity made it similar to the teaching of the Essenes, a view shared by David Flusser in our own time. Without actually identifying him as an Essene, K. Kohler described Jesus and his teaching as "the acme and the highest type of Essenism."[22] With the discovery of the Dead Sea Scrolls some scholars believed they could establish the connection, but, as we have noted, there were radical differences between the teaching and practices of Qumran and those of Jesus. The pacifistic spirit of the Essenes would certainly find its counterpart in the message of Jesus, as well as their sincere piety and works of charity.

Unquestionably it would be difficult to imagine Jesus in the Essene setting which is drawn for us by Irving Zeitlin. He writes, "Wherever they found themselves, similar principles of community organization were implanted. At the head were superiors whom the rank and file members unconditionally obeyed. Those who desired to enter the order were presented with a small hatchet, an apron and a white robe, and were required to undergo a year of probation before being admitted to the ritual ablutions.... Only adult men were accepted as members, though the community did take in children to educate them in the principles of the order."[23]

Philo testified that their philosophy had an influence beyond their own Judaism, and in the overall exchange of thought between people, Jesus may well have been impressed by Essenism; yet cannot be classified as an Essene. Renan commented that Christianity is Essenism that succeeded, but James H. Charlesworth feels his dictum was "simplistic and distorted" since Christianity did not evolve out of one "sect" on the fringes of a normative Judaism.[24]

## Jesus, a Jewish Hasid?

A. N. Wilson writes: "For Vermes, and those who think like him, Jesus comes alive again as a recognizable Jew of the first century. I may as well start by confessing that this is the Jesus in whom I have come to believe.... A *hasid* was an heir of the prophetic tradition. He had peculiar insights into man's relationship with God, and he had the charismatic power of healing."[25] The *hasidim* indeed were known to heal the sick, cast out devils, control the weather, as Elijah, and were noted for their quarrelling with the religious hierarchy in Jerusalem. One of those was Hanina ben Dosa who is reputed to have healed the son of Gamaliel, who, when requested to respond to the situation, went to his room to pray, and emerged to announce that the child's fever had departed from him.[26] The story has a strong similarity to that of the healing of an official's son recorded at John 4:46ff. Hanina is said to have lived just ten miles north of Nazareth and was so fervent in his devotions that he would not interrupt his prayer even when a snake coiled itself around his ankles. He and another *hasid* by the name of Honi, who lived at the time of Pompey, are credited with the ability to make rain appear out of cloudless skies. Curiously, a Talmudic reference in Tosefta—Hullin, 22-23 points to a Rabbi Elazare ben Damah, who was offered healing by a man named Jacob (or James) "*in the name* of Yeshu."

Geza Vermes who describes Jesus as "the paramount example of the early Hasidim or Devout" also refers to Galilee as a place of 'sophisticated religious ambiance' which was apt to produce holy men of the Hasidic type.

We should pause here for an important lesson. Critics who are tempted to reject the Gospels' record of Jesus' works, on the grounds that they contain a mythical element, must relate to similar claims to the miraculous made by Jewish writers on behalf of other persons besides Jesus. Are these likewise to be rejected, or do they in fact add credibility to the four Gospel writers who so often have been accused of making up stories to reinforce their claims for the divinity of Jesus? Or will the critics settle for the miraculous element but not the implied theology? The point is that the integrity and historical accuracy of Matthew, Mark, Luke and John are not to be outrightly dismissed simply because of a sceptic's rejection of miracles. And why the reluctance to credit Jesus with the supernatural? In his teaching about his own unique relationship with the Father he attributes his works to the same source.

## Jesus, a Zealot?

Did the Jewishness of Jesus extend to his being a political revolutionary, and a rebel leader against Rome whose followers could be potential terrorists? After all, he had said that he had come not to bring peace, but a sword. In the same context Jesus indicated that he would set a man against his father, a daughter against her mother; and that he who loves father or mother more than his Lord is not worthy of him (Matthew 10:34). Incidentally, this is one of his less Jewish sayings, since the unity and welfare of the family has always been upheld in their communities. Clearly Jesus was previewing the divisions that

## The Controversial Jesus

his Gospel would create—not in a militant attack against Rome, but as a consequence of his personal demands on individual lives for true discipleship and total commitment.

Even the author of the Epistle to the Hebrews took up the illustration of the word of God being in essence a divisive tool, or a two edged sword which splits open our inmost thinking (Hebrews 4:12-13). Again, Jesus' order to purchase two swords, as recorded in Luke 22:36, on the very day he was to be arrested, cannot possibly be regarded other than as a means of testing his disciples' perception, or as a symbolic act intended to show the futility of force. The sword, Peter and the others had to learn, was not the weaponry of the kingdom of God.*

The Zealots may have derived their title from Phinehas, a grandson of Aaron, who was known for his great 'zeal' for the Lord when he slew an Israelite and his Midianite woman who had flouted Moses' commands. Certainly the Maccabees were their heroes, having shown their zeal for God's law by ridding the land and the temple of the Hellenists in the time of Antiochus Epiphanes. Josephus describes them as brigands and murderers, and cites them for having put people to death as collaborators with Rome, completely without the Sanhedrin's confirmation of the said crimes. (*War* 4:138-46). The Zealots fought in guerilla fashion (*War* 3:170; 6:357), and their actions often provoked savage reprisals on innocent people. Judas the Galilean, a known leader of the Zealots, is referred to in Acts 5:37, where Gamaliel declines to associate the arrested disciples with the same political movement. However, because of the number of Zealot leaders who came from Galilee, the word Galilean became a synonym for Zealot.

We must address the argument, which repeats itself from time to time, that Jesus and his disciple band were in fact Zealots, and that Jesus

---

* As we shall see, it is argued that Matthew and Mark avoided the use of the word 'Zealot' to conceal any suggestion of an identity of the Jesus party with violence, yet all four Gospels testify to the sword confrontation of Peter with the servant of the High Priest. Admittedly the command of Jesus to purchase swords is strange. Was it to make sure that he would be turned over to the Roman authorities, and not be judged only by Caiaphas, the Chief Priest?

was arrested, tried and executed simply as a rebel against Rome. After all, didn't Pilate fix that superscription to the cross, "Jesus, King of the Jews"? Nor did Jesus deny his kingdom teaching, even if Pilate did not understand what was meant by Jesus' statement, "My kingship is not of this world; if my kingship were of this world, my servants would fight, that I might not be handed over to the Jews." (John 18:36).

As early as the eighteenth century Hermann Samuel Reimarus, of Hamburg, adopted the view that Jesus was a leader of the Zealots, was in no way divine, and ended a political failure. He believed that the Gospel stories of Jesus had been a concoction. Others who have followed the same line of argument, have alleged that attempts were made by the Gospel writers to transfer the blame for the death of Jesus from the Romans to the Jews. The four Gospels, and particularly the fourth, were being viewed, and continue to be seen by many, as anti-Semitic. Thus if it can be proven, once and for all, that Jesus was a Jewish patriot who died at the hands of a national enemy, Jewish people would be relieved of all responsibility for this person's execution. It then becomes not merely an academic question, but an issue of the greatest consequence to Jews and Christians alike.

S. G. F. Brandon published his book *Jesus and the Zealots* (Manchester: Manchester University Press) in 1967, and drew attention to the call for swords at the time of Jesus' arrest, also to the fact that a Zealot was a known member of his disciple band. Not only so, but it was pointed out that Luke describes Simon (not Cephas) as a Zealot, while Matthew (10:4) and Mark (3:18) call him Simon the Cananaean (RSV). This name 'Cananaean' is derived from the Hebrew word for zeal or zealous, and means Zealot. Brandon insisted that Mark had deliberately suppressed an identity which would have aroused the suspicions of the Roman authorities by deliberately avoiding the use of the Greek (zelotes) equivalent of the Hebrew. Luke, on the other hand, has no inhibitions about using the Greek word in both his Gospel (6:15) and in the Acts of the Apostles (1:13). It might be thought that the danger had passed by the time of Luke's writings; and this, interestingly, would also argue for an early date for Mark. But this is not the issue.

The obvious point is surely just this. If Jesus and his disciples were Zealots, there would be no need to single out any one of them

# The Controversial Jesus

as such. The fact is that fishermen, a hated pro-Roman tax-collector, another political opportunist in the person of Judas Iscariot, who may have been of the Sicarri (dagger) band, Nathanael, a student and an Israelite "in whom was no guile" (John 1:47), represented a heterogeneous group of men seeking for something other than what they had known. Imagine two such opposites as a Zealot and a (pro-Roman) tax gatherer! They were seekers willing to embark on a very different kind of venture of faith. They were a proto-microcosm of what was to be the Church.

In 1971 Brandon issued a paper as a sequel to his book which was entitled " 'Jesus and the Zealots': a Correction" (N.T. Studies 17: July, 1971) repudiating the implications of his former argument. In 1988 Irving Zeitlin produced a work, *Jesus and the Judaism of His Time*, in which he carefully reviewed many of Brandon's positions, and commented "We must agree, then that insofar as the Brandon thesis depicts Jesus as a Zealot or para-Zealot, it is misleading and wrong."[2]

More recently in 1983, R. H. Eisenman published a work of research *Maccabees, Zadokites, Christians and Qumran* which postulated a configuration that involves the early church with the entire Jewish movement in its rebellion against the Romans in the years 66-70 C.E. He attacked current scholarship, alleging that "Unfortunately for the premises of modern scholarship, terms like Ebionim, Nozrim, Hassidim, Zaddikim ... turn out to be variations on the same theme. The inability to relate to changing metaphor ... has been a distinct failure in criticism."[28]

Let us select one of these terms, the Zaddikim. It goes back to the Zadokite priesthood, and beyond that to Zadok, a priest in the reign of David the King. The Qumran community freely used the term, no doubt with the desire to see the Zadokite priesthood restored to Jerusalem. Eisenman points out that Nozrim is derived from the phrase *Nozre ha Brit* meaning 'Keepers of the Covenant' an expression adopted by the Qumran sect. Then he connects the word Nozrim with Nazarenes in the New Testament, in preference to its traditional connection between Nazarene, a follower of Jesus with Nazareth, the place of his upbringing.

Baigent and Leigh in their book, *The Dead Sea Scrolls Deception* clearly commit themselves to the view, "Contrary to the assumptions of later tradition, it has nothing whatever to do with Jesus alleged upbringing in Nazareth, which, the evidence (*or lack of it*) suggests, did not even exist at the time.* Indeed, it seems to have been the very perplexity of early commentators encountering the unfamiliar term 'Nazorean' that led them to conclude Jesus' family came from Nazareth, which by then had appeared on the map."29

Three responses are required here:

1. The existence of Nazareth. It is true that Nazareth is not mentioned in the Old Testament, nor in Josephus or Philo, or the early literature of the rabbis in the first and second centuries C.E. However, to create a thesis based on the assumption that there was no such place is totally unjustified, and we must express profound regret that Baigent and Leigh casually cast doubt on its existence. The question is satisfactorily dealt with in John Meier's *A Marginal Jew: Rethinking the Historical Jesus*, where he writes "Despite Nazareth's obscurity, archaeology indicates that the village has been occupied since the eighth century B.C.E., though it may have experienced a "refounding" in the second century B.C." The footnote also goes on to confirm the philological derivation of *Nazoraios* from Nazareth, a position supported by Raymond Brown, W. F. Albright and other noted Semitists.30

2. Josephus refers to many Galilean villages without naming them all. John Dominic Crossan stresses this in his *The Historical Jesus—The Life of a Mediterranean Jewish Peasant*, that Nazareth and these villages must not be seen as isolated entities but as satellites of a provincial capital, namely Sepphoris. Crossan further noted the findings of Bellarino Bagatti who excavated at Nazareth beneath the demolished older church of the Annunciation and other adjacent properties. He discovered tombs of the Middle Bronze Period, silos with ceramics of the Middle Iron Period, and ceramics and constructions of the Hellenistic

---

*In their earlier publication, *The Messianic Legacy* (1986), the authors stated that "an overwhelming body of evidence indicates that Nazareth did not exist in biblical times" and probably didn't appear until the third century (C.E.).

Period (c. 332-63 B.C.E.).[31]

Two contemporary historians who have written books under the title *Jesus*, Michael Grant in 1977, and A. N. Wilson in 1992, both accept Nazareth as having existed in Jesus' time, and as the place of his upbringing. The one-liner by Baigent and Leigh, casting doubt on the biblical record, is obviously unjustified and seriously misleading.

3. Eisenman's associating the word Nazarene with the Qumran adoption of the Hebrew phrase for 'Keepers of the Covenant', as above, has the further difficulty of Paul being charged in Acts 24:5 as an agitator among all the Jews throughout the world, and a *ringleader of the sect of the Nazarenes*. Clearly the use of the word here implies the Christian sect and not Qumran. It is Eisenman's obsession that Paul was the great deviant from the Jewish faith, and most probably the Liar, or "Man of the Lie" of the Dead Sea Scrolls. According to this view Paul is the real enemy of Qumran. If such were the case, he would not have been regarded as one of their leaders so late in his career before being sent to Caesar. Or again, if the charge against Paul had mistakenly associated him with Qumran, Luke would surely have avoided the use of the term.

If a personal parenthesis is permitted here, I would suggest that we pay great respect to all our theologians and researchers who deal with the complexities of their subjects. Also, that we offer our sympathies to seminary students who have to find their weary way through such labyrinths of mind-boggling hypotheses which, at times, lead absolutely nowhere, and sometimes into sheer error. But for pastors to be maligned because they fail to pass on this kind of mesmerising muddle to their congregations is an unfair charge. Yet, worse still, is when a hypothesis, already discredited, becomes part of a best-seller to the unsuspecting public. As S. G. F. Brandon showed scholarly integrity by cancelling out his previously held view about Jesus and his followers being militant Zealots, so all of us should be willing to honestly review our positions, and to recant these if it is found to be necessary.

Baigent and Leigh, following upon Eisenman, have revived the same argument that the Zealots and the early Christians were either identical or in close relationship. Their theory goes on to link the early Judaean Christians with Qumran, and Qumran with a military operation—in liaison no doubt with the Zealots. This position will be further addressed in our chapter *The Cross and the Kingdom*. Meanwhile a very balanced opinion by Geza Vermes is worth quoting:

> There is no evidence, in my reading of the gospels, that would point to any particular involvement by Jesus in the revolutionary affairs of the Zealots, though it is likely that some of his followers may have been committed to them and have longed to proclaim him as King Messiah destined to liberate his oppressed nation.[32]

As our study progresses it will become increasingly evident that the person of Jesus defies any attempts to reduce him to a single category. As Charlesworth correctly assessed when he said that Christianity developed out of many Jewish currents, "there was no one source or trajectory." [33] We should affirm that Jesus was first a Jew, yet more than a Jew, and in the words of William Blake:

> I am sure this Jesus will not do
> Either for Englishman or Jew.

## Jesus, a Magician?

To go from the sublime to the ridiculous, we must take into account, albeit briefly, the view of Morton Smith set forth in his book *Jesus the Magician* [34]

Not surprisingly he dismisses the story of the turning of the water into wine, and says "it has been shown to have been modelled on a Dionysiac myth." McDowell and Wilson respond by stating that "The reader should understand that the myth is almost certainly from the second century and is probably a deliberate attempt to keep the Dionysiac worshippers from becoming Christians"[35] Baigent and Leigh see it differently and go on to suggest that the wedding in Cana of Galilee may have been Jesus' own marriage celebration. To propose a marriage, and a progeny as Barbara Thiering does, would be helpful to their notion that a human descendant, or descendants of Jesus, or of his family, will emerge at the end of the age to rule the world.

The variations between popular writers and their interpretations

## The Controversial Jesus

of Jesus become almost entertaining. One might say that in rejecting the miracles of the Bible they show great ingenuity in the creation of their own myths.

A.N. Wilson regards the miracle at Cana as a parable, "and this story is told not to entertain us with Jesus' party tricks, but to tell us something."[36] He thoughtfully likens the waterpots to old Israel, and the wine to Jesus himself since God is making a new Israel. Of course Jesus did have recourse regularly to the parabolic method, and he might have chosen to keep this event only in story form. The fact is that something unusual happened here, as in numerous other cases, which came to be understood as messianic 'signs'. These were truly acted out occurrences for people to see and to judge. Consider the stilling of the storm which forced the disciples to ask what manner of man was this, and the feeding of the multitude which aroused many to make him a king then and there! King Herod, we should recall, was glad when Jesus was brought before him, since he desired to see a 'sign'.

Nor can it be denied that the performing of some of his other miracles provoked significant theological controversy and sometimes hostility, as in the case of the healing of the paralytic recorded in Mark 2:1-12. A magician normally performs his acts in order to add to his popularity. In this case, Jesus responded to his critics by forcing them to answer whether it would be easier to heal the man or to forgive his sins. To this they stubbornly affirmed that only God could forgive sins.

It has been suggested that Jesus used hypnotism, and without disparaging a practice which has known therapeutic value, the extent of his miracles would surpass the limits of hypnotism, e.g. the raising to life of the young man of Nain, the daughter of Jairus, and his friend Lazarus. Significantly, Jesus frequently forbade a healed person to publicly advertise the event. His practices seemed contradictory, yet in cases where the action was purely humanitarian and done in reasonable privacy, this was often his instruction. It has been suggested, and wisely, that Jesus had more to accomplish than simply to establish himself as a faith healer. Magic does not explain the life, words and works of this man Jesus.

Nor would magic account for his own resurrection, though some have resorted to such ideas as the swoon theory or the use of drugs, as in the cases of Hugh Schonfield and John Allegro.* To propose that a person could be subjected to crucifixion, the most agonizing form of execution, after being forced to carry his cross, then to survive the ordeal under the watchful eyes of the Romans, is to show a credulity which also believes in the miraculous!

Another example of non-religious fantasy is A. N. Wilson's suggestion that the disciples probably mistook Jesus' brother, James, for Jesus, and mistakenly reported that they had seen the Lord. I wonder how long it took them to wake up to their misapprehension, and once that happened, as inevitably it would, whatever did they think of themselves? Besides, James was probably not with them in the first days following Jesus' resurrection. Paul, in his outline of the sequential events of the resurrection appearances in 1 Corinthians 15:1-9, tells us that James (like Thomas) was not with the disciples in the first instance. This should not be so surprising to us since James, the brother of our Lord, belonged to a family which had expressed doubts and misgivings regarding Jesus' behaviour (cf. Mark 3:21 and John 7:5 plainly reading "For even his brothers did not believe in him"). We have every reason to believe that it was the fact of the resurrection which convinced James of his brother's messiahship, since there was little mention of him earlier.

Of course there were magicians in the days of Jesus just as surely as the Egyptians had them in the time of Moses. We read of Simon the magician in Acts 8:9ff, and Elymas the sorcerer in Acts 13:6-8. In the case of Simon, Luke introduces him as one who thought himself to be "somebody great", a not unusual trait in the profession.

In areas of the charismatic and the para-normal, some phenomena cannot be easily, if at all, explained, but the high moral teachings of Jesus could hardly emanate from someone who knowingly used his personal gifts and power to falsely impress people and thus to deceive them. Compassion was natural to him, and the energies which flowed from him touched people at their point of need. Jesus was no mere

---

*Schonfield authored the book *The Passover Plot* (New York: 1965), and Allegro produced his work *The Sacred Mushroom and the Cross: A Study of the Nature and Origins of Christianity Within the Fertility Cults of the Ancient Near East* (London: 1970).

# The Controversial Jesus

magician and certainly not a trickster.

## Jesus, a Prophet?

The office of prophet was important and strongly influential in the religious and political life of Israel. A prophet could rebuke the king, as Nathan did when David had sinned against Uriah, the husband of Bathsheba (2 Samuel 12:1ff). Prophets anointed kings, and sometimes outlived them in terms of impacting the people of Israel. It was after the death of Uzziah that Isaiah reached his zenith. Prophets not only predicted the course of the nation, but would warn Israel of her enemies, even to the point of naming these as God's instruments of discipline against his own people. Jewish prophets had messages for nations outside of Israel as per Jonah who was sent to Nineveh. They were not always respected but often persecuted, and even regarded as traitors as in the case of Jeremiah who warned Judah of its impending disaster. Jesus referred to Jerusalem as the city which killed the prophets and stoned those who were sent to her (Matthew 23:37). Jesus paid great respect to John the Baptist, the fiery prophet who preceded him. The common people saw Jesus as a prophet, and as someone who spoke with authority "and not as the scribes" (Mark 1:22).

Jesus saw himself as a prophet, for when he preached in his own home territory, the people took offence at 'the carpenter' whose family they knew so well. In response to this situation Jesus uttered his unforgettable statement that "a prophet is not without honor except in his own country and in his own house" (Matthew 13:57).

Old Testament prophets were known for their powerful denunciation of the evils of the day, the greed of the rich, the oppression of the poor, and the hypocrisy of political and religious leaders. Jesus showed the same prophetic courage. There are scholars today who cringe at the thought of Jesus being judgmental, and they try to relegate these 'hard sayings' such as the woes against the Pharisees, to unknown writers who, they will claim, must have added these pronouncements to the ipsissima verba of Jesus. True, he taught that we must not judge lest we be judged, and he is surely condemning the person who is prone to criticise others. Yet the obvious corollary to Jesus' assumption of the prophetic role would be the right to judge, and to do it eloquently and passionately, which he did.

At Luke 24:19, we find Cleopas had been convinced that Jesus was "a prophet mighty in deed and word before God and all the people." Few have difficulty with Jesus' identity as a prophet, except for a current school of thought which seeks to deny his Jewishness while stressing the Hellenistic influence of the Cynics in the regions of Galilee where Jesus was raised. This, too, will be duly considered in the present chapter.

For Christians who see a close relationship between the Old and New Testament faiths, it is only natural that Jesus is to be regarded as one who falls into the category of Deuteronomy 18:15-18, and pre-eminently so:

> The Lord your God will raise up for you a prophet like me from among you, from your brethren—him you shall heed.... I will raise up for them a prophet like you from among their brethren; and I will put my words in his mouth, and he shall speak to them all that I command him. And whoever will not give heed to my words which he shall speak in my name, I myself will require it of him. But the prophet who presumes to speak a word in my name which I have not commanded him to speak, or who speaks in the name of others gods, that same prophet shall die.

This pronouncement was understood to apply to the entire succession of Hebrew prophets, each of whom, however, would be tested by his strict adherence to the words given to him by God. Nevertheless, the implication is that his words would augment the Law. It is doubly significant that Jesus stresses his own commitment to the Father's will in the message he brought, at the same time claiming a unique authority.

> Do you not believe that I am in the Father and the Father in me? The words that I say to you I do not speak on my own authority; but the Father who dwells in me does his works ... for I have given them the words which thou gavest me, and they have received them and know in truth that I came from thee; and they have believed that thou didst send me (John 14:10; 17:8).

Those of the Jewish faith, and true to the Torah, are likely to have

## The Controversial Jesus

extreme difficulty with these words of Jesus since, after all, he seemed to be in frequent conflict with the keepers of the Law in his day. If Jesus were a true prophet, how could this be? The fact is that he showed allegiance to the Law to the extent of saying that not one iota or dot ("jot or tittle") would be removed from the Law until all was fulfilled (Matthew 5:18). He went on, "Whoever then relaxes one of the least of these commandments and teaches men so, shall be called least in the kingdom of heaven; but he who teaches them shall be called great in the kingdom of heaven" (5:19).

David Flusser vouches for the faithfulness of Jesus to the Law when he writes, "The Gospels provide sufficient evidence to the effect that Jesus did not oppose any prescription of the Written or Oral Mosaic Law, and that he even performed Jewish religious commandments"[37] He attributes the mistaken impression that Jesus did counter the Law to the exaggerated wording contained in the Gospels; this wording reflecting the later and growing rift between the synagogue and the church."[38] Such is the view of Flusser.

Perhaps we can better understand the situation by following the statement of Jesus, as recorded in Matthew 5:20: "For I tell you, unless your righteousness exceeds that of the scribes and Pharisees, you will never enter the kingdom of heaven." Even if this verse had been added by the later church, we would still need to ascertain what is really intended. Is this a call to a more fundamental legalism, or is there another explanation? The answer surely lies within a similar context, described for us in Matthew 15:1-9, where Jesus quoted from the prophet Isaiah as he took issue with the Pharisees for their having made void the word of God by the traditions of men:

> And the Lord said: 'Because this people draw near with their mouth and honour me with their lips, while their hearts are far from me, and their fear of me is a commandment of men learned by rote; therefore, behold, I will again do marvelous things with this people, wonderful and marvelous; and the wisdom of their wise men shall perish, and the discernment of their discerning men shall be hid (Isaiah 29:13-14).

Time and again Jesus felt it necessary to stress the inner righteousness of the heart, even as Jeremiah the prophet had expressed in his significant prediction (31:31-33):

> Behold the days are coming, says the Lord, when I will make a new covenant with the house of Israel and the house of Judah, not like the covenant which I made with their fathers when I took them by the hand to bring them out of the land of Egypt. But this is the covenant which I will make with the house of Israel after those days, says the Lord: I will put my law within them, and I will write it upon their hearts, and I will be their God, and they shall be my people.

Jesus was no lawbreaker, but declared he had come to fulfil the law. Yet he and his disciples often incurred the displeasure and condemnation of the Pharisees for their seeming laxity, particularly in matters of sabbath observances. In contrast to this was Jesus' high view of marriage and his strong reluctance to permit divorce—a strictness which did not accord with the followers of Hillel, and may have been even a trifle too conservative for the school of Shammai.

Obviously Jesus was concerned more about matters of the heart, and inner motivation, than with the technicalities of interpretation, and less with the letter of the law than with the spirit and purpose of the law. In our contemporary society, the vigorous application of certain of the Levitical and Deuteronomic laws is deemed unworkable, e.g. capital punishment for all intentional murder (Deuteronomy 19:12-13), the putting to death of a brother, son, daughter, wife or friend who adopts a religion outside of Judaism and entices others to do the same (13:6-11); and the stoning to death of a rebellious son (21:21). The problem of literal obedience may help us to see the difficulties that confronted Jesus in his dealings with the religious authorities of his day. He sought the fulfilment of the Law but by means of a motivating love.

Neither was Jesus anything of a wimp when it came to the essentials of human morality and punishment for crimes. He gave grave warnings to any who would offend "one of these little ones" (Matthew 18:15), suggesting that the person was deserving of capital punishment for abuse of children! Positively stated, Jesus made it clear that whatever we do to any of the least of our brothers we do to him (Matthew 25:40). He was truly a prophet of righteousness, justice and fairplay, with an intense concern for the poor, the deprived and the handicapped of the world.

## Jesus, a Cynic?

This brings us to a fresh and unconventional view of Jesus. It has been largely promoted by Burton L. Mack, whose book *The Lost Gospel* seeks to recover the early and authentic sayings of Jesus, largely by rejecting all Jewish-oriented sayings of the Gospels on one side, and those sayings which he and some fellow scholars consider to have been added later by the church.[39] John Dominic Crossan travels in the same direction, but he does allow somewhat for the Jewishness of Jesus, yet wishes to demonstrate that he was little other than a pacifistic peasant whose travelling and preaching style closely resembled that of a Greek Cynic. His controversial work *The Historical Jesus: The life of a Mediterranean Peasant* was followed three years later with his *Jesus: A Revolutionary Biography* in which he revised some of his opinions but continued to reject the Gospels' records of the miracles, the Last Supper, of the idea of an atoning death and certainly of the resurrection of Jesus. He maintains that Jesus, as a social reformer, was against political hierarchies as such, and encouraged instead the establishment of an egalitarian society, or what he likes to call "a brokerless kingdom of nobodies"

The same scholars appreciate the teaching of Jesus to love our enemies and to turn the other cheek, and they would praise his pacifism. They applaud his call to the disciples to a life of poverty. In their travels they were to take "no bread, no bag, no money in their belts" (Mark 6:8) Such, they aver, typified the life-style of the Cynics.* However, it becomes obvious that they select those words of Jesus which make them feel comfortable, and to discard other sayings which conflict with their own preconceptions of Jesus. References to messianism, authority to forgive sins, Jesus' attitude to the Law and related issues

---

\* In point of fact the Cynics did carry food and such money as was given to them on their itineraries, and actually regarded this practice as a mark of their independence. "This suggests, if anything, a reaction by Jesus against the Cynic modus operandi." See Ben Witherington III, *The Jesus Quest*: p.72.

which would be of the utmost interest to the Pharisees and others of the Jewish community, are overlooked or minimized. One is forced to ask if Jesus spoke without having an audience. There had to be reaction and no doubt of the kind which our Gospels actually report. The most serious deficiency in Mack and Crossan's position is their failure to provide an adequate explanation of the factors which led to the execution of Jesus, an act which did not parallel the treatment of known Cynics of the time. Their omissions leave large black holes in the picture of Jesus they paint for us. This is also typical of the entire enterprise of the Jesus Seminar. Ben Witherington III, professor of New Testament at Asbury Theological Seminary, observes:

> It has long been the consensus of most scholars that if there are two things Jesus certainly spoke about they are the Son of Man and the kingdom of God. Yet these subjects hardly surface in the Jesus Seminar's discussions of important topics. [40]

The pressing need for a total picture of Jesus, his words and works, his relationships with his contemporaries, and the reasons for his crucifixion, was clearly outlined in E. P. Sanders' book *Jesus and Judaism*, published as early as 1985. Richard B. Hays, writing in *First Things* (No. 43, The Institute of Religion and Public Life, New York, N.Y., 1994: p.46) appropriately comments: "the Seminar inexplicably ignores Sanders' methods and conclusions."

Whereas the editors of *The Five Gospels* assert that the publication of their work "represents a dramatic exit from windowless studies and the beginning of a new venture for scholarship,"* it might be better described as leaving a well lit room to descend into a cellar where no one can easily distinguish one thing from another. They have in fact applied a rigorous surgical procedure to the four gospels, based on their claim that Jesus' original sayings are to be found *primarily* in the hypothetical document known among theologians as 'Q', and in the apocryphal Gospel of Thomas. It is quite incredible that only one saying of Jesus of all those recorded in Mark is given full accreditation

---

* Eds. Robert W. Funk & Roy W. Hoover. New York: Poleridge/Macmillan, 1993, p.1.

in *The Five Gospels*. It is the one which reads "Pay the emperor what belongs to the emperor, and God what belongs to God" (12:17).

'Q' (short for Quelle in German meaning 'source') is a hypothetical reconstruction which for many years has been assumed to exist prior to the writing of our gospels. The assumption is well justified since certain materials found in the gospels of Matthew and Luke bear a striking resemblance and presumably came from a common source. Early researchers in this area included Karl Lachmann (1835), Christian Wilke (1838), H. J. Holtzmann (1863), and Bernard Weiss (1907). Major work was done in our own century by Adolf von Harnack, B. H. Streeter and Rudolf Bultmann. Harnack actually published a little book entitled *The Sayings of Jesus*, which may well have been the original purpose of 'Q'—a collection of Jesus' ethical teachings, rather than anything of a biography, much in the same way that Mao Tse Tung's words were specially preserved in the Little Red Book.

The title of Burton Mack's book, *The Lost Gospel* may suggest to the uninformed reader that a recent discovery has been made of further material to augment the Gospels we already have. In actual fact these sayings can not be regarded as 'lost' since, in God's providence, they are already contained in our traditional New Testament. This does not apply, of course, to the apocryphal Gospel of Thomas which was discovered among other Gnostic writings at Nag Hammadi, Egypt in 1945. The reader will be well acquainted with the fact that numerous works appeared in the second century, and beyond, which took Jesus as their theme, some of which were novelty rather than history. Not a few had clear and obvious tendencies towards Gnostic heresy.

Comprehensive works on extracanonical sayings of Jesus have been assembled by William D. Stoker and Joachim Jeremias. The latter comments: "The bulk of it (the corpus of *agrapha*) is legendary, and bears the clear mark of forgery.... The range of material which is of any use to the historian is remarkably small."[41] An example of the sheer imaginativeness of *apocrypha* is conspicuous in the *Infancy Gospel of Thomas*, which represents the child Jesus "as a self-willed little brat who, throwing a tantrum, makes a child who runs up against him drop dead."[42] John P. Meier goes on to describe this kind of literature as "pop" literature designed for "religious" entertainment. He also chides the press and book publishers who in recent years have been "selling" apocryphal works to the public under the guise of New Testament research and the quest for the historical Jesus. He bluntly states "This is a misuse of useful material. There is nothing here that can serve as a source in our quest for the historical Jesus."[43]

An intriguing touch of romance characterizes the so-called *Gospel of Philip* (second half of the third century), as something of a modern Harlequin paperback. The disciples are made to ask Jesus why he kisses Mary Magdalene on the mouth, and why he loves her more than all the disciples! Not far removed from this reputed incident, this *Gospel* calls God a man-eater!*

Paradoxically, we are finding that greater faith is being placed by some modern writers in works which for years have been regarded as novel, often fictitious and unreliable, besides being farther removed in time from the life of Jesus and the beginnings of the early church. A notorious example of forgery is the case of the so-called *Gospel of Barnabas*. James C. Charlesworth explains:

> The study of the historical Jesus has had an impact on international affairs. Some in the Middle East who hate Judaism and Christianity claim that the Gospel of Barnabas, a massive work of 222 chapters, alone contains the original gospel of Jesus. Barnabas, counted among the twelve in his gospel, receives Jesus' secret teachings, reports that Judas is the one who is crucified, and that Jesus prophesied the coming of Muhammad. [44]

David Sox examined this so-called gospel and provided ample evidence that the work is a medieval forgery written by an enthusiastic convert to Islam![45] Christians must be aware, not only of cults which seek to pervert the faith within church circles, but more so of those who invoke most questionable documents to undermine the public's confidence in Christianity.

Let us now return to a consideration of the Gospel of Thomas, which Burton L. Mack and others prefer over our canonical Gospels, believing

---

* See N. T. Wright, *Who Was Jesus?* Grand Rapids: Eerdmans, 1992, pp.30-31.

## The Controversial Jesus

it to be an earlier source of Jesus' teachings. The following are representative quotes from the work which are reprinted here to enable the reader to decide for himself or herself how reliable it may be or otherwise.

Prologue: These are the hidden sayings that the living Jesus spoke and Judas Thomas the Twin recorded.

1. And he said, 'Whosoever discovers the interpretation of these sayings will not taste death.'

12. The followers said to Jesus, 'We know that you are going to leave us. Who will be our leader?' Jesus said to them, 'No matter where you are, you are to go to James the Just, for whose sake heaven and earth came into being.'

19. Jesus said, 'Fortunate is one who came into being before coming into being. If you become my followers and listen to my sayings, these stones will serve you. For there are five trees in paradise for you; they do not change, summer or winter, and their leaves do not fall. Whoever knows them will not taste death.'

30. Jesus said, 'Where there are three deities, they are divine. Where there are two or one, I am with that one.'

31. Jesus said, 'A prophet is not acceptable in the prophet's own town; a doctor does not heal those who know the doctor.'

53. His followers said to him, 'Is circumcision useful or not?' He said to them, 'If it were useful, children's fathers would produce the already circumcised from their mothers. Rather, the true circumcision in spirit has become valuable in every respect.'

77. Jesus said, 'I am the light that is over all things. I am all: From me all has come forth, and to me all has reached. Split a piece of wood; I am there. Lift up the stone, and you will find me there.'

84. Jesus said, 'When you see your likeness, you are happy. But when you see your images that came into being before you and that neither die nor become visible, how much you will bear!'

114. Simon Peter said to them, 'Mary should leave us, for females are not worthy of life.' Jesus said, 'Look, I shall guide her to make her male, so that she too may become a living spirit resembling you males. For every female who makes herself male will enter heaven's kingdom.'*

As already mentioned, this gospel has been added to the work of the Jesus Seminar in its publication of *The Five Gospels,* and it may be just that—chronologically a fifth and later production which combines some early sayings of Jesus with Gnostic theology typical of the mid or late second century. Take for instance Saying 31, the first part of which is certainly a word of Jesus, but the addition is very much open to question, doubt and confusion, viz. "a doctor does not heal those who know the doctor." It may be reminiscent of Jesus' other statement about those who feel they are well, but have no need of a physician, which makes good sense. R. T. France describes these joint sayings (31) in the Gospel of Thomas as "curious and slightly incongruous."[46]

It may occur to the reader that some of these sayings represent a hodge-podge of contradiction. Saying 12 highly favours James the Just, known to be a stout defender of Judaistic traditions in the early church, yet Saying 53 about circumcision is quite Pauline! It is also very difficult to believe that Jesus would issue such an exaggerated and fanciful statement about the importance of James his brother, as the leader to whom everyone must go after his own ascension. The tradition that the Holy Spirit would guide his followers is much more believable:

> And when they deliver you up, do not be anxious beforehand what you are to say; but say whatever is given you in that hour, for it is not you who speak, but the Holy Spirit" (Mark 13:11).

> These things I have spoken to you, while I am still with you. But the Counselor, the Holy Spirit, whom the Father will send in my name, he will teach you all things, and bring to your remembrance all that I have said to you (John 14:25-26).

---

*\* The Gospel of Thomas.* New Translation by Marvin Meyer and Interpretation by Harold Bloom (San Francisco: Harper Collins, 1992), pp.23-65.

# The Controversial Jesus

Saying 114, as most will agree, is troublesome. It stands out in the sharpest contrast to Jesus' known attitude towards women in all of our four Gospels. The story of the woman who anointed Jesus with spikenard ointment, which Judas and others complained was a waste, shows how he commended the woman for being more discerning than his own disciple (Mark 14:3-9). He endorsed her act by declaring that she would be memorialized wherever the Gospel was preached.

In our present quest to find out whether Jesus was more of a hellenized Cynic than he was Jewish, it is important to observe that there is no hint of pantheism in his teaching. The birds of the air and the crops of the land, etc., are all the Father's creation and under his care. However, Saying 77, "Split a piece of wood; I am there. Lift up the stone, and you will find me there" is strong evidence of non-Jewish Gnostic or eastern thinking. The church, let it be said, had to do battle with the Gnostics whose ethereal philosophizings came to question whether Jesus was a real human. This phantom-thinking of theirs is challenged by John in his first letter where he stresses that Jesus partook of our flesh and came by "water and blood" (1 John 4:2; 5:6). John further affirms the physical reality of the one whom he knew in Galilee, when he writes "we have seen with our eyes ... and touched with our hands" (1:1).

We can be sure that Jesus was no mere assimilationist of Hellenism, nor of Greek mythology, neither can he be reduced to an itinerating Cynic. Mack is careful, of course, to challenge the modern caricature of the ancient Cynics which, he says, "usually calls to mind the unsavory figure of Diogenes of Sinope and dwells upon his habits of biting sarcasm and public obscenities."[47] He claims that the Cynics were the Greek analogue to the Hebrew prophets, playing the role of critics of conventional values and oppressive forms of government. He provides us with amusing cases of their humour and of their carefree way of living as beggars. Crossan gives much space to Hellenistic influences which operated in the Galilean cities of Sepphoris and Tiberias—the pride of the generally disliked Herod Antipas, but he fails to give sufficient emphasis to traditional Judaism which continued in the older towns and villages of Galilee and which even received the attention of the Judaea-based Pharisees (cf. Josephus, *Life*, 197 ff).

The same writers, however, confess to the fact of Jesus' calling of twelve disciples does not correspond to the typical Cynic. Of these travelling philosophers Crossan writes, "... they showed little sense of collective discipline, on the one hand, or of communal action on the other. Jesus and his followers do not fit well against *that* background."[48]—an honest observation which greatly weakens his own thesis. Likewise Mack admits to the same difficulty: "In the case of the Jesus people, however, signs of social formation can be detected even among the core aphorisms of Q1.... This feature of the Jesus movement appears to be distinctive."[49]

Mention of "Q1" obligates us to conclude this chapter by referring to the recently evolved theory held by Burton L. Mack and John Kloppenborg[50] that Q itself must be divided into different time frames, the earlier sections being actual sayings of Jesus, while the second and third *may* be the thoughts of the members of the Jesus community as it faced more and more difficult times. Thus their sense of rejection is said to have aroused *in them* a judgmental attitude towards their opponents, finally producing the apocalyptic section which foresees the judgment of the world and the return of the victorious Son of Man. Jesus, then, is seen as one who would never have uttered any undue condemnations; and those difficult, judgmental and apocalyptic sayings in the Gospels are no more than the frustrated expressions of the persecuted Jesus community!

Unbridled speculations of this kind can and will surely lead to an unprecedented arbitrariness in scholarship. Craig L. Blomberg, in an article entitled *The Seventy-four Scholars: Who does the Jesus Seminar really speak for?* writes: "People dropped out for various reasons. Some expressed discomfort with how the most radical fringes of New Testament scholarship were disproportionately represented.... Others voiced disagreement with Funk's propagandistic purposes of popularizing scholarship in a way designed to undermine conservative Christian credibility."[51]

We began by saying that there is abroad today an apparent desire to diminish the importance of Jesus and to dilute his message. In so doing they have hid the real person from our sight. Methinks the old adage is true, that as God first created man in his own image, man quickly returned the compliment by making God in *his* image. Jesus,

I am sure, refuses to be reduced to the form of an idol or to a statue of our making, or worse, to play the role of a ventriloquist's dummy and be made to say only what his critics will allow him to say. Such negative attitudes towards Jesus of Nazareth, however, are sometimes only a modern reflection of the opposition he himself encountered as he traversed Galilee, Judaea and Jerusalem. Holy man, moral teacher, spiritual leader, strong prophet, Son of God, he was destined to play the part of the suffering servant and the man of sorrows who was acquainted with grief. Remaining silent before his accusers, he was led as a sheep to the slaughter. And for very good reason we have hid our faces from him. Shame should consume us, when we realize how we have ignored with contempt his love for people, and his call to repentance, forgiveness and restoration. We have tried to conform him to our mean concepts, and to use him to advance only our own crooked agendas, whether religious, political or personal. The treatment accorded to this man in whom was found no fault, is a frightening exposure of the subtle deceptions, the unspeakable cruelties and the heinous crimes of which humankind is capable.

It is a proven paradox, however, that faced with the real Jesus we ourselves are changed and this is the incredible miracle of the Gospel.

"Sir, we wish to see Jesus" (John 12:21).

## Notes

[1] Vermes, G. *Jesus the Jew: A Historian's Reading of the Gospels*, 1973; reprinted, New York: Collins, 1977, p.50.

[2] Montefiore, C. G. *What a Jew Thinks about Jesus*. The Hibbert Journal, vol. 33 (1934-5), p.516.

[3] Montefiore, C. G. *The Old Testament and Its Ethical Teaching*. The Hibbert Journal (1917-18), p.242.

[4] See Hans Kung *Signposts for the Future*. ET by Edward Quinn. New York: Doubleday, 1978, p.71.

[5] Friedlander, G. *The Jewish Sources of the Sermon on the Mount*, 1911; reprinted, New York: Ktav, 1969, p.266.

[6] Flusser, D. *Jesus* ET by R. Walls. New York: Herder & Herder, 1969, p.7-8.

[7] Kaminka, A. Quoted from the periodical *Ha-Toren* (August, 1922) by H. Danby, *The Jew and Christianity*. London: Sheldon, 1927, p.103.

[8] Lapide, P., & Luz, U. *Jesus in Two Perspectives*, ET by Lawrence W. Denef. Minneapolis: Augsburg, 1985.

[9] Lawrence H. Schiffman in *Understanding the Dead Sea Scrolls* ed. H. Shanks. New York: Random House, 1992, pp.218-219.

[10] Ibid., p.221.

[11] Hagner, D. *The Jewish Reclamation of Jesus*. Grand Rapids: Zondervan, 1984, pp.229-233.

[12] Ibid., p.231.

[13] Ibid., p.231.

[14] Ibid., p.232.

[15] Maccoby, H. *Revolution in Judaea*, 1973; reprinted, New York: Taplinger, 1981, pp.106-7.

[16] Zeitlin, Irving M. *Jesus and The Judaism of His Time*. Cambridge: Polity Press, 1988, pp.11-12.

[17] Ben-Chorin, Schalom. *Bruder Jesus: Der Nazarener in judischer Sicht*, Munich: 1967.

[18] Lawrence H. Schiffman in *Understanding the Dead Sea Scrolls*, p.219.

# The Controversial Jesus

[19] McDowell, J. & Wilson, Bill. *He Walked Among Us.* Nashville: Nelson, 1993, p.220.

[20] Zeitlin, Solomon *The Rise and Fall of the Judaean State.* vol 3, Philadelphia: 1978, p.187 ff.

[21] Vermes, G. *Jesus the Jew,* p.35.

[22] Kohler, K. *Jesus of Nazareth—In Theology.* The Jewish Encyclopedia, ed. I. Singer. New York: 1901-1906, 7:169.

[23] Quoted by Irving M. Zeitlin from Schurer *History of the Jewish People,* pp.555ff. Also Josephus *Antiquities* 18:21 and *War* 2:120.

[24] Charlesworth, James H. *Jesus Within Judaism.* New York: Doubleday, 1988, pp.74-75.

[25] Wilson, A. N. *Jesus.* London: Harper-Collins, 1993, p.xvii.

[26] Vermes, G. *Jesus the Jew,* p.75.

[27] Zeitlin, Irving M. *Jesus and The Judaism of His Time,* p.160.

[28] Eisenman, Robert H. *Maccabees, Zadokites, Christians and Qumran.* Leiden: 1983, p.44 n. 30.

[29] Baigent, M. and Leigh, R. *The Dead Sea Scrolls Deception,* New York: Simon & Schuster, 1991, p.174.

[30] Meier, John P. *A Marginal Jew: Rethinking the Historical Jesus.* New York: Doubleday, 1991, pp.300-301, n.77.

[31] Crossan, John Dominic. *The Historical Jesus: The Life of a Mediterranean Jewish Peasant.* San Francisco: Harper, 1992, p.18.

[32] Vermes, Geza. *Jesus and the World of Judaism.* Philadelphia: Fortress, 1983, p.12.

[33] Charlesworth, James H. *Jesus Within Judaism,* p.75.

[34] Smith, Morton. *Jesus the Magician.* New York: Harper & Row, 1978, p.25.

[35] McDowell, J. & Wilson, Bill. *He Walked Among Us,* p.334.

[36] Wilson, A. N. *Jesus,* p.61.

[37] Flusser, D. *Jesus.* Encyclopedia Judaica, ed. C. Roth. Jerusalem: 1971, 10:13.

[38] Ibid., 10:12-13.

[39] It should be noted that Norman Perrin was a pioneer in current redactionism, a method which, however, has been exploited by some far-out thinkers. Cf. *Rediscovering the Teaching of Jesus.* New York: Harper & Row, 1967.

[40] Witherington III, Ben. *The Jesus Quest: The Third Search for the Jew of Nazareth.* Downers Grove, Ill.: InterVarsity Press, 1995, p.55.

[41] Jeremias, Joachim. *Unknown Sayings of Jesus.* p.120.

[42] Meier, John P. *The Marginal Jew,* p.115.

[43] Ibid., p.123.

[44] Charlesworth, James H. *Jesus Within Judaism.* pp.25-26.

[45] Sox, D. *The Gospel of Barnabas.* London: 1984.

[46] R. T. Frances in the Tyndale New Testament Commentary, *Matthew.* Leicester: IVP.; Grand Rapids: Eerdmans, 1985, p.232.

[47] Mack, Burton. L. *The Lost Gospel.* San Francisco: Harper, 1993, p.114.

[48] Crossan, John Dominic. *The Historical Jesus.* p.421.

[49] Mack, Burton L. *The Lost Gospel.* p.121.

[50] Kloppenborg, John. *The Formation of Q: Trajectories in Ancient Wisdom Collections.* Philadelphia: Fortress Press, 1987.

[51] Blomberg, Craig L. *Christian Research Journal,* Vol. 17, No. 2, Fall 1994; Christian Research Institute, Irvine CA.

CHAPTER FIVE

# The Founder of the Faith

> And I tell you, you are Peter, and on this rock I will build my church, and the powers of Hades shall not prevail against it (Matthew 16:18).

> For no other foundation can any one lay than that which is laid, which is Jesus Christ (1 Corinthians 3:11).

The idea that the apostle Paul was the real founder of the church, and not Jesus, has circulated for some time, but a recent writer has given it fresh impetus. Hyam Maccoby in his book *The Mythmaker* pursues the argument that Paul effectively displaced Jesus in the early formation of the church and of its doctrines. Not only so, but Maccoby, like Paula Fredriksen and others, maintains that Paulinism greatly influenced the writing of the Gospels. It is also pointed out that Paul is the hero of the Acts of the Apostles, but we must retort that the person of Jesus of Nazareth, his death and resurrection, are paramount in the preached message.

The importance of the apostle Paul cannot, and should not be downplayed, but to accord to him the distinction of founding the church is an exaggerated absurdity. Paul is regularly accused of obscuring the real Jesus by importing mythological concepts of a virgin birth,* a deified saviour, a warfare between spiritual powers in heavenly places, and a dualism which was essentially Gnostic (see pp. 148-151). He is further accused of denigrating the Law of Moses by emphasising salvation *sola fide,* by faith alone.

Dr. Maccoby betrays his low view of Paul when he comments, "Like many evangelical leaders, he was a compound of sincerity and charlatanry."[1] He alleges that Paul was never a Pharisee rabbi, but was "an adventurer of undistinguished background."[2] He asserts that Paul's dialectic represented a 'non-Pharisaical use of argument.'"[3] For a striking comparison which comes from a fellow Jewish academic, the reader is invited to consult the booklet *Paul, Rabbi and Apostle* where Pinchas Lapide states that Paul's style "reveals unmistakably rabbinic thought forms and lets Pharisaic dialogue patterns shimmer through."[4]

Maccoby insists, however, that Paul had an exaggerated sense of his own academic status, and in addition he probably misrepresented his own biography in order to increase the effectiveness of his missionary activities. To support his viewpoint he draws on materials from the Ebionite sect, which according to Solomon Zeitlin made its appearance sometime in the second century (C.E.).[5] It was a likely successor to earlier Judaistic Christians who are described by Justin Martyr (c. 150 C.E.), as recognizing the messiahship of Jesus, but only as a man. They were known for their observance of circumcision, of the Sabbath and dietary restrictions, but were shunned by gentile Christians. Later, Irenaeus towards the end of the century protested the group known as Ebionites who insisted that Jesus was not born of

---

* In Galatians 4:4 Paul seems more concerned to stress the humanity of Jesus when he writes: "God sent forth his Son, born of woman, born under the law", but at vs.21-23 he significantly contrasts the births of Abraham's two sons, which in Isaac's case, was other than 'normal' to the human experience. Here Paul underscores the element of the supernatural. We might take from this that the birth of the child of promise can be viewed as a precursor of the birth of Messiah. Of significance within the same context (Gal. 4:27) is Paul's quote from Isaiah 54:1-3.

## The Founder of the Faith

a virgin, and that he became the Messiah only at the time of his baptism. It was they who rejected the apostle Paul and called him "an apostate from the Law." Some of their allegations were obviously calculated to be injurious to the image of Paul, but this was nothing new since Paul himself had freely written about his Judaistic opponents many years before.

It will be necessary for us to discover how early the division took place between the Judaean Christians who insisted on the keeping of the Law, particularly the rite of circumcision, and those who held to the view that Christ's death and resurrection had inaugurated an entirely new era of salvation. Fundamentally we must find out if these distinctions go back to Jesus himself. Certainly he alluded to the fact that new wine could not be put into old bottles (Mt. 9:17; Mark 2:22; Luke 5:37-38). This statement along with many others would indicate that the breach did start most definitely with Jesus, and not with Paul. James D. G. Dunn holds to this view in his book *Jesus, Paul and the Law*, and he argues cogently for the primacy of a faith which was transmitted to the early disciples and later received by Paul. Dunn takes into account the view of Wilhelm Wrede who once described Paul as "the second founder of Christianity."[6] Wrede, of course, maintained that the Pauline influence was the stronger; but for us as Christians, and certainly for Paul himself, the radicalness of Jesus which led to his death, was the ground and basis of the new faith.

Some Jewish scholars, going as far back as Reimarus, describe Jesus as a patriot and a political revolutionary. Understandably there is a reluctance to acknowledge that Jesus could have been a religious radical and one who was at variance with the religious authorities of his day. Yet the Hebrew prophets had often placed themselves in the same kind of situation, even to the point of condemning the sacrifice abuses of the priests. In any event there is ample evidence that Jesus had his disagreements with the Pharisees, as also he had with the Sadducees and the Temple priests, facts which predate Paul's entry on the scene.

Dunn significantly points out that the five principal issues in the second chapter of Mark seem to be the authority claimed by Jesus, implicitly or explicitly, in matters of healing and forgiveness, consorting with sinners, fasting and the sabbath.* As the title of our previous chapter indicated, Jesus was highly controversial, and his provocative teaching must have given the authorities of the day, both religious and political, much uneasiness and annoyance. That they were ready to put him away, can hardly be attributed to Pauline manipulation either of the initial events or of their subsequent record.

Our first task has been to investigate Maccoby's charge that the theological presuppositions of Paul "were already before the writers of the Gospels and coloured their interpretations of Jesus' activities.... Paul is, in a sense, *present from the very first word* of the New Testament" (my italics).[9] Thankfully, in his next sentence, he seems to moderate his view, and writes: "This is, of course, not the whole story, for the Gospels are based on traditions and even written sources which go back to a time before the impact of Paul...."

Now we must turn to the connecting link between Jesus and the conversion of Paul, again to find if there was any primitive evidence of a radical recognition by the church that its future would be other than a continuation of traditional Judaism. There is such evidence in Acts of the Apostles, chapter 11. At verse 2 we are told that the 'circumcision party' remonstrated with Peter, "Why did you go to uncircumcised men and eat with them?" Peter defended his position and gave testimony that the Holy Spirit had come upon the Gentiles "just as on us at the beginning" (11:15). Perhaps even more significant is the reference to a great number of Greeks in Antioch who believed the Gospel. It was there that the disciples were first called Christians (11:20-26).

Surprised by this surge of success among the Gentiles, the church in Jerusalem sent Barnabas to enquire into the occurrence. He found to his satisfaction that the grace of God was in evidence among them. No mention whatever is made of circumcision, exactly identical to the case of the conversion of Cornelius in chapter ten, where only baptism

---

*Dunn claims that "there is widespread agreement as to the pre-Markan nature of the traditions utilized by him in 2:1-3:6 .... All five of the narrative sections focus on controversies between Jesus and his critics, particularly the Pharisees."[7] Vincent Taylor and Norman Perrin are cited in support of the independent origin of this Markan passage.[8]

was administered to him and his household. Dunn maintains that "without authorization from the original Jesus-tradition it is difficult to see how such a departure gained the acceptance it did within the earliest Christian communities of Palestine."[10]

We can be very sure that this development in the practice of the primitive church was not at all the invention of Paul, any more than the glorious fact of the resurrection which was proclaimed right from the beginning, and well before Paul's experience on the Damascus road. Paul is not to be credited nor blamed for the first steps in the new faith and he is honest enough to acknowledge his dependency on the earlier traditions as in 1 Corinthians 15:3-10:

> For I delivered to you as of first importance what I also received, that Christ died for our sins in accordance with the scriptures, that he was buried, that he was raised on the third day in accordance with the scriptures, and that he appeared to Cephas, then to the twelve. Then he appeared to more than five hundred brethren at one time, most of whom are still alive, though some have fallen asleep. Then he appeared to James, then to all the apostles. Last of all, as to one untimely born, he appeared also to me. For I am the least of the apostles, unfit to be called an apostle, because I persecuted the church of God.

Frankly, the above testimony of the apostle does not savour of an egostical pride, whatever may have induced Hyam Maccoby to think otherwise of Paul; for here we have a positive affirmation of the church's true foundation, that of Jesus himself, and of the priority in time of those apostles who were before Paul.

Our second task in this area of discussion must be to ascertain precisely what was the real underlying cause of tension and increasing friction between the early Christian believers, which later prolongated into the solidifying of a distinctly Judaistic segment of the church. In some cases, a complete return to the old Judaism took place, as the epistle to the Hebrews painfully indicates (cf. 6:6). This defection is even described as a fresh crucifying of the Son of God. Paul is dealing with the same problem among the Galatians, some of whom had been persuaded to be circumcised. In response to this development he writes, "Now I, Paul (*himself a circumcised Jew*), say to you that if you receive circumcision, Christ will be of no advantage to you.... You are severed from Christ, you who would be justified by the law; you have fallen away from grace" (5:2-4). The argument is plain. As Gentiles, to receive salvation, circumcision was not a requirement; and to yield to the Judaizers, who were following Paul on his missionary journeys, these Galatians were unwittingly denying the experience into which they had entered, thus nullifying the meaning of the cross. This is why Paul writes earlier in the same epistle:

> O foolish Galatians! Who has bewitched you, before whose eyes Jesus Christ was publicly portrayed as crucified? Let me ask you only this: Did you receive the Spirit by works of the law, or by hearing with faith? (5:1-2).

It became axiomatic for Paul to contrast the crucifixion of Jesus, as the means of salvation for the Gentiles, with the covenantal sign of circumcision which had been given to the children of Abraham, of which he was one. More than that, however, the cross represented God's final sacrifice for sin and the provision of forgiveness for all, Jew and Gentile, who had become transgressors. The Law, given by Moses, was augmented by the sacrificial system to ensure ritual purification and to cover the sins of transgressors. Whether Paul realised it or not, the entire Jewish sacrificial system would shortly collapse with the destruction of the Temple, and this would force a change in the religious practices of the Jews. He was certainly aware of the idea of substitutionary atonement, as it is outlined in Isaiah 53:5. where a very solitary figure, generally known as the Suffering Servant, is introduced:

> But he was wounded for our transgressions, he was bruised for our iniquities; upon him was the chastisement that made us whole, and with his stripes we are healed. All we like sheep have gone astray; we have turned every one to his own way; and the Lord has laid on him the iniquity of us all (Isaiah 53:5-6).

The idea of vicarious suffering is indisputably present here, and it is understood by Christians as representing Jesus himself. John the Baptist had announced him as the lamb of God, while in Petrine theology,

## The Founder of the Faith

the sacrificial view of Jesus as the unblemished lamb is very clear (1 Peter 1:19). The author of the epistle to the Hebrews has this to say: "But as it is, he (Christ) has appeared once for all at the end of the age to put away sin by the sacrifice of himself" (9:26). And in Jesus' own self-consciousness, he was to give his life as a ransom for many (Mark 10:45). It is, therefore, not merely a Pauline thought, though presently we will see that the cross became central in Paul's theology.

Before proceeding to that consideration, we must give profound respect to the Jewish understanding of the Isaiah portion, namely that the strange and unnamed figure is a symbol of Israel as a suffering people. Protestant theologian Helmut Gollwitzer gave utterance to his deep feelings when he wrote "If anyone has been a community of the cross during these centuries, it is the Jews, who were so often struck down by the community of the crucified" (*Der Ungekundigte Bund*).[11] Yet while the suffering figure may well depict the unspeakable agonies of a people, even within Jewish circles there are optional interpretations. Hyam Maccoby assists us when he writes in *Early Rabbinic Writings* "In the earliest extant Jewish exegesis, that of the Targum, the passage (*Isaiah 53*) is indeed interpreted as referring to the coming Messiah, but not a suffering Messiah." However, "after the failure of the Bar Kokhba revolt, the Jews themselves began to interpret the passage as referring to a suffering Messiah, who would be afflicted with leprosy."[12] It is the Christian view that Jesus personified human suffering in a remarkably unique way, and that in his vicarious death he has and will justify many.

Paul himself had found deliverance from guilt in the death of Christ as millions of others have found in their experience. Religious devotee as he had been, he now vowed that he would glory in the cross (Galatians 6:14). The cross had become more meaningful to him than circumcision or even baptism, as he states in 1 Corinthians 1:17-18:

> For Christ did not send me to baptize but to preach the gospel, not with eloquent wisdom, lest the cross of Christ be emptied of its power.... For the word of the cross ... is the power of God.

Paul is much more a realist than a ritualist. He is well aware that not all circumcised Jews or nominally baptized Christians live up to their respective faiths. Hypocrisy can afflict both, and Paul is no doubt aiming for the circumcision of the heart, and an intelligent acting out of the symbolism of baptism. Well do we all know that badges and symbols can be misread, even by those who wear them, and Paul is penetratingly conscious of this when he resumes his argument in the second chapter of Romans at verse 25ff:

> Circumcision indeed is of value if you obey the law; but if you break the law, your circumcision becomes uncircumcision. So, if a man who is uncircumcised keeps the precepts of the law, will not his uncircumcision be regarded as circumcision? Then those who are physically uncircumcised but keep the law will condemn you who have the written code and circumcision but break the law.... He is a Jew who is one inwardly, and real circumcision is a matter of the heart, spiritual and not literal. His praise is not from men but from God.

Paul would seem to be treating us to a lesson in logic. To get the complete picture, it is necessary to remember that Paul believes the Gentile, outside of the Law of Moses, has a sense of right and wrong. He postulates, if you like, a natural law. To the Jew this would be known as the Noachic covenant, or the law of conscience, which was given to all humankind before the time of Abraham.

This is the appropriate moment to listen carefully to a parallel argument, but one which comes to a very different conclusion. Maccoby reminds us that "Judaism did not offer one covenant but two.... The second covenant was the Noachic covenant, by which a Gentile could achieve salvation without becoming converted to full Judaism." He continues, "It is true that the Noachic was a second best: only by full conversion could a Gentile achieve not only salvation but membership of the Priest nation."[13] He goes on, "But Judaism already offered Gentiles a way to become entirely equal to the Jews: by full conversion to Judaism."

Here we must refer to L. H. Schiffman's article "At the Crossroads: Tannaitic Perspectives on the Jewish-Christian Schism" where he indicates that it was essential for male converts to Judaism to be circumcised."[14] Maccoby's case sounds very neat, though to some it will savour of spiritual elitism; nor does it answer to Paul's complaint that a circum-

## The Founder of the Faith

cised person who transgresses the law is himself under condemnation. Here the argument would inevitably lead into the contingencies of the sacrificial system of Judaism, which we now know was about to end.

The crux of the matter, then, is the necessity (or otherwise) of circumcision for a Gentile, who, having acknowledged his sin and repented, is being received into the new fellowship of the church. Paul is being very consistent by saying 'no' to this, because forgiveness has already been vouchsafed to him through Christ's sacrifice. In the church, however, he will not be regarded as a second class citizen, for as the Pauline maxim in Galatians 3:28 reads:

> There is neither Jew nor Greek, there is neither slave nor free, there is neither male nor female; for you are all one in Christ Jesus.

I am perfectly convinced that, as a Jew, Paul was willing to subordinate himself to the ritualistic practices of Judaism, as well as to be faithful to the Law. This can be seen in the cutting of his hair for the keeping of a vow at Cenchreae (Acts 18:18). and on his final visit to Jerusalem (Acts 21:15-26) when he observed the necessary days of purification. Paul's consistency in observing Jewish practices is well illustrated in his agreeing to have Timothy circumcised, whose mother was a Jew, but refusing to have the same applied to Titus who was a Greek. There is no question that circumcision was the paramount cause of disagreement in the early church, and even prior to Paul coming on the scene, as already discussed.

In retracing our steps to the founder of the church, do we have any pronouncement from Jesus on the subject of circumcision? The answer is in the negative. From this we might assume that, as a Jew and having been circumcised himself, he would feel that it was an accepted feature of the Law and did not call for any change.

On the other hand, Jesus would be well aware of the fact that Gentiles generally were uncircumcised. Perhaps he considered it a non-issue. If his ministry was confined to Israel alone, there was no need to discuss circumcision. If, on the other hand, he believed that Gentiles would have a place in the kingdom of God, something surely ought to have been specifically said about circumcision, if indeed it were a rite of admission to that kingdom. There is no indication that Jesus included it in his command to his disciples to teach their followers "to observe all that I have commanded you" (Matthew 28:20).

There are three routes we can follow. One, if Jesus was the apocalyptist anticipating a sudden end to the age, as Albert Schweitzer had thought, instructions about circumcision would not have been a pressing necessity. Two, if the attitudes and behaviour of his fellow Jews were displeasing to Jesus, circumcision would be of less importance to him as an ethicist. We are close to a clue just here, for it was in one of Christ's tense moments when a crowd insisted that they were the children of Abraham, he retorted with his stinging statement: "If you were Abraham's children, you would do what Abraham did.... If God were your Father, you would love me.... You are of your father the devil, and your will is to do your father's desires" (John 8:39-42). It must be kept in mind that circumcision was the sign of the Abrahamic covenant. For Jesus, as for John the Baptist (Matthew 3:9-10), righteous behaviour was of greater consequence than religious ritual.

In an unforgettably threatening statement, Matthew records Jesus' prediction that the kingdom of God would be taken away and given to a nation producing the fruit of it (Matthew 21:43). Such a drastic statement would imply that circumcision by itself, Temple worship, the sacrificial system, and all that was held dear by the Jewish community would hardly save the Jewish nation from those around her. Nor would it be the first time that the spiritual bankruptcy of Israel, and her disobedience to God, would cause her to be uprooted and sent into exile.

Third, we must discover what interaction Jesus did have with Gentiles. There is the case of the Centurion who had built a synagogue for the Jews in Capernaum, and whose servant Jesus had healed. The account ends with a compliment which Jesus gives to the Centurion, "I tell you, not even in Israel have I found such faith" (Luke 7:9). Some redactionist critics would claim that the authors of the Gospels went out of their way to place Jesus in situations which would impress the Roman authorities, even to the extent of putting down the Jews; but this story is actually favourable to both. An overture to the Romans was certainly not the motif of another incident which reveals Jesus' attitude towards Gentiles. This particular dialogue includes difficult statements

## The Founder of the Faith

which critical scholars must accept as original sayings of Jesus.* He had brought his disciples into Gentile territory where they meet with a Syro-Phoenician woman who pleads for the healing of her child. Jesus appears to brush her off by saying that he has been sent only to the lost sheep of the house of Israel. No doubt his disciples received this comment with satisfaction. Here she pleads with Jesus again, "Lord, help me!" upon which he virtually adds insult to injury, "It is not fair to take the children's bread and throw it to the dogs." At this she cries out in desperation "Yes, Lord, yet even the dogs eat the crumbs that fall from their master's table." Eventually Jesus responds to the woman's pleas, and Mark records his final comment to her. "For this saying you may go your way; the demon has left your daughter."

No doubt Jesus was testing the woman's faith, but, for the most part, this incident was so out of keeping with Jesus' normal compassionate style when confronted with such situations. Obviously it was designed to be a lesson to the disciples. It is no secret that in the religious vocabulary of the time, dogs and gentiles were interchangeable terms, and here Jesus is putting this woman and her daughter in the category of little dogs. The disciples, impressed no doubt by his statement about being sent only to the sheep of Israel, asked him to send her away. She was an embarrassment to them. The fact is that Jesus continued the engagement, and finally responded to the woman's faith. How the disciples must have wondered at this condescension of Jesus, but the lesson would be well remembered when they themselves were thrust into the Gentile world after Pentecost. God responds to the faith of the non-Jew, as Peter also found out how God had listened to the prayers of Cornelius and was prepared to bestow on him and his family the gift of the Holy Spirit (Acts 10:1-48).

That Jesus had a thought for humanity at large as well as for "the lost sheep of the house of Israel", and for the needs and weaknesses common to both, does not require a lot of imagination. Already he had astonished the Pharisees and many others when he chose to identify with the despised elements of society, e.g. tax-gatherers and prostitutes. He knew what was in the heart of man, and even to his own people he

---

* See Matthew 15: 21-28 and Mark 7: 26-30

had to say, "If you, then, who are evil, know how to give good gifts to your children, how much more will your Father who is in heaven give good things to those who ask him!" (Matthew 7:11).

Here he states the universality of evil in humankind and the Father's unconditional love for all. Christians believe that these two opposites—man's sin and God's love meet uniquely and redemptively at the cross. This message had to break out of the confines of Judaism, and we should not be surprised that the Great Commission instructed the disciples to go into all the world and preach the good news of God's love and forgiveness, beginning in Jerusalem, and on through Judaea, Samaria and to the ends of the earth (Matthew 28:19-20; Acts 1:8).*

## Servants of God—Jew and Gentile

The sum of all this discussion ends with two options. Firstly, to recognize the purpose of God to reach the Gentile world via the Jew. Isaiah envisaged the time when Israel would "Arise and shine; for your light has come, and the glory of the Lord has risen upon you. For behold, darkness shall cover the earth and thick darkness the people; but the Lord will arise upon you, and his glory will be seen upon you. And the nations shall come to your light, and kings to the brightness of your rising" (60:1-3). Zechariah saw a day when " ... ten men from the nations of every tongue shall take hold of the robe of a Jew, saying, 'Let us go with you, for we have heard that God is with you'" (8:23).

Dare we ask the question, How enthusiastic were the Jewish people about inviting Gentiles to share their knowledge of God in Old Testament and inter-Testamental times? They acknowledged 'righteous' Gentiles as in the case of Cyrus of Persia to whom they gave the title 'anointed' or 'messiah'. But for most it seems that Zechariah's words were not yet to be acted upon. Indeed the outlook of the Qumran community toward the Gentile world was one of bitter hostility against 'the enemies of Israel.' People of the Diaspora, however, had influenced

---

* In a significant Gentile encounter Jesus states that many will come from east and west and sit at table with Abraham, Isaac, and Jacob, while *the sons of the kingdom* will be cast out (cf. Matthew 8: 11, 12, and Luke 13: 28-30).

## The Founder of the Faith

many 'God-fearers' among the Gentiles, and these were accommodated in synagogue worship. Tacitus tells us that Judaism in Rome had achieved notable missionary success (Hist. 5.5); but overall it has to be said that no widespread, concerted effort to teach and to convert Gentiles from their polytheistic religions was undertaken by the Jews prior to the times of Jesus. The influence of monotheistic Judaism had been profound, but no missionary enterprise comparable to the scale of evangelism of the later church had been carried out.* Christians believed that Jesus entered history in "the fulness of the times" as part of the strategy of destiny. It was no mere coincidence that this Jew should have a distinctive message for the Gentile world just at a juncture in Israel's history which would seriously impinge on her worship patterns with the loss of the Temple and of Jerusalem for two thousand years to come. A comment from Franz Rosenzweig is helpful here: he has said that it was not Judaism, but Christianity which carried the Hebrew Bible to the remotest islands in harmony with the prophecy of Isaiah 42:6,[15] while Pinchas Lapide, as already noted, has committed himself to the view that "the Christ event leads to a way of salvation which God has opened up in order to bring the Gentile world into community of God's Israel" (see p. 61). If circumcision was the seal and symbol of the Abrahamic Covenant to his seed, per se, why should a conflict over circumcision have created such an awesome gulf between Jew and Christian?

If any two groups ought to have lived together with mutual respect it ought to have been Judaism and Christianity. Sadly this has not been the testimony of history, but Paul affirms a strange but undeniable interdependency of the two in the classic chapters of Romans 9, 10 and 11. Indeed at 11:25-29 he warned the Gentile Christians not to be arrogant about their election, as, unfortunately, the Jews had been in theirs:

---

* Opposite views can be found between the writings of Louis Feldman's *Jew and Gentile in the Ancient World* (1993), and Scot McKnight's *A Light among the Gentiles: Jewish Missionary Activity in the Second Temple Period* (1991). See Bibliography.

> Lest you be wise in your own conceits, I want you to understand this mystery, brethren; a hardening has come upon part of Israel, until the full number of the Gentiles come in, and so all Israel will be saved; as it is written, 'The Deliverer will come from Zion, he will banish ungodliness from Jacob'; 'and this will be my covenant with them when I take away their sins." As regards the gospel they are enemies of God, for your sake; but as regards election they are beloved for the sake of their forefathers. For the gifts and the call of God are irrevocable.

Paul did not attempt to abrogate the Law for the Jewish people, and he solidly affirmed "the law is holy, and the commandment is holy and just and good" (Romans 7:12). Here he is in full compliance with Jesus and his stated respect for the Law. However, there was also another important area of agreement between Jesus and the converted Paul, and that was their common concern for the sinners who had fallen short of the Law's requirements, both of Israel and of the Gentile world. Sadly the religious establishment of the day showed more concern about maintaining its own self-image of righteousness than caring for the lost, the poor and the outcasts of society. If this were true of the Pharisees, the Sadducean priestly establishment was also an object of contempt to many of the Jews, while the Zealots were resolved to destroy the Roman army of occupation.

The pre-converted Paul was part of this sad and confused scene. All in all, Judaism was not fulfilling its prescribed role of being a light to the Gentiles. How then could Paul have done other than he did after his meeting with Jesus and receiving this call from him?

> And the Lord said, 'I am Jesus whom you are persecuting. But rise and stand upon your feet; for I have appeared to you for this purpose, to appoint you to serve and bear witness to the things in which you have seen me and to those in which I will appear to you, delivering you from the people and from the Gentiles—to whom I send you, to open their eyes that they may turn from darkness to light and from the power of Satan to God, that they may receive forgiveness of sins, and a place among those who are sanctified by faith in me' (Acts 26:15-18).

# The Founder of the Faith

Paul was not the founder of Christianity, and to those who sought to exalt him, or Cephas or Apollos, he asks the ultimate and decisive question "Is Christ divided? Was Paul crucified for you?" As James in his epistle describes himself as "a servant of God, and of the Lord Jesus Christ" (1:1), so also does Paul (Romans 1:1; Philippians 1:1).

That there was a Jesus of Nazareth, a figure of history, one who was crucified under Pontius Pilate, who rose from the dead, and who captivated the love of those who followed him, there can be no doubt.

Listen again to the unified witness of the early church. In the Petrine tradition, testimony is given that "we were eyewitnesses of his majesty" (2 Peter 1:16); from James comes this word of adoration "... hold the faith of our Lord Jesus Christ, *the Lord of glory*" (James 2:1); from John the assurance that "we have seen with our eyes, ... we have touched with our hands, the word of life ... which was from the beginning" (1 John 1:1); and, finally, this crescendo of praise from Paul:

> He is the head of the body, the church; he is the beginning, the first-born from the dead, that in everything he might be pre-eminent (Colossians 1:18).

## Master and Servant

Paul always acknowledges Jesus as his Lord. He describes himself as his servant, slave and prisoner. He thus acknowledges the authority of the one to whom he has committed himself. If there is any traceable egotism in the apostle it can never be found in his relationship with Christ. In offering advice on marriage, for instance, he talks of giving it "by way of concession, not of command" (1 Corinthians 7:6), but in dealing with the question of separation and divorce, he prefaces his advice: "to the married I give charge, *not I but the Lord,* that the wife should not separate from her husband."

He willingly submits to the teachings given by Jesus:

> Love one another with brotherly affection.... Rejoice in your hope, be patient in tribulation, be constant in prayer.... Bless those who persecute you; bless and do not curse them. Rejoice with those who rejoice, weep with those who weep; do not be

haughty, but associate with the lowly; never be conceited. Repay no one evil for evil.... Do not be overcome by evil, but overcome evil with good (Taken from Romans 12:1-21).

In the same portion Paul exhorts the Christians: "if your enemy is hungry, feed him; if he is thirsty give him drink"; but this word already appears in Proverbs 25:21. Indeed many of Jesus' words, as we have acknowledged, derive from the Old Testament Scriptures with which he was well acquainted from his upbringing. The point here is that Paul is no flamboyant evangelist who has no sense of accountability. He is a *disciple* who disciplines himself lest, as he puts it, "after preaching to others I myself should be disqualified" (1 Corinthians 9:27). It is noteworthy, however, that his prior allegiance is to Christ rather than to the Law, and in the same Corinthians chapter he provides us with an insight into his own personal motivation:

> To the Jews I became as a Jew, in order to win Jews; to those under the law I became as one under the law—that I might win those under the law. To those outside the law I became as one outside the law—not being without law toward God but under the law of Christ—that I might win those outside the law. To the weak I became weak, that I might win the weak. I have become all things to all men that I might by all means save some (vs.19-22).

## The Authority of the Risen Jesus

It is true that Paul says he knows Christ no longer after the flesh, but after the spirit, which is translated in the RSV as "even though we once regarded Christ from a human point of view, we regard him thus no longer" (2 Corinthians 5:16). This isn't a form of Gnostic mysticism, as some may imply, it is rather a statement that the Jesus who really walked through Galilee and Judaea is now the risen one, and as such his spirit of grace and love will be imparted to us. Verse 14 reads: "For the love of Christ controls us." This is a profound acknowledgment of Christ's authority over his people, yet an authority which is in the nature of a compelling love.

Jesus himself combined a sense of his own authority with an incredible love for people. As we have seen, his healings were acts of

# The Founder of the Faith

great compassion, yet his authority over demons and disease, along with his claim to forgive, unsettled the religious people around him. Even a Roman centurion, who had power to command his men, recognized a superior authority resident in Jesus. When Jesus entered the Temple the chief priests, scribes and elders came to him and asked him by what authority was he doing these things. He answered their question with a question demanding of them what they thought of John's baptism—whether it was from heaven or of men. Diplomatically they avoided an answer, to which Jesus responded by saying "Neither will I tell you by what authority I do these things" (Matthew 21:23-24).

Let us make no mistake, Jesus was a formidable leader, a controversialist, and one who had the ability to command the love, the respect and the obedience of those who followed him. He issued the Great Commission to evangelize the world (Matthew 28:18). At the same time, he acknowledged that his was a "given" authority which came from the heavenly Father to whom he himself was perfectly obedient, even to the death of the cross. "Therefore," writes Paul, "God has highly exalted him and bestowed on him the name which is above every name, that at the name of Jesus every knee should bow … and every tongue confess that Jesus Christ is Lord, to the glory of the Father" (Philippians. 2:9-11).

## Servant of the Church

> For we preach not ourselves, but Jesus Christ as Lord, with ourselves as your servants for Jesus' sake (2 Corinthians 4:5).

Just as Peter, in writing to the churches of the Diaspora, reminds their leaders that they are not to "lord it" over the flock, but rather to "Tend the flock … not as domineering over those in your charge but being examples to the flock" (1 Peter 5:2-3), so also Paul recognizes his servant role. Frequently he writes with a moral authority, as we should expect from a leader, but he subordinates himself and his own behaviour to the Lord he serves. He asks the Corinthian Christians to be followers of him as he is of Christ:

> Give no offense to Jews or to Greeks or to the church of God, just as I try to please all men in everything I do, not seeking my own advantage, but that of many, that they may be saved. Be imitators of me, as I am of Christ (1 Corinthians 10:32-11:1).

Where he may seem to be pompous is when he responds to attacks on his qualifications as a Jew and as an apostle, reminding his critics of his past lineage, his persecution of the church as a zealous Jew, and of the genuine reality of his conversion to Christ. He thus invites them to scrutinize his past, which many at that time could confirm. It might be added here, that criticisms which were later levelled at Paul, some of which amounted to slander, were easy to make years after his martyrdom when he could not defend himself. The reader may guess that I am referring particularly to the Ebionites (see p. 245 footnote).

Paul viewed himself as a caring leader, and essentially a servant of those he was guiding in the faith, and even describes himself as a nourishing nursemaid (1 Thessalonians 2:7) to the babes in Christ (1 Corinthians 3:1). For reasons other than any natural humility, Paul played a low-key part. A clear example of this is seen in his respectful approach to the church at Rome:

> First, I thank my God through Jesus Christ for all of you, because your faith is proclaimed in all the world. For God is my witness, whom I serve with my spirit in the gospel of his Son, that without ceasing I mention you always in my prayers, asking that somehow by God's will I may now at last succeed in coming to you. For I long to see you, that I may impart to you some spiritual gift to strengthen you, that is, that we may be mutually encouraged by each other's faith, both yours and mine (1:8-12).

The obvious reason for Paul's humble and very respectful approach is that he was not the founder of the church at Rome, as he had been in many other places. This is a tremendously important point to make with those who ascribe to him a dominance in the formation of the early church generally, and specifically in the case of its doctrines and practices. We learn from Acts 18:1-2 that Paul first met friends from the church in Rome when he was in Corinth. These were a Jew named Aquila, and his wife, Priscilla, who had been banished from the capital because of Claudius the emperor. He had issued a decree, which Suetonius, the historian, tells us was due to tumults raised by the Jews in Rome over one called 'Chrestus'. This helps us to see that the Gospel had reached that city by the late 40s, and certainly well prior to Paul's epistle to that church.

## The Founder of the Faith

This is of exceptional value to us in establishing that the original gospel, as it went out across the Mediterranean world, was not just the product of Paul. It will also help us to see what theological disagreements, if any, were being discussed in the church at Rome. Judging by Paul's letter, there was no dissension over the teachings of Jesus, the fact of his death, nor of the accepted truth of his resurrection. It will be recalled that Paul found it necessary to write a whole chapter on the subject of the resurrection to the Greek Christians in Corinth, because of some disputations there. It would seem that in the case of the church at Rome, it was accepting of the basic *kerygma*. Where there was concern it was in the area of the Law and circumcision; and this is not in any way surprising since this church had obvious Jewish associations.* First, we must note the tense used at 16:17:

> I appeal to you, brethren, to take note of those who create dissensions and difficulties, in opposition to the doctrine which you have been taught.

Paul was writing this letter to a church which had been taught by others than himself, and he endorses what the church has received from them. Currently the church was in a state of dissension, (*dichostasia*, lit., a stand up division between two persons). It was, as we know, a common practice for Judaizers to follow Paul on his travels to preach a 'revised edition' of his gospel. In this case, however, disagreement had broken out prior to Paul's planned visit to Rome.

Paul's treatment of the Law and of circumcision, and of natural law among the Gentiles is salutory. Here is an assembly of believers located in Rome who must relate to the Gentile elite, the civil service of Caesar's household, and to the intelligentsia of the capital of the empire. What of their laws, and their sense of right and wrong, the *lex Romana*? And what about conscience as their guide, etc.? Paul responds to this very adequately. He speaks up in favour of the privileges of the Jew as the recipients of the written law. He recognizes the

---

*Francis Watson in *Paul, Judaism and the Gentiles* (p.94) avers that two distinct Christian congregations existed in Rome, one Jewish and one Gentile.

law of conscience in the Gentile. And he addresses the problem of both having sinned against God. He recognizes the immense difficulties that even well-meaning people have in living according to the Law, himself included; and he rejoices in God's provision for forgiveness in Christ, and for the gift of the Holy Spirit to energize us for holy living in everyday situations. Circumcision is again focalized for a congregation made up of both Jews and Gentiles, and Paul writes:

> Circumcision indeed is of value if you obey the law; but if you break the law, your circumcision becomes uncircumcision. So, if a man who is uncircumcised keeps the precepts of the law, will not his uncircumcision be regarded as circumcision. Then those who are physically uncircumcised but keep the law will condemn you who have the written code and circumcision but break the law (Romans 2:25-27).

Earlier in the same chapter, Paul has been particularly stern in dealing with fellow Jews who have broken the law and who have betrayed their God-given trust to the Gentiles:

> You who boast in the law, do you dishonor God by breaking the law? For, as it is written, 'The name of God is blasphemed among the Gentiles because of you' (vs. 23-24).

This quote could be from Isaiah 52:5, or Ezekiel 16:27, and more likely from Ezekiel 36:22, which reads: "Therefore say to the house of Israel, 'Thus says the Lord God: 'It is not for your sake, O house of Israel, that I am about to act, but for the sake of my holy name, which you have profaned among the nations to which you came.'" Basically, Paul is saying that the Jews have privileges of being the bearer of God's oracles, and correspondingly they have the greater moral responsibility to the nations around them. Thus, circumcision, he is saying, is secondary to the witness of a good life, which is now expected of all Christians, both Jewish and Gentile. This may seem to be too neat an argument, but it is both logical and irrefutable, and Paul consummates it with these words :

> Or is God the God of Jews only? Is he not the God of Gentiles also?

# The Founder of the Faith

Yes, of Gentiles also, since God is one; and he will justify the circumcised on the ground of their faith and the uncircumcised through their faith (3:29-30).

Of course, the remarkable thing about the church at Rome was its ability to have both Jews and Gentiles worshipping as Christians, which, by the way, was the experience of the early Palestinian church, though not without strain, as we have seen from our readings in the Acts of the Apostles. Surely we are servants of God together for the sake of the Jew who died for us all!

## Paul the Pastor

We conclude with this short portrait of a man who recognized his accountability to his Lord for the care of the church. Along with other Christians, he believed he had the mind of Christ (1 Corinthians 2:16). Additional to the parallels in teaching between Jesus and Paul already noted, the following should be included. Then we should proceed to observe how Paul acted as a pastor to use his judgment in problem areas where cultural differences called for special consideration.

1. *The Love of God.* Jesus reiterated the command to love God and our neighbour. He also called upon us to love our enemies. He urged his disciples to love one another even as he had loved them, even to the point of laying down his life for them. Paul takes up this very theme in Ephesians 5:25 when he urges husbands to love their wives "as Christ loved the church and gave himself up for her...." He sees himself as the object of Christ's love when he declares "He loved me and gave himself for me" (Galatians 2:20). He is the writer of the exquisitely beautiful chapter on love, 1 Corinthians 13, which Henry Drummond called "the greatest thing in the world."

2. *The Sin of Man.* Jesus was known as the friend of sinners. He said that he had come not to call the righteous but sinners (Mark 2:17). He told the story of the self-righteous Pharisee and the Publican who prayed "God be merciful to me a sinner" (Luke 18:13). Paul has often been blamed for creating a different gospel, and one which unduly emphasizes our sinfulness and our need for forgiveness. In fact

his teaching is entirely in keeping with Jesus' own view of his mission and of man's need of salvation.

3. *The Call to a Holy Life.* Jesus urged his disciples to be perfect even as their heavenly Father is perfect (Matthew 5:48), and Paul called for a life of holy obedience to the perfect will of God (Romans 12:1).

4. *Respect for the Civil Authorities.* Jesus' famous saying of rendering to God that which is God's, and to Caesar what is Caesar's (Luke 20:25), finds its corresponding Pauline injunctions in Romans 13:1-7.

5. *Life beyond Death.* Many sayings of Jesus have to do with an afterlife of judgment and reward. Paul also writes of the blessed state of the believer after death (1 Corinthians 2:9; Colossians 1:5) and of the judgment seat of Christ (2 Corinthians 5:1-10). Eschatalogical similarities between Paul and Jesus are clearly identifiable (e.g. the 'Small Apocalypse' of the Synoptic Gospels and Paul's teaching in First and Second Thessalonians).

It is at this point, however, that we should recognize a liberty which Paul takes in his moral teaching to the church. He is not a 'revisionist' of the message of Jesus, but as a pastor he is seen to be wrestling with his Lord's absolutes and the cultural problems of the church in the city of Corinth.

We have already noted how in 1 Corinthians 7:6 and 7:10 a distinction is made between his giving advice at a counselling level, and his respect for the strictness of his Lord's commandments on marriage. Here he upholds the prohibition of Jesus against divorce, yet within two verses (12-16) he offers permission for a believing spouse to accept the departure of an unbelieving partner, presumably because of irreconciliation or, more likely, moral incompatibility.

Corinth was known as "the cesspool of iniquity", and its one thousand religious prostitutes from the Temple of Aphroditus would parade the city daily in solicitation for clients. Sexual activity seems to have been excessive, and Paul advises each Christian to have his or her own Christian spouse (cf. 1 Corinthians 6 15-20; 2 Corinthians 6:14). Such was the problem that Paul went so far as to suggest that those who were single should remain so because of the distressing situation

## The Founder of the Faith

(1 Corinthians 7:26), but in no way should this be understood as advocacy for celibacy as the rest of the chapter will show. Jesus also accepted the fact that the single state might be preferred in certain situations. He states this in Matthew 19:10-12, which immediately follows his positive teaching on marriage. Jesus and Paul are not at variance. Paul upholds both marriage and the option of the single state, and does not allow one to cancel out the other. Those who think that Paul imposed a 'non-Jesus' asceticism on the church should recognise that the apostle leaves the matter entirely to individual choice. Richard Longenecker has stated it well:

> Nowhere does he speak of marriage as sub-spiritual because of the material aspect in it causing defilement. Nor could Paul agree that celibacy was to be normal or even the best procedure for every Christian. If the Corinthians were to accept such a tenet, they would have become 'slaves of men' rather than 'freemen in Christ' (1 Corinthians 7:23). Both celibacy and marriage were callings of God.[16]

Where there is an apparently serious difference, it is in their respective attitudes to women. Jesus was very much a liberator of women in his Jewish setting. Even his disciples were surprised by his having conversation with a Samaritan woman of questionable repute and honoring the woman who anointed him in Bethany, at the same time rebuking his male disciples for their insensibilities (Mark 14:3-9). On this latter occasion he gave command that the incident should be memorialised wherever the Gospel would be proclaimed. He delighted in the fellowship of Martha and Mary, and he was known to have delivered Mary Magdalene from demons. He showed compassion to an adulteress when her accusers were ready to stone her. Women were with him at the crucifixion, and they were among the first to be at the tomb.

By way of contrast Paul is seen to be almost rabbinical in his restrictions on women. They are to wear a head-dress in worship, they are to keep silence in the church, and they are to be submissive to their husbands. At 1 Corinthians 14:34 he adds "even as the law says." It is true that in synagogue worship the women were the spectators, or onlookers, but as such they were not to distract the men by their chatter. However, we should be careful to note that in the eleventh chapter Paul recognizes the right of a woman to pray and to prophesy (Gk. *propheteuo*: to preach or publicly expound). Paul pays profound respect to women, such as Euodia and Syntyche (Philippians 4:2), whom he describes as yoke fellows and co-labourers in the Gospel (lit. *en to euangelio*), or, in the preaching of the Gospel.

William Barclay points out that in Paul's letter to the Romans, of the twenty four names of friends who receive his commendation, six are women. He writes: "If we really wish to see Paul's attitude to women in the Church it is a passage like this that we should read, where his appreciation of the work that they were doing in the Church shines and glows through his words."[17] Most interesting is his entrusting of this masterpiece of an epistle to the care of a woman called Phoebe (Romans 16:1-2), who bears a twin title of deacon (Gk. *diakonos*, masculine and therefore the office) and *prostatis*, a sponsor, patron or patroness. This prominence given to a woman on Paul's part was quite 'un-rabbinical' and in significant contrast to the saying "Were the words of the Torah to be burned, they should not be handed over to a woman."

One must allow for the fact that Paul was helping the Corinthian church to emerge from a society which was morally corrupt, hopefully to attain to a degree of respectability acceptable to Jewish believers and other God-fearers. The contrast between this Gentile society and the morality of the Jewish synagogue was extreme, and Paul himself must have been concerned about the developing character of the infant church. But beyond endorsing some conventional practices which would be viewed as "decent and in order" (cf. 1 Corinthians 14:40), Paul was opening doors of opportunity to women in worship, ministry and service which had never taken place within Judaism itself. A quiet revolution was taking place, and one which began not with Paul but with Jesus.

Critics have the right to judge, but those who hasten to diminish great figures of history like Jesus and Paul, are doing humankind a sad disservice. Some would describe Jesus as a prophet, others as a wandering Cynic, a Zealot and rebel leader, or a misguided pseudo-messiah. The ever heightening controversy demonstrates that Jesus cannot be confined to any one of these categories, whether complimentary or critical. The exclamation of doubting Thomas needs to be

## The Founder of the Faith

heard again, "My Lord and my God!" (John 20:28). Others have endeavoured to set Paul of Tarsus against Jesus, accusing him of misrepresenting his master's intentions, of corrupting his message and founding a religion which Jesus had never intended. Most Christians do not see it this way, not at all. We are unspeakably indebted to that over-arching providence of God in the sending of his beloved Son for the redemption of the world, and in the choice of a Jew who would courageously carry that message to the world of the Gentiles.

> But how are men to call upon him in whom they have not believed? And how are they to believe in him of whom they have never heard? And how are they to hear without a preacher? And how can men preach unless they are sent? As it is written, "How beautiful are the feet of those who preach good news"(Romans 10:14-15; cf. Isaiah 52:7).

## Notes

[1] Maccoby, Hyam. *The Mythmaker: Paul and the Invention of Christianity*. New York: Harper and Row, 1986, p.17.

[2] Ibid., p.15.

[3] Ibid., p.92ff.

[4] Lapide, Pinchas and Stuhlmacher, Peter. *Paul, Rabbi and Apostle*. Minneapolis: Augsburg, 1992, p.34.

[5] Zeitlin, Solomon. *The Rise and Fall of the Judaean State*, vol. 3. Philadelphia: 1978, p.359.

[6] Dunn, James D. G. *Jesus, Paul and the Law*. Louisville: John Knox, 1990, p. 37.

[7] Ibid., p.12-13.

[8] Taylor, Vincent. *The Gospel according to St. Mark* Macmillan: 1952, p.92. Perrin, Norman. *The New Testament: An Introduction*. Harcourt: 1974, p.145.

[9] Maccoby, H. *The Mythmaker: Paul and the Invention of Christianity*. p.4.

[10] Dunn, J. D. G. *Jesus, Paul and the Law.* p.29ff.

[11] Gollwitzer, H. *Der Ungekundigte Bund.* Stuttgart: 1962, p.48

[12] Maccoby, Hyam. *Early Rabbinical Writings.* Cambridge University Press: 1988, p.202.

[13] Maccoby, Hyam. *Paul and Hellenism.* London: SCM., 1991; Philadelphia: Trinity Press, pp.172-5.

[14] Schiffman, Lawrence H. *At the Crossroads: Tannaitic Perspectives on Jewish-Christian Schism.* Jewish and Christian Self-Definition, vol. 2. Philadelphia: 1981, pp 125-127.

[15] Quoted by Pinchas Lapide in *Paul, Rabbi and Apostle.* Minneapolis: Augsburg, 1992, p.52.

[16] Longenecker, Richard N. *Paul, Apostle of Liberty,* 1964; reprinted 1976, Grand Rapids: Baker, p.238.

[17] William Barclay in The Daily Study Bible; *The Letter to the Romans.* Edinburgh: Saint Andrew Press, 1955, pp.231-232.

CHAPTER SIX

# The Cross and the Kingdom

Once upon a time we sang *Good King Wenceslas,* and we read stories like *Snow White and the Seven Dwarfs,* and little girls would dream of Prince Charming who might come their way. Even in the real world a royal title, be it king or queen, prince or princess, duke or duchess, represented a mark of respect, of authority and often of adulation as in the case of young David of Israel. "Saul has slain his thousands, and David his ten thousands" the women chanted as he returned from his battle with Goliath. There have been good kings and bad kings, And can we leave out the good queens like Esther of Persia and Victoria of England? The trend today, however, is downward. The Czars have ceased in Russia, the Kaisers in Germany, and quite recently the British royalty has been in the throes of scandal.

Monarchs could also be tyrants. Some of the Pharoahs of Egypt were, as was Nebuchadnezzar of Babylon, and not a few of the Caesars of Rome; but the time came when people began to protest their state of subjugation and to demand some form of constitutional rights. So it was in England when the barons forced King John to sign the Magna Carta in 1215. But indulgent and oppressive monarchial aristocracies survived in European countries until the French Revolution, when the masses took their full measure of revenge at the bloody guillotine. The breakaway of the American colonies from Great Britain signalled a highly significant move towards real democracy with the production of the masterly Constitution of the United States. Yet in Europe non-royal and inhumane dictatorships arose like Napoleon Bonaparte who brought humiliation to his nation, Adolf Hitler who brought terror to the Jews and the worst ever war to the world at large, and Josef Stalin who ruled with murderous might in the Soviet Union, a system originally designed to bring equality to all.

Modern history has been an ongoing story of finding the balance between authority and liberty, between order and anarchy, between management and labour, between the politburo and the proletariat, and so on. This is why we must try to understand what the Bible means by the kingdom of God.

Psalm 103 tells us that "the Lord has established his throne in the heavens, and his kingdom rules over all" (v.19), obviously a declaration of God's sovereignty over his creation. In the early experience of the Israelites, there was a deliberate avoidance of appointing a king, preferring rather a kind of collectivism between the twelve tribes. However, in Samuel's time, the people felt that the regime of the judges had failed them. They took justifiable exception to the misbehaviour of Samuel's sons who "did not walk in his (God's) ways, but turned aside after gain; they took bribes and perverted justice" (1 Samuel 8:3). The elders gathered together and confronted Samuel at Ramah: "Behold, you are old and your sons do not walk in your ways; now appoint for us a king to govern us like all the nations" (8:4). The Lord's response is expressed in his words to Samuel, "Hearken to the voice of the people in all that they say to you; for they have not rejected you, but they have rejected me from being king over them" (v.7).

Two things emerge from this statement: first, the people's choice represented a rejection of God's rule; but, second, their wishes were to be carefully regarded and acted upon, and with divine sanction. As Israel's history progresses, the hope persisted that David's kingdom would endure for ever. When the time came for Solomon to be selected as his father's successor, David addresses the assembly. "He (the Lord) said to me: "It is Solomon your son who shall build my

## The Cross and the Kingdom

house and my courts, for I have chosen him to be my son, and I will be his father. I will establish his kingdom for ever if he continues resolute in keeping my commandments and my ordinances, as he is today" (1 Chronicles 28:6-7). Paradoxically, this promise of permanence was dependent on Solomon's own integrity. Without doubt Solomon surpassed all in wisdom, yet his reign was not flawless, and, subsequent to his death, the kingdom split between the north and the south. If anything the succession of kings thereafter reflected a monotonous sequence of success and failure, of good and bad.

Still the conviction persisted that God would give his people a king, or messiah, who would rule from the throne of David, and whose kingdom would be everlasting. This is eloquently described by the prophet Isaiah:

> For unto us a child is born, unto us a son is given; and the government will be upon his shoulder, and his name will be called 'Wonderful Counselor, Mighty God, Everlasting Father, Prince of Peace,' Of the increase of his government and of peace there will be no end, upon the throne of David, and over his kingdom, to establish it, and to uphold it with justice and with righteousness from this time forth and for evermore (9:6-7)."

The phrase 'Kingdom of God' was not in common biblical usage, however, until the coming of John the Baptist and Jesus of Nazareth. At a time of impending change and upheaval, a voice was heard from the wilderness of Judah, "Repent, for the kingdom of heaven is at hand.... Prepare the way of the Lord, make his paths straight" (Matthew 3:2-3). Then reads Mark, chapter 1:14-15, "Now after John was arrested, Jesus came into Galilee, preaching the gospel of God, and saying, 'The time is fulfilled, and the kingdom of God is at hand; repent, and believe in the gospel."

Clearly there was great expectation of the opening of a new chapter in the history of Israel as crowds came from Jerusalem and all Judaea to be baptized of John in the river Jordan. He, in turn, pointed forward to someone whom he described as one "Mightier than I, whose sandals I am not worthy to carry" (Matthew 3:11). Yet, as seems common to many promising reform movements, tragedy struck John who was arrested and executed by Herod Antipas. Josephus records his murder and attributes it to John's great popularity with the people, at a time when Herod feared an uprising (Ant. 18:115-9). Of course, Herod's profligate behaviour was widely known, and led later to war with Aretas, the Arabian prince whose daughter Herod had divorced to marry Herodias, his own brother's wife. John the Baptist, according to our Gospels, had vehemently preached against this marriage. Jesus' attitude was also one of censoriousness which can be gathered from his reference to Herod as "that fox" (Luke 13:32). Both John and Jesus were truly fulfilling the Hebrew prophets' prerogative to rebuke kings on moral grounds.

This was an important principle operating in Israel's political system, and, in quite a different setting, it was duplicated when Andrew Melville rebuked his sovereign, James the Sixth, and son of Mary Queen of Scots. In the personal interview extended to him by the king, Melville laid forth in his broad Scottish tongue "And therefore, Sir, as divers times before, so now again I must tell you, there are two Kings and two kingdoms in Scotland. There is Christ Jesus the King, and His kingdom the Kirk, whose subject King James the Sixth is, and of whose kingdom not a king nor a lord nor a head, but a member."* The supposition, of course, was that the king was subject to the moral law of God, and Melville saw this personified in Christ, but goes on to equate the Kirk or the Church with the kingdom of God. In the first instance we agree, but in the second we can only comment that in Protestant Scotland separation of church and state was not even a consideration.

It is also possible for emperors, kings, princes and political leaders, who are committed to a given religion, to persuade themselves that they are acting on God's behalf. Constantine fell into this category as did the sovereigns who enlisted their subjects in the Crusades. It was a feature of medieval times. Even Luther, in the midst of the Reformation,

---

*"And thairfor, Sir, as dyvers tymes befor, sa now again I mon tell yow, their is twa Kings and twa kingdomes in Scotland. Thair is Chryst Jesus the King, and His kingdome the Kirk, whase subject King James the Saxt is, and of whase kingdome nocht a king nor a lord nor a heid, bot a member."—Alexander Smellie, *Men of the Covenant* (London: Banner of Truth, 1960), p. 236.

## The Cross and the Kingdom

obtained the support of German princes to establish his religious regime in opposition to the political power of the Vatican. So also Cromwell, the self-styled Protector of the Commonwealth, believed he was a leader acting for God. And in our own time, Muslim Khomeinies seem prepared to declare a holy war on the 'decadent' west in the cause of Allah, while terrorists are already fulfilling their missions of murder in the fervent belief that a divine reward awaits them if they should die in the dastardly deed. Is this what the kingdom of God is all about?

The Jews, too, have often embarked on mistaken adventures led by self-styled messiahs. There was the famous revolt of Bar Kokhba in the first part of the second century resulting in a repetition of the 70 C.E. destruction of Jerusalem. In the fifth century the pseudo-messiah Moses of Crete led many to a drowning death in the Mediterranean Sea. In the seventh century Persian Jewry was stirred by a messianic movement headed by Abu-Isa, who led his adherents against the authorities. Similar endeavours were made by Juda Yudghan of Hamadan, Persia, Serene of Syria, and Abraham Abulafia of Spain who proclaimed 1290 as the year of Israel's redemption. All were failures, including a seventeenth-century rising under Shabbetai Tzevi of Smyrna, who persuaded whole Jewish communities to follow him to Palestine. Even the Gentile world became aroused, and many were led to believe that the end of the world was approaching. In the end, however, in order to save his own life, this false messiah accepted the Moslem religion, causing widespread disillusionment among his fellow Jews.

In returning to the times of the Qumran community, we have observed the highly militant character of the War Scroll, and the aggressive expectations of the Jews to see their enemies brought down and destroyed (see pp. 44-45). They were completely confident of divine intervention and the mighty assistance of Michael the archangel, as their troops would enter battle.

Again let it be said, there is no evidence that this movement and that of the Zealots, had the organised support of the Christian community, despite the efforts of Eisenman, Baigent and Leigh to establish a firm connection. The Christians in coming centuries would in fact make the same kind of mistake by equating religion and nationalism, but in the Jewish rebellion of 66-70 C.E. history has on record that as a body they moved away from Judaea to Pella, a city in Perea, east of the river Jordan.[1] Indeed, as already noted, they were even considered by some to have been informers to the Roman authorities.[2] Similarly in the later rebellion of Bar Kokhba, his indignation was aroused by the failure of the Christians to enlist in defence of Judaea against the Romans.

> We have Shmeul Safrai's acknowledgment that when this revolt began in full force in 132 C.E., "General conscription was introduced, and the Judeo-Christians who refused to bear arms were severely punished." (*A History of the Jewish People*, H. H. Ben-Sasson, ed.; Cambridge, Harvard University Press, 1976, p. 332).

Robert Eisenman correctly describes the Qumran Scrolls as representing the historical reality of a violent first-century nationalistic messianism, but he wants to convince the world that the members of the Qumran community were in fact the early Christians. He tells us it is a mistake to see these early Christians as "little people walking around with halos around their heads and monks' robes."[3] I'm not sure who has seen them this way, but neither have we visualised them as fanatical warriors whose mission was to destroy the Romans. Eisenman's argument, of course, goes beyond the catastrophe of the Jewish War of 66-70 C.E. As already pointed out by Neil Asher Silberman, he also believes that Judaism and Christianity both compromised with Rome in the interests of their own self-preservation, and duly revised their respective outlooks towards the empire, if not also their theological positions.

To believe, then, that many of Jesus' pacifist statements were the product of a later "assimilationist" church would suit his case very well, but it is a position impossible to sustain. For one thing, it cuts across the findings of other researchers (including those of the Jesus Seminar as well as Burton Mack), which affirm that the non-retaliatory pacifist-style sayings of Jesus are most certainly original. Secondly, the same type of teaching by Paul, as in Romans 13 which called for submission to the civil authorities, was written long before the fall of Jerusalem. His exhortation, identical to Jesus' command to render to Caesar what is Caesar's, was not something reactionary to a failed militant confrontation which had taken place in Palestine. It was an essential part of the behaviour code of the early Christians.

# The Cross and the Kingdom

Yet we need to account for the ongoing persecution of the Christians. Let it be said that it was not because of sedition or of a suspected military conspiracy against Rome, as Pliny's letter to Trajan proves, but because of the Christians' refusal to bow to Emperor worship as the martyrdom of Polycarp clearly revealed (see p. 287).* Perhaps we should ask if Eisenman has matched his theories with known historical data, or are the remarks of Neil Asher Silberman within the same context nearer to the truth? "There may be mistakes and overstatements. Certainly many of Eisenman's proposed connections are based on intuitive leaps rather than on demonstrated textual evidence ..." 4

From all of the foregoing discussion it becomes urgent and imperative that we move along to very clear definitions of the kingdom of God as Jesus conceived it to be. We simply cannot ignore the fact that Jesus' teaching centred largely on the kingdom theme. John Dominic Crossan acknowledges this in his earlier work *In Parables* (p.22). The kingdom teaching of Jesus was distinctive and radically different from conducting warfare on God's behalf, a concept so popular in his day among the Zealots.

## The Kingdom—What it is not.

One way of defining an object in any guessing game is to get the participants to describe what it isn't. An elephant may look like a mouse—in colour yes; in shape, somewhat; in size, definitely not! A cartoon appeared in an English fun magazine showing a little mouse standing alongside a huge elephant, and whispering, "But I've been sick!" Excuses are all very well, but in the case of finding out what the kingdom of God is all about we must be profoundly serious. It is no exaggeration to say that both history and destiny depend on it.

The word *kingdom* immediately conjures up pictures of a sovereign with his or her crown and sceptre, an entourage of courtiers, ladies in waiting, and, of course, a large, beautiful palace. Soldiers

---

*The persecution of the church in varying degrees of intensity continued for over two hundred years until April, 311 C.E. when Galerius, in conjunction with Constantine and Licinius issued an edict of toleration to Christians.

must be in that picture, as guards of the monarch, and as an emblem of the strength and power of the nation.

Jesus was *not* that kind of a king. His kingdom was to bring liberty to captives, deliverance from oppression, comfort to the afflicted, healing for the sick, provision for the poor, and justice for all. It was to be a great human rights' movement, whose citizens' hearts had been changed and whose lives would transform the world around them. They were to be 'the salt of the earth' and 'the light of the world'. The church was to be a city set on a hill for the weary traveller to find rest and refreshment. This kingdom was to be in fact a replica or at least a reflection of life in heaven—and so the Lord's Prayer, "Thy kingdom come; thy will be done on earth as it is in heaven."

The one thing that it was *not* to be and that was an authoritarian institution, which, regrettably the church has so often become. Of course, organisation is needed for such an enterprise, and even Jesus used method and planning as in the feeding of the many thousands. We are told that he made them sit down, and had his disciples arrange them in ranks of fifty. Yet Jesus was insistent that rulers in his kingdom would be servants. In his response to James and John, the sons of Zebedee, who wanted chief seats in the kingdom he had this to say:

> You know that those who are supposed to rule over the Gentiles lord it over them, and their great men exercise authority over them. But it shall not be so among you ... whoever would be great among you must be your servant, and whoever would be first among you must be slave of all. For even the Son of man also came not to be served but to serve, and to give his life as a ransom for many (Mark 10:42-45).

Here indeed was a revolutionary type of kingdom. The first would be last, the last would be first, and the humblest would be the greatest. These dicta were not formulated by a low class peasant who wanted revenge on the establishment of his day, but the enunciation of a principle which, if and when implemented, would make government something human and caring, honest and accountable to all. I used to be amused at the phrase customarily used by the U.K. civil service personnel in the signing of an official letter,

## The Cross and the Kingdom

I am,
Your obedient servant,

A friend of mine had an encounter with an income tax official whose demeanour did not betray any such humility. My friend temporarily lost his self-restraint and sarcastically described the official as a 'civil serpent' and *not* a 'civil servant'!

We must take one obvious inference from Jesus' teaching, and it is that no one has the right to rule over another unless he is willing to serve. And if this principle is against the grain of human nature, which it certainly is, then at least it must prevail within the kingdom of God and in the interaction of the disciples. By the way, is it not remarkable that these particular sayings of Jesus, which are critical of the rulership of Gentiles, should be preserved in our three Synoptic Gospels when it is frequently alleged that the writers wished to avoid offending the Roman authorities? Little wonder that this kind of kingdom, and the kind of 'king' who stood before Pilate, left him bewildered and probably amused. Yet Jesus refused to deny the title, which forced Pilate to take the action he did. The cry from the crowd, as recorded by John (19:15), "We have no king but Caesar" no doubt added to his determination to dispose of this problem person.

John Dominic Crossan writes about a brokerless kingdom and a 'kingdom of nobodies'. He draws from the beatitude "Blessed are the poor in spirit, for theirs is the kingdom of heaven", and stresses the word '*ptochoi*'—poor to the point of beggary.[5] Here is a group of people which has no claim to power and nothing with which to bargain its position in society. Yet they are chosen to be the citizens of the kingdom, a description which happens to parallel Paul's words in 1 Corinthians 1:26-29:

> For consider your call, brethren; not many of you were wise according to worldly standards, not many were powerful, not many were of noble birth; but God chose what is foolish in the world to shame the wise, God chose what is weak in the world to shame the strong. God chose what is low and despised in the world, even things that are not, to bring to nothing things that are, so that no human being might boast in the presence of God.

Burton L. Mack makes reference to the Stoic use of the term kingdom by way of internal self-control; and goes on to remind us that the travelling Cynic's staff was described by Epictetus as his 'sceptre'.[6] There could be a resemblance to either of these concepts in the teachings and life-style of Jesus, "no bread, no bag, no money in their belts; and sandals only, with only one tunic" (cf. Mark 6:9).* However, Crossan and Mack are agreed that the calling and training of twelve disciples as a team was uncommon to the Cynics. Besides, this particular sending forth of his disciples appeared to have a special purpose in mind. It was a strategy of urgent outreach to the surrounding towns and villages, and, if the textual context can be trusted, as surely it can, the movement attracted Herod's attention (v.14).

There was something more designed and purposeful about Jesus' mission, than would fit the description of either the Cynic or the Stoic, and this 'something' would eventually challenge the power of government—not by way of a militant revolt, but in terms of Jesus' manifesto of love and humility. If this seems so inconceivable, one may think of William Wilberforce, who disarmed the lords of slavery without the shot of a gun, or Mahatma Gandhi who overcame the dominion of the British Raj in India, and of Martin Luther King who marched without an army from Selma to the grand liberation of his black brothers and sisters all across the United States.

Jesus promised a different kind of kingdom; a kingdom, he said, not of this world, or "my servants would fight" (John 18:36). And Jesus offered himself, not merely as a martyr, but as the Messiah whose death would change people's ideas about kingdoms, and government and power. Tragically, it took a long time for Israel to discover this lesson as militant messiahs continued to surface; and Gentile nations continue with their power struggles for economic and political supremacy. Little wonder that Jesus prayed the prayer on the Roman cross, "Father forgive them, for they know not what they do." He had reason to feel sorry for humanity in all of its blindness and stupidity.

---

*The Cynics did in fact carry bag and food with them as marks of their independence. See Ben Witherington III, *The Jesus Quest*, p.72.

## The Cross and the Kingdom

## The Kingdom—What it is.

A definition: The rule of God in the lives of people.

1. *A Call for Reform.* It was not a call to arms, as some would like to think since they favour Jesus as a Zealot. Both John the Baptist and Jesus, in announcing the kingdom called for repentance, and a turning away from evil and injustice. While John demanded that taxgatherers collect no more than was legitimate (Luke 3:13), Jesus induced Zachaeus to restore more than he had wrongfully taken. Both called upon those who had two coats to give to those who had none. John condemned violence, and Jesus encouraged non-retaliation. Of course, there was much more to it, but these observations will help us to see that kingdom preaching was expected to have an immediate moral impact, much in the same way that Dr. Billy Graham, and other responsible evangelists, call for a changed life-style in those who profess conversion.

2. *A Movement of Mercy.* The beatitudes, as they are recorded for us by Matthew, present to us the qualities of the kingdom of heaven. As we recognize that the commandments given to Moses came from God whose splendour was seen at Mount Sinai, so here we are made acutely aware of the high idealism of the teachings of Jesus, and of the other-worldly atmosphere from whence they also came. In contrast to the laws on tablets of stone, which stressed God's prohibitions of disobedient behaviour (Thou shalt *not*, etc.), here we have crystal clear portraits of personality positives for those who are citizens of the kingdom of heaven. Here is a beautiful list of virtues to be cultivated.

Just as negative forms of the Golden Rule, e.g. Do *not* do to others, what you yourself *dis*-like, had been enunciated by Rabbi Hillel (*Shabbath* 31a; cf. Tobit 4:15), and others; so Jesus preached it in positive form at Matthew 7:12, and describes it as a summary of the law and the prophets. This lays on his disciples, and all his subsequent followers the imperative of doing to others, and for others, what they themselves perceive to be the best in their own interests. This goes a long way beyond the avoiding of those behavioural traits which we personally dislike and fear in others, to a commitment on our part to actively seek for others those things which we like for ourselves. The concept of mercy was radically expanded from feeling sorry for people to doing for them all that we can. Nor was mercy to be sought from God and kept for oneself, but rather something which we will extend to others The beatitudes of Jesus were not only forward steps in the evolution of ethics, but direct exhortations for the children of men to be, and to act, as does their heavenly Father—a tall order, no doubt, but one which is intended to be functional in the new kingdom relationships.

Matthew records these:

> 'Blessed are the poor in spirit, for theirs is the kingdom of heaven.
>
> 'Blessed are those who mourn, for they shall be comforted.
>
> 'Blessed are the meek, for they shall inherit the earth.
>
> 'Blessed are those who hunger and thirst for righteousness, for they shall be satisfied.
>
> 'Blessed are the merciful for they shall obtain mercy.
>
> 'Blessed are the pure in heart , for they shall see God.
>
> 'Blessed are the peacemakers, for they will be called the children of God.
>
> 'Blessed are those who are persecuted for righteousness' sake, for theirs is the kingdom of heaven.
>
> 'Blessed are you when men revile you and persecute you and utter all kinds of evil against you falsely on my account. Rejoice and be glad, for your reward is great in heaven, for so men persecuted the prophets who were before you.'

It is agreed that the beatitudes are in a very Jewish setting. Jesus is not breaking with the past, as we can see from the last of these sayings, but he is emphasizing that what the earlier prophets had urged, and for which they often had suffered, *must* be manifested in the lives of the subjects of his kingdom. Hypocrisy is to be shunned. Truly he is calling for the ideal, and some may think the impossible, but this only shows the radicalness of his views, and how unpopular they could be. He is portraying a veritable heaven on earth, and a glorious revolution in attitudes and relationships. That he expected it to happen is further seen from his statement that his disciples were not to call him "Lord,

## The Cross and the Kingdom

Lord" and fail to do the things he had commanded (Matthew 7:21). Even an affirmation of their love for him, was to be measured by their obedience to his commandments (John 15:10). Only when Christians recognize the lordship of Christ, can they hope to fulfil these demands. Thus the ethics of Jesus cannot be separated from the person of Jesus. It was the disciples' close experience of him, and their affection for him, which inspired them to rise to these heights. And, let us remember, that the provision of forgiveness was to be available to them when they failed, yet this was never to become an easy escape route from the challenge of the good life.

The experiment, despite human failures, has worked and history does attest to the care of the sick by Christians, the erection of hospitals in numerous countries; of mercy being shown to the poor, to widows and orphans; of peacemakers among the Mennonites and the Quakers, and of the many, many saints who have truly hungered for holiness. The cruelties of the Roman gladiators who hacked helpless victims to death for the entertainment of the spectators, came to a halt only when Honorius the monk rushed into the arena in protest and was killed in the process. This isn't all that the kingdom of heaven was about, as we shall see, and the apostle Paul takes up the theme that " ... the kingdom of God does not consist in talk but in power" (1 Corinthians 4:20).

*3. A Mystery communicated through the use of Parable.* Attempts at defining all that Jesus meant by the kingdom are not easy. Being a present and a future reality, a personal and an eschatalogical phenomenon, he resorted to story form. Jesus was very adept at this, though the parabolic method was also part of the rabbinic tradition.

E. P. Sanders and Margaret Davies observe:

> Jesus' teaching was on the whole not exegetical: it did not consist of commenting on the Scripture, and this distinguishes his parables from many rabbinic ones, though the distinction is not absolute. Not all parables told in Hebrew were exegetical in nature, as the one from Ecclesiastes shows. It is fair to say, however, that Jesus' parables were superior: on the whole they are simply better than those found in any other body of literature. The stories are apt, clear and forceful; and the point usually striking.[7]

Several of the Kingdom parables appear in 'Q', such as The Mustard Seed, the Yeast and the Flour, the Invitation to the Banquet, and the Parable of the Talents. Even the Jesus Seminar is generously prepared to acknowledge six of the parables as unquestionably original to Jesus, but others are consigned to the pink, grey or black areas. Sanders and Davies believe that some of the interpretations given to the parables are likely to have been added by the Gospel writers as editorial comments; yet, on the other hand, they make an important point when they add: "In the text of the gospels, however, there is no indication that some early Christian wanted to step forward and claim for himself the ingenious interpretation: it, like the parable itself, is attributed to Jesus".[8] Over all, we can be sure that these parables are verily the creation of Jesus, and more, they represent the key to our understanding of his view of the Kingdom.

Two significant works on the subject of the parables of Jesus were published in the 1960s, one by C. H. Dodd and the other by Joachim Jeremias. Whereas it was recognized that a number of the parabolic teachings of Jesus were futuristic, or eschatalogical, others had to do with our everyday living, and how God would expect us to behave in a variety of situations. Greed, for instance, is condemned in the parable of the farmer who built greater barns; while responsibility to use the gifts God has given us is well illustrated in the parables of the talents and the pounds.

Elsewhere Jesus talks about the kingdom of heaven being among us as a present reality, or within us as an experience. This last concept would represent God's rule in our hearts. John's Gospel equates being born again with entering the kingdom. In his initial announcements, Jesus proclaimed that the kingdom of God was at hand, or imminent. Yet at the last supper he predicts that he will not again drink of the vine until he would drink it new in the kingdom (Mark 14:25).

After his resurrection, the disciples asked Jesus, "Lord, will you at this time restore the kingdom to Israel?" He declines to give them a direct answer other than to assure them that they will receive power to accomplish the task he has given them. Significantly he told them, "It is not for you to know times or seasons which the Father has fixed by his own authority" (Acts 1:7), as though suggesting that the restoration of the kingdom to Israel would be a future event, but not necessarily in the current time period. Here we must relate to the hard saying at Matthew 21:43, "Therefore I tell you, the kingdom of God will be taken away from you and given to a nation producing the fruits of righteousness."

Additional to this difficult verse is the parable of the Wicked Husbandmen, which foresees the killing of the son of the owner of the vineyard by the tenants, then followed by a reference to Psalm 118 associating the victim with "the stone which the builders rejected". Many scholars have found this parable highly controversial, and some would place it in the later church period, written with the full knowledge of the fall of Jerusalem.

James H. Charlesworth argues on the contrary that it "reflects Galilee precisely as Jesus would have experienced it. Galilee before 30 C.E. was significantly different from Galilee after 66 C.E. In the earlier time Herod had established new forms of *tenant* farming. He habitually confiscated farms from his numerous Jewish enemies and turned them into large royal estates, especially in the great fertile Plain of Esdraelon, just south of Nazareth. These tenant farms were owned by absentee landlords, usually Herod's own wealthy friends." Obviously Jesus was using a setting in his parable about which all his listeners were well aware. Charlesworth also points out that "The connection between the Parable of the Wicked Tenant Farmers and the rejected-stone motif from Psalm 118 is early. It immediately follows an independent saying of Jesus in the Gospel of Thomas (logion 66); but it is Mark the Evangelist who frames the parable and clarifies the interpretation."[9] This all adds up to three things. Jesus saw himself as the son, foresaw his own rejection and death, yet anticipated a significant and positive outcome.

This is why we have chosen the title of this chapter to read "The Cross and the Kingdom". It is abundantly clear that Jesus himself, and later his apostles, recognized the association, while John, in his Gospel, includes the statement of Jesus that a corn of wheat must fall into the ground and die before it can bear fruit (John 12:24). In the context of this saying Greeks were present, and the message they received was that Christ's death would bring the fruit of salvation to the world at large. The kingdom of God was to be worldwide, and no longer confined to the nation Israel.

This exciting view, however, left the disciples puzzled about the status of Israel, as we have seen from their question in Acts 1:7. Understandably, Jerusalem was still for them the centre of the world, and the Temple had not been destroyed. After all, wouldn't the Messiah reign from Jerusalem, and what about their respective places in the hierarchy of power, as the sons of Zebedee had asked before? What kind of a kingdom could extend into the vast Gentile world, and how could they achieve this? It had to be something very different. They had no army but they were promised spiritual power for the task, as we read at Mark 9:1:

> And he said to them, 'Truly I say to you, there are some standing here who will not taste death before they see the kingdom of God come with power.

Obviously this applied to the spectacular event which occurred on the day of Pentecost. Yet contrary to the traditional expectations, there was no sign of the wolf lying down with the lamb, and the plowing of spears into pruning-hooks, with peace prevailing throughout the world. Instead they were told that they would be persecuted, imprisoned and called upon to carry their crosses even as Jesus had carried his. In fact their message was to be a message of a cross and of a kingdom, and only after this mission was completed would the messianic age dawn with the return of the Son of Man (Mark 13:26; cf. Matthew 24:30).

> And this gospel of the kingdom will be preached throughout the whole world, as a testimony to all nations, and then the end will come ( Matthew 24:14).

## A Slight Diversion

A fascinating, if not totally fanciful idea, has been put forward by Michael Baigent, Richard Leigh and Henry Lincoln in their book *The Messianic Legacy.* Here they part company with Robert Eisenman who, as we shall see later, is very unsure about Jesus—who he was, and if he was. They are prepared to accept the reality of Jesus and the record of his genealogy tracing him to David, king of Israel. They write: "In contrast to a conventional revolutionary, Jesus must be seen as what the Gospels themselves acknowledge him to be—a claimant to the throne of David, a rightful king...."[10]

So far, so good, but a surprise awaits the reader. For these authors, (not altogether unlike Barbara Thiering who claimed that Jesus had married Mary Magdalene, and became the father of three children), Jesus *may* have had a physical progeny! Whether or not he did have brothers after the flesh, as our Scriptures clearly indicate—James, Joses, Judas and Simon (Mark 6:3)—their thesis is that the members of his family were his true successors and leaders of the early church. They would have children, and Eusebius, the fourth century historian, reports that the Desposyni—the descendants of Jesus' family (though not necessarily of Jesus himself) were traceable in the time of the Emperor Trajan (ca.98-117 C.E.). [11]

The three authors then take their readers through a winding trail of assumptions, to tell us that a physical descendant of Jesus, possibly in our own time, will be presented to the world as the real Messiah and the rightful king! It is their expectation that this person will embody all the great teaching of Jesus, and that he will lead us into the paths of peace. Of course, it is also the wish of these writers that the false doctrines, which they believe have been manufactured over the years by the traditional church, will be superseded by a fresh rediscovery of Jesus' high moral code. While they are to be commended at least for their faith in a historical Jesus, they deliberately ignore other reliable sources in the New Testament which tell us that Jesus said that he himself would return at the end of the age—and not just one of his relatives! Meantime, he looked on all who did his will as his brothers and sisters (Mark 3:35), and gave us due warning about false prophets who would come in his name, an epidemic of which we have seen in our time.

> And then if any one says to you, 'Look, here is the Christ!' or 'Look, there he is!' do not believe it. False Christs and false prophets will arise and show signs and wonders, to lead astray, if possible, the elect. But take heed; I have told you all things beforehand (Mark 13:21-23).

> And when I go and prepare a place for you, I will come again and will take you to myself, that where I am you may be also (John 14:3).

> Men of Galilee, why do you stand looking into heaven? This (same) Jesus, who was taken up from you into heaven, will come in the same way as you saw him go into heaven (Acts 1:11).

I like the term "rightful king", because for me it implies that the one who laid down his life in love for his people, and for the world at large, is the one who has the right to rule. Fortunately the world has seen many good rulers, as well as bad ones, and the testimony of the late Queen Victoria of England is deeply moving. She is reported to have said, on hearing the message about the return of Christ, "I wish he would come in my lifetime, so that I could lay my crown at his feet!"   Here is the kingdom of God at work where a person in authority, humbly and sincerely submits to the higher authority of God's will. This attitude is rare today. All too many public figures prefer to play God than to obey him.

Our three writers are accurate, however, in their charge that the church has often failed to properly interpret the mind of Jesus, having become highly doctrinaire and politically authoritative. They remind us of the submission of the church to Constantine, extending to him and to many monarchs the so-called divine right of kings. This union of church and state led indeed to such atrocities against Jews and Muslims as the Spanish Inquisition,* the persecution and murder of tens of thousands of French Huguenots, and the martyrdom of Protestant 'heretics' from central Europe across to England.

If only the words of Jesus had been obeyed, "It shall not be so among you", but the church copied the world, instead of changing it. The call to repentance applies as much to the church as it does to everyone else. The cross which adorns our churches must be seen as a humbling reminder of our own guilt before God. The cross is not a flag or an emblem of national pride, but a blood stained 'stop-sign' to bring a halt to our sinful stratagems. It is meant to be a vivid reminder of our potential for all manner of evil. If men could crucify the inno-

---

* Pope Sixtus IV protested the severity of Ferdinand and Isabella's execution of the Inquisition. This awful event in history, however, still attests to the dangers of a domineering religious establishment and of a nation presuming to act on God's behalf.

## The Cross and the Kingdom

cent Son of God, we are capable of anything. Nor is the cross to be an instrument of accusation against the Jews, since, after all, it was predetermined by God to address the sins of all humanity. This is the clear New Testament teaching (Acts 2:23, cf. 1 Corinthians 2:7,8; Acts 3:17-18), even if it has been ignored far too often.

In this sense Jesus reigns from the cross. His kingdom is to be composed of those who repent and turn from their sins. The lifechanging effectiveness of the cross can be measured in some degree by the words of Isaac Watt's beautiful hymn:

> When I survey the wondrous cross
> On which the prince of glory died,
> My richest gain I count but loss,
> And pour contempt on all my pride.

Nor is it a symbol to be confined to the church. It is surely no coincidence that nations at war have welcomed the sign of the Red Cross. The organisation was founded by Jean Henri Dunant, a dedicated Christian, who was appalled at the carnage of the Battle of Solferino in 1862, and resolved to bring compassion to the wounded and the dying. So began the International Red Cross which led to the signing of the Geneva Conventions for War in 1949 by fifty eight governments including the Vatican. This is the kingdom of God at work, where mercy follows tragedy, love prevails over hate, and, hopefully, forgiveness will follow grievous hurt. Carl Jung wrote about the Christian contribution to civilisation:

> The domestication of humanity has cost the greatest sacrifices. We do not realize against what Christianity had to protect us.... We should scarcely know how to appreciate the enormous feeling of redemption which animated the first disciples, for we can hardly realize in this day the whirlwinds of the unchained libido which roared through the ancient Rome of the Caesars. [12]

## The Kingdom and the Future

Yet what we have now is not the messianic era when humankind will at long last "learn war no more." It is the common expectation of the Old and New Testaments that human history, with all of its suffering and strife, will consummate with the coming of Messiah. And how we yearn for the time when peace will prevail and the knowledge of the Lord will cover the face of the earth, as the waters cover the sea. Among the messianic, or royal Psalms of the Old Testament are numbers 2 and 110 which read in part:

> Why do the nations conspire, and the peoples plot in vain? The kings of the earth set themselves, and the rulers take counsel together, against the Lord and his anointed, saying,
>
> 'Let us burst their bonds asunder and cast their cords from us.' He who sits in the heavens laughs; the Lord has them in derision, Then he will speak to them in his wrath, and terrify them in his fury, saying, 'I have set my king on Zion, my holy hill.' I will tell of the decree of the Lord; He said to me. 'You are my son, today I have begotten you. Ask of me, and I will make the nations your heritage; and the ends of the earth your possession' (Psalm 2:1-8).
>
> The Lord said to my lord: 'Sit at my right hand, till I make your enemies your footstool.' ... The Lord has sworn and will not change his mind, 'You are a priest for ever after the order of Melchizedek. The Lord is at your right hand' (Psalm 110:1,4-5).

These royal Psalms would celebrate the coronation of the king, an event which was marked by an anniversary with each new year. In the times of Solomon, the Temple and the palace stood side by side. Through the Davidic covenant, the reigning king was the adopted son of God, his representative, almost his vice-regent, on earth.[13] Israel was both a monarchy and a theocracy. While the primary setting of the second Psalm has reference to the contemporary king of Israel, the dramatic opening paragraph has an obviously wider meaning. Here we read of a conspiracy of the gentile nations (*goyim*) at large, and all the kings of the earth, against Jahweh and his Messiah.

The point to be noted is that the Messiah himself will be the object of conspiracy and conflict. This is a picture of rebellion, not merely against Israel, but against God and his chosen one. Throughout her history Israel has suffered at the hands of the Gentiles (B.C.E. and C.E.), but the marvellous promise here is that her Messiah will be vindicated of God, and will eventually inherit the gentile nations (v.8).

The Christian interpretation of these Psalms has much merit. It is agreed that Jews and Christians share the same anticipation of the kingdom of God eventually ruling the world, and that this will be achieved by the coming of Messiah. Where we differ lies in our respective views of the Messiah. Far be it from Christians to borrow on a strictly Hebrew concept, yet this must be permitted since the Psalm under consideration has much to say about the relationship of Messiah to the Gentiles.

A lesser known belief among Jews is that of two messiahs, and a study that has been revived by the examination of the Dead Sea Scrolls. James C Vanderkam, in referring to the Manual of Discipline 9:9-11, writes of "the Messiahs of Aaron and Israel ... The more prominent messiah is the priestly one—the Messiah of Aaron. The second and apparently lower-ranking messiah is the lay one—the messiah of Israel. Precisely what the messiahs would do, other than officiate at the messianic banquet, is not clear."[14] Another comes from a rabbinic interpretation of Zechariah 12:10 which suggests that the pierced figure described here, is 'Messiah son of Joseph' (b. Sukkah 52a). Hyam Maccoby further explains "This is a reference to a tradition that there would be two Messiah figures, one descended from Joseph and the other descended from David, of the tribe of Judah. The Messiah son of Joseph would be killed in an apocalyptic battle, but the Messiah son of David, would then be successful in establishing a messianic kingdom."[15]

In Christian thinking there is only one Messiah, traceable as the Suffering Servant of Isaiah 53, the one mocked and pierced in Psalm 22, and the one put to death and mourned as an only son in Zechariah 12. Christians also believe that Jesus fulfilled the role of the priestly Messiah after the order of Melchizedek, alluded to in another of the Royal Psalms (Psalm 110:4; cf. Hebrews 5:6), this following his death and resurrection through the interval of time until his return to reign as King of kings and Lord of lords (Revelation 19:16).

In all of this, however, we simply must not lose sight of the message of the second Psalm which pinpoints the Messiah as the one against whom the nations would wage their warfare, but by whom also they shall be brought into obedience to God. This, we believe, is the task of the church in its call to the Gentiles to be reconciled, and for this reason the apostles ('*apostoloi*', from *apo-stello*, the sent-out ones) were commissioned to go into all the world and to make disciples of all nations.

If it is complained that this has taken an undue length of time, we can only respond that God's persuasiveness is matched by his patience. The second epistle of Peter offers an appropriate comment in this regard:

> But do not ignore this one fact, beloved, that with the Lord one day is as a thousand years, and a thousand years as one day. The Lord is not slow about his promise as some count slowness, but is forbearing toward you, not wishing that any should perish, but that all should reach repentance. But the day of the Lord will come like a thief (3:8-10).

So often the Christian faith has been strongly resisted, and Christians persecuted in the process of their evangelizing of the nations. Often the kingship of Jesus has been no more welcomed among Gentiles than it was by Pilate in his day. Critics have scorned the church for its missionary activity around the world as an invasion of primitive cultures, though in today's world Christian relief agencies are gratefully received amidst the heartbreaking suffering of tribal and other conflicts.

No doubt the missionary outreach to the nations was a more formidable undertaking than had been realised by the early Christians. The church was clear, however, that the return of its Lord would be contingent upon the completion of its task (Matthew 24:14), and the expiry of "the times of the Gentiles" (Luke 21:24). Paul is absolutely clear, too, about the necessity of completing "the full number of the Gentiles" to be reconciled, as he puts it in Romans 11:25-26, after which Israel will come into her own natural inheritance. Again, if it is objected that two thousand years are just too long to wait, then we might ask our critics whether their complaint is not so much against the church as it is against God himself, who might have ushered in his kingdom by force a very long time ago, perhaps even in 70 C.E. It was the wisdom of the ancient Isaiah who declared "God's ways are not our ways" (55:8-9), while Paul affirmed his faith in the mystery and the majesty of God when he wrote:

# The Cross and the Kingdom

> O the depth of the riches and wisdom and knowledge of God! how unsearchable are his judgments and how inscrutable his ways! (Romans 11:33).

## A Personal Complaint

I have a problem with critics who are prone to put down evangelical Christians because of their zeal to preach the Gospel of reconciliation. This zeal is not a militant one, and historically their methods have been non-political. Their motivation comes from the realisation that God loves the world and gave his Son for its redemption (cf. John 3:16). These people are generally classified as 'fundamentalists', a term which has a very different connotation in other religious contexts often implying terrorism. This is grossly unfair and unfortunate since these are the very Christians who have deliberately avoided the political 'enthronement' of Christianity. Generally speaking, the evangelicals, and the so-called free churches (as in the U.K.), represent that segment of the faith which has advocated freedom of religion, and separation of church and state, well illustrated in the founding of the Rhode Island community by Roger Williams.

Of course, in the present milieu of scepticism, a Christian is, so to speak, "damned if he does, and damned if he doesn't" I mean by this, that Christians who historically have advocated a strong religious establishmentarianism, i.e. by way of a state church, are condemned; and equally those who take a very different view, and who seek to extend the kingdom of God by individual persuasion rather than by any form of religious, social or political compulsion. The apostle Paul had something relevant to this issue, when he wrote, "Let every man be fully convinced (or, persuaded) in his own mind" (Romans 14:5). And this approach is certainly the one which typified the ministry of Jesus himself. He neither looked to the authorities of his day, whether political or religious, for the advancement of his cause, nor did he seek to create a duplicate pattern of power for his church.

However, from both traditions there have come those individuals and groups which have sought to bring the benefits of the Gospel to the world—healing the sick, clothing the naked, and saving the lost.

Mother Theresa is a marvellous example of one who brings the kingdom of Heaven into a neglected and otherwise hopeless corner of this world. In a past generation General William Booth took his son, Bramwell, to a London east end tavern filled with drunks, and confidently announced to the young man, "Son, this is our kingdom!", and the subsequent record of the Salvation Army is well known.

Perhaps now that we are living in a post-Christian era, we will experience a revival, not only of the old paganisms, but of uncontrolled sensuality, uncurbed self-will, and vicious outbreaks of violence This brings us to a necessary consideration of the apocalyptic warnings of Jesus as recorded in the Synoptic Gospels (Matthew 24, Mark 13 and Luke 21), which hint at a worsening moral situation despite the propagation of the Gospel. In the pastoral epistles there are similar warnings:

> But understand this, that in the last days there will come times of stress. For men will be lovers of self, lovers of money, proud, arrogant, abusive, disobedient to their parents, ungrateful, unholy, inhuman, implacable, slanderers, profligates, fierce, haters of good, treacherous, reckless, swollen with conceit, lovers of pleasure rather than lovers of God (2 Timothy 3:1-4).

Inevitably we are forced to ask why there is an ongoing and apparently unceasing opposition to God's righteousness and to his judgments. His Messiah remains an object of contention, both intellectual and moral, as evidenced by the dialectical games we play, and the contemptible verbalizing of the name 'Christ' and 'Jesus Christ' as common curse words, a practice all too common in our entertainment media. It is the view of this writer that all our crass conduct and the cruelties of humankind—our greed, deceits, animosities, violence, our wars and dreadful holocausts, are gross sins not only against each other, but primarily they are an insult to God. David the king confessed "Against thee, thee only, have I sinned, and done that which is evil in thy sight."(Psalm 51:4). The Gospel is essentially a call for worldwide repentance as a prelude to the coming of the kingdom of God in its final form.

It would seem that over the centuries God has given humankind the opportunity to experiment with various types of government and to devise their own ways to run the world. The writer of the eighth

# The Cross and the Kingdom

Psalm declares that man, made a little lower than *elohim,* has been given the responsibility to act as God's caretaker. Some political idealists have endeavoured to order God's world without reference to him, but it hasn't worked. Long before the collapse of the U.S.S.R., Richard Crossman writing in *The God that Failed,* reviewed the honest search among one-time Marxist intellectuals for a Communist utopia:

> They saw it at first from a long way off—just as their predecessors 130 years ago saw the French Revolution as a vision of the Kingdom of God on earth; and, like Wordsworth and Shelley, they dedicated their talents to working humbly for its coming. They were not discouraged by the rebuffs of the professional revolutionaries, or by the jeers of their opponents, until each discovered the gap between his own vision of God and the reality of the Communist State—and the conflict of conscience reached breaking point.*

Jesus' teaching solidly links his kingdom and conscience together. The world has suffered too often and too long from rulers who have little or no conscience. Some politicians today believe that government can not or should not legislate morality, but woe betide any government which is itself scathed by immorality and loss of integrity.

The promise remains that God will yet place his king over the affairs of men. In anticipation of Messiah's return, the twenty fourth Psalm chants twice over "Who is this king of glory?" as though there are questions in the minds of the inhabitants of Jerusalem as to who this is, but back comes the resounding answer "The Lord of hosts, he is the King of glory." Of all the figures of history, we may ask, who has the right to rule over our humanity? Is it not too much of a coincidence that Jesus who, more than anyone else, spoke about the kingdom of God, and who himself was crucified as 'king of the Jews', should also declare that he would return? This is the Son of God who condescended to share our humanity and to identify with our sin and our suffering. He

---

\* Contributors to *The God that Failed* (New York: Harper and Row, 1950) were Andrew Gide, Richard Wright, Ignazio Silone, Stephen Spender, Arthur Koestler and Louis Fischer

is the one who absorbed our hatreds yet prayed for our forgiveness. The Scriptures tell us that he died to redeem the world. Indeed the Cross might even be viewed as the driving in of a stake to reclaim a planet which had disowned its Creator and had rebelled against his will.

Jesus was no usurper of power, in contrast to the many who have claimed the right to rule other people. How different he was from those who set themselves up in high places to oppress those who are under them. How intoxicated they become with authority. Jesus contended with Pilate, despite his boast he could crucify him, that the power he had was not inherent but only derived (John 19:11). In the end it was Pilate who came to ask Jesus "What is truth?" (John 18:38).

In Psalm 110, the Lord says to David's Lord "Sit at my right hand, till I make your enemies your footstool" (v.1.). The Christian understanding of this Psalm is that Messiah is the one who in the ultimate will be vindicated by God. The rejected one will become the anointed one, the servant will become master, and the crucified will be given the King's crown. Christ will be the victor, and he alone will be recognized as the true interpreter of history, unlocking the mystery of it all.

> ... [and] I saw a strong angel proclaiming with a loud voice, 'Who is worthy to open the scroll and break its seals?' And no one in heaven or on earth or under the earth was able to open the scroll of to look into it.... I saw a Lamb standing, as though it had been slain.... And when he had taken the scroll ... they sang a new song, saying, 'Worthy art thou to take the scroll and to open its seals, for thou wast slain and by thy blood didst ransom men for God from every tribe and tongue and people and nation, and hast made them a kingdom and priests to our God, and they shall reign on earth (Taken from Revelation 5:2-10).

This is the superbly exciting climax to the Christian philosophy of history, dramatized in apocalyptic language, declaring that the meaning of all human destiny centres around the Lamb of God and the Lion of Judah (5:5). Nor is it intended to be exclusive to the Christian movement within history, since the same Book of Revelation identifies the Lamb with an assembly of one hundred and forty four thousand who stand with him on Mount Zion (14:1; 7:4-8), representing all twelve

## The Cross and the Kingdom

tribes of Israel—from Judah, Reuben, Gad, Asher, Napthtali, Manasseh, Simeon, Levi, Issachar, Zebulun and Joseph to Benjamin.

Other major religions might well take exception to what they would regard as an extravagant claim on the part of both Jews and Christians to hold the messianic key to the history of the entire world. Of course Marxists have come close to making the same kind of claim, and for this reason they have fervently propagated the teachings of Marx, Engels and Lenin, to create a worldwide following. And their impact has been widespread, though not without serious setbacks, and hideous inhumanities to their opponents. Mao Tse Tung committed himself to the view that political power comes out of the barrel of a gun—obviously another kingdom of violence.

On the basis of free discussion, entirely without the force or fear of arms, and devoid of pride, religious people must be mature enough to consider the claims of all the world faiths, along with the moral and social values of each in turn. At the very least an inter-faith conference should be able to declare a moratorium on terrorism. If such a move cannot succeed among those who claim to be God's representatives on earth, then we should bow our heads and confess to a terrible sense of shame. Since it is the religious view of humankind which declares us to be made in the image of God, it follows that how we treat one another is how we are treating God. One of the great parables of Jesus is graphically illustrative of this truth:

> When the Son of man comes in his glory, and all the angels with him, then he will sit on his glorious throne. Before him will be gathered all the nations, and he will separate them one from another as a shepherd separates the sheep from the goats.... Then the King will say to those at his right hand, 'Come, O blessed of my Father, inherit the kingdom prepared for you from the foundation of the world; for I was hungry and you gave me food, I was thirsty and you gave me drink, I was a stranger and you welcomed me, I was naked and you clothed me, I was sick and you visited me, I was in prison and you came to me.' Then the righteous will answer him, 'Lord, when did we see thee hungry and feed thee, or thirsty and give thee drink? And when did we see thee a stranger and welcome thee, or naked and

clothe thee? And when did we see thee sick or in prison and visit thee?' And the King will answer them, 'Truly, I say to you, as you did it to one of the least of these my brethren, you did it to me' (Taken from Matthew 25:31-40).

We must be prepared to "Come, and reason together", and this process should be welcomed by Christians, Jews and Muslims each of whom fervently believes in a prophetic significance to the city of Jerusalem. We are well aware of the potential explosiveness of the situation which exists between Israel and the Muslim world, so much so that the peace of Jerusalem is pivotal to the peace of our entire planet. The Gulf War witnessed provocative acts by Iraq against Israel, while years before Israel had attacked a nuclear plant in Iraq on the pretext that it had to defend itself against the possible use of nuclear weapons on its people. At the same time other countries have protested Israel's suspected development of her own nuclear devices. The Old Testament prophet Zechariah foresaw a day when Jerusalem would be "a cup of reeling to all the peoples round about ... and a heavy stone" for all nations. (12:2-3), while Jesus identified the expiry of the occupation of Jerusalem by the Gentiles as a prelude to his return (Luke 21:24), and significantly added:

> So also, when you see these things taking place, you know that the kingdom of God is near (21:31).

Not only is Jerusalem significantly controversial to all three religions, Judaism, Islam and Christianity, but so also is the person of Jesus. Carl Henry writes:

> Any theological redefinition of personhood (i.e. of Jesus Christ) has important theological consequences for both Christian-Muslim and for Christian-Jewish dialogue. [16]

The Koran agrees that Jesus was born of the virgin Mary by a miraculous act of Allah (Sura 3:47), and further concedes to his miracle-working powers and to his ascension, though not to his death by crucifixion. Islam, Henry believes, must yet come to terms with the totality of its own perception of Jesus, and, we might add, with its expectations of the future as well. If Jesus is to be taken seriously, so

# The Cross and the Kingdom

also are his prophetic utterances which relate to the end of the age and to the final establishment of the kingdom of God. We live in a time of un-precedented global crisis—morally, environmentally and in terms of man's ability to destroy whole populations. One other paragraph from the sayings of Jesus has an ominously authentic ring about it as we survey the world in which we live today:

> And there will be signs in sun and moon and stars, and upon the earth distress of nations in perplexity at the roaring of the sea and the waves, men fainting with fear and with foreboding of what is coming on the world; for the powers (Gk. *dunameis*) of the heavens will be shaken. And then will they see the Son of man coming in a cloud with power and great glory (Luke 21:25-27; cf. also Mark 13:19-27).

The cosmic proportions of this event are further alluded to in Matthew 25:26-27 where Jesus warns against false prophets and false Christs, among them no doubt pseudo-gurus and treacherous cult leaders, and declares that his coming will be as visible and unmistakable "as the lightning comes from the east and shines as far as the west." It cannot be denied that Jesus' eschatological teachings make him our contemporary. Surely we are obligated to give him not only a careful and respectful hearing but also a place of honour throughout the nations.

The praises of the first Palm Sunday choristers need to be echoed loudly today: "Blessed is he who comes in the name of the Lord! Hosanna in the highest!"

## Notes

[1] Eusebius, *Ecclesiastical History*

[2] Zeitlin, Solomon. *The Rise and Fall of the Judaean State*, vol. 3. Philadelphia: The Jewish Publication Society of America, 1978, p.187.

[3] Quoted by Neil Asher Silberman in *The Hidden Scrolls*. New York: Grosset/Putnam, 1994, p.190.

[4] Ibid., p.189.

[5] Crossan, John Dominic. *The Historical Jesus: The Life of a Mediter-

*ranean Jewish Peasant.* San Francisco: Harper, 1991, Pt.III, pp.225-416.

[6] Mack, Burton, L. *The Lost Gospel: The Book of Q and Christian Origins.* San Francisco: Harper, 1993, pp. 126-127.

[7] Sanders, E. P. and Davies, M. *Studying the Synoptic Gospels.* London: SCM., and Philadelphia: Trinity Press, 1989, p.184.

[8] Ibid., p.23.

[9] Charlesworth, James H. *Jesus Within Judaism.* New York: Doubleday, 1988. pp. 140-148.

[10] Baigent, M., Leigh, R., and Lincoln, H. *The Messianic Legacy.* London: Corgi/Transworld, 1987, p.52.

[11] Ibid., p.131.

[12] Quoted by Arnold Lunn and Garth Lean in *The New Morality,* London: Blandford Press, 1965, pp.20-21.

[13] Lawrence E. Toombs in *The Interpreter's Bible* (One Volume), Nashville: Abingdon, 1971, Third printing, 1980, p.258.

[14] James C. Vanderkam in *Understanding the Dead Sea Scrolls,* ed. Hershel Shanks. New York: Random House, 1993, p.196.

[15] Maccoby, Hyam. *Paul and Hellenism.* London: SCM., 1991, p.63.

[16] Henry, Carl H. *The Identity of Jesus of Nazareth.* Nashville: Broadman Press, 1992, p.110.

CHAPTER SEVEN

# The Grand Affirmation

(God) has fixed a day on which he will judge the world in righteousness by a man whom he has appointed, and of this he has given assurance to all men by raising him from the dead (Taken from Paul's Address to the Athenians, Acts 17:31).

Paul, a servant of Jesus Christ, called to be an apostle, set apart for the gospel of God which he promised beforehand through his prophets in the holy Scriptures, the gospel concerning his Son, who was descended from David according to the flesh and designated Son of God in power according to the Spirit of holiness by his resurrection from the dead (Paul's Letter to the Romans 1:1-4).

We can be very sure that it was the resurrection of Jesus which accounted for the astonishing turnaround in the life of this Jewish Benjamite, scholar and one who boasted of being a Hebrew of the Hebrews. He might well have settled for Jesus as a prophet to Israel in his day, but the claim of the early Christians that this Jesus had risen from the dead was a matter of keen dispute among the Jews. The Christians found themselves being actively persecuted by those fellow-Jews who rejected their claim. Saul of Tarsus was among them and seems to have been distinguished by his fanatical opposition to the young church. In the carrying out of orders from Jerusalem, he was suddenly confronted by the risen Jesus. The words "I am Jesus whom you are persecuting" must have rung like church bells in the mind of Paul all the rest of his life.

It must be noted that it wasn't the teaching of Jesus, per se, that challenged Saul. It is unlikely that they had met with each other. At least there is no record of such an acquaintance. Nor was it Saul's meeting with the Christians he was persecuting, although it can be argued that a martyr's testimony, even that of Stephen, must have impacted him. This is an interesting conjecture, but it was unquestionably the blinding experience on the Damascus Road which stopped him in his tracks and forced him to re-evaluate his actions. He gives personal testimony to this fact again and again in his letters to the churches.

If the cross was central to the teaching of the early church in terms of its message of reconciliation, so also was the resurrection of Jesus crucial to the disciples as God's own vindication of the suffering and death of his Son. It will be argued, and convincingly so, that the scattered disciples would never have regrouped to preach their message unless their own doubts had been erased. The resurrection was a corner stone of the *kerygma*, the Gospel message, right from the start. This was the thunderous proclamation of Peter on the day of Pentecost recorded for us in the second chapter of Acts. Without the resurrection the disciples' witness to Jesus would have whimpered to a mere silence for fear of their lives.

Ironically, however, in today's Christian world there are those unbelieving believers who reject the fact of the resurrection while claiming to uphold the teachings of Jesus. Even in the latter case, however, one cannot be exactly sure as to their interpretation of his teachings.

A stalwart critic of those who take a fundamental stand on the actuality of the resurrection of Jesus is the Episcopal Bishop of New Jersey, John Shelby Spong, who has written *Resurrection: Myth or Reality? A* fellow Episcopalian, of the Church of England, N. T Wright, effectively responded with his publication of *Who Was Jesus?* which champions the traditional view. In no way does Bishop Spong seek to undermine the Christian faith *as he understands it*, but the following two quotes from his book will amply illustrate the doubtful direction in which he is travelling.

# The Grand Affirmation

> Angels who descend in earthquakes, speak, and roll back stones; tombs that are empty; apparitions that appear and disappear; rich men who make graves available; thieves who comment from their crosses of pain—these are legends all. Sacred legends, I might add, but legends nonetheless.[1]

> No, the Jesus of history did not say and do these things. What we have in the Gospel story of Jesus is a midrashic interpretation of his life and death based upon an ancient biblical image.[2]

The bishop is a believer in the ascension of our Lord, and cites Paul in support of his thesis. Despite his earlier expressed doubts about the virgin birth,[3] he surprisingly quotes from the famous passage where the apostle teaches the oneness of Christ with God before his human birth (Philippians 2:5-11). He does so because he believes that the remainder of the same portion illustrates his point of an immediate 'spiritual' ascension to God after the death of Jesus on the cross: "Therefore God has highly exalted him, and bestowed on him the name which is above every name." He comments on page 56, "There was no sense of an empty tomb for Paul."[4] Of course Jesus' appearance to Paul was considerably later than the Easter event, and his lack of reference to the historical tomb is not particularly significant. In Acts 13, however, a speech by Paul delivered in the synagogue of Antioch of Pisidia includes the following:

> And when they had fulfilled all that was written of him, they took him down from the tree, and laid him in a tomb. But God raised him from the dead; and for many days he appeared to those who came up with him from Galilee to Jerusalem, who are now his witnesses to the people (Acts 13:29-31).

Nevertheless Spong seeks to sustain his argument that the resurrection and ascension constituted a single event, that the physical body of Jesus was perishable and "was probably dumped unceremoniously into a common grave, the location of which has never been known—then or now"[5] Why, we may ask, does the bishop want to reject the resurrection as we have always understood it? He is quite right to stress that flesh and blood do not inherit the kingdom of God, a point well established by Paul in 1 Corinthians 15, where he too emphasizes that our bodies are sown in weakness, but raised in power; they are sown in dishonour and raised in glory. Spong indicates that he is wrestling with what he believes to be inconsistencies and discrepancies in the Gospels' records of incidents accompanying the resurrection.

He notes, for instance, that in Matthew's account Mary Magdalene and the other Mary are mentioned, while Mark records the presence of Mary Magdalene, Mary the mother of James, and Salome. Luke states that Mary Magdalene, the other Mary, Joanna, and some other women visited the tomb. Spong figures that neither Matthew nor Mark knew who Joanna was. He reminds us that the fourth Gospel refers only to Mary Magdalene alone at the tomb. In all four reports, Mary Magadalene is placed first, and surely we must allow the various authors some latitude in their reporting of names of the several women who had involved themselves at the tomb on that first day of the week. It should not be surprising to us that there was much running to and fro, excitement mingled with fear, even before the women ventured to find the disciples who were in hiding following the crucifixion. In a man's world it is significant that the women were acknowledged at all. We should note that Paul makes no reference to them in his list of those to whom Jesus appeared, a list obviously calculated to focus on church leaders of the time, namely, Cephas, the twelve, James and "all the apostles" (1 Corinthians 15:3-9).

We must ask ourselves if difficulties of this kind justify the position taken by Spong when he writes: "It took some sixty years to make this journey from the crucifixion of Jesus to the literalness of the empty tomb as the proof of his resurrection...."[6] Dr. Spong must certainly realize that the oral tradition of these incidents would start very soon after the event as the young church went out to proclaim the wonder and the mystery of what had happened. Such reporting would not be left to the imaginations of the next generation. Yet in outright opposition to this obvious fact, he further writes:

> At its very core the story of Easter has nothing to do with angelic announcements or empty tombs. It has nothing to do with time periods, whether three days, forty days, or fifty days. It has noth-

# The Grand Affirmation

ing to do with resuscitated bodies that appear and disappear or that finally exit this world in a heavenly ascension.[7]

Compare this with Paul's early survey of church teaching about the resurrection, and note his emphasis **on the third day** as being a precise moment when Christ was raised (1 Corinthians 15:4). In the same chapter Paul clearly states the objectivity of the appearances of Jesus when "he was seen of over five hundred brethren at one time" (v.6). Obviously the bishop is not in the same camp as the apostle, as he may have supposed.

This compels us to note other interesting and important differences in their respective concepts.

1. Soul immortality was something quite familiar to the Greeks, whereas the idea of resurrection, as we find it in both the Old and New Testaments, was much less acceptable to their way of thinking. We can observe this in the strongly negative reaction of the Athenians to Paul's preaching in the Areopagus:

> The times of ignorance God overlooked, but now he commands all men everywhere to repent, because he has fixed a day on which he will judge the world in righteousness by a man whom he has appointed, and of this he has given assurance to all men by raising him from the dead. Now when they heard of the resurrection of the dead, some mocked; but others said, 'We will hear you again about this' (Acts 17:30-32).

2. Had Paul been addressing a predominantly Jewish audience he would not have met with quite the same mockery over the idea of resurrection. Even in such a case, however, there might have been the Sadducean element which rejected any doctrine of resurrection. In contrast the Pharisees were firm believers in angels and in resurrection. In the Old Testament the idea of resurrection is hinted at in Job 19:23-26 (cf. 14:14), Psalm 16:9-10, Daniel 12:2, and figuratively in Ezekiel 37:1-14.

3. The concept of resurrection, however, must not to be confused with theophanies and angelophanies where God or 'the angel of the Lord' would appear in some visible form as in the case of the burning

bush (Exodus 3:2-6), or in the story of the three faithful Jews in Nebuchadnezzar's fiery furnace (Daniel 3:25), with the appearing of a fourth person like the Son of God (or, 'a son of the gods'). In the New Testament an example would be the temporary appearance of Moses and Elijah on the Mount of Transfiguration.

If the resurrection of Jesus were to have been understood in terms of soul immortality which, after all, would apply to everyone generally, or else as a theophany, Paul would never have described the risen Jesus as the 'firstfruits of them that slept.' Again, it was a unique event where the corrupting process natural to all physical bodies would be interrupted, as the apostle states so clearly in Acts 13:30-37.

> But God raised him from the dead.... And as for the fact that he raised him from the dead, no more to return to corruption, he spoke in this way, 'I will give you the holy and sure blessings of David.' Therefore he says also in another psalm (16:10), 'Thou wilt not let thy Holy One see corruption.' For David, after he had served the counsel of God in his own generation, fell asleep, and was laid with his fathers, and saw corruption; but he whom God raised up saw no corruption.

It cannot be overemphasized that Paul regards the resurrection of Jesus as something categorically different from the immortality concept of the Greeks, and likewise quite distinguishable from the Hebrew experience of theophanies. Nor was it for him midrash, and he would not be unfamiliar with the method. We see him utilize something of this form of commentary in Galatians 4:21-31* He honestly confesses that the phenomenon of the resurrection is a *mystery* (1 Corinthians 15:51), but as a pragmatist he insists that it is real, historical and pivotal to the new faith.

> Now if Christ is preached as raised from the dead, how can some of you say that there is no resurrection of the dead? But if there is no resurrection of the dead, then Christ has not been raised;

---

*Midrash was essentially an expository commentary on scripture, but it never included the invention of stories which were clearly seen as non-literal in intent. See N.T. Wright, in *Who was Jesus?*, p.73.

## The Grand Affirmation

if Christ has not been raised, then our preaching is in vain. We are even found to be misrepresenting God, because we testified of God that he raised Christ.... If Christ has not been raised, your faith is futile and you are still in your sins (1 Corinthians 15:12-17).

It would have been easier for Paul to have stepped over to the Greek mindset which preferred only the concept of soul immortality, thereby making his preaching acceptable to the Gentiles. Similarly, he could have avoided stressing the message of the cross—an offence to many of his fellow Jews; but both aspects of the Gospel, the death and the resurrection of Christ, represented redemption from past sin, and the reality of the new life. Again it has to be said that this was not original or unique to Paul as he himself freely admits in 1 Corinthians 15:3-5, 8:

> For I delivered to you as of first importance what I also received, that Christ died for our sins in accordance with the Scriptures, that he was buried, that he was raised on the third day in accordance with the Scriptures and that he appeared to Cephas, then to the twelve.... Last of all, as to one untimely born, he appeared also to me.

Evangelicals would endorse one aspect of Bishop Spong's thesis and it is the fact that Jesus entered the realm of the immortal with a spiritual, glorified body. In our human context of time and space, however, this body could visibly materialize itself in unexpected places (cf. John 20:19; 21:4). Following his resurrection Jesus himself refuted the idea that he was only a spirit (Luke 24:39). We therefore reject Spong's inference that Jesus' natural body remained in whatever tomb, grave or wasteland it had been put. Likewise we must take exception to his proposition that stories of happenings surrounding the mystery were trumped up by the Gospel writers just to convince a new generation of Christians. Finally, we frankly disbelieve his absurd explanation of the beginnings of the church.

In his chapter 19, entitled *But What Did Happen?* Spong looks for the 'big bang' that started it all. The big bang, however, takes the form of quiet suggestive whispers in the mind of Simon Peter (or Cephas) who, overwhelmingly impressed by the sheer goodness and wonder of the man Jesus, and by his own sense of failure and betrayal, goes back to his fishing in Galilee. Night after night out on the lake he meditates on the past three years, finds for himself some Scriptures which helped to explain the death of this good man, and suddenly found renewed hope within himself. "That was the dawn of Easter in human history" says Spong. "It would be fair to say that in that moment Simon felt resurrected.... So Simon rallied his mates with his vision, and together they decided that now they must go up to Jerusalem for the feast of Tabernacles, and in that setting they must share this vision with others so they also might see."[8]

This is a pathetically inadequate explanation. The disciples must have known that to return to Jerusalem within fifty days of the crucifixion of their master would have placed their own lives in serious jeopardy. And to do so only on the basis of Simon's mental deductions! Would the other disciples have trusted the very one who had denied Jesus in the Judgment Hall of Pilate? Wouldn't it have been easier to have remained in their home territory and to have continued to espouse the goodness of the late Jesus of Nazareth, if this was all that had impressed them?

The biblical rationale for the courageous behaviour of the once-terrified disciples, namely the resurrection of Jesus, and the empowering gift of the Holy Spirit, makes the only sense. Morever, if these early Christians had reactivated in Jerusalem to restate the messianic claims of Jesus, it seems extraordinary that the Jewish authorities failed to obtain the immediate support of Pilate to have them arrested. Or was Pilate so tired of the whole affair that he declined to intervene? Resurrection, he might have argued, was a question of theology and not of politics. Even so, however, it would remain a highly contentious issue for the religious authorities, and one sufficient to have had the disciples stoned to death, as in the case of Stephen. The reality of the resurrection of Jesus in the experience of the disciples was the catalyst for their powerful, public and unapologetic proclamation on the day of Pentecost.

Bishop Spong's dismissal of the resurrection as we have always understood it is only part of his story. Along with other critics he is prepared to question the real existence of persons and incidents which the Gospels portray as related to the death and resurrection of Jesus. Two examples will illustrate this type of argument.

# The Grand Affirmation

1. He writes: "There are many elements in this story that cause me to wonder about the historicity of Judas Iscariot.... Judas seems like to be a creation of midrash" 9 (p. 242). He then proceeds to suggest that the betrayal of Jesus may have been invented to make the behaviour of the other disciples less shocking by comparison. The bookcover comment is also quite sensational, claiming that Spong can trace "the Christian origin of anti-Semitism to the Church's fabrication of the ultimate Jewish scapegoat, Judas Iscariot." This, I believe, is a twisted concept which is not at all proven in Spong's book, nor in any reading of Scripture itself. Both of these assertions must be looked at closely.

Firstly, Spong picks up on the idea that comments made by Matthew and Luke (the latter in Acts 1:16-20) relative to Judas' betrayal of Jesus are drawn from the prophet Zechariah (cf. also Psalms 69:25 & 109:8).

> Then I said to them, 'If it seems right to you, give me my wages; but if not, keep them.' And they weighed out as my wages, thirty shekels of silver. Then the Lord said to me, 'Cast it into the treasury (or, 'to the potter', a Syrian variant reading), the lordly price at which I was paid off by them.' So I took the thirty shekels of silver and cast them into the treasury in the house of the Lord. Then I broke my second staff Union, annulling the brotherhood between Judah and Israel (Zechariah 11:12-14).

The meaning of the Zechariah passage, including its authorship and date, is unclear and has been much discussed by Old Testament scholars. Certainly it describes one loyal shepherd who is aghast at the money making trickery of other shepherds. Farther along in the book this good shepherd is described by the Lord as "the man who stands next to me" (RSV), or as "my fellow" (KJV). This same person becomes smitten and wounded in the house of his friends, or colleagues (13:7). The resemblance to the person of Jesus, his betrayal and suffering cannot be denied.

The messianic character of chapters nine to fourteen is acknowledged by most scholars. Evangelicals endorse the view that Jesus was well read in the Hebrew prophets and that he correctly applied many of the messianic passages to his own life and ministry. Spong admits that Jesus must have been an incredible and outstanding person, having had a stupendous influence on Cephas and let us add, on many, many others as well. We fervently believe that Jesus did not need to be made famous by the afterthoughts of his disciples, important as these were, or by the later attempts of the Gospel writers to associate him with the Old Testament.

Of course there was nothing wrong in searching for messianic parallels in the Old Testament, especially if the readers were from a Jewish background. Matthew, more than any of the other evangelists, seeks to establish correspondences between the life of Jesus and the Old Testament prophecies, but in so doing he freely acknowledges his sources, and does not in any way conceal his intentions. This pattern of things, however, is an altogether different genre from the hypothesis that events were invented by the Gospel writers merely on the basis of Old Testament precedents, thereby leading to something of a clandestine composition.

I suppose the basic question here is whether the egg came before the chicken, or the chicken before the egg. Was the Old Testament simply a happy hunting ground for materials out of which the Gospel writers could manufacture a portrait of an entirely fictitious Jesus, and indeed his supporting cast? To find an exit from what can become a hopelessly circular argument, let it be said that the gospel which least of all leans upon the Old Testament is Mark. He is concerned to provide only the facts in simple and straightforward vocabulary, unembellished by cross-references and the like. Thus in his gospel no exact amount of money is stated for the reward given to Judas for his act of betrayal. His commentary simply reads:

> Then Judas Iscariot, who was one of the twelve went to the chief priests in order to betray him to them. And when they heard it they were glad, and promised to give him money. And he sought an opportunity to betray him (Mark 14:10-11).

Since Mark was the earliest of the Gospels, it helps us to establish the principle that the event precedes the interpretation of the event. Mark is concerned only with the incident, the deed and the action. Whatever additions may have been added by Matthew and Luke by way of Old Testament quotations, or in terms of their own interpretation, the event was already an established fact.

## The Grand Affirmation

Before we proceed to Bishop Spong's second case, a further objection must be raised against the insinuation that the Judas story was concocted as an act of anti-Semitism. The pre-Christian Zechariah message pertained to God's judgments on the unfaithful of Judah and Israel, and the split which took place between the northern kingdom and the south. It was, if you like, an internal problem which was being addressed by a Hebrew prophet to God's people. Denunciation of their fellow-Jews was not unusual among the Hebrew prophets.

Stories of traitors are common to most cultures, but the treachery of one person does not imply guilt of the whole nation. It has even been suggested, though not by Spong, that the use of the name Judas was an attempt to implicate all Jews in his dastardly deed. This is a foolish idea since one of the brothers of Jesus is named Judas (Mark 6:3), while another apostle is described as Judas "not Iscariot" (John 14:22); and the last epistle of the New Testament bears the name of the writer, Jude, who describes himself as "a servant of Jesus Christ, and brother of James," Had there been a desire on the part of the early Christians to disassociate from this particular Jewish identity, the name might well have been avoided, but such was not the case.

2. Spong's second example comes from the story of Joseph of Arimathea who offered his tomb for the body of Jesus. Spong goes to work on this tradition in similar fashion to the Judas story. He writes "There is a strong probability that the story of Joseph of Arimathea was developed to cover the apostles' pain at the memory of Jesus' having had no one to claim his body and of his death as a common criminal" [10] Such a story would have thus alleviated their emotional distress over the memory of their own failure at a time when their leader most needed their support.

In this way the writers of the Gospels are accused of searching for an Old Testament precedent which they are quite prepared to adapt to the embarrassing situation in which the disciples found themselves. Hindsight is easy of course, but it might have been better for the writers to have concealed altogether the treachery of the disciples in their desertion of Jesus, than to have come up with this kind of pseudo-therapy for their bad conscience. The fact that their failure in the hour of need is recorded is a tribute to the honesty of the Gospel writers. By the same token, we have no reason to doubt the truth of the Joseph of Arimathea account.

Whereas in his assessment of the Judas story as a stereotyping of the Jewish people, and therefore anti-Semitic, no such conclusion can be drawn from this vignette of Joseph of Arimathea, "a respected member of the (Jewish) Council" (Mark 15:43). Indeed the exact opposite is true, and the same applies to the place of respect given in John's Gospel to Joseph and Nicodemus, another leader of the Jews, both of whom had shown interest in and favour toward Jesus.

Employing the same questionable line of investigation to find the source of such a story, Spong cites the burial of king Asa, third king of Judah following the parting of the northern and southern kingdoms, as described in 2 Chronicles 16:14:[11]

> They buried him in the tomb which he had hewn out for himself in the city of David. They laid him on a bier which had been filled with various kinds of spices prepared by the perfumer's art, and they made a great fire in his honor.

Thus we are asked to believe that the burial story of Jesus was formulated only by searching the Scriptures for such a vague similarity as this! The matter is not deserving of further comment, other than to point out that tombs in the rock areas around Jerusalem, and the use of spices were not uncommon practices.

We have already observed Spong's suggestion that post-resurrection material took up to sixty years to complete (our page 172), but mention of both Judas Iscariot and Joseph of Arimathea appears in all four of our Gospels. In my judgment this strongly indicates that the origin of these traditions was well before 70 C.E., and that they were widely known across all of the Christian communities. This strikes a blow at those who want their readers to believe that many of these stories were very late, and, being after the fall of Jerusalem, were unverifiable. My point is that they had already circulated at a time when many witnesses were alive and resident in pre-70 Galilee and Judaea, and in the other territories where the church had advanced. To have foisted these stories on the later church would have been at the risk of serious contradiction.

In the last analysis Bishop Spong's understanding of Jewish midrash is severely challenged by N. T. Wright, of Oxford, who points

## The Grand Affirmation

out that nowhere does he acknowledge Geza Vermes, Jacob Neusner and Philip Alexander, all of whom are known experts in this field.[12] Wright further comments that "Alexander's articles form, in fact, a direct and devastating rebuttal of the use of 'midrash' by Michael Goulder and others, upon whom Spong places great reliance."[13]

The reader must judge for himself/herself as to the intellectual credibility of scholars themselves, even to the point of questioning their motivation. A frank statement by Bishop Spong may be helpful to us in the formation of our opinions: "Perhaps we need to be reminded that our ultimate goal is not objectivity, certainty, or rational truth. It is rather life, wholeness, heightened consciousness, and an expanded sense of transcendence."[14] Elsewhere he writes, "once you enter the midrash tradition, the imagination is free to roam and to speculate."[15]

This all suggests to me the ecstasy of a hot-air balloon experience, rising high, resplendent with psychedelic colours, but totally at the mercy of the shifting winds. In no way am I overlooking the 'out-of-body' experience of the apostle Paul, described in 2 Corinthians 12:1-10, but this did not divorce him from the realities of life, its adversities and the objectivity of history. Paul did not drift into the nebulous, but he remained firmly faithful to the earliest records and traditions of the young church relating to the ignominious death and the bodily resurrection of Jesus.

Christian faith is already superbly life-affirming in a most profound and holistic sense. It recognizes the relationship of the physical to the spiritual. It is idealistic and pragmatic. It insists on both faith and works. It is inspirational and it is strongly ethical. It is transcendent and it is down to earth. It has a high view of God but it meets humans at our points of need. It exalts righteousness but bends to those broken in the battle of life.

The doctrine of the resurrection must not be allowed to evaporate into the ethereal and the invisible, since its message is essentially the same as the meaning of the other miracles which Jesus performed. His acts of healing provided a new impetus to the care of the sick and the infirm. Blindness in the ancient world had been considered a curse of the gods, while the dreaded disease of leprosy ostracized its victims from the rest of society. Jesus restored sight to the blind and he touched the leper. He revolutionalized contemporary attitudes toward disease and those who were deprived of the faculties God had intended for them. There is a recurring phrase in the Gospels describing the acts of Jesus as making people whole.

Similarly Paul's teaching on the body as the temple of the Holy Spirit endorsed the importance of our physical nature, reminding us also that "the body is not meant for immorality, but for the Lord and the Lord for the body" (1 Corinthians 6:13). It is in this very context that Paul holds tenaciously to the reality of Christ's resurrection and in the same chapter adds a challenging corollary to our social behaviour and the non-abuse of our bodies:

> For he must reign until he has put all his enemies under his feet. The last enemy to be destroyed is death.... If the dead are not raised, 'Let us eat and drink, for tomorrow we die.' Do not be deceived 'Bad company ruins good morals' (1 Corinthians 15:25-33).

In no way does he deny the corruption of death, however, but he has an optimisim which is paralleled in Romans 8:18-23 that the travail of human suffering will eventuate in the abolition of 'the bondage of decay' so that the whole creation will one day enjoy 'the glorious liberty of the children of God.' Even for our scientifically sophisticated generation this must appear to be a bewildering mystery, but the clear implication is that our physical world is yet to be transformed, renewed and made to participate in a great resurrection process. With all due respect to Bishop Spong I doubt that his call for more transcendental thinking can surpass the grandeur of Paul's expectations for the future.

Indeed we ourselves as Christians may find all of this to be quite incomprehensible, but the inescapable lesson which emerges is that the apostle Paul was in no way a day-dreaming Gnostic. On the contrary he had his feet firmly planted on physical reality. He also had his share of affliction, hardship, pain and persecution, but he refused to reach for some hallucinatory escape hatch. Instead he sought to comfort others with the comfort wherewith he had been comforted in Christ (2 Corinthians 1:3-7), and this was the quality of courage and commitment which characterized the early Christians. They knew that they had to carry their cross even as Jesus had done, but that with him they

## The Grand Affirmation

would triumph in the establishing of the kingdom of God on earth. And so the church, despite its human failings, became a powerful civilizing influence in our world, and the end is not yet. The prayer of Jesus awaits its final fulfilment,

> Thy will be done on earth, as it is in heaven.

The resurrection of Christ has exciting implications for our times and this is certainly not the moment in history for the church to repudiate the miraculous and to resign its mandate. As the community of the resurrection, we are to call the world to repentance, reform and glorious renewal. Spring must follow winter, and rays of hope must stream from our cathedrals, churches and the whole body of Christ in brilliant defiance of the dark clouds of doubt and despair which hang low over our world today. In a saving, redeeming and transforming way we must reject a drug culture which abuses the bodies and the minds of our younger generation, and spreads over it a dark cloak of evil confusion, self-mutilation, violence against others and suicidal self-destruction. This is the dreadful and horrifying opposite to the Gospel of Resurrection, and is patently the Devil's lie. The resurrection of Jesus Christ is God's grand affirmation of life, and of eternal life.

> I believe in God the Father Almighty, Maker of heaven and earth, and in Jesus Christ His only Son, our Lord, who was conceived by the Holy Ghost, born of the Virgin Mary, suffered under Pontius Pilate, was crucified, dead and buried; He descended into hell; the third day He rose again from the dead. He ascended into heaven and sitteth on the right hand of God the Father Almighty; from thence He shall come to judge the quick and the dead. I believe in the Holy Ghost: the holy catholic Church; the communion of saints; the forgiveness of sins; the resurrection of the body; and the life everlasting. Amen.
>
> (The Apostles' Creed).

## Notes

[1] Spong, John Shelby. *Resurrection: Myth or Reality?* Harper San Francisco, 1994, p. 233.

[2] Ibid., p. 141.

[3] Spong, John Shelby. *Born of a Woman: A Bishop Rethinks the Birth of Jesus* Harper, San Francisco, 1992.

[4] Spong, John Shelby. *Resurrection: Myth or Reality?* p.56.

[5] Ibid., p.225.

[6] Ibid., p.78.

[7] Ibid., p.21.

[8] Ibid., pp.253-260.

[9] Ibid., p.242.

[10] Ibid., p.225.

[11] Ibid., p.223.

[12] Wright, N. T. *Who Was Jesus?* London: S.P.C.K., 1992; reprinted 1993, Grand Rapids: Eerdmans, p.72.

[13] Ibid., p. 72.

[14] Spong, John Shelby. *Resurrection: Myth or Reality?* p.100

[15] Wright, N. T. *Who Was Jesus?* p. 72. See also Spong, John Shelby, *Resurrection: Myth or Reality?* Chapter 1

CHAPTER EIGHT

# Men, Myths and Morality

With all the wisdom of the sages, the guidelines of lawmakers, the outcries of the prophets against injustice, the lessons of historians, and the persuasiveness of Jesus Christ, what in the world is it that hinders humankind from attaining moral excellence? Homo sapiens bears the distinction of being made in the image of God, the Bible claims, yet our record of evil and of destructiveness surpasses anything we know in the animal world. Anthony Storr, noted psychiatrist, has written the following indictment of our humanity in his book, *Human Aggression*:

> In truth, however, the extremes of 'brutal' behaviour are confined to man; and there is no parallel in nature to our savage treatment of each other. The sombre fact is that we are the cruellest and most ruthless species that has ever walked the earth; and that, although we may recoil in horror when we read in newspaper or history book of the atrocities committed by man upon man, we know in our hearts that each one of us harbours within himself those same savage impulses which lead to murder, to torture and to war.[1]

We have a remarkable range of behaviour between the good and the bad, between sacrificial self-giving and aggressive possessiveness, between an endearing humility and an insufferable egotism, between being saints and sinners, and acting either like angels or devils. We can build cathedrals for the worship of God and we can create gas ovens to exterminate a whole race of people. We are both Dr. Jekyll and Mr. Hyde, and little wonder that the apostle confessed "For I do not the good I want, but the evil I do not want is what I do.... Wretched man that I am! Who will deliver me from this body of death?" (Romans 7:19,24). Pope's *Essay on Man* (Epistle II, l.) graphically expresses the poignancy of the paradox:

> He hangs between: in doubt to act or rest
> In doubt to deem himself a God, or beast;
> In doubt his mind or body to prefer;
> Born to die, and reas'ning but to err;
> Alike in ignorance, his reason such,
> Whether he thinks too little or too much;
> Chaos of thought and passion, all confused;
> Still by himself abused, or disabused;
> Created half to rise, and half to fall;
> Great lord of all things, yet a prey to all;
> Sole judge of truth, in endless error hurled;
> The glory, jest and riddle of the world!

In ancient times humans may have thought themselves to be the sport of the gods, or else that they could somehow supplicate the gods to favour them in their distresses. In the Hebrew experience it was realised that man had a recognizable responsibility to act in ways which would be morally acceptable to God, and this sense of accountability continued on in the Christian faith. But with the prevalence of contemporary atheism, man is seen to be on his own, and in no way beholden to a higher power. This release from the *superstition* of religion, as some would see it, has only served to increase man's own moral dilemma.

The existentialist philosophers Kierkegaard and Nietzsche were among the first to concern themselves with the oncoming world of man's ascendancy and the inevitable sense of 'aloneness' that humankind would feel. Living in a world of his own creation—a technological, secular and materialistic society, led to Nietzsche asking "Do we not now wander through an endless Nothingness?" For him it was a good thing for man to be the master of his own fate, yet he betrayed an awesome fear of the alienation it would produce. Indeed Nietzsche's great confidence in man's innate qualities convinced him of 'superman', and marked out the pathway which accelerated the rise of both Marxist and fascist systems; and the nihilism, which he himself feared, duly followed. Kierkegaard, in contrast, maintained that man's true self could only be preserved by identification with God. Karl Jaspers also warned us that the price we pay for our technological progress is anxiety, a dread of life perhaps unparalleled in its intensity and increasing "to such a pitch that the sufferer may feel himself to be nothing more than a lost point in empty space, inasmuch as all human relationships appear to have no more than a temporary validity." [2]

Much of the foregoing has been fulfilled in our time, and we stand amazed and ashamed at the behaviour of the human animal in the twentieth century. We have come terrifyingly close to nuclear annihilation, we have witnessed genocide on an unprecedented scale, and struggles between power groups go on unabated. Man has highlighted himself in remarkable ways even to landing himself on the moon, but, overall, we are neither impressed nor amused. Today's 'information highway', with its incalculable potential for systematising the results of research, etc., will be subject to the very temptation posed to Adam and Eve in the Garden of Eden. Take the fruit of the tree of knowledge and choose to become gods yourselves. Knowledge is not to be despised, but its use by the wrong people for wrong purposes will always be something to be feared. A big factor at this point in man's history is the 'dethronement' of God by secular humanism in western society. There are powerful advocates of this philosophy who have only contempt for 'religious' people. In their arrogance they will scoff at such biblical quotes as 'the fear of the Lord is the beginning of wisdom' (Proverbs 1:7). They have forced a view of human sexuality which is more concerned to place condoms in schools than to having responsible lectures given on mothercraft and family responsibilities for the males. Of course it is a point of view, and as such it has the right to be considered in a freethinking society, but only so long as its consequences are also fully encompassed within the courses of such a curriculum.

Temptation to any kind of evil generally starts with what seems to be a relatively innocent invitation to a desirable pleasure. Adolf Hitler persuaded the highly intelligent German people that his Third Reich would bring them a super culture. Timothy Leary persuaded the hippie youth of America to opt for drugs rather than for a stupid war in Vietnam, and the idea didn't seem so evil at the time. In the first case catastrophe befell not only Germany, but the Jewish people in particular, and the world at large. In the second case, North American society is plagued today with robberies and murders by people who have to feed their drug habit. Incidentally, it may interest the reader to note a relatively hidden verse in the Book of Revelation, 9:21, which reads "nor did they repent of their murders or their sorceries (lit. *pharmakeia*—the practice of drug-abuse), or their immorality or their thefts." I remember hearing a New England minister saying "Man cannot be as evil as he is, without some assistance!" He was no fanatic, but he was contending for the existence of Satan as the mastermind behind so many of man's self-defeating schemes. Nor was he advocating a simplistic view of human behaviour as something which could be brushed off with the typical remark "The Devil made me do it." We bear responsibility for the evil we undertake, but man is that unique creature who is open and vulnerable to an infinite variety of ideas about which he has to make his own choices.

The Jewish rabbinical view of man emphasizes the choice factor and sees in him two natures, or better, two inclinations one of which is to evil (*Yetzer hara*), and the other to good (*Yetzer hatov*). The essential meaning of the Adam and Eve story is that we human beings are creatures of choice, and are accountable for the decisions we make. Surprisingly, however, in rabbinical teaching "the effect on human nature of Adam's fall is generally denied or at best minimized, and great stress is laid on man's ability to attain righteousness without outside help.... Instead of the Fall of man (in the sense of humanity as a whole), Judaism preaches the Rise of man; and instead of Original Sin, it stresses Original Virtue (*Zchut Abbot*), the beneficial hereditary influence of righteous ancestors upon their descendants."[3] Similarly, any serious dualism between God as the embodiment of all good, and Satan as a self-existing entity of evil powerfully arrayed against God, is either rejected or downplayed. Satan is only the adversary who is himself appointed by God to put men to the test. God's sovereignty is in no way compromised by the existence of Satan. Yet if there is a people who should be convinced of these two realities, the fallen-ness of human nature, and the atrocious power of evil, it is the persecuted nation of Israel. The evil within human nature is recognized by David, as expressed in the penitential Psalm:

> For I know my transgressions, and my sin is ever before me. Against thee, thee only, have I sinned, and done that which is evil in thy sight, so that thou art justified in thy sentence and blameless in thy judgment. Behold I was brought forth in iniquity, and in sin did my mother conceive me (Psalm 51:3-5).

Jeremiah the prophet also attested to the utter deceptiveness of the human heart when he wrote:

> The heart is deceitful above all things, and desperately corrupt; who can understand it? (17:9).

Jesus, optimistic as he was and merciful to all who had sinned, underscores the universality of sin embedded in human nature when he made the observation:

> If you then, who are evil, know how to give good gifts to your children, how much more will your Father who is in heaven give good things to those who ask him (Matthew 7:11).

The Bible does not have a completely despairing view of human nature. On the contrary it teaches that God continues to communicate with us through his Word. We are still made in his image, and capable of responding to his truth even if it demands repentance on our part. All the same, the hideousness of human sin is not to be minimized, and we are solemnly reminded of God's judgment on the generation of Noah when "The Lord saw that the wickedness of man was great in the earth, and that every imagination of the thoughts of his heart was only evil continually" (Genesis 6:5). The Old Testament view of the sins of Sodom and Gomorrah finds its counterpart in

Paul's letter to the Romans, chapter 1:24-32. The apostle also alludes to the universality of sin when he declares that all have sinned and have fallen short of the glory of God (Romans 3:23).

Teaching in the Old Testament about Satan, evil and the demonic may be considered limited, but there is sufficient to alert us to the greatness of the problem. In the book of Job Satan does play the role of 'the devil's advocate' and is permitted by God to test righteous people, having the right to appear in the presence of God to make his charges or accusations. The First Book of Samuel tells us that God was displeased with Saul, and sent him an evil spirit. Later in that well known tragedy of Israel's first king, we learn that he consulted with the woman medium of Endor. In her seance she had a vision of "a god coming up out of the earth", whom Saul identified as Samuel. Perhaps this story can be put on the same plain as Shakespeare's Macbeth, but in the Old Testament it is stated as a fact. It is an acknowledgment of the spirit world.

At Zechariah 3:1-2 we read, "Then he showed me Joshua the high priest standing before the angel of the Lord, and Satan standing at his right hand to accuse him. And the Lord said to Satan, "The Lord rebuke you, O Satan! The Lord who has chosen Jerusalem rebuke you! Is not this a brand plucked from the fire?" The prophet Isaiah takes a serious view of the evil influence which has inspired the king of Babylon to make him think that he is equal to and even above God:

> How you are fallen from heaven, O Day Star, (or Lucifer) son of Dawn! How you are cut down to the ground, you who laid the nations low! You said in your heart, 'I will ascend to heaven; above the stars of God I will set my throne on high; I will sit on the mount of assembly in the far north; I will ascend above the heights of the clouds, I will make myself like the Most High' (14:12-14).

A similar denunciation of the king of Tyre occurs in the book of Ezekiel, but linked to an angel who walked in the Garden of Eden:

> "Because your heart is proud, and you have said, 'I am a god, I sit in the seat of the gods, in the heart of the seas,' yet you are but a man, and no god, though you consider yourself as wise as a god—you are indeed wiser than Daniel; no secret is hid from

you.... You were the signet of perfection, full of wisdom and perfect in beauty. You were in Eden, the garden of God.... On the day you were created they were prepared, with an anointed guardian cherub I placed you; you were on the holy mountain of God; in the midst of the stones of fire you walked. You were blameless in your ways from the day you were created, till iniquity was found in you"(Chapter 28:2-3; 13-15).

Allowing for poetic licence, the inescapable inference in these passages is that kings and rulers can be intoxicated with a sense of power that emanates from the world of angels and demons. The book of Daniel plainly teaches that the archangel Michael is the spiritual force set for the protection of the Hebrew people (12:1) in the great contests of history. At 10:13 Daniel describes 'the prince of Persia' who withstood God, but who in turn was rebuked by Michael. Just as Michael was in no way a human leader for Israel, neither is the prince of Persia to be so perceived. Today we may talk of the psyche of a nation, where a people can be stirred into a frenzy of patriotism. Certainly we cannot deny the incredible 'spirit' that propelled the Nazi movement to power accompanied to the beat of martial music, waving banners, and marching soldiers in their thousands. The element of the demonic, however we understand it, cannot be ignored and should not be underestimated.

Paul speaks of principalities, powers, the world rulers of this present darkness, and the spiritual hosts of wickedness in the heavenly places. (Ephesians 6:12), while Revelation describes Satan as the one who goes out to deceive the nations (18:23; 20:3). Hyam Maccoby in his work *Paul and Hellenism* takes the apostle Paul to task for his dualism which he considers to be excessive, attributing it to the influence of Greek Gnosticism and not to Judaism. In citing such portions of New Testament Scripture as Roman 8:38, 1 Corinthians 15:24; 1 John 5:19 (not Pauline) and Colossians 2:15 he believes that these "show that the Pauline view of Satan went far beyond that of the most Jewish dualistic writings. Instead of regarding Satan as, at most, a fallen renegade angel, working surreptitiously against the purposes of God in a world, which on the whole, was under God's domination, Paul regarded Satan as the ruler of this world and of the regions of the heavens contiguous to the earth."[4]

If Paul is guilty of Gnosticism, we need to ask if he was in line with Jesus in his view of Satan, and how the scribes of the day regarded Beelzebub, or Be'el-ze-bul, whom they viewed as the evil inspiration behind Jesus (Mark 3 :22). Likewise we need to take into account the use of the expression 'Belial' or 'sons of Belial' as found in the Dead Sea Scrolls. William Sanford LaSor points out that the Qumran community viewed all nonmembers as "sons of darkness", "sons of perversion", "men of the pit" and "the men of Belial's lot."[5] He points out that in these cases they had official Judaism in mind, while in the War Scroll the people of God would pursue and destroy the enemy to eternal destruction, specifically "for all the lot of Belial."[6] Presumably this latter would refer to Israel's Gentile enemies.

Language, we well know, was often a weapon of contempt in the world of the Middle East, as it can be in other primitive societies around the world. Thus we might assume that the scribes were only indulging in verbal abuse of Jesus by calling him the prince of demons, while in similar fashion Jesus himself accused certain of the Jews that they were of their father, the devil (John 8:44; cf. 8:48 where they call Jesus a Samaritan and a devil). On the other hand, Jesus took the first charge seriously (Mark 3:22-30), and claimed that God's house was not divided, that the intruder 'the strong man' should be bound, and that the scribes' attributing of his miracles to the devil, rather than to the Holy Spirit, was unpardonable blasphemy. Jesus took Satan very seriously as 'the prince (or, 'ruler') of this world', a saying preserved for us, not in the Pauline tradition, but in John 14:30. Paul's dualism, in my judgment, is not to be dismissed as an un-Jewish Gnostic addition to his theology.

We must return to LaSor's observation from the Scrolls that real spiritual beings are meant by 'the prince of lights', on one hand, and Belial, or 'the angel of darkness' on the other. His summation reads: "God is blessed for His works and judgments, and also because He made Belial, the angel of hostility, to hinder, and then made him to fall into darkness (1Qm 13:1-5)."[7] As for Jesus in his encounters with Satan and the demons, he never treated them as something illusory or unreal. In the record of his forty day temptation in the wilderness, Jesus testifies to the claim of Satan to offer him the kingdoms of this world, if only he would bow to him. As noted, Maccoby takes strong exception to Paul's description of Satan as "the god of this world " (2 Corinthians 4:4), as though he were some kind of Demiurge (a Gnostic lesser god); but Paul's use of the expression parallels a Qumran view that Belial is an angel of darkness. Here in this paragraph of 2 Corinthians Paul writes of the blinding of the minds of unbelievers, "to keep them from seeing the light of the gospel of the glory of Christ, who is the likeness of God" (4:4).

We have reached the point in our discussion of the nature of evil where we ought to take a position. Evil can be regarded as merely the result of bad decisions on the part of humans, or something endemic in human nature, or a moral condition induced by spiritual influences, and/or an entity in itself—an intelligence which operates against God and the performing of his will. In a chapter entitled "*Toward a Psychology of Evil*", M. Scott Peck shares this view with his readers:

> The problem of evil is a very big mystery indeed. It does not submit itself easily to reductionism.... Moreover, the size of the puzzle is so grand, we cannot truly hope to obtain more than glimmerings of the big picture.... Bear in mind also that just as the issue of evil inevitably raises the question of the devil, so the inextricable issue of goodness raises the question of God and creation.... A sense of awe is quite befitting. In the face of such holy mystery it is best we remember to walk with the kind of care that is born both of fear and love.[8]

This is a very honest and humble assessment, and it would be true to add that serious thinkers of the late twentieth century have every reason to view the phenomenon of evil with the utmost gravity. Two world wars, the advent of nuclear and biological weaponry, the holocausts of millions of innocent people, and the strong undercurrents of organized crime operating on all five continents, are ominous signs of political corruption, social disintegration and widespread destruction of life. This unique and beautiful planet has become a grim battlefield, and a terrifying scene which is best described by the apocalyptic language of the book of Revelation.

If *homo sapiens* alone is responsible, how can we hope for the saving of our world, other than by divine intervention? Of course another super-dictator may yet emerge to orchestrate our chaos into a monstrous Big Brother 'fourth reich' to enslave the entire world. Strangely enough, this would coincide with a biblical anticipation of the Antichrist who is predicted as having zero tolerance for any who will not comply with his diabolical system (cf. Revelation 13:16-18).

It is not in my purpose to dogmatize on whether this person belongs to past history or is yet to come. It is, however, my deep conviction that if Satan is the great evil manipulator who has lurked behind the stage of world history in every age, then it becomes imperative for all of us to renounce evil, to reject his stratagems and to return to an intelligent and genuine worship of the true and living God. Only as we honour our Creator, will we learn to desist from destroying the earth he has given to us. Our urgent priority must be to seek the kingdom, or rule of God and his righteousness, even as Jesus urged (cf. Matthew 6:33).

## Myths and Morality

Creation stories and apocalyptic themes are often viewed as myths which have their place in religious thought and serve to explain the beginnings and endings of things. They are common to most faiths. In the case of Judaism and Christianity, Robin Lane Fox [9] believes that both the accounts of creation in Genesis and the stories of the birth of Jesus in the New Testament are merely pictorial representations of events which no doubt happened, but not at all in the way depicted in Scripture.

We have no difficulty in saying that Genesis was never intended to be a textbook on physics or biology, or $H_2O$ might have been a preferred term to the Hebrew word *mayim* for water. Language and concepts were used that would be easily intelligible to all generations, describing not how God created the earth but providing an answer to why he did. In the case of Fox's rehearsal of old arguments against the nativity stories of Jesus' birth, I would refer the reader to a recent publication by Josh McDowell and Bill Wilson entitled *He Walked Among us—Evidence for the Historical Jesus*, also Alan Richardson's article on the Virgin Birth in *A Dictionary of Christian Theology*, and Donald Baillie's classic *God was in Christ*. [10]

But to place the teaching of the Old and New Testaments relative to the mystery of evil in the category of the mythological is not acceptable.

## Men, Myths and Morality

Evil is not merely in our imagination, and the biblical treatment of it bears no real resemblance to the graphic Greek myths of the gods and the figurative battles they fought usually out of lust, spite or jealousy. To the modern mind these would seem closer to opera, while the biblical concepts would better fit the lawcourts. The Judaeo-Christian outlook, however, is not just strictly and sternly legalistic. It also acknowledges a dramatic element. It perceives our world to be a stage on which is acted out a struggle between forces good and evil, with human beings deciding the outcome. The pendulum of history, we know, swings between good and evil, according to the circumstances of any given era and the moral climate of the time. It is significant that both Judaism and Christianity are confident that good will triumph in the end.

The fundamental difference between them, however, is that the latter believes God has chosen to enter the fray personally and has stepped on to that stage in the person of his Son. He has voluntarily placed himself in the arena of vulnerability; he has accepted the gauntlet of challenge from Satan. Thus Jesus, truly human and of the seed of the woman (cf. Genesis 3:15), must affirm his constant and complete obedience to the Father, in vivid contrast to the rebelliousness of Satan. This he has done, and by this means he deprives the Adversary of the right to hold men and women in bondage. The Gospel, or the Good News is one of release and redemption. And still more, Jesus Christ, already the Saviour, is finally destined to be the rightful ruler in place of the Usurper. The thought is well expressed in the hymn:

O loving wisdom of our God, when all was sin and shame,
A second Adam to the fight, and to the rescue came.

Here God is seen to be more than a spectator to the human conflict and to our testings and suffering; he becomes a participant. He is dwelling among people, to sit where we sit, to be acquainted with our grief and to carry our sorrows. The issues at stake are too important for him to be uninvolved. Of course the doctrine that God became man, or the Word became flesh, is regarded by some to be purely mythical. Then let us indulge ourselves in a little speculative adventure of our own.

Imagine the scene when Satan exceeded his mandate from God

his creator and actively rebelled against him. Could not God have destroyed him instantly? Yet if he had done so, a shock wave would have reverberated through the universes to unsettle all of the created beings. The mystified response of these angels, principalities and powers could well have been, "Here is One who instantly exterminates his opponents, while he tells us that he is a God of love! Who can trust him?"

The writer to the Hebrews tells us that God cannot deny himself. If this is so, he had to find a way either to persuade his enemy to be reconciled, or to disenfranchise him of his power.

So God thought that he should make a world in which creatures, uniquely adapted for decision making, would play their part in this drama of vindicating either God or Satan. So He convened a council of the Godhead and said, "Let us make man in our own image." The story goes on to tell us that many of those 'special beings' chose the good life, but others yielded to the temptations of the Adversary. Then came the moment when God saw that the stage was set for a personal duel, one in which his own Son would engage himself and die at the hands of a ruthless and implacable Enemy.

In this way he demonstrated to his heavenly hosts, the irreconcilability of Satan, God's own patience with him, and the willingness of a member of the Godhead to suffer voluntarily the penalty that the Enemy ought to have received when he rebelled. And now God had the moral justification to strip the Devil of his usurped authority, and, when it pleases him, to commit Satan to the Lake of Fire. And the moral to this parable is that never again throughout all the ages of eternity, would an angel be tempted to rebel and wreak the same awful havoc on any of God's worlds. Nevermore, Amen.

A semblance of this very theme is traceable in Paul's letters to the Ephesians and to the Colossians. In the first instance he is quoting from Psalm 68 which rejoices in the triumph of God over his enemies (vs. 17-18), and the deliverance of the captives (v.6).

Therefore it is said, 'When he ascended on high he led a host of captives, and he gave gifts to men.' In saying, 'He ascended, what does it mean but that he had also descended into the lower parts of the earth. He who descended is he who also ascended far above all the heavens, that he might fill all things' (Ephesians 4:8-9).

He disarmed the principalities and powers and made a public example of them, triumphing over them in it [the cross] (Colossians 2:15).

Before rushing off hastily and gleefully to the game of demythologizing the Scriptures, some secular thinkers and a few theologians as well, need to give second thoughts to those modern myths which have not fulfilled themselves, but which in fact have led to widespread disillusionment. Worse still there have been those myths like Marxism and fascism which have been positively identifiable as the cause of political mass murders and untold suffering for whole nations. Friedrich Nietzsche and his 'death of God' philosophy had a surprisingly wide appeal for both far-leftists and far-rightists. In his *Assorted Opinions and Maxims*, published in 1879, he appealed to the racial pride of German youth and urged them to turn from Christianity when he wrote:

> For youthful, vigorous barbarians Christianity is poison; to implant the teaching of sinfulness and damnation into the heroic, childish and animal soul of the ancient German, for example, is nothing other than to poison it.[11]

Not only was this a false myth, but it constituted brutish advice which bore a bitter fruit for Jews and Germans only sixty years later. Clark Pinnock provides us with an enlightening chapter in his book *Reason Enough* when he deals with the question of mistaken mythologies:

> Marx and Freud, for example, can be seen in these terms. Each of them has devoted considerable talent and effort to construct a life and world view to fill up the vacuum left by the "death of God." They offer us surrogate theologies, suited to secular thinking and intended to capture the allegiance of post-Christian men and women. That they are antireligious should not blind us to the fact that they offer new mythologies, profoundly religious in nature

> and scope and aimed at replacing traditional religion in modern culture.... For my part, I think Marx's prophecy of the new Eden is an illusion. Instead of bringing greater humanization, it has brought systematic terror on a new scale.... With Freud, too, we are dealing with a highly mythological and religious surrogate theology. That is especially obvious in the rich use Freud makes of myths in his work. Some of his basic notions did not arise out of controlled experiments but from an imaginative leap of faith.[12]

Pinnock notes Freud's use of the Greek myth of Oedipus to suggest that every male child is eager to kill his father and jump into bed with his mother! Fortunately, post-Freudian psychology has revisionists like Rollo May, who stresses the ethic of intention, and Roberto Assagioli, who talks about walking to the door of religion and letting the individual open it, in significant contrast to Freud's earlier dismissal of religion as a neurosis.

It was Ernest Renan who once said "The twentieth century will spend a good deal of its time picking out of the waste basket things which the nineteenth century threw into it."[13] And still much of our twentieth century thinking needs to be re-examined As already observed, contemporary humanism may prove to be little more than a masochistic myth which engineered the wholesale destruction of its own species.

The Second Letter to Timothy tells us that the time will come "when people will not endure sound teaching, but having itching ears they will accumulate for themselves teachers to suit their own likings, and will turn away from listening to the truth and wander into myths" (4:3-4).

## The Acid Test

> A sound tree cannot bear evil fruit, nor can a bad tree bear good fruit.... Thus you will know them by their fruits (Matthew 7:18-19).

We turn from myth to morality, though not for a moment implying that myths, parables or other story forms are devoid of any moral value. In the last analysis, however, any religion, faith or philosophy has to be judged by its truthfulness, honesty and beneficial effect on people. It must be interested not only in the well-being of its own devotees, but in the improvement of society in general, and eloquent in its advocacy of justice for all.

Any religion or political philosophy which is intolerant of those who do not agree with it, to the point of becoming terrorist in its activities, should disqualify itself as a member of our civilization. Jesus rebuked James and John, his disciples, who wanted to call fire down from heaven on a Samaritan town because it refused Jesus an entrance. Typical of his responses, Jesus actually used the Samaritan figure in a parable to drive home the fact that those we may regard as farthest removed from us racially and culturally are neighbours we are to love. Today we live in the global village, and, more than ever before, it is imperative to implement this marvellous message he gave to us almost two thousand years ago.

Countless women and children in our times continue to be the victims of abuse and inequalities, and the greatest champion of their dignity and worth was unquestionably Jesus. Some talk proudly of our post-Christian era, but in doing so we need to ask what were things like in the pre-Christian era. As far as women were concerned, Aristotle regarded a female as 'a kind of mutilated male.' He wrote: "Females are imperfect males, accidentally produced by the father's inadequacy or by the malign influence of a moist south wind."[14] Even in Jewish circles, it was a common prayer for a rabbi to give thanks that he had been born "neither a Gentile, a slave nor a woman."

As far as children were concerned, infanticide in Greece and Rome was common, especially of unwanted females, a situation which still has its parallels in today's world. The Gospel which begins with the Christ child revolutionized western society in terms of caring for the young, born and unborn. It proclaimed God's sanctifying of human birth. Michael Ramsay, when Archbishop of Canterbury, addressed the Church Assembly in 1967 and said: "We shall be right to continue to see as one of Christianity's great gifts to the world the belief that the human fetus is to be reverenced as the embryo of a life capable of coming to reflect the glory of God...."[15] Up until 1959 the Christian influence was quite pervasive as can be detected in the United Nations' Declaration of the Rights of the Child, part of which insisted that the child needs "special safeguards and care, including appropriate legal protection, before as well as after birth."

The medical profession itself is drifting from the updating of the Hippocratic Oath by the Declaration of Geneva (1948) which included the clause "I will maintain the utmost respect for human life from the time of conception" (Quoted by John Stott in *Involvement: Social and Sexual Relationships in the Modern World*, Vol 2; New Jersey: Revell, 1985, p.189.

We have come a long way since then along a road that is strewn with millions of aborted fetuses, a road which spans the very areas which once were known to be Christian. Little wonder that a likely corollary to all of this is the rise in murders, rapes, and savage attacks on women and children. Life has become cheap and bodies disposable! This is not to argue in favour of over-population, when, after all, there are acceptable methods of contraception. It is a protest against the ruthlessness of indiscriminate rupturing of human life, brain, flesh and tissue. Nor is it an endorsement of those who have taken in hand to murder staff members in abortion clinics, which only adds to the bloody stains of the execution chambers.

In this chapter we have focussed on the issues of women and children since these most conspicuously illustrate that in a time when it is fashionable to deny God, so is it easy to deny life itself—its wonder, its growth and its beauty. Is it coincidental that many radical supporters of abortion-on-demand are found in the ranks of those who are quick to dub the virgin birth of our Lord Jesus as mythical? Not all, of course, who question the incarnation story do it for this reason, and it is equally true to say that not all who believe in the virgin birth are necessarily opposed to abortion on certain specific grounds. One such reason could be when a pregnancy is due to a violent rape assault. The point to be made here is that even if some choose to regard the virgin birth of Jesus as a myth—a position not accepted by this writer, the Bethlehem event remains a powerful witness to the truth of the value of any and every child. Deny that miracle, and, in the climate of today's thinking, the likelihood is that many will lose reverence for the wonder of the birth of any child. Many idealistic humanists will disagree, but statistics of child abuse indicate that a major deterioration is occurring in our society. Ultimately what we believe determines what we think and how we behave.

Let me register a plea for the continuation of the joyous celebration

## Men, Myths and Morality

of Christmas. Voices are being raised in opposition to the Christian festival which is enjoyed by millions as one of the happiest seasons of the year. As part of the celebration the real Saint Nicholas, a kindly and generous old bishop, has been transformed commercially into a "Ho, Ho," mythical money-making Santa Claus. The Christian community doesn't complain, even though it is a travesty of the truth. Nor should any non-Christian feel threatened by the beautiful story of the child in a manger. Let's have Chanukkah and let's have Christmas, even if there are those around us who don't believe in either of these miracles. The chances are that these same folk believe in other myths which may not have such happy results as the value-systems they are seeking to eliminate.

Finally, it should be said to the credit of Christianity that exploitation of children as slave labourers during England's industrial revolution was brought to an end by Lord Shaftesbury, an earnest believer. He also had labour laws passed to stop the forced recruitment of women and boys for work in the coal mines. Even yet, however, in some of the world's non-Christian environments, appallingly slave-like conditions continue for women and children who are denied even minimal human rights.

Let those thinkers and writers who seem intent on dismantling the Christian faith ask themselves if they are equally sincere about exposing other *myths* around the world which have tragic effects on their native peoples?

## Notes

[1] Storr, Anthony. *Human Aggression* Harmondsworth, U.K.: Penguin, 1975, p.9.

[2] Karl Jaspers in *Man Alone*, eds. Eric and Mary Josephson, New York: Dell, 1962, pp. 15-16.

[3] Kac, Arthur W. *Rebirth of the State of Israel*, 1958; Grand Rapids: Baker, revised 1976, pp. 184-186.

[4] Maccoby, Hyam. *Paul and Hellenism*. London: SCM., 1991, P.40
55 LaSor, William Sanford. *The Dead Sea Scrolls*, 1956; reprinted 1972, Chicago: Moody, p.69.

[6] Ibid., p.173.

[7] Ibid., p.100.

[8] Peck, Scott M. *People of the Lie: The Hope for Healing Human Evil.* New York: Simon and Schuster, 1981, pp.41-42.

[9] Fox, Robin Lane. *The Unauthorized Version: Truth and Fiction in the Bible.* New York: Knopf/Random, 1992.

[10] McDowell, J. and Wilson, B. *He Walked Among Us.* Nashville: Nelson, 1993; Richardson, A. *A Dictionary of Christian Theology.* London: SCM., 1969; Baillie, Donald M. *God Was In Christ: An Essay on Incarnation and Atonement.* London: Faber and Faber, 1948.

[11] Nietzsche, Friedrich. *Assorted Opinions and Maxims,* published in 1879 as the First Supplement to *Human, All Too Human,* 2nd edition published in 1886 and quoted in *A Nietzsche Reader,* ed. R. J. Hollingdale (Harmondsworth, U.K.: Penguin Books, 1977, pp.172-173.

[12] Pinnock, Clark H. *Reason Enough.* Burlington: Welch, 1985, p.26-27.

[13] Quoted by E. Stanley Jones in *Abundant Living* London: Hodder and Stoughton, 1950, p.92.

[14] Aristotle. *The Generation of Animals,* II. iii. Loeb Classical Library, trans. A. L. Peck. London: Heineman, 1943, p.175; quoted by John Stott in *Involvement,* vol.2, Old Tappan: Revell, 1985, p. 128.

[15] Quoted by John Stott in *Involvement: Social and Sexual Relationships in the Modern World.* Old Tappan: Revell, 1985, p.206.

CHAPTER NINE

# The Proof of Experience

> For this gospel I was appointed a preacher and apostle and teacher, and therefore I suffer as I do. But I am not ashamed, for I know whom I have believed, and I am sure that he is able to guard until that Day what has been entrusted to me (St. Paul, 2 Timothy 1:12).

In a personal interview with Neil Asher Silberman, Robert Eisenman was asked what he thought of the role that a historical personality named Jesus of Nazareth may have played in the creation of a distinctively Christian faith. Silberman tells us that his answer was candid: "I really don't see him because the material we have about him has been so artificialized and worked over and mythologized and undergone retrospective theological transformation that to get to any human being called Jesus with any substantiality is, as I've said from the beginning, an impossibility."[1]

On reading this, my initial reaction was an instant recall of Matthew Henry's cliche, 'None so blind as those that will not see'; but then I rebuked myself since, after all, this was the verdict of a scholar. Yet, as we have seen, another scholar, David Flusser, who taught classical philology at the University of Prague before becoming professor of Comparative Religion at Hebrew University in Jerusalem, is profoundly assured that the Gospels are reliable historical sources for the life of Jesus (see my pp. 82 and 99). Like a game of tennis, the ball flies between one court and another, and this analogy is not so inappropriate when we turn to a paragraph in *The Messianic Legacy:*

> By the twentieth century, however, Jesus and his world had become 'fair game', not for luridly sensational purposes, but as valid points of enquiry and exploration for serious, internationally acclaimed literary figures.[2]

Authors Baigent, Leigh and Lincoln follow this up with mention of Hugh Schonfield's *Passover Plot*, in which he argued that Jesus staged his own mock crucifixion, and Morton Smith's controversially belittling *Jesus the Magician*. Earlier they allude to *The Last Temptation*, in which the Nobel Prize winning author Nikos Kazantzakis depicted Jesus as facing crucifixion yet visualising what might have been if he had married Mary Magdalene, for whom he had lusted all through the book.[3]

So one writer says he cannot really find a historical Jesus in the Gospels, another says he can, and others jump on the band wagon of entertaining sensationalism. It is important for us to find scholars who face up to all the intricacies of their research, but who retain a reliable perspective in the process. Robin Lane Fox is one who is known for his independent, critical and non-conservative views of biblical literature. He responds to those who seek for additional sources of information outside of our Bible to verify the scriptural record:

> It is not only that we have no evidence outside the Bible for Moses, Joshua, or any of the Judges; we have none for David or Solomon either.[4]

Significant to our thesis, however, he goes on to write:

> When we come to the New Testament, we are within reach of primary sources. The texts tell us about people in a historical setting which we know independently: we do not face the problem of a Solomon or Joshua, and we need not wonder whether Jesus

## The Proof of Experience

of Nazareth lived and could have visited the places which the Gospels name.[5]

Not for a moment does this imply that these Old Testament characters never lived. It does mean that trust has to be placed in the biblical authors even if they represent our only sources. The important point to be made here is that we have, if we must have, solid grounds for believing in Jesus as a historical figure. In his case we have extra-biblical primary sources. Yet even without these, the records of the New Testament are regarded by numerous reputable Christian scholars as adequate and reliable, and their writers as significantly inspired and ethically motivated. They do not deserve to be placed under suspicion by sceptics, an exercise which monotonously recurs from time to time. The anvil will surely outlast the hammers that beat on it!

The time has come to weigh the motivation of those of Jesus' followers who have given, and those who continue to give sincere witness to the reality of his presence in their lives. And many have done so at the price of laying down their lives. Some may die for a good cause, some because of their belief in a future reward, and others because they have been deceived, but no responsible and honest person will die for what he or she knows to be a deliberate lie unless perhaps to protect someone they love. The risen Christ did not need any protection. Nor were the early Christians suicidal. They wanted to go on living, witnessing and serving their Lord; but death, if it were inevitable, was willingly accepted by them because of their belief in the fact of Jesus, crucified and resurrected. This reality they could not and would not deny. James of Zebedee, Stephen, James the Just, Peter and Paul,—all martyrs, did not die because a lie had been fabricated by any one of them.\*

There is the classic case of the risen Lord appearing to Saul on the road to Damascus, which led to his conversion from being a persecutor

---

\*The moving scene of Polycarp's martyrdom in Smyrna (156 C.E.) is preserved for us in the *Martyrium Polycarpi*. It tells of the frenzied cries of the crowd, both Gentiles and Jews, for his killing. Rejecting the demand that he make sacrifice to Caesar, the old sincere bishop said "Eighty and six years have I served him (Christ), and he hath done me no wrong; how then can I blaspheme my king who saved me?" Polycarp was burned to death.

of the church to becoming a great Christian leader. This is frequently downplayed as a hallucinatory experience, or perhaps an occurrence due to epilepsy or to the workings of his sub-conscious following his part in the death of Stephen. The late Dr. Martin Lloyd Jones, of Westminster Chapel, London, and formerly a Harley Street medical specialist, once retorted that if epilepsy could turn a murderer into a missionary, and a man of intense hatred into the writer of the love chapter of 1 Corinthians 13, then he might just wish for an 'epidemic of epilepsy'!

Let's take a leap over the centuries to find Augustine, who for years had followed his lusts, coming suddenly to find a compelling desire for a life of saintliness, a Bernard of Clairvaux who wrote the hymn "*Jesus, Thou Joy of Loving Hearts*, a John Newton who had been a slave trader but impacted by Jesus, and in testimony to the remarkable change in his life wrote the hymn "Amazing Grace".

To return for a moment to the Eisenman-Silberman interview, the comment was made that Jesus, presumably "an obscure and quickly quashed messianic pretender was 'turned into the lover of Gentiles, lover of Roman centurions, lover of tax collectors, the lover of prostitutes. 'What', asks Eisenman, 'can I say about any of that matter? It's all preposterous.'"[6] If it was preposterous then, it has continued to be so when one looks at the astonishing record of the conversions of some of the most unlikely people.

Blaise Pascal's secret of an ecstatic experience came to be known to the world after his death. He recorded it as having taken place on November 23, 1654, from about half past ten in the evening until about half past twelve. The words he wrote included such exclamations as "*FIRE ... God of Abraham, God of Isaac, God of Jacob, not of the philosophers and scholars ... Certitude. Certitude. Certitude. Feeling. Joy. Peace. God of Jesus Christ, Deum meum et Deum vestrum. My God and your God*" (John 20:17) [7]

From a mathematician, noted physics scholar and philosopher, as Pascal was, we turn to an English clergyman who felt a great emptiness in his all too formalized profession—that is until May 24, 1738, when he went "very unwillingly" to a Moravian meeting in Aldersgate Street, London. There something happened which changed John Wesley into a man who changed England in his day. In his Journal he tells us

# The Proof of Experience

"About quarter before nine, while he (the preacher) was describing the change which God works in the heart through faith in Christ, I felt my heart strangely warmed. I felt I did trust in Christ, Christ alone for salvation; and an assurance was given me that He had taken away *my* sins, even *mine*, and saved *me* from the law of sin and death". Historically, it has been said that the Wesleyan revival transformed England, and saved it from the bloodshed of a French revolution.

In our own generation we need to hear of what might be called the intruding presence of Jesus into the lives of C. S. Lewis and Malcolm Muggeridge. Lewis shares with us the moments of an introspective mood when he writes in *Surprised by Joy:* "For the first time I examined myself with a seriously practical purpose. And there I found what appalled me; a zoo of lusts, a bedlam of ambitions, a nursery of fears, a harem of fondled hatreds. My name was legion."[8] Then follows his testimony to an instant conversion experience: "I know very well when, but hardly how, the final step was taken. I was driven to Whipsnade one sunny morning. When we set out I did not believe that Jesus Christ is the Son of God, and when we reached the zoo I did."[9] An intellectual of distinction, he did not choose to rationalize away his encounter with Jesus.

Malcolm Muggeridge, correspondent for the *Manchester Guardian*, editor of the British humor magazine *Punch*, and a highly individualistic thinker, confessed to his utter disillusionment with both communism and capitalism as systems which could bring Utopia to earth. Without any claim to a spectacular type of conversion he came to recognize that "the Christ figure enshrines the only sure and certain truth in an age of skepticism, shifting values, and gross materialism"[10] In the last half of the twentieth century Muggeridge became an outstanding apologist for the Christian faith. In the context of our closing discussion the following excerpt from his book *Jesus Rediscovered* is so very fitting.

> Having seen this other light, I turn to it, striving and growing toward it as plants do toward the sun. The light of love, abolishing the darkness of hate; the light of peace, abolishing the darkness of strife and confusion; the light of creativity, abolishing the darkness of destruction. Though, in terms of history, the darkness

falls, blacking out us and our world, You have overcome history. You came as light into the world in order that whoever believed in You should not remain in darkness. Your light shines in the darkness, and the darkness has not overcome it. Nor ever will. [11]

And so the numbers grow of those who are willing to step on to the witness stand to tell of their encounter with Jesus of Nazareth, a company of people from every race and nation, and from a worldwide diversity of cultures.

Nor does he reject us if in our searching we resist him. Lin Yutang, raised a Christian but turned Confucianist wrote a best seller entitled *Why I am a Pagan,* but later returned to Christianity because he wished "to re-enter that knowledge of God and love of God which Jesus revealed with such clarity and simplicity."[12]

Strange though it may seem, Jesus is quite accustomed to people playing games with him, going right back to the Roman soldiers who made him "King for a Day" and thrust a crown of thorns on his bleeding head. He is, however, the silent conqueror who is able to penetrate the defences of a political hatchet man of the White House. Charles W. Colson is another contemporary evidence of Jesus the Saviour who forgives the sinner, restores his dignity, and imparts a compassionate desire to serve others.

In affectionate respect to the Jewishness of Jesus, I conclude with an impressive tribute made by one of today's foremost Hebrew scholars:

> Second to none in profundity of insight and grandeur of character, he is in particular an unsurpassed master of the art of laying bare the inmost core of spiritual truth and of bringing every issue back into the essence of religion, the existential relationship of man and man, and man and God[13] (Geza Vermes).

What he said and what he did compel us to ask who he was. Indeed the very questions which Jesus himself posed in his day persist even to our own time, "Whom do men say that the Son of man is?" (Matthew 16:13), "But who do you say that I am?" (ibid., 16:15), and "What do you think of the Christ? Whose son is he?" (ibid., 22;42). Some today will say that he was a prophet, others that he was a cynic with the

# The Proof of Experience

wisdom of a sage, while Christians declare him to be the Son of God, the Word made flesh, and the express image of Him who is invisible. Without doubt the controversy will continue until he comes again. And even if heaven and earth were to pass away, he tells us that his words will remain for ever. How could he have been so confident? The answer must depend on who he was, and is, and always will be.

## Notes

[1] Silberman, Neil Asher. *The Hidden Scrolls*. New York: Grosset/Putnam, 1994, pp. 198-199.

[2] Baigent, M., Leigh, R., and Lincoln, H. *The Messianic Legacy*. London: Corgi/Transworld, 1987, p.16.

[3] Ibid. p.16.

[4] Fox, Robin Lane. *The Unauthorized Version: Truth and Fiction in the Bible*. New York: Knopf/Random, 1992, p.253. Fox's views in this area already call for revision. In an article by Marlin Levin, Felice Maranz and Richard N. Ostling, entitled "Is the Bible Fact or Fiction?", the following quote appears in *TIME* magazine, December 18, 1995, p. 41: "In what may be the most important of these discoveries, a team of archaeologists uncovered a ninth century B.C. inscription at an ancient mound called Tel Dan, in the north of Israel, in 1993. Words carved into a chunk of basalt refer to the "House of David" and the "King of Israel." It is the first time the Jewish monarch's name has been found outside the Bible, and appears to prove he was more than mere legend."

[5] Ibid., p.243

[6] Silberman, Neil Asher, Ibid., p.199.

[7] Taken from *Great Shorter Works of Pascal*, transl. Emile Cailliet and John C. Blankenagel. Philadelphia: Westminster Press, 1948. See pp. 117, 220, 228.

[8] Lewis, C. S. *Surprised by Joy*.1955; reprinted London: Harper Collins, 1977, p.181.

[9] Ibid., p.189.

[10] Kerr, Hugh T., and Mulder, John M., eds. *Conversions*, 1983; reprinted, Grand Rapids: Eerdmans, 1985, p.251.

[11] Ibid., p.254; taken from *Jesus Rediscovered*, New York, Doubleday, 1969.

[12] Ibid., p.205.

[13] Vermes, Geza. *Jesus the Jew*, 1973; reprint, Philadelphia: Fortress, 1981, p.224.

CHAPTER TEN

# The Controversy Continues

1. A Response to *The Real Jesus: The Misguided Quest for the Historical Jesus and the Truth of the Traditional Gospels*
Author: Professor Luke Timothy Johnson.

Many conservative scholars may have breathed a deep sigh of relief with the publication of Johnson's critique of the doubtful techniques employed by the Jesus Seminar. Yet some had second thoughts. On the book cover N. T. Wright offers this word of significant congratulation:

> The intellectual power of this book presents a challenge to unthinking piety; its deep Christian devotion, with no loss of scholarly precision, challenges unthinking reductionism, not least that of the 'Jesus Seminar.'

However, Wright later exercised his academic freedom in a *TIME* magazine article, dated April 8, 1996, where he took issue with one of Johnson's pivotal positions that "Christianity has never been able to 'prove' its claims except by appeal to the experiences and convictions of those already convinced."[1] This he calls poppycock and adds the comment: "He kicks the ball back into his own net by mistake." Johnson indeed is seen to come all too close to the Bultmannian error, which inferred that we "know almost nothing concerning the life and personality of Jesus," since the sources are said to be fragmentary and often legendary. Further on in his book Johnson echoes Bultmann's call to search for the existential rather than the historical Jesus. This must surely come as a disappointment to those who are eager to know what Jesus really taught in his travels through Galilee and into Judaea before his crucifixion in Jerusalem. What did he *really* say about justice and authority, marriage and divorce, the Law and the sinner, war and peace, and many other pressing topics?

At the outset Dr. Johnson demonstrates every effort to rescue the Gospels and the Acts of the Apostles from the vicious arbitrariness of the Jesus Seminar which, he charges, has tossed out their narratives as "mythical fabrications based on faith"[2] He would seem to be playing the role of a faithful sentry standing on guard for the integrity of the Scriptures by keeping at bay those mischievous scholars who wait to do havoc to his protected treasure. At the same time he disassociates himself from the fundamentalists who, he observes, "wrongly stake all Christian faith on the literal historical accuracy of the Bible."[3] Obviously he is looking for a middle of the road position which allows for myth as well as fact in the text of the New Testament.

He would naturally place parables in the category of the illustrative since these are only stories and not actual events. Yet even fundamentalists would agree to this, though preferring words other than myth, e.g., allegory, story, dramatization or lesson. Here we ought to inject a verse from 2 Peter 1:16, which resists any attempt to 'mythisize' any occurrence which the early disciples believed to be 'real'. In this case reference is being made to the tradition of the glorification of Jesus on the Mount of Transfiguration, an event which took place before his death and resurrection.

> For we did not follow cleverly devised myths when we made known to you the power and coming of our Lord Jesus Christ, but we were eyewitnesses of his majesty.

Whatever the date of the composition of this epistle, we can recognize its deliberate rejection of a developing tendency to introduce mythical

## The Controversy Continues

elements to the Gospel. Here the writer refers to a truly unforgettable experience recalling exactly the words spoken, "This is my beloved Son, with whom I am well pleased; listen to him" (cf. Matthew 17:5). It must be observed, however, that in *The Real Jesus* Dr. Johnson seeks to establish a distinction between the "real" and the "historical" which leads, not surprisingly, to a rather protracted study in semantics. He writes:

> The term history manifestly cannot be used simply for "the past" or "what happened in the past."... History is rather the product of human intelligence and imagination. It is one of the ways human beings negotiate their present experience and understanding with reference to group and individual memory.[4]

He proceeds to remind us that history is an interpretive activity which often misses a great deal of things "like compassion, alienation, meaning and value, love and hope." Johnson's reservations about the limited value of history is further illustrated by his comment: "What is most important, however, is that the serious historian knows and acknowledges that historical knowledge deals only in degrees of probability, and never with certainty."[5] In turning specifically to research of the Gospel documents, Johnson pays high tribute to the erudition of the renowned scholar and fellow Roman Catholic, John P. Meier, but questions what he considers to be "false inferences, manifesting symptoms of a condition that might be diagnosed as 'creeping certitude.' " By this he means that even the best of historians (and theologians) can be propelled by overriding anticipations of finding "patterns of meaning."[6]

It remains to be seen whether this oscillation of Johnson between his announced intention to present *the real Jesus*, and his apparent lack of confidence in history, will be judged by scholars to be the strength or the weakness of his work. If anything, it seems to give a measure of consent to the very assumptions and techniques used by the Jesus Seminar which elsewhere he is condemning. Interestingly, N. T. Wright has this to say: "The street level of what Johnson is saying is, 'We can just *believe* the Bible and don't need to *worry* about it.' But it plays right into the hands of the Seminar, and there's a huge price to be paid for that."[7]

Without denying that any history is a collection of known data duly handled, or mishandled by the writer, and subject to his or her own subjective evaluation of causes and effects of the given events, the reasonable expectation is surely that facts will be somehow woven into the printed or published record. In our day of mass communication and information explosion one would hope that facts will be meticulously and accurately preserved even more than ever. Nor must the painstaking care of early chroniclers be minimized, not forgetting the rabbinic practice of a scroll being buried ceremoniously because of copyist errors in the text.

Johnson of course is correct when he infers that the real Jesus cannot be confined to the historical perspective. A historian may feel that he or she cannot include the records of Jesus' resurrection, even if they are supported by many witnesses, since such a supernatural event is beyond his or her level of understanding and cannot be fitted into his or her mental grid. Johnson is making the point, and rightly so, that only faith can truly grasp the truth of the risen and ascended Lord, but surely this does not mean that the resurrection is to be rejected as an *event*. Indeed the apostle Paul tells his Corinthian readers that if Christ did not rise, then their faith is useless:

> If Christ has not been raised, then our preaching is in vain and your faith is in vain. We are even found to be misrepresenting God, because we testified of God that he raised Christ, whom he did not raise if it is true that the dead are not raised. For if the dead are not raised, then Christ has not been raised. If Christ has not been raised, your faith is futile and you are still in your sins (1 Corinthians 15:14-17).

Paul, as an evangelist, does not moderate his preaching of the resurrection to the intellectual Athenians in his Areopagus address, even though resurrection was alien to their philosophical concepts. Luke Timothy Johnson commits himself to the position: "I will argue that Christian faith has never—either at the start or now—been *based on historical reconstructions of Jesus,* even though Christian faith has always involved some historical claims concerning Jesus. Rather, Christian faith (then and now) is based on religious claims concerning the present power of Jesus."[8] Yet it has to be stated that, as in the above case, Paul dramatically recalls the backsliding Galatians to the historic fact of the cross:

# The Controversy Continues

O foolish Galatians! Who has bewitched you, before whose eyes Jesus Christ was publicly portrayed as crucified? (3:1).

Christian faith cannot and must not be divorced from historical fact, though we are well aware of the insufficiency of history alone to generate faith. Paul puts it well when he declares that faith comes by hearing, and hearing by the Word of God (i.e. the record of God's saving acts: Romans 10:17), yet the miracle can only happen when that hearing is "of faith" (Galatians 3:2). To this extent we can agree with Johnson that "even the best and most critical history—is not the necessary basis of religious faith."[9] We must certainly subscribe to Johnson's view, and the biblical view, that our faith is not placed merely in a historical figure but in the living Christ. Paul affirms this in 2 Corinthians 5:16: "... even though we once regarded Christ from a human point of view, we regard him thus no longer." But in so saying Paul is in no way repudiating the early and authentic historical traditions of the primitive church pertaining to Jesus of Nazareth, and all of this Johnson acknowledges in his Chapter 6 (pages 156-165).

It will be disconcerting to some that Johnson holds to the view that it is quite irrelevant to debate whether Jesus "back then" predicted his death and resurrection. He suggests that "It is equally silly, in this context, to debate whether Jesus 'back then' predicted his return, for that return is predicated on his being the living and powerful Lord, and it is in the light of that truth that we await God's final triumph through him."[10] He also throws some doubt on the reported statement by Jesus on the return of the Son of Man, as one which may have been placed in the mouth of Jesus by the Gospel writer. The reason Johnson develops this dialectical approach is to by-pass sayings in the Gospels which some critics, especially those of the Jesus Seminar, claim could never have been uttered by Jesus in the time frame prior to his death.

It has to be said, however, that in each of the Synoptic Gospels the eschatological teaching of Jesus in what is known as the Little Apocalypse (Matthew 24; Mark 13; and Luke 21), is given in response to the disciples' enquiry about the future of the Jerusalem Temple. It is placed in a natural setting and it seems to me that no reason exists to doubt that Jesus' forecast of the fall of the Temple was an authentic part of his teaching later on in his three year ministry. After all the cleansing of the Temple was a provocative act on his part, and was surely one of the major causes of his arrest and subsequent death. It must have been the subject of intense and heated discussion by his disciples, culminating in an unforgettable lesson given by Jesus to them before his crucifixion.

A most welcome contribution to the study of the historical Jesus is Johnson's ability to establish the essential inter-relationship between Jesus and Paul, even if neither the two had met until the remarkable event on the Damascus road. Johnson is strong in his dismissal of the view that Paul was a perverter of the pure message of Jesus and that he had compromised "the radical itinerant mission of Jesus with the urban realities of Greco-Roman culture." [11]

He demonstrates how Paul had the utmost respect for Jesus whom he called Lord, and warned that "... no one speaking by the Spirit of God ever says 'Jesus be cursed!'" (1 Corinthians 12; 3). He affirmed the humanity of Jesus "born of a woman, born under the law, to redeem those who were under the law (Galatians 4:4). In terms of the relationship of Jesus to his fellow Jews, Johnson adds the quote "Christ became a servant to the circumcised to show God's faithfulness to the Patriarchs (Romans 15:8), while reminding us that Jesus was "descended from David according to the flesh" (Romans 1:3). Paul attributed the death of Jesus to a condemnation by earthly rulers: "none of the rulers of this age understood this; for, if they had, they would not have crucified the Lord of glory" (1 Corinthians 2:8). Paul's allusion to Psalm 69:9 in Romans 15:3 records that Jesus underwent abuse and humiliation, adding numerous references to his death by crucifixion throughout his writings (cf. 1 Corinthians 1:23; 2 Corinthians 13:4; Philippians 2:8; Galatians 3:1). He refers to the burial of Jesus (1 Corinthians 15:4; Romans 6:4) and he asserts the reality of the resurrection duly witnessed by others (1 Corinthians 9:1; 15:4-8; Galatians 1:15-16). Johnson provides us with a valuable summary of Paul's awareness of Jesus and of his mission, and he enumerates many of the identical resemblances between Paul's ethical teaching and that of Jesus as we discussed in Chapter 5, *The Founder of the Faith*.

He also opens wide a window to the work of the Holy Spirit and shows how Christians are to operate on the basis of having the mind

## The Controversy Continues

of Christ and to live according to the law of Christ. He makes a strong case for the evidence of a morally transformed life as the greatest proof of the power of the living Christ in the world of today. He expresses it beautifully when he writes:

> The "real Jesus" is therefore also the one who through the Spirit replicates in the lives of believers faithful obedience to God and loving service to others.[12]

One would just wish that Dr. Johnson had included more discussion of the Dead Sea Scrolls issues in relation to the person of Jesus and the beginnings of Christianity. He devotes several pages to the bizarre theories of Barbara Thiering arising out of her superficial and highly imaginative treatment of the Scrolls, but he makes no mention of Robert Eisenman and others who have forced their own interpretation of Jesus as a patriotic nationalist, even a Zealot, and the church as possible provocateurs prior to and during the Jewish War of 66-70 C.E. Nor does Johnson include the names of distinguished scholars, such as Hershel Shanks and Lawrence Schiffman, who have taken an opposite position to the foregoing. Perhaps Johnson thought it sufficient simply to observe that "... the sober conclusion of the best-informed scholars (who are not members of a cabal seeking to keep the truth from the public) is that the Dead Sea Scrolls do not shed any direct light either on Jesus or on the development of Christianity."[13] In this statement he could be absolutely justified.

> The continuing controversy goes to prove that the Jesus of the first century remains the intriguing and controversial figure of today!

**2. A Response to:** *"James, the Brother of Jesus: The Key to Unlocking the Secrets of Early Christianity and the Dead Sea Scrolls."*
**Author: Professor Robert Eisenman**

In the current series of responses to today's critics of the New Testament faith, it is vital to address ourselves to Robert Eisenman's *James, the Brother of Jesus*. The author is Professor of Middle East Religions and Archaeology and Director of the Institute for the Study of Judeo-Christian Origins at California State University. The work, consisting of 1,074 pages, must be one of the largest in size to be published by Penguin Books in paperback. It is impressively erudite though at times monotonously repetitive.

Dr. Eisenman is known to have been one of the more controversial researchers of the Dead Sea Scrolls, whose views are by no means universally recognized in the company of competent scholars. He aligned himself with such writers as Michael Baigent and Richard Leigh who published their *The Dead Sea Scrolls Deception* in 1991. In that work they alleged a conspiracy on the part of the Vatican to suppress the full findings of the International Team appointed to the tasks of excavation and translation of the Scrolls at Qumran. This accusation was later found to be groundless.

In the arduous process of reading *James, the Brother of Jesus*, the enquiring mind will be compelled to ask what is this writer's motive. Professor Eisenman appears determined to discredit Christianity by proving his case that the Gospels, and even more the Acts of the Apostles, are the products of late first century writers who on occasions have borrowed the *names* of historical persons, removing them from their true context and relocating them in order to produce a propaganda presentation of Jesus and the early church. The very existence of Jesus he calls into serious question. The impact of this book is not to be underestimated, as will be seen from the following quotes by leading journalists. These are included in a Preamble to the book itself:

> Robert Eisenman's *James the Brother of Jesus* is less a book than an irresistible force. Once opened ... [it] bulldozes your prejudices, flattens your objections, elbows aside your counter-arguments, convinces you (*Toronto Globe and Mail*).
>
> A tremendous work of historical scholarship ... Expert, Unparalleled ... Great ... This book will live and live and live (A. Auswaks in the *Jerusalem Post*).
>
> Careful ... Passionate ... So logical and so compelling, one wonders how this demythologized, internally consistent

## The Controversy Continues

understanding of Christianity could have been kept out of sight for so long (*The Scotsman*).

To add to Robert Eisenman's scholarly distinctions we must note that he is a Visiting Senior Member of Linacre College, Oxford University, and a National Endowment for the Humanities Fellow at the Albright Institute of Archaeological Research in Jerusalem.

So convinced of his own conclusions about the beginnings of Christianity, and specifically in the area of New Testament origins, that Eisenman resorts to outbursts of indignation which are not exactly typical of scholars. This must mean, however, that his convictions about his subject are deep rooted and call for respect, but also for a thorough investigation by other clear and honest thinkers. At times the reader will sense that the author is being driven by a strong spirit of resentment against that system of thought which we call Paulinism, and which Eisenman believes has utterly corrupted the original Jewish-Christian faith. It is imperative for those of us who are Christians to pay heed to his powerful arguments and to acknowledge those that are valid, but to reserve judgment when Eisenman's dialectic becomes more hypothetical than empirical.

Let us sample a few of his accusations.

In expressing doubt about Luke's account of the interview between Jesus and Herod, Eisenman declares:

> Luke's story about an intervening interview by 'Herod' with Jesus, like all the others, is simply preposterous fiction. Even worse, it is malevolent, aimed at whitewashing Herodians and focusing vilification on 'the Jews' (563).

Challenging the reliability of the Book of the Acts, he writes:

> ... either one accepts Acts' presentation as it is, full of history repetitions, and rewriting, or admits there are huge holes in it, mistaken historical information, bodily liftings from other sources, and oversimplification verging on dissimulation or outright fallaciousness (530).

> Here someone is overwriting with definite knowledge. Such is the playfulness of the writers of Acts' pseudo-history.... [Eisen-

man is alleging the story of the Ethiopian eunuch to be a pure fiction and indeed a parody on a well known Jewish convert, and son of a Gentile queen]—particularly as these words have been taken by endless numbers of people including even Muslims, as 'the Word of God' for the last almost twenty centuries—it will be seen as offensive in the extreme (918-9).

Again the precision of the geographical details in the Pseudoclementine Recognitions is superior to Acts.... in Acts we have to do with disembodied spirits, tablecloths from Heaven, individuals supposed to be on their way to Gaza, but ending up in Caesarea instead, 'Ethiopian' eunuchs, 'a prophet called Agabus'. and similar flights of fancy (593).

Eisenmen's resentment reaches white-heat intensity when he attacks Paul's use of imagery, as in 2 Corinthians 3:7-18. Here the apostle recalls the moment that Moses' face had shone because of his being in the presence of God, and how Aaron and all the Israelites were afraid and did not want to draw near. After delivering God's message to the people, Moses veiled his face intimating the end of the glory of that moment. Paul proceeds to remind the Israelites of the later hardening of their hearts despite the Sinai revelation, a fact well illustrated in Psalm 95:8-11, where God declares his loathing of that generation and vows it shall not enter his rest. To complete the story, the Book of Exodus reveals that on returning into the presence of God, Moses removed the veil from his face, implying that God's servant enjoyed the privilege of an unimpeded relationship with God (Exodus 34:32-35). What might well arouse Eisenman's indignation is Paul's claim that Christians now enjoy the same open access to God by the Spirit. However, the sheer inappropriateness of Eisenman's exaggerated rhetoric, as below, is all too apparent.

Regardless of the thrust of the various imageries being used or the rightness or wrongness of the polemics involved, no more scurrilous accusation has ever been recorded by the founder of one major world religion against that of another (650).

First, the story of the veiling comes initially from Moses' own testimony as we have it in the Book of Exodus; and, second, Christians do not

# The Controversy Continues

regard Paul as the founder of their religion. Third, the Johannine tradition also expressed the identical view that as the Law came by Moses so did grace and truth come by Jesus Christ (John 1:17). The suggestion of a transition from one glory to another was surely stated squarely by Jesus himself when he said that new wine was not to be put in old bottles.

Dr. Eisenman is to be commended for his extensive use of New Testament Scriptures as back-up support for many of his arguments. We must accord to him the right to do this, but reciprocally we must ask for the right to cite Old Testament portions which allude, as many do, to the failures of Israel to keep the Law, the need of a fresh and drastic purging of the Temple and of the priests as per Malachi, and the coming of an exciting New Covenant as per Jeremiah. Each other's comparisons of our respective faiths, Jewish and Christian, must not be viewed as deliberately demeaning and destructive, but as positive and progressive. John Robinson, who bade farewell to the Pilgrim Fathers in 1620, declared that he believed God would always have fresh light to break forth from his Word. Anything less than this expectation will tend to produce a narrow mind, a dogmatic defensiveness, suspicion or even paranoia, and, in the last analysis, a bitter intolerance. Robinson's pronouncement was given against a background of religious persecution of the sixteenth and seventeenth centuries in Europe.

Eisenman castigates Paul for being what he considers to have been a traitor to Judaism, when in fact Paul was acting on his own evaluation of the Old Testament faith. He respected the prophets, had kept the Law, but became an advocate of freedom. He exhorted the Galatians to stand fast in the liberty into which they had come in Christ (Galatians 5:1), that is freedom from sin, but also freedom from the bondage of religious legalism. Jesus, too, had preached about being made free by the truth (John 8:31-18)—a freedom which would rise above the limitations of racial identities. Paul was not the only one who saw the beginning of a new religious era.

However, all of this constituted a threat to established religion. At different intervals of history both Judaism and Christianity have shown their proclivity to intolerance and hostility. The secularist, let it be said, is entitled to make his/her own judgments on the phenomenon of religious strife, and to measure each religion by its benefits to the humankind which it professes to serve in God's name. The dictum of Jesus still holds, "By their fruits you shall know them" (Matthew 7:16). The apostle Paul comes in for scathing criticisms by Eisenman on the grounds that he was pro-Roman and a perverter of the Jewish faith. Yet the results of Paul's interpretation of the faith produced a church which yielded the fruits of righteousness and peace in a pagan society, while religious fanatics in Judaea had brought destruction on Jerusalem. If Paul is to be condemned, then Josephus must also be seen as a traitor to his Jewish people, yet the fact is that the insights of both these men might have saved Jerusalem, the Temple, and all the people from the catastrophe of 70 C.E.

It is against this background of events that Eisenman wrestles with his own perceptions of what really happened in the first century. It is something much more than whether James was a brother, or a cousin, to Jesus. Indeed, as it will be seen, the existence of Jesus is opened to question by this writer, who is bent on portraying James as the model and epitome of moral rectitude, and one who is clearly identifiable as a devotee of the Law of Moses. His argument becomes even more complex, if not contradictory, when simultaneously he dismisses Paulinism as a miserable maladaptation of Judaism, and proceeds to blame the Jewish War of 66-70 C.E. on Christian Jews rather than on Jewish Zealots. Given this interpretation of events, one is almost compelled to believe that it was a dismal outlook for both the Jewish and Gentile forms of Christianity which were emerging. But there was more to the new faith: there was a resurrected Christ.

We must address ourselves first to Eisenman's fluctuating views on Jesus. He believes it is near to impossible to establish a real history of Jesus. "Unfortunately, the facts themselves are shrouded in mystery and overwhelmed by a veneer of retrospective theology and polemics that frustrates any attempt to get at the real events underlying them" (xxii). He even contends that the brother relationship between James and Jesus "may turn out to be the only confirmation that there ever was a historical Jesus" (xxiii).

This is Eisenman's starting point but at the end of his book he writes "In Jesus' case, however, the reply probably is in the affirmative, that he *did* exist, most of all because *Paul refers to him in his letters,* though this reticently" (926). This is most gratuitous, but his dialectic

## The Controversy Continues

throughout seems intended to create doubt upon doubt. Even in this last statement, Eisenman gives a twist to Paul's appreciation of Jesus suggesting that there was some reluctance on his part. Anyone familiar with Paul's writings has to be impressed by the apostle's respect, love and gratitude for the Lord Jesus Christ, a title which appears *repetitively* in his letters to the churches. Nor must it be forgotten that the person of Jesus was uppermost in the minds of the Jerusalem Christians, even James himself whose epistle summons the believers "to show no partiality as you hold the faith of our Lord Jesus Christ, the Lord of glory" (2:1), and this was written in the context of taking care of the poor, a matter which was dutifully observed by Paul and by both the Gentile and Judaean Christians. Nor is there any trace of a split between these groups over the person of Jesus. As we shall see, just before his tragic death in 62 C.E., James was being urged to dissuade the people from following Jesus. In no way did he yield to this demand.

Basically, Eisenman gives credence to the historicity of Jesus only in terms of his brother relationship with James. Thus the most he can say about him is "Who and whatever James was, so was Jesus" (963). He even disputes the name given to Jesus since, along with the title 'Christ', or 'anointed One', it too may well have been an epithet given to him by the emerging church. "In fact the very name 'Jesus', may be simply allegorical, as Eusebius himself suggests, derived from the Hebrew word meaning 'Saviour' ('Yeshu'a')" (926). Scholars will recognize that Eusebius in no way questioned the historicity of Jesus, nor did he suggest that the name was a theological afterthought of the church, nor allegorical in the exact sense of the word. This portion of Eusebius' Ecclesiastical History to which Eisenman refers is a simple reminder that the Old Testament Joshua (the equivalent of 'Jesus'), was seen to be a 'saviour' of his people from their bondage in Egypt, and, particularly as Moses' successor in the leading of Israel into the promised land. The indisputable fact is that many Jewish sons were given the name Joshua, though initially it had a clear 'Saviour' connotation.[14] Why Eisenman wants to deprive the Man of Galilee from having been given the name Jesus by his parents is impossible to understand. Josephus lists no less than thirteen persons in his historical record who bore the name 'Jesus', including at least six who were Jewish priests, one a governor of Tiberias, and one a ringleader of robbers.[15]

The strong predisposition to doubt permeates so much of the book, *James, the Brother of Jesus*. If the writer makes the very existence and the identity of Jesus a matter of denial, we should not be in any way surprised at the far out stratagems he will devise to explain what he considers to be a myth.

## A. Jesus, as seen by a radical Redactionist

We can have no argument against historians and others who seek to reconstruct events from whatever materials are available to them. Generally we also allow them the freedom to introduce their own ideas as to the causes and the consequences of events and of actions taken by people of that generation. It has been a constant discipline among New Testament scholars to conduct research of this kind on the four books we call Matthew, Mark, Luke and John. They have sought to discern between what Jesus actually said and did, and any embellishments which the authors may have added, even by way of their own interpretations.

With Robert Eisenman, however, we must be aware that he makes it his primary position that much of what is written in the Gospels about Jesus is really a throwback from James, the brother of Jesus, or other sources. This would apply, for instance, to the words of Jesus on the cross, "Father, forgive them for they know not what they do." It is recorded by Hegesippus that James uttered these very words as he was being dragged to his death. The terms of address are slightly different: "I beseech you, O Lord God and Father, forgive them for they know not what they do." It is Eisenman's assumption that James' words are being put into the mouth of Jesus, rather than the more likely possibility that James is following in the train of his Master.

At the scene of the crucifixion the Centurion's exclamation that Jesus was a righteous man, is also seen to be a title more befitting of James. Although Eisenman has stated that whatever James was, is what Jesus must have been, certainly in terms of Judaistic fidelities, it is clear Jesus is given a very secondary place. Of course it is Eisenman's intention to identify James as the Righteous Teacher of Qumran. He quotes from Eusebius and Epiphanius who tell us that James was known by two important cognomens, *The Righteous One* (Heb. *Zaddik*; Gk.

## The Controversy Continues

*Dikaios;* and Latin *Justus*); the second is Oblias, or holiness as from the womb (353). He also reminds us how Josephus described James as a man whose righteousness was above that of other men.

It is interesting that an individual called Simeon the Righteous was known around 200 B.C.E. He is described in the apocryphal book of Ecclesiasticus which speaks of his righteousness in highly exalted terms, and pictures him in his High Priestly vestments which "shone like the sun shining on the Temple." His son Onias also named 'the Zaddik', the righteous, was martyred under Antiochus Epiphanes (175-163 B.C.E.). Traditionally it was he who gave the Messianic sword of vengeance to Judas Maccabee thus triggering the famous revolt. The book of Ecclesiasticus for long had been known in the Greek, but a Hebrew edition was found in the Cairo Genizah in 1896, and later in the discoveries at Qumran. It is generally recognized that the Dead Sea Scrolls were written between 250 B.C.E. and 68 C.E., and attempts to identify the Teacher of Righteousness are far from unanimous in their findings.

Another important example of alleged transpositioning of James' words back to Jesus is that of James' Proclamation in the Temple as it is preserved for us in Eusebius, quoting from Hegesippus. It starts with the demands of the religious leaders:

> 'Stand, therefore, upon the Pinnacle of the Temple that you may be clearly visible on high and your words readily heard by all the people, for because of the Passover all the tribes have gathered together and numbers of Gentiles too.' So the aforesaid Scribes and the Pharisees made James stand on the Pinnacle of the Temple, and shouting to him, cried out, 'O just One, whose word we all ought to obey, since the people are led astray after Jesus, who was crucified, tell us what is the Gate to Jesus?' And he answered shouting out loudly, 'Why do you ask me concerning the Son of Man? He is now sitting in Heaven at the right hand of the Great Power and is about to come on the clouds of Heaven.'

Eisenman contends that the Pinnacle mentioned here is what gave the Gospel writers the idea of the devil's temptation of Jesus in the wilderness. The devil, we read, urged him to cast himself down to prove the promise contained in Psalm 91:11,12. In other documents, including the apocryphal Pseudoclementines and the Second Apocalypse of James, James' fall does not take place from the Temple pinnacle but only down the steps of the Temple. Eisenman would have us believe that the exaggerated version would come later, as we have it in Matthew and Luke, and being applied to Jesus and not to James. But since Hegesippus' writings are traceable to as late as 150-180 C.E., it can also be argued that he has conflated the respective accounts which lay before him, one of Jesus' temptation and the other of James' death* It is a known fact that Jesus made more than one visit to Jerusalem, and we know that he had carefully observed the great Temple of Herod (Mark 13:1-3). It is not at all unlikely that just such a temptation to do the spectacular did occur to the young prophet of Galilee, altogether without any thought of what would later happen to James. We believe the temptation to have been very real.

More importantly and, I believe, more conclusively for our present discussion, it must be pointed out that Eisenman's confidence in Hegesippus obligates him to acknowledge that James fully recognized Jesus to be the Son of Man now seated at the right hand of God. At the same time we must reject Eisenman's suggestion that James' references to the *Son of Man* coming on the clouds of Heaven were retroactively transferred back to Jesus in Mark's Gospel (13:6), a work of early composition, and to Stephen in Acts of the Apostle (7:55,56). All this savours of a self-contradictory arbitrariness. Worse, it asserts that Jesus had little if any contribution to offer, and that the Gospels are unreliable second hand records of what others have said and done.

E. P. Sanders has put it well, "In the text of the gospels, however, there is no indication that some early Christian [writer] wanted to step forward and claim for himself the ingenious interpretation." This statement pertained to the interpretation given to the Parable of the Sower and the Seed, but it can be extended to the mass of teaching which Jesus shared with the people. If his parables, beatitudes, and sermons are attributable to someone else, who then is the ghost writer? Specifically, when it comes to the issue of Jesus' teaching on the Son of Man, this

---

* Ignatius quoted from Matthew ca. 115 CE. Luke was included in the Marcion Canon in 140 CE.

# The Controversy Continues

concept is as early as the book of Daniel (written probably around 200-160 B.C.E..), where the prophecy relates to a figure who acts with divine approbation in the establishing of an everlasting kingdom (7:13,14). The vision here is exactly that of the Son of Man coming with clouds of glory. It is an insult, as well as an absurdity, to claim that the historical Jesus could never have uttered what is credited to him in the Gospels, and that his life story had to rely on the imaginations and originalities of people who lived decades, or even a whole century, after his time. It is one thing for a writer to *invent*, and quite another to *recall*, whether by using oral or written traditions. It is going too far for any redactionist actually to repudiate the existence of a historical character by attributing all or most of his sayings and doings to someone else.

## Jesus and Miracles

Robert Eisenman does not take a position of denial when it comes to the supernatural, but, again, this does not mean that he takes as real or literal the miracles reported of Jesus in the Gospels. Again fascinated by all that happened to James, Eisenman sees a significance about James' wearing of white linen, *and being brutally assaulted by a 'laundryman's club.'* He thinks there is a possible connection between this and the record in Mark's gospel of the Transfiguration scene where Jesus' garments became "glistening, intensely white, as no fuller on earth could bleach them" (9:3). Again, another throwback of what happened to James is being applied to Jesus, implying that Mark has connected the white of James' vestment to the garment that Jesus wore, and coloured so white that only a 'laundryman' could produce.

This, it is being seriously suggested, had formed a vivid picture in the Gospel writer's mind, and so he simply transferred it to Jesus. I cannot refrain from commenting that this would suggest to me the mind of a contemporary sceptic even more subtle and imaginative than any of the Gospel writers! Eisenman applies the same principle to the figure in white who appeared at the tomb of Jesus.

As a reinforcement of his argument he now turns to the Pseudoclementine *Recognitions* which describe a strange and remarkable happening to the graves of some of James' followers who had been buried near the town of Jericho. It will be recalled that after an attack on James in Jerusalem, during a time of great persecution, a large number of devotees, said to have been five thousand, retreated to the town of Jericho.

> In the meantime, James' Community has gone outside Jericho to visit the graves of some fellow brethren which miraculously 'whitened of themselves every year', thereby restraining the fury of their enemies, because they 'were held in remembrance before God' (PseudoClementine Recognitions 1:71).

Eisenman writes with respect and reminds us "that the blessed dead should be 'remembered before God', as alluded to in connection with the 'miraculous whitening' of the brothers' tombs", and that such a custom along with the use of the colour white is part of the Yom Kippur observances even to the present time (686-7).

Eisenman then takes us from the tombs at Jericho to the Damascus Road where, according to the Acts' account, Saul is confronted by the risen Christ, at which point there is a brilliant light, brighter than the light of the midday sun shining on him. He brings these events together and states that the correspondence between the two "should not be missed". Presumably this is another invitation for the reader to speculate that one is original and genuine, and that the story in Acts is but a rewrite of the brightness of the Jericho rock used to embellish and dramatize whatever happened to Saul.

Thus three of the New Testament stories, viz., the Transfiguration of Jesus, the appearance of a man, or an angel, 'in white' announcing Jesus' resurrection, also the bright light on the Damascus Road are all taken from this Pseudoclementine report of a whitening of the Jericho tombs. Only this last event, however, is to be considered to be fact, albeit supernatural, while the other three can be dismissed as poor copies!

From elsewhere in Eisenman's book we can gather that his belief in miracles is sustained by his references to Honi the Circle-Drawer (or Onias the Righteous, ca. 63 B.C.E.) known for his ability to alter the weather and to cause rain to fall, not unlike the reputation of Elijah to prevail with God in terms of rain and drought. Any reader of the New Testament is well aware of James' reference to this in his letter, and his exhortation to believers to pray effectually. James himself laid no claim to have this power in himself, but Epiphanius (367-

## The Controversy Continues

404 C.E.) is one of the writers who elevates James to a lofty degree in the high priesthood in Jerusalem, and claims that 'during a drought, he lifted his hands to Heaven and prayed, and at once Heaven sent rain' (78.14.1). It was also Epiphanius who made the proud claim that James wore the mitre of the High Priest. James, of course, is recorded in Josephus as having been killed by Ananus, the High Priest.

In the area of miracles, Josephus pays tribute to Jesus when he writes: "At this time there appeared Jesus, a wise man. For he was a doer of startling deeds, a teacher of people who received the truth with pleasure." Over the years scepticism has been expressed that the *Testimonium Flavianum* has suffered from interpolations. This is discussed in my Chapter Two, pages 25-26; but whether or not Josephus originally made reference to Jesus as the Messiah here—which is sometimes disputed, it is vitally important in the present discussion to acknowledge that he certainly did so in the very passage of his *Antiquities* on which Eisenman bases his entire thesis, namely Book 20:9.1. There we read: "these things happened to the Jews in requital for James the Righteous, who was a brother of Jesus who is called Messiah." Quite apart from the question of messiahship, the point to to be made here is that Eisenman is totally disregarding of the miracles attributed to Jesus in the Gospels, or the startling deeds ackowledged by Josephus. This is not surprising when initially he has expressed his personal doubts about the very existence of Jesus.

Interestingly, Hegesippus provided a strong affirmation of Josephus' testimony to Jesus, also of the Jewish historian's own integrity in this account when he wrote:

> That there was at that time a wise man, if it be lawful to have him called a man, a doer of wonderful works. If the Jews do not believe us let them at least believe their own writers. Josephus whom they esteem a very great man, hath said this, and yet hath he spoken truth after such a manner; and so far was his mind wandered from the right way, that even [though he] was not a believer as to what he himself said; but thus he spake, in order to deliver historical truth, because he thought it not lawful for him to deceive.... However it was no prejudice to the truth that he was not a believer; but this adds more weight to his testimony,

that while he was an an unbeliever, and unwilling this should be true, he has not denied it to be so.[16]

In contrast to Eisenman's silence on the 'startling deeds' of Jesus, he underscores the miraculous works of Honi, the rainmaker, and correctly identifies a faint connection with James the Just who himself urges his people to pray even as Elijah had done in a time of drought (Epistle of James 5:17). This may well have had reference to the famine which occurred in Palestine in the late 40s C.E. Eisenman wishes, however, to establish a traditional link between James and Honi, or Onias the Righteous, and thus to reinforce his argument that James is the Qumranic "Teacher of Righteousness". Two things render his assumption suspect. One, James makes no reference to Honi, but rather to Elijah. Two, James does make reference to Jesus twice in his epistle (1:1; 2:2), and the Qumran writings do not make any mention of Jesus at all. This fact in itself must certainly distance the Qumran community from the early church even if their respective movements were contemporary in the first century C.E. The beginnings of Qumran, of course, date back more than a one hundred and fifty years before the time of Jesus.

Further, the miracles of Jesus were not confined to the control of nature, be it rainmaking as in the case of Honi, or the calming of the waves in a storm on the Lake of Galilee as recorded in the Gospels, but the overwhelming emphasis of Jesus' powers was in the area of healing the sick. This feature is inextricably linked with the spirit of compassion which characterized his overall ministry. This fact, too, impacted the early church and has had a significant influence on our Western society. Not only do the Gospels give their witness to the miracles of healing, but James again in his epistle, encourages the church to continue to pray for the sick, and to lay hands on sick persons for their recovery. In a word, for Eisenman to celebrate Honi, good man as he was, and to entirely neglect Jesus of Nazareth represents a regrettable imbalance, and an inexcusable prejudice. Of course, the view of Jesus as a healer and one who cares about justice, the care of the poor, as the strong advocate of the marriage institution and the gentle protector of children, is not exactly the image Eisenman wants to project when he seeks to identify Jesus with the cause of Judas the Galilean and his political insurgents,

## The Controversy Continues

the Zealots. It is a much repeated argument in *James, the Brother of Jesus* that the Fourth Philosophy, as described by Josephus, was the militant movement which was most responsible for the violence which unmistakeably led to the destruction of Jerusalem.

This Judas was at the height of his power about the time Jesus was born. He is usually identified with Judas Sepphoraeus who broke into the arsenal at Sepphoris in 4 B.C.E. It was at the time of the Census of Quirinius (mentioned in Luke's Gospel 2:2) that Judas vented his opposition against taxation to Rome, and thus revived a militant nationalism. Josephus tells us that the movement had the support of young men and that "the nation was infected by it to an incredible degree."[17] Two sons of Judas the Galilean, James and Simon, were crucified around 48 C.E. Though the movement became fanatical and murderous, it began with a strength of religious conviction for righteousness and freedom for the land of Israel.

In his attempt to identify the Jesus movement with Judas the Galilean, Eisenman dismisses the idea that the early Christians were "little people walking around with halos around their heads and monks' robes" (See my page 144). Not all will agree with Eisenman's etymological identification of the name Iscariot with the *Sicarii* who were known for street executions by means of the specially shaped dagger they carried under their cloaks, but our New Testament does not conceal the existence of Judas Iscariot, per se. In John 6:71, he is described as 'the son of Simon Iscariot'. In the Acts of the Apostles' list of disciples a Simon 'the Zealot' is mentioned, and one can assume that among the early followers of Jesus some were of a given political stripe. The fact that they are so identified, however, in no way means that the Jesus' company was part of that movement. Indeed the contrary must be true, for then there would be no need to single out those who bore the name, be it *Iscariot* or *Zealot*. (See the earlier discussion on Simon the Zealot or 'Cananaean', p. 90.) We must demonstrate that the Jesus' Party was distinctive, yet at the same time recognizing that parallel concerns were entertained by several groups within the Judaism of that day.

## B. Eisenman's Name Game

This author goes to great lengths to postulate his theory that the church was a major force, besides others, to cause the Jewish War of 66 C.E., and the horrendous destruction of Jerusalem in 70 C.E., followed by the mass suicide of the defenders of the fortress Masada. One of his techniques is to find names which he believes he can match with disciples of Jesus or with associates of Paul. An intimation of what is coming later in his book appears as early as page 61 "Other individuals connected to Paul and mentioned also in (Josephus') *War* are Stephen, Philip, Silas, Niger and, in our view, Paul himself." Let the reader be warned the likeness between these persons and the New Testament characters bearing the same name is not even recognizable. The question of Stephen will be considered in a separate chapter, but a brief review of the Niger, the Philip and the Silas who appear in the *War* will surely satisfy an enquirer that these persons were in no way followers of Jesus.

Niger was a leader across Jordan in Perea of the Idumaeans who fought with valour against the Romans. In the War he had identified with the Zealots until a great rampage was carried out by both the Idumaeans and the Zealots resulting in the killing of Ananus and the other High Priests. Eisenman observes Josephus' report of Niger's execution and tells us that the details "can only bring to mind Jesus' in the Gospels" (538):

> Frequently crying out and pointing to the scars of his wounds, he was dragged through the centre of the city. When he was brought outside the gates ... in his dying moments, Niger called upon them [the Jews] the vengeance of the Romans, famine and pestilence, to add to the horrors of the war, and besides all that, internecine strife.

The complete irrelevance and inappropriateness of Eisenman's comment about a similarity with the crucifixion of Jesus is self evident. Nor is there anything of the forgiving spirit of Jesus in the outpouring of Niger's condemnation on his persecutors. Eisenman goes on to explain himself, suggesting that there is a similarity with the Little Apocalypses (contained in the Synoptic Gospels) and the times of terrible tribulation and ecological disaster depicted there. Be it noted, however, that Jesus never called down fire from heaven on Jerusalem, nor on the Samaritan town which rejected him (Luke 9:52-56). Here

## The Controversy Continues

he rebuked his disciples, James and John, for their vengeful spirit. Yet he foresaw, and with much sorrow, the inevitable destruction of Jerusalem. He and this Niger had nothing in common. There was a Simeon called Niger who took part in the laying on of hands of Paul and Barnabas in Acts 13:1. He is not mentioned again in the Scriptures, but even Eisenman confesses that the implied connection between him and leader of the Idumaeans "might be simply coincidental" (537). His lack of dogmatism at this point is both wise and welcome. Again, Niger was a name in common usage, as also was Simeon.

Philip, in the Acts of the Apostles, is known as one of the deacons selected to assist in a dispute over distributions to the widows in the church, both Jewish and Hellenistic. As such he was obviously recognized for his organizing abilitiy. He also appears as an energetic evangelist. Eisenman likens him to 'Philip the *Strategos*' of Agrippa II's army in Caesarea, and believes that for the above reasons the author of Acts has chosen to transfer this name to a worker, real or imaginary, in the early church.

Then comes Silas, who, according to our writer, "may or may not bear a relationship to Paul's companion Silas" (538). Eisenman now cites the case of a Silas who was arrested by Herod Agrippa I because of his pretence of being Agrippa's equal, and was later executed.

We must ask if there is any truth to this extraordinary claim that the New Testament authors in composing their materials well after 66-70, as is claimed by many liberal scholars, actually rewrote or overwrote names of other individuals into their texts? What motives would they have for doing this, especially if the name titles so borrowed belonged to characters who were either distinguished for their brutality or undistinguished by way of their ugly demise? Or were the Scripture writers ignorant of the histories of the persons whose names they utilized? Or is it much, much more likely a possibility that more than one person in the same generation bore the same name?

Two other examples of Eisenman's 'transference' of identities are those of Agabus, the prophet mentioned in Acts who gave warning of the impending famine (11:28), and Epaphroditus whom we know to have been a friend to Paul during his imprisonment in Rome, sent to the apostle by the church in Philippi. Eisenman is convinced that the author of Acts deliberately borrowed and altered the name of Abgarus, king of Edessa, and known as "the Great King of the peoples beyond the Euphrates",[18] whose Queen Helen sent assistance to Judaea during the famous famine. Since these names belong to recorded history we must again ask why an author would see any advantage to the devious procedure Eisenman is suggesting. Agabus is mentioned later in the Acts as warning Paul of his impending arrest (21:11). Some scholars, including Eisenman, believe that the 'we' passages in the Book of Acts are more reliable than the earlier chapters, and here we must add that Agabus appears in both sections. There is really no justification for Eisenman's distortion of the facts, though the accuracy of his research on the conversion of King Abgarus to the Christian faith, and the conversion of his wife to Judaism, is to be commended.

S. F. Hunter, writing in The International Standard Bible Encyclopaedia, describes Epaphroditus, with its meaning of "lovely" corresponding to the Latin *Venustus* ('handsome'), and states that it was "very common in the Roman period." However, Eisenman is determined to identify the New Testament Epaphroditus as the personal secretary of Nero, who is said to have assisted the emperor in his suicide. This same Epaphroditus is said to have lived on until Domitian's reign and was executed by him when he was known as Josephus' reputed publisher. That a serious persecution of the church took place under Domitian is a matter of record, but Eisenman makes an initial mistake in assuming Paul's friend Epaphroditus to be part of Caesar's household. It is true that Paul sends salutations from Christians who are among Caesar's household (Philippians 4:22), but these he sends by Epaphroditus to the Christians in Philippi from where this messenger had come to assist Paul. Moreover, Paul assures the Philippian church that *their* Epaphroditus, who had been ill and near to death on his visit to Rome (Philippians 2:25-30), is now well recovered and longing to return home. There is no way, and certainly no reason, for Paul to have duplicated the name of an eminent Roman and to have applied it to an individual who obviously belonged to the community of Christians in the city of Philippi. It is equally unlikely that the Emperor's secretary would have been a 'runner boy' for Paul the prisoner all the way from Rome to Philippi!

How very thankful we can be that God, in his wisdom, used the

# The Controversy Continues

medium of personal letters, written by real people to real places dealing with real situations. Not only are the Pauline epistles important for doctrine, but they represent the earliest record we have of the development of the church. Invented names would have been challenged by the very recipients of those letters. We are not impressed by Eisenman's name game, which implies a deliberate juggling of personal identities. It would be no exaggeration to say that he reaches for straws in the wind with both hands and tries to tie these straws together.

A more serious case is the allegation that Stephen, the first recorded Christian martyr, may have been an invented figure. Eisenman avers that his name was extremely suitable. In the Greek it means 'a crown', and thus represents a recognition of one who has attained some great distinction and is worthy of special honour. The name must have had special meaning for Paul since in his first letter to the Corinthians he refers to such a person, whose household he had baptized (1:16). The implied question is: Did Paul so dote on this name that he, or else his biographer, Luke, decided it should be adopted for the 'fictitious' figure who would play the part of a martyr at the hands of angry Jews, as the story of Stephen portrays? A common assumption among many scholars is that Paul influenced Luke in the writing of both his gospel and the Acts. Eisenman believes that this accounts for anti-Semitic innuendoes in the Acts. This criticism is hard to sustain when in one case, 'the Jews' are blamed for Paul's hurried escape in a basket from Damascus (Acts 9:23), while Paul himself pinpoints the blame rather on the city Governor under the jurisdiction of the Arabian King Aretas (2 Corinthians 11:32), even if some Jews in Damascus may have been involved.

Eisenman goes on to offer a further hypothesis as to the identity of this 'stand-in' Stephen (453). He suggests that the name could be a rewrite by the author who took his cue from Josephus in his report of a murderous attack on one named Stephen, a servant of the emperor, by rampaging Zealots in the vicinity of Jerusalem.[19] But if this is so, he claims that the chronology of Acts is out of sync, yet it is no secret that Josephus himself was not always reliable in this respect. To return, then, to his earlier thesis, that the name of a Christian convert in far away Corinth was imported into the story of Acts 7 to provide an identity for a fictitious martyr, Eisenman is asking us to stretch our imagination to the point of absurdity. His *modus operandi* is seriously suspect. Interestingly, when it comes to establishing the historicity of James, the brother of our Lord, he uses confirmatory material in Eusebius' *Ecclesiastical History*, but in the case of Stephen he makes no effort to quote from Eusebius, Book II. 1, where the historian acknowledges:

> Stephen's martyrdom was followed by the first and greatest persecution by the Jews themselves of the Jerusalem church.

Could, and did, this stoning take place? Eisenman refers to a Talmudic source which claims that stoning for blasphemy did not take place in the forty years before the destruction of Jerusalem. However, this seems invalid when we recall Ananus' demand for the stoning of James in 62 C.E. In *Mishnah Sanhedrin* we learn that if a priest served in a state of uncleanness, it was permissible for the young men among the priests to take him outside the Temple and to split open his brain with clubs.[20] This exactly befits the story of the killing of James the Just. Josephus reports another stoning, that of Menachem, the son or the grandson of Judas the Galilean, carried out by collaborating high priests who resisted his wearing of the royal purple and the presumptuous claim to the Throne of Israel. This occurred just prior to the retreat of the *Sicarri* to the fortress Masada towards the end of the War. In spite of these known stonings, Eisenman employs all of his sceptical skills to deny the biblical account of Stephen's martyrdom, and we must discover why this is so.

Stephen's speech certainly represented a massive verbal attack on the Jewish establishment. He accused them of having become the betrayers and murderers of 'the Just One' whose coming had been predicted by the Hebrew prophets (Acts 7:52). The speech is a lengthy account of the history of Israel, and Eisenman thinks this could not have been delivered by a non-Jew. Yet the preamble to the address reads, "Brethren and fathers hear me. The God of glory appeared to *our* father Abraham." In assuming that he was a 'Hellenistic' Jew, we can be sure he would be intensely investigative of the history of his own religion now that he was in Jerusalem. Such, probably, was Stephen's experience prior to his encounter with people of the new faith, or of 'The Way' as early Jewish Christianity was being called. It is significant that prior to his being

## The Controversy Continues

brought before the Council to answer the charge of blasphemy, he is found in crucial debate with Hellenistic Jews in the Synagogue of the Libertines, or the Freedmen (6:9ff), which is commonly understood to mean the gathering place of Jews who had returned from the Diaspora. Eisenman sarcastically alludes to this Synagogue of the Hellenists when he comments "whatever this is supposed to mean in Jerusalem" (186).

As a matter of archaeological interest, F.F. Bruce, tells us of a Hellenistic Synagogue in Jerusalem from the period preceding 70 C.E., known by the Greek inscription set up by its founder Theodotus and discovered on Ophel 1913/14.[21] He explains that freedmen were former slaves or the children of former slaves, who had been emancipated by their owners. Many Jews who were taken captive to Rome at the time of Pompey's conquest of Judaea in 63 B.C.E. were subsequently emancipated. Some, if not many, would certainly have resettled in Jerusalem. If so, despite their Hellenization, they would be ardent opponents of anyone who would have dared to speak against the Temple as Stephen did.

Clearly this is one of the most provocative speeches in all of the New Testament, and delivered by what Eisenman describes as an 'archetypical Gentile convert' to Judaism (610). He takes great satisfaction in a discrepancy which appears in Luke's record of the speech, and suggests that such a mistake would have given rise to the most incredible derision that a Jewish Sanhedrin audience could offer. In reviewing the histories of the patriarchs Stephen is reputed to have said that the remains of Jacob were carried out of Egypt and laid to rest in the sepulchre which Abraham had bought for a sum of money from the sons of Emmor. Jacob was in fact buried at Hebron, in the cave of Machpelah, which Abraham had bought from Ephron the Hittite. Joseph, his son, was buried at Shechem, in the piece of ground which Jacob had bought from the sons of Hamor. According to Josephus (*Ant.* 2.199), the other sons of Jacob were buried at Hebron.

Looking closely at the text (Acts 8:15-16) one can see a plurality of persons, viz. "as well as our ancestors, and *they* were brought back to Shechem, and laid in the tomb that Abraham had bought...." F. F. Bruce describes this record as a telescoping of two separate purchases of land. It is only fair to say that Stephen must have felt great tension, knowing that his critique of Israel's history would be explosively controversial. It was delivered to a tense and unsympathetic audience resulting in an outburst of furious anger. For his courage he paid with his life. The reconstruction of precisely all that Stephen had said would not be easy. Eisenman correctly points out that Luke appears to be drawing from Joshua 24:32, but this excerpt refers only to Joseph. Yet Luke may still be faithful to the original speech when he pluralizes the company to include Jacob, the father. This problem, however, is no justification for denying the existence of Stephen.

The fact that the Pseudoclementine *Recognitions* fail to make any mention of Stephen provides Dr. Eisenman with a further argument in support of his claim to the fictitiousness of the alleged first martyr of the Christian church. *Recognitions* tell us much about the early church, but not always reliably so. However, there is a striking similarity between this source and the Acts. In the first case Acts 8:1-3 records an outbreak of serious persecution and of the scattering of Christians from Jerusalem immediately after the death of Stephen. Significantly we learn from *Recognitions* of a sudden migration of Christians from the city to Jericho, five thousand in all, by reason of the activities of an unnamed 'Enemy' who is said to have physically assaulted James the Just. Here Robert Eisenman identifies with a view that this Enemy was none other than Saul of Tarsus. Without any undue or fanciful suppositions the scenario can be unravelled.

Until Stephen's condemnation of the moral vicissitudes of Israel, something so offensive to the Jerusalem religious establishment, the early Christians were tolerated by the Jewish community. The apostles continued to observe their prayer times at the Temple (Acts 3:1), while in chapter six (v.7) it is stated that many priests sided with the new faith in spite of opposition from the High Priest and the Sadducees. A leader of the Pharisees actually interceded for the safety of the apostle Peter and his companions (5:34-40). It needs to be recalled that Peter's preaching allowed for the fact that the Jewish rulers had acted against Jesus *in ignorance* (3:17-18). In stark contrast, Stephen, a Hellenist, accused the nation of repeated disobedience to God. This aroused bitter hostility and his murder is what surely triggered the hurried evacuation of Christians from the city.

# The Controversy Continues

It takes little imagination to see that the pro-Judaistic chronicler of *Recognitions* had little reason to give honorable mention to Stephen, and certainly none to the speech he delivered. No doubt there were those who wanted the church to go on ostensibly functioning as a Jewish sect, as indeed the later Ebionites wished. The Stephen episode represented a significant turn in events, whether for better or worse; but there is no justification for rejecting the truth and sequential accuracy of the biblical account of Stephen's martyrdom, of Saul's self-confessed part in the execution, and of his continuing harrassment of the church (Acts 8:1). Eisenman pursues his unconvincing theory to the extent of claiming that the story of Stephen's murder was but a mere rewrite of the *actual* stoning of James which took place as far along as 62 C.E. He cites such similarities as "rushing their victim" and his "kneeling down to pray,"—facts and phrases which have been common to the ordeal of many martyrdoms.

## C. An Author's Selected Sources

The reliability of an author's sources is a crucial issue. We have to ask why Eisenman places such confidence in the Pseudoclementine literature when many notable scholars reject this material as seriously inferior. He writes:

> It can be objected that the Pseudoclementines are not history but fiction.... But this is what we are dealing with in regard to most documents from this period, except those with outright historical intent like Josephus. On this basis, the the Pseudoclementines do not differ appreciably from more familiar documents like the Gospels or the Book of Acts (Page 76).

He proceeds to tell his reader that the first ten or fifteen chapters of Acts are so imaginary that as history they cannot be entertained 'with any degree of certitude'. His summation of the situation, as he sees it, is less than generous, except to add to uncertainty:

> The Pseudoclementines are no more counterfeit than these [as above]. But that is just the point—all such documents must be treated equally, according to the same parameters.

Personally, I believe we have another criterion that must be observed in our respective evaluation of these documents. Just as Robert Eisenman asserts that the writings of Luke are under a Pauline influence, so we must ask on whose behalf, or for whose benefit, were the Pseudoclementines written. Otherwise put, To which audience were these writings being addressed? This will surely help us to ascertain not only their historical accuracy but the quality of their material, whether embellished for romantic, sentimental and entertaining purposes, or thorough in terms of thought-out issues which characterized a given situation and the results which followed. Chapter 15 of Acts is an excellent example of the latter of these, where the Jerusalem Council resolved the disputes between James and Paul, and issued clear instructions for all the churches, both Jewish and Gentile.

It is no secret that the Pseudoclementines bear in the direction of what Eisenman terms Jamesian Christianity, which later was the pride of the Ebionites. These Jewish Christians quite idolized James the brother of Jesus, and little wonder, for he was clearly a man of undisputed righteousness and one who suffered much opposition from the pro-Herodian Jewish priesthood of the time. Eventually he was murdered by the High Priest. He would be seen as a patriotic nationalist when zeal for the Law became a paramount factor. In the final visit of Paul to Jerusalem, James actually obligated him to demonstrate his fidelity as a Jew, and to act in such a way as would dismiss the suspicions of Jewish Christians who believed he had compromised the faith:

> On the following day Paul went in with us to James; and all the elders were present.... And they said to him, "You see, brother, how many thousands there are among the Jews of those who have believed; they are all zealous for the law, and they have been told about you that you teach all the Jews who are among the Gentiles to forsake Moses, telling them not to circumcise their children or observe the customs. What then is to be done? They will certainly hear that you have come. Do therefore what we tell you" (Acts 21:18-23).

Paul acceded to their requests and, as a Jew, performed the rites of purification. Later in the same context, however, the elders simply

# The Controversy Continues

reiterated the demands of the Jerusalem church to lay no additional burden on the converted Gentiles than the avoidance of things offered to idols, from blood and from what is strangled, and from sexual immorality (Acts 21:25; cf. also 15:28,29). Circumcision as an universal obligation was not included.

All the same, circumcision became an ongoing and bitter controversy, and one which continued to set Jewish Christians against Gentile Christians. For the present, however, it is important to recognize the integrity and the accuracy of the Acts' account. In no way does it conceal the problems between these two leaders. Nor should we underestimate the likely strain between these men, *if* indeed James had been physically assaulted by Paul in the latter's violent persecution of Christians *prior* to his own conversion to Christ. This tradition may help us to understand something of the leadership crisis which developed, besides the excessively elaborate accolades laid at the feet of James by the Jewish Christians. Eisenman acknowledges this fact when he writes: "For this reason, James has been described by more contemporary, hostile 'Christian' reactions as 'the Pope of Ebionite fantasy' "(566).[22]

However, he retorts with the cynical remark that what is pictured in the PseudoClementines "is less fantastic than some of the things we are asked to believe about Jesus in the Gospels...." I doubt that the Ebionites would have gone this far in demythologizing Jesus, since at least they were known to have accepted his messiahship while rejecting any suggestion of superiority of Jesus over Moses. Their view of his divinity, if one can use the term, was adoptionist, i.e. by the descent of the Holy Spirit on him at Baptism, and not by a virgin birth; yet as a kind of second Adam, or primal Man, he assumed 'a Jewish Body' (*Recognitions* I, 60).

A conflict of ideas, not only about Paul but also about Jesus, soon produced its own brands of literature. A determining factor in all of this must certainly be early dating as over against much of the apocryphal literature which belongs to the late second and third centuries. There is a general agreement among scholars about the primitiveness of the Gospel of Mark, probably written well before 70 C.E. or soon after; also the clear evidences of an early record of Jesus' teachings named 'Q', which is contained within the Synoptic Gospels. After all, the early church would wish to have had word pictures of Jesus and not just oral tradition, especially as it moved into the Gentile areas very distant from where it all happened. There is an actual extant excerpt from the Gospel of John dated as early as the first quarter of the second century. The nature of that particular find suggests that this Gospel was well in circulation at the turn of the century.

It is extremely important to recognize a significant development in the move towards codices as over against the use of scrolls, occurring as it did in the first and second centuries C.E. Indeed some scholars have suggested that there was something tantamount to 'a Christian invention' of codices. Harry W. Gamble traces the dominance of the codex for early Christian literature back to Pauline usage, for the quick transmission of his letters to the churches, these having been written in the early 50s on into the 60s.[23]

This is not to say that scholars who attach equal importance to such works as the Gospel of Thomas, found in Nag Hammadi in 1948, cannot also claim early dates for their selected materials. However, the subject matter of all manuscripts calls for a very close scrutiny of particular expressions which may disclose theological or even mystical developments of a later period than first thought. Some sayings which occur in the Gospel of Thomas may fall into this category, even suggesting the possibility of Gnostic influence. (See my pages 104-106, noting especially the Gospel of Thomas sayings Nos. 30, 31 and 114.) In the controversies over Gnosticism, John Dominic Crossan has this to say:

> What we need to do is not continue an unproductive debate between Gnostic versus non-Gnostic, but see if it is possible to describe the theology of the Gospel of Thomas in such a way that it could later go in either direction.[24]

This is an agreeable suggestion and it leans in favour of judging the value of a document by its theology, and, we might add, by its high ethical content where it shows consistency with the spirit of Jesus' teachings. However, Crossan's statement, as it stands, also recognizes the trap of circular arguments of critics which start from an unverifiable base. He further observes that presuppositions are inevitable but can be tested by the structures built on top of them.

Wrong presuppositions, he admits, will yield wrong conclusions,

## The Controversy Continues

and he summarizes his position: "Same judgment for me, you, and everyone else". Even on this basis, however, many of us would still judge the Gospel of Thomas to be useful in its agreement with the Synoptic Gospels, but suspect by reason of its peculiar statements. Incidentally, Crossan sees 28 percent of the Gospel of Thomas as having parallels in the Q Gospel, and 37 percent of the Q Gospel having parallels in the Gospel of Thomas (248).

It is necessary at this point to ask which Gospels, epistles and other treatises bring to our attention the real issues Jesus dealt with, and those over which the early church had to wrestle. In respect to the second category, there is no denying that the New Testament epistles—Pauline, Petrine, Jamesian and Johannine are mirrors of the first century C.E. They reflect unmistakably the developing theology of Christianity, and the kind of impact Christian leaders were making on the Mediterranean world, both Jewish and Gentile. These are of real historical value, and they should not be downplayed. This is not to overlook discussions which have stretched over many years as to possible interpolations to the original text, and the question of the use of pseudonyms. We deeply believe, however, that God chose the medium of the letter, and not merely the meditational monologues of individualistic monks, mystics or other holy men.

Here we must return to Eisenman's deliberate choice in favour of apocryphal works which he has admitted are not without flaws. As the index of his book indicates, despite its subtitle, *The Key to Unlocking the Secrets of Early Christianity and the Dead Sea Scrolls*, he has more quotes from the Pseudoclementines than he does from the Dead Sea Scrolls. Of course one must be appreciative of the fact that he has published other works which concentrated intensely on the Scrolls, and it is only fair to say that the Scrolls probably have less to say about the early Christian church than may have been supposed. His firm conclusion that James the Just is the Teacher of Righteousness in Qumran and Ananus is the Wicked Priest calls for more responses from other major scholars.

Among the apocryphal works which Eisenman uses to advance his propositions are the Pseudoclementines (*Recognitions* and *Homilies*), works of fiction falsely attributed to Clement of Rome. It is acknowledged that they were written at the end of the second century or the beginning of the third. Included is a letter purportedly written by Peter to James which includes a violent verbal attack on the apostle Paul. It is manifestly Ebionite, and therefore calculated to strengthen the position of some Jewish Christians in their contest against the Gentile church. In using this material, Eisenman is very honest about the doubtfulness of much of its content He writes:

> What is important is that we are speaking here of literature, in this case, Hellenistic romance of a familiar genre.... Because this is a novel or Hellenistic romance does not mean that it is entirely devoid of historical fact (71).

He further admits that there is garbling of materials, "either purposefully or otherwise", and that mythologization has taken place, "yet Clement of Alexandria [not the earlier Clement of Rome, whose name is used as a pseudonym for this work] is a useful link in the process of transmission and another firm testimony to James' importance in first-century Palestine and other areas in the East heir to traditions relating to him" (72). The fact of Eisenman's inordinate preference for a third century work as over against one of the first century is unmistakable when he writes:

> It should be appreciated that the reason Mark's name came to appended to the second Gospel is because he was considered to have been Peter's secretary [the Papias tradition], regardless of whether we can speak in any firm way of the historical Peter or even Mark (71).

Another set of dubious works Eisenman employs is that of the Protoevangelium, or the *Protoevangelium Jacobi* a title given in the sixteenth century to the book which was known by Origen as the *Book of James*. It is commonly accepted as spurious. It develops the ideal of Mary's perpetual virginity by attributing the 'brothers of Jesus' to a former marriage which Joseph had with a wife other than Mary. However, Eisenman uses this to point out that the concept of Mary's 'perpetual virginity' really stemmed from the 'real' virginity of James the Just! This work, Eisenman acknowledges, contradicts even the Gospels as we have them since they are perfectly clear that Jesus had brothers (844), even as Paul himself acknowledges James to be 'the Lord's

# The Controversy Continues

brother' (Galatians 1:19).

Like the Protoevangelium, the Two Apocalypses of James emphasize the perpetual virginity of Mary. Here in fact Mary is portrayed as telling us that James was a 'milk brother' or a step brother to Jesus. One would expect the greatest reluctance on Eisenman's part to use this kind of legendary material which John P. Meier describes as "a hilarious mishmash of the infancy stories of Matthew and Luke, with a heavy dose of novelistic folklore that betrays ignorance of the very Jewish institutions being described." [25] However, again it suits his purpose to use the Apocalypses which emphasize the importance of James, who is said to have received a kiss of knowledge from Jesus. Here James plays a central role in a conversation in the first person, and it is here that we are told that it was James, and not Thomas, who commissioned Addai, or Thaddaeus, to evangelize the Edessenes. Incidentally, this Second Apocalypse adds more gruesome detail to James' death by stoning:

> ... stretching him out and placing a stone on his abdomen, they all jumped on it, saying, 'You have erred!' Then, they raised him up, since he was still living, and made him dig a pit. They made his stand in it. After having covered him up to his stomach they stoned him like this.... (62:1-4),

and it follows with a picture of James stretching out his hands and delivering a long prayer" (951). Such was an added touch to the cruel use of the laundryman's club.

It must surely be the wish of the reader to find an exit from these meanderings in areas of literature which have elements of fact overlaid with bias, legend, and excessive sentimentality. We must find our way

---

\* The extent to which the Ebionites would go to discredit the apostle is seen in their story that Paul had no Pharisaic background or training, that he was the son of Gentiles, converted to Judaism in Tarsus, went to Jerusalem when an adult, and attached himself to the High Priest as a henchman. Eager to obtain the hand of the High Priest's daughter, he was refused and then sought fame by founding a new religion! This story has been reproduced by Hyam Maccoby in *Paul the Mythmaker* (pp. 17, 60, 174-183). He claims that "this account, while not reliable in all its details, is substantially correct."

out from the confusing maze of pseudo writings which, on one hand, set James against Paul to the denigration of the latter;* and, secondly, those which are seen to support James at the same time advocating a strong sexual asceticism limited at first to the Virgin Mary, but later developed into a condition of salvation. Compare the warning in 1 Timothy 4:3 against those departing from the faith who would both forbid marriage and the eating of meats. The church had a difficult course to follow, not only to preserve the teachings of Jesus, but to protect itself from extremists on the left and on the right, each of whom were writing their own gospels, epistles and propagandist novels.

We must then return to the fresh air atmosphere of the initial controversies between Paul and James, completely uncomplicated by the views of later writers, and in this way to determine what the real issues were and how exactly they were resolved in the historical Jerusalem Council in the mid first century. Plainly stated, the findings of this Council did not condone abstinence from marriage, but rather the avoidance of fornication; nor did it forbid the eating of meats, but those sacrificed to idols and those strangled. The drinking of blood was also forbidden, but circumcision was not required of the Gentiles. As is so human, however, people took sides in the aftermath of these decisions. Paul became less than strict in regard to the meats issue, while those following James become more entrenched in their conviction about the absoluteness of circumcision. Animosities would increase as arguments developed to justify each position, while some points of contention would become so progressively exaggerated as to constitute unhelpful absurdity, or, at least, a departure from the decisions of the Jerusalem Council. And hence the flood of confusing literature in the second and third centuries.

## D. The Mystery of the Ethiopian Eunuch

One further assertion of incredulity on the part of Robert Eisenman must be examined, and this pertains to his belief that the story of the baptism of the Ethiopian Treasurer is not only fiction, but represents a mischievous parody on Izates, son of Queen Helen of Adiabene. Helen was married to King Abgarus of Edessa. It would seem that both Abgarus and Helen had undergone conversion experiences, and

## The Controversy Continues

these are associated with teachers, one by the name of Ananias and the other who is unnamed. According to Josephus a form of Judaism was being taught in which the worship of God was more important than circumcision. Eisenman suggests that Ananias could be the same person who assisted Saul of Tarsus in his conversion to Christianity (907).

While tradition does hold to the Christianizing of Agbar, Rabbinic sources claim that Helen turned to Judaism. However, she was averse to the circumcision of her favourite son, Izates. Josephus tells the story of Eleazar, a Galilean teacher, who went in to find Izates reading the passage in Genesis 17:10-17 commanding Abraham to circumcise all the males in his entourage 'and any stranger not of his seed' that was with him (919). In the story Eleazar then asks Izates whether he understood what he was reading, and proceeds to warn him against the impiety of neglecting this command. Eisenman rightly notes the similarity of Philip's question to the Eunuch who is found reading a scroll of Isaiah. The setting is very different, one in a palace, and the other on a chariot, but, admittedly, the question was the same, "Do you understand what your are reading?" (Acts 8:30). Yet, one might ask, how else would the same enquiry have been put to either of these men?

What Eisenman is seriously alleging is that the writer of the Acts is intentionally demeaning the Jewish requirement of circumcision, and chooses to make a mockery of the Eleazar-Izates encounter and of the practice of circumcision in general. Here comes a eunuch, and though he cannot be admitted to 'the congregation of the Lord' by reason of the Deuteronomic prohibition against eunuchs and bastards (23:1), Philip invites him to enter the Christian faith by way of belief and by baptism. Are we then to believe that this was a kind of bad joke on Luke's part, or are we to view it as an example of providential benevolence? We shall see.

Later on, in the Uprising against Rome, Izates' son, Kenedaeos, along with a brother, Monobazus, was killed fighting against the Romans. Eisenman alleges that Luke has taken the name of Kenedaeos and turned it into 'Kandake' thus adding insult to injury. Luke is now charged with misinformation and malice because of this veiled insult against Kenedaeos, 'a non-Jew and convert, who none the less was a valiant freedom-fighter and real martyr for his adopted people' (919). Eisenman declares that the author of Acts is ridiculing a sacred Jewish heritage, at the same time deceiving many people, including the Muslims, who have taken this story of the Ethiopian to be a fact of history (919).

All the aspects' of the argument must be considered. On page 917 Eisenman states "Of course, there were no *Ethiopian Queens* at this time—except in pages of biblical archetype a thousand years earlier—and none certainly who *sent their agents* or *messengers to Jerusalem*." On the next page he writes: "There was *almost* certainly no 'Ethiopian Queen' in existence at this time. Certainly not one named 'Kandakes', or anyone remotely resembling her." Although there is a sign of less dogmaticism in his second statement, as italicized, he continues to link the name Candace, or Kandake, the name of a queen as we have it in the Acts of the Apostles, with 'Kenedaeos', the name of a man who is a recognized hero in Jewish history, although quite forgotten by the Jewish people (918).

All of this obligates us to a study in depth, as far as that is possible, and certainly a consideration of what may be valid alternative explanations. Contrast the etymology of the name Candace as described by Ben Witherington in his commentary on the Acts:

> Actually the term "Candace" is not a personal name but apparently a transliteration of an Ethiopic title (*k[e]ut[e]ky*) as applied to a royal line of queens over the various generations. [See Cadbury, *Book of Acts in History*, p. 16.] [26]

Significantly Eusebius, the historian, commits himself to a confirmation of the biblical record about the Eunuch story:

> For as the annunciation of the Saviour's gospel was daily advancing, by a certain divine providence, a prince of the queen of Ethiopians, as it is a custom that still prevails there to be governed by a female, was brought hither, and was the first of the Gentiles that received the mysteries of the divine word from Philip (Eusebius of Caesarea; ca.260-340).

Elsewhere Eisenman does make use of Eusebius, and at times questions his accuracy, but he offers no refutation of this statement about a dynasty of queens in Ethiopia.

That the author of the Acts of Apostles may have chosen to

## The Controversy Continues

include this incident in the opening portion of his work as a profound illustration of the openness of the Gospel to all, irrespective of race or social status, is something all Christians would accept and appreciate. If, in the process, he has decided deliberately to contrast it, and embarrassingly so, to the Izates' case of self-circumcision, we have to feel very uncomfortable and deeply apologetic. All we can say here is that nowhere in the Book of the Acts is attention drawn to Eleazar or Izates. Mention of them might have invited Luke's readers to make their own judgment as to whether Luke is consciously and deliberately demeaning someone else in telling the story of the eunuch. Let it also be reiterated that Luke always faithfully records the respect Paul had for James' demands for his purification as a Jew, and the decision of the Jerusalem Council not to force circumcision on Gentile converts. It is difficult to imagine that either of these important issues would be made a subject of derision by the author of Acts.

An interesting observation made by Eisenman is that the eunuch was reading from the prophet Isaiah, which he reminds us was one of the main source books for Christians to find their Old Testament proof texts. The chapter was the fifty-third which describes the Suffering Servant as one who would be despised and rejected, oppressed and afflicted, yet is also the one who would bear the iniquities of all, and by whose stripes we are healed. Hardly a more appropriate set of verses could be found for this man made a eunuch. Though holding a responsible position, he would be seen as a member of a deprived class of persons. Surely most of us can sense an over-arching kindly Providence rather than an ironical joke in this account of Philip's encounter with a eunuch. Here the universality of God's saving grace was being proclaimed, and without respect of persons or cultures.

The sceptical mind, however, may insist that all this is just part of a Christian ploy, and is an inexcusable misuse of Scripture simply to fit an imaginary situation. On the contrary, this portion of Scripture is particularly sacred to Jew and Christian alike and would not be so abused. The idea of vicarious suffering is a concept common to both faiths. It is inconceivable that the author of Acts would incorporate into this chapter a trumped up 'put down' of a Mesopotamian prince and his mother, and as a calculated insult to Judaism over a question of circumcision. A final blow to this erroneous idea is the plain fact that baptism and circumcision were not regarded as inter-related by the infant church. Let it be recalled that both John the Baptist and the disciples of Jesus were baptizing fellow Jews who, obviously, were circumcised persons. Baptism was another matter.

## E. Anti-Semitism in the New Testament

A major part of Eisenman's thesis is that Paulinist Christianity, otherwise described by him as 'Overseas Christianity', constituted a Hellenization of the Jewish faith. Though a much milder invasion of Jewish religion and customs than that of the conquest of Judah by the tyrannical Antiochus Epiphanes (176-164 B.C.E.), all the same it was something to be regretted and deplored. In both cases Hellenism was the enemy. He claims that even the authors of the Gospels were, in the main, Greek and not Jewish, though Jewish names like Matthew and John were selected to give them some kind of authenticity. As far as the Pauline epistles are concerned he seeks to build a case against the 'Jewishness' of Paul whose claim to be a Benjamite is deliberately downplayed. He even suggests that there is a strong hint that 'Saul' may have been an agent for Rome before the outbreak of the 66 C.E. War.

Anything of the above should not surprise us when we realize that his initial premise suggests that, if there was a historical Jesus, the record we have of him is likely to be the creation of the imaginations and ideas conceived by men of letters toward the end of the first century C.E.

In our view, these various positions place Eisenman on the horns of several dilemmas. He has every praise for James, who is clearly stated to be 'the brother of Jesus', because he does not deviate from the Law of Moses. At one point our writer has declared that whatever James was, Jesus was, yet he charges the Jesus of the Gospels with antinomianism. He commends James for his faithful adherence to the Law and his resistance to the pro-Herodian Sadducean priesthood, yet blames his Zealot associates, and the circumcision-fanatical *Sicarii,* described by Josephus as brigands and murderers, as the cause of the Jewish War. He is seriously at odds with Paulinist Christianity on one side, but is out to prove that Jewish Christianity's messianism triggered much of the trouble. He speaks well of Qumran, at the same time he chooses to overlook the

## The Controversy Continues

excessive war mindset of that community as revealed in the War Scroll. He tries to establish a possible ongoing connection of the Jewish Christians with Bar Kochba who brought fresh destruction on Jerusalem in the Second Revolt against Rome in the 130s C.E., when history clearly records that the Palestinian Christians of that time were actually punished by this false messiah because they refused to fight with him. [27]

That there were troubles within Israel long before the advent of Christianity is evident to any reader of Jewish history. There is the great story of the Maccabean revolt against Antiochus and the succession of the Hasmonean king-priests who saw themselves as "reliving the Book of Joshua, reconquering the Promised Land from the pagans, with the Lord at their elbow. They lived by the sword and died by it in a spirit of ruthless piety." [28] John Hyrcanus (134-104 B.C.E.) believed that he was called of God to restore the Davidic kingdom and to evict all foreign cults. He razed the Samaritan temple on Mount Gerizim and demolished the city of Samaria. He burned the Greek city of Scythopolis and massacred whole populations "whose only crime was that they were Greek-speaking." [29]

His son, Alexander Jannaeus (103-76 B.C.E.) continued this policy of expansion, and invaded the territory of Decapolis and northwards through Galilee into Syria. To his conquered peoples he offered the options of conversion, expulsion or massacre. A faithful promoter of a rigorous Judaism, still he encountered serious troubles from within. In his capacity of High Priest he refused to perform the libation ceremony, and pious Jews pelted him with lemons. This ignited his indignation, and Josephus tells us that he slew about six thousand people. A civil war ensued that lasted six years and cost 50,000 Jewish lives. Josephus then describes what he calls "one of the most barbarous actions in the world." [30] Alexander, when feasting with his concubines, in the sight of all the city, executed by crucifixion eight hundred Pharisees; and while they were still alive he ordered the throats of their children and wives to be cut for the dying husbands to witness.

In the next generation at the time of the Roman conquest, 63 B.C.E., another split occurred between Jewish nationalists and anti-nationalists, those for Aristobulus II (67-49 B.C.E.), and those for his older brother, Hyrcanus II (76-31 B.C.E.), who was the only Maccabean supporting the Pharisees. The people gave their support to Aristobulus who refused to abase himself before Pompey. The Pharisees waited for their opportunity of revenge on the zealot supporters of Alexander and Aristobulus II, so they joined with the Romans in the storming of the Temple. Josephus tells us that the Romans stood back in bemused astonishment as the pro-Zealot priests were cut down while they performed their Temple rituals.[31] In 37 B.C.E. when Herod, to become Herod the Great, was given an army by Mark Anthony, the leaders of the Pharisees prompted the people to open the gates but he met with resistance. However, as one who was determined to become 'King of the Jews', he prevailed and thus the Pharisee-dominated Sanhedrin, as described in the New Testament, came to power.

That the land of Judaea must have been a baffling conundrum to the Romans is an understatement. In 49 C.E. the Claudian decree which evicted Jews from Rome indicates that it was over one named 'Chrestus', presumably Christ. Obviously the Emperor could not distinguish between Jew and Christian. Eisenman admits that such seems to have been the case as far on as Domitian and Trajan who could not discern between the "two conflicting strains of Messianism, one virulent and nationalistic; and the other more Hellensitic, benign, and other-worldly....", i.e., one Jewish and the other Christian (787). If, by the way, Paul was an agent for Nero, as Eisenman absurdly suggests, we could safely assume that the Emperor would not have regarded the Christians in Rome as any kind of a threat. We know that Josephus was a friend of Nero's wife, Poppea. We also know that Nero kicked her to death even though she was pregnant. Not long afterwards he took out his inane spite on the Christians, as Tacitus dramatically reports.

We mean it as a compliment when we say that Jews are known to disagree among themselves. It is part of an ongoing heritage of religious convictions, moral judgments and free speech, but the process can be bewildering to the non-Jew. It is indeed part of their God-given calling to be settled in alien lands, often to be found in opposition to the political establishment, be it monarchic, autocratic or democratic. A strong nationalism is seldom welcomed by 'the wandering Jew' who so often has found himself misunderstood, maligned and persecuted by paranoid but powerful political and religious figures. This situation spans all of

## The Controversy Continues

the history spectrum from the Pharaohs of Egypt, through Haman of Persia, under the Greeks and Romans, into the church-dominated Middle Ages, and on sadly to the Hitlerian holocaust. In a sense we have now come full circle in our times when Israel is once again a nation among the nations of the world, yet significantly divided within herself between religious and secular Judaism.

Perhaps we are on the eve, not only of a new millennium, but of the advent of a new world order with its centre in Jerusalem. Such, indeed, is the eschatological expectation of many Bible reading Christians and Jews. This is no digression since, as Eisenman points out, pending the fall of Jerusalem in 70 C.E., both Josephus and Rabbi Yohanan ben Zacchai surprisingly attached the sacred 'Star prophecy' of a messianic world ruler to Vespasian, the Roman general later to be Emperor! Needless to say, it was a terribly false prediction. In our century, however, we have witnessed the revival of the nation Israel, with an international focus on Jerusalem. There is a significant background of teaching in the New Testament which points to a revival of the nation Israel and a restoration of its glory (Romans 11:1-3, 11-12, 15, 25-29). A re-emergence of Jerusalem, the 'holy' and 'beloved' city, is also envisioned once the times of the Gentiles have expired (Luke 21:24; Romans 11:25 & ff.; Revelation 11:1-4; 20:7-9). This important underlay of eschatology must not be overlooked when examining the alleged problem of anti-Semitism in the New Testament.

It cannot be denied, however, that many references to 'the Jews' in the Gospels, Acts and the Pauline epistles are manifestly judgmental. Of course it is also true to say that some astonishing condemnations of the Jewish people have come from their own prophets, but this is an 'in-house' issue.

1. The Gospels. Matthew has been described as the most philo-Semitic of the Gospels, and certainly it is rich in its Old Testament quotations. However, Jesus' pronouncement of woes on the Pharisees is given more attention and space than by Mark, Luke or John. Yet Eisenman does not see this as anti-Semitism since, as a Dead Sea Scrolls scholar, he is aware of similar sharp and uncomplimentary criticisms levelled against the Pharisees, or other fellow-Jews, by the Qumran community.

But he does take exception to the last two verses of Matthew chapter 28, which to him represent Paulinist interference and should not be regarded even as historical. These verses pertain to the Great Commission to go into all the world and make disciples of all nations. Understandably, and with a sense of bitter resentment, he refers to Matthew's inclusion of the cry said to have been raised by all the people present at Jesus' trial before Pilate:

> His blood be on us and on our children.

Known by Jews as 'the blood-libel', we too have to ask ourselves, Did these people really say this? Yet the fact that it comes to us from the hand of the author closest of all the Gospel writers to Jewish Scriptures and customs, forbids us to outrightly deny its authenticity. There are many 'hard sayings' in our Scriptures which, as Christians, we must take to heart, even as Jews accept the judgments of their own prophets. The term 'blood' was in very common usage among the Israelites, as in the story of the prostitute Rahab and the spies who were reconnoitering Jericho:

> If any one goes out of the doors of your home into the street, his blood shall be upon his head, and we shall be guiltless; but if a hand is laid upon any one who is with you in the house, his blood shall be on our head (Joshua 2:19).

It needs to be remembered that ideas of responsibility and of retribution in the Old Testament could be grim indeed, and one can be quite astonished at such blood-curdling pronouncements against God's elect people as appear in the Law itself (Deuteronomy 28:15-68).

2. Mark's Gospel. Eisenman confines his criticism of this gospel to the author's mention of the rending of the veil of the Temple. He feels that this indeed happened, but not until the destruction of Jerusalem in 70 C.E. In any event for him, it represented the humiliation of the Jews and he treats it as a further insult to have it associated with the crucifixion of Jesus.

3. John's Gospel is regarded by many as the most anti-Semitic, and certainly it makes mention of 'the Jews' as such, rather than singling out,

## The Controversy Continues

for instance, the Pharisees, the Sadducees and the Scribes, as over against all the Jewish people. Thus in chapters 6 and 8, this general designation is alluded to eight times. However, if this gospel is of later date, and was written for a Gentile audience, the use of a general designation is not surprising. This is not to say that John fails to make specific mention of these groups, but not as repetitively as in the case of the other Gospels. Eisenman avoids any in-depth analysis of John's alleged anti-Semiticism. He does sum up his overall view of the four Gospels, as follows:

> There are some of the things we shall never know, but the Gospels as we have them—whoever produced them—at their core are just too anti-Semitic to have been produced by anyone other than Gentile (Page 800).

For many years the view was upheld that of all four Gospels, the fourth was the least Jewish. John was a common name in Palestine in the days of Jesus, but his gospel was thought by many to have been thoroughly Hellenistic, even Gnostic, with its emphasis on logos (the Word), and on the dualism of light and darkness, etc. With the discovery of the Dead Sea Scrolls, however, scholars have recognized a significant identity of concepts and of vocabulary, shared between the Scrolls and this gospel. A. M. Hunter, who at one time disputed the authorship of John, has written:

> To put the matter in one sentence, the Scrolls have established its essential Jewishness.... The trend of recent studies has been to make the Evangelist's links with Palestine much stronger than many of us have allowed. [32]

A. N. Wilson, writer of the controversial book *Jesus*, also remarks about the similarity of terms instanced by John's use of the Greek word *opsarion*, known to have been used in 'Galilee of the Gentiles' instead of the customary word for fish, namely, *ichthus* (See my page 39). These few concrete observations force us to question Eisenman's generalized statement, as above, about the non-Jewishness of the Gospels. It might be added, that whether or not John happens to be the author of the Book of Revelation as tradition has it, the prominence given to Israel, to Jerusalem, and to the Twelve Tribes, (even if in somewhat pictorial and symbolic forms), establishes something far removed from anti-Semitism.

4. The Acts of the Apostles. We have already considered an important verse, viz. Acts 9:23 (see page 235, line 18ff). Like the apostle John, and certainly Josephus, the term 'Jews' could be used by a historian just as we use other collective nouns describing a given nationality.

5. The Epistles or Letters of Paul. First Thessalonians 2:14-16 is an embarrassment to many Christians who consider it to be blatantly anti-Semitic:

> For you, brothers, became imitators of the churches of God in Christ Jesus that are in Judea; for you suffered the same things from your own countrymen as they [the churches in Judaea] did from the Jews who killed both the Lord Jesus and the prophets, and drove us out; they displease God and oppose everyone by hindering us from speaking to the Gentiles so that they may be saved. Thus they have constantly been filling up the measure of their sins; but God's wrath has overtaken them at last.

Eisenman is kind enough to suggest that the passage, or a part of it at least, could be an added interpolation. It would seem to suggest a time concurrent with, or subsequent to the destruction of Jerusalem; yet there is no evidence of textual tampering. First Thessalonians is an early letter of Paul, and it does reveal that opposition to his missionary evangelism was as severe in the Gentile countries as it is reputed to have been against the infant church in Judea. Paul here shows intense anger, but it is a mistake for Eisenman to suggest that he calls the Jews 'the Enemies of all mankind.' It was of course Tacitus who called the Jews 'haters of the human race'. Here Paul's bitter complaint is that they seem to be doing everything possible to hinder his outreach to the Gentiles. Paul is supremely concerned to bring the Good News to the Graeco-Roman world, and he devoutly resents the fact that these people are being denied this blessing by Jews who are standing in the way. Perhaps today he might have been regarded as a spokesman for free speech. However, unlike Peter in his Day of Pentecost address, Paul in no way excuses the Jews for their part in the killing of Jesus, at

## The Controversy Continues

least not in this passage. Compare Acts 2:23; and later 3:17:

> ... this Jesus, delivered up according to the definite plan and foreknowledge of God, you have crucified and killed by the hands of lawless men [or, men outside of the Law].... And now, brethren, I know that you acted in ignorance, as did your rulers.

It is when we turn to the three chapters, 9-11, of Romans that we are given a clearer insight of Paul's view of the Jew in history:

> I am speaking the truth in Christ, I am not lying; my conscience bears me witness in the Holy Spirit, that I have great sorrow and unceasing anguish in my heart.... They are Israelites, and to them belong the sonship, the glory, the covenants, the giving of the law, the worship, and the promises; to them belong the patriarchs, and of their race, according to the flesh is the Christ. God who is over all be blessed for ever. Amen (Romans 9:1-5).

One wishes that Eisenman would have concentrated less on the fact that Paul says he is not lying (which he uses to bolster his own suspicion that Paul is 'the Man of the Lie' in the Habakkuk *Pesher*), and more on the apostle's clear affirmation of the privileged place of the Jew in the mystery of God's purposes. A milder critique of Paul appears on page 58:

> But what might strike the reader as more surprising still, the anti-Semitism of Gentile or Pauline Christianity is directed as much or even more towards the Jewish Apostles or the Jerusalem Church, particularly James, as it is towards the Jews outside it. Paul is not so much concerned with Jews outside the Church who are for him largely an irrelevant nuisance.

While we find the last comment to conflict with what Paul has just said in the ninth chapter of his letter to the Romans, Eisenman is correct in pointing out the apostle's impatience with those who seemed to follow him and to seek to Judaize his Gentile converts. His letter to the Galatians makes this abundantly clear. Having become Christians, he asks, how can they hope to improve on the salvation they have already received by faith, by acceding to circumcision? He resists those Jewish reactionaries who seem to be hard to define as to whether they themselves were making any kind of profession of Christian faith. The fact remains that in the early stages of the infant church, it was not so much a Hellenizing process of Jews, as a Judaizing of Christians.

Eisenman has his own definition of anti-Semitism, and it is fascinating. He proceeds to argue that a Jewish document can be sectarian "that is, anti-Pharisee or even anti-Sadducee as the Dead Sea Scrolls most certainly are and the Gospels at their most authentic sometimes are, but it cannot be anti-Semitic" (59). At this point Eisenman is prepared to include Paul in this very category, though still questioning whether he was really a Jew! The argument draws further on Josephus who, as a Jew and as a historian, is critical of many things which have happened within his own nation and among his own people, but who is in no way anti-Semitic. Perhaps we can say that Eisenman is not unduly troubled by a 'lover's quarrel.'

Pleasant, agreeable and conciliatory as this position is, one has to hope for the ultimate emergence of a satisfactory resolution of opposite yet thought-to-be equally valid opinions. The truth is that Eisenman is unrelenting in his attacks on Paul. For him Paulinism represents a total negation of what Judaism is, and always will stand for. Again, Paul is a liar, and, according to Eisenman's interpretation of the Habakkuk *Pesher* he is the builder of that dreadful city of blood alluded to in Habakkuk 2:12. Let it be remembered that the original Habakkuk could belong to the time of Nebuchadnezzar in 598 B.C.E., while a suspected revision of chapters one and two is thought to have taken place in the reign of Zedekiah (597-586). [33]

The *Pesher* commentary found in the Dead Sea Scrolls is obviously much later, but exactly when has not been established. In any event, the chapter which Eisenman takes to make his point about Paul's heretical corruption of the Jewish faith, building instead a false religion on the basis of blood, should be read. It describes someone who is arrogant, with a pride that is contrary to the principle of justification by faith, greedy, and who plunders the nations. He gets evil gain 'to set his nest on high', to be safe from the reach of harm' (2:9) and *he will build a town with blood and found a city on iniquity*. He makes his neighbors *drink of the cup of his wrath,* making them drunk to gaze on their shame.

Quite obviously there is a high degree of assumption on Eisenman's

## The Controversy Continues

part to use this to describe Paul's character and his known activities in the first century C.E. Audaciously he focuses on Paul's 'cup of the Lord', and identifies the 'town of blood' as none other than the church itself, which is seen to be a city of iniquity because of its departure from the Law. He insists that the cup of the Lord usually represents judgment and wrath outpoured on evil. Even in the New Testament 'drinking the cup' as a metaphor, meant for James and John their willingness to suffer persecution and martyrdom. But, in contrast, David the King tells us in an exultant moment, that he will lift up the cup of salvation, and call upon the name of the Lord, and this in return for all his bountiful blessings (Psalm 116:12-13). We are well aware that Paul himself drew from the same chapter in Habakkuk to declare that 'the just shall live by faith', for him a cardinal doctrine. It would be a coincidence indeed if he had derived inspiration from the same chapter which, according to Eisenman, condemns him in the teachings of the Qumran community. Such an application of this portion of Habakkuk *pesher* is patently illogical, and exposes Eisenman's argument to be far-fetched.

Eisenman, however, feels entitled to declare his opposition to a theology of blood, with the cup of the New Covenant at its centre. Of course there have been those who believe that something of cannibalism is suggested in John 6:52-56, where Jesus was urging his followers to eat of his flesh and drink of his blood, but one must follow through to verse 63 which qualifies his remarkable *analogy:*

> It is the spirit that gives life, the flesh is of no avail; the words that I have spoken to you are spirit and life.

Even when Jesus first invited the disciples to drink with him the New Covenant in his blood, it had to be understood purely symbolically since, as yet, Jesus' body had not been broken, nor his blood been shed. Moreover, when Paul gives us what we call the Words of Institution in the First Letter of Corinthians, eleventh chapter (where he alludes to a practice already well established and traditional in the young church), he warns against any who drink unworthily. There is no way that the church, in Paul's mind, is to be a town of blood and a city of iniquity. Both of these expressions suggest the taking of a city by force and the shedding of blood(s), with iniquity and violence to prevail. This is something far removed from the celebration of Communion or the Eucharist. Besides, this sacrament has a powerful ethical outworking. It calls for self-examination and the searching of one's soul for any sin, lest we should be making a mockery of the blood of Christ shed for our redemption. We are not to drink the cup of the Lord and the cup of demons (11:21). This is a summons to high morality and to holy living. We must reject the grossly erroneous connection that Eisenman seeks to make between Habakkuk and 'the Cup of the Lord.' We might add that any view of the Eucharist, or Communion, which is thought to provide Christians with 'cheap grace', easy forgiveness and a carte blanche permission to live as they please, is as heretical as it is unholy. In the same Corinthians chapter Paul solemnly warns against any such misunderstanding and misbehaviour. It is the cup of the New Covenant, with all the attendant moral obligations assumed in that covenant of the heart (Jeremiah 31:33). With so much downplaying of Paul, any uninformed reader might think that he had nothing to say about the sanctity of marriage, sexual morality, purity of conversation, justice, compassion, the prohibition on lying, and the living of a life well pleasing to God.

Blood, though never to be drunk, is most meaningful in Jewish thought and experience—from the sprinkling of the blood of the Passover lamb on the doorposts of the enslaved Israelites to the sprinkling of blood from the animal sacrifices in the Temple. These were things not to be despised, and surely the same holds for the sanctity of the Christian's observance of the Lord's Supper. In his Epilogue (959), Eisenman finally alludes to the similarity of the 'Cup' imagery between the Qumran community and the early church, and this he does without any condemnation of the practice. Lawrence Schiffman significantly comments that these meals, "conducted regularly as part of the present-age way of life of the sect, were preenactments of the final messianic banquet which the sectarians expected in the soon-to-come end of days."[34] The presiding priest would bless the firstfruits of the bread and new wine (Manual of Discipline 6:4-6).

We turn now from one sacred area to another. In his first epistle, Peter pays respect to the shedding of the blood of Christ as the means of atonement and redemption. He relates this to the need of an animal 'without blemish' in keeping with Jewish sacrificial practice (1 Peter

## The Controversy Continues

1:18,19). Historically, Peter was not only one of 'the pillars' of the Jerusalem church, but he became a missionary with a particular pastoral care for the Jews of the Diaspora (1:1,2).

Peter, like Paul, however, does not escape the criticisms of Robert Eisenman. He is attacked, not on his use of the 'blood' analogy, but in respect of his views on the Spirit. Our critic points to what he regards as Peter's misappropriation of Joel's prophecy about the Spirit of the Lord being 'poured out' on all flesh (Acts 2:17; Joel 3:1-5).

> And it shall come to pass afterward, that I will pour out my spirit on all flesh; your sons and your daughters shall prophesy, your old men shall dream dreams, and your young men shall see visions, even upon the menservants and maidservants in those days, I will pour out my spirit.

He is entirely correct in his insistence that this Scripture should be seen strictly within a Zionist context, that is as a promise to Israel's sons and daughters. The essential Jewishness of the early apostles must be recognized, also their own admitted surprise that there came an infusion of the Spirit on the Gentiles, as in Peter's experience with the household of Cornelius (Acts 10:44-48). After this it was reported to the church in Jerusalem:

> So when Peter went up to Jerusalem, the circumcision party criticized him, saying, 'Why did you go to uncircumcized men and eat with them?' ... 'As I began to speak [to these men], the Holy Spirit fell on them just as on us at the beginning. And I remembered the word of the Lord, how he said, 'John baptized with water, but you shall be baptized with the Holy Spirit.' 'If then God gave the same gift to them ... who was I that I could withstand God?'

Here we need to discuss two serious difficulties. One, why does Eisenman betray an aversion to the expression 'pouring out' by associating it with the vocabulary of the Dead Sea Scrolls which, he claims, invariably applies to the pouring out of judgment? Thus he contrasts 'the waters of Lying being poured out on Israel' in the Damascus Document, with the Holy Spirit being poured out on the Jerusalem Community, as recorded in Acts 2:17-18 and 2:33 (206). He notes that *this* 'pouring out' in the Damascus Document, column 8, is associated with 'lying visions', 'wine', 'poison', 'venom', 'vipers' and 'Gentiles', 'walking in windiness', or the 'Spirit and the Spouter of Lying spouting to them.' Of course it is Eisenman's opinion that the Qumran writer of these indictments is fuming at Paul, 'the Liar.' However, for Eisenman to equate, unless merely grammatically, the *pouring out* of the Spirit' and 'waters of Lying being *poured out* on Israel' is unfortunate and misleading. Not only does Joel use the expression 'pouring out' of the Spirit, but so also does Zechariah:

> And I will pour out on the house of David and the inhabitants of Jerusalem a spirit of compassion and supplication, so that, when they look on him whom they have pierced, they shall mourn for him, as one mourns for an only child (12:10).

This is the second serious difficulty alluded to above. We must ask if the implication of Eisenman's position on the Holy Spirit is nothing short of an exclusion of non-Jews from the benefit of this gift from God. Before proceeding that far, however, we can sense in Eisenman's writings a strong reluctance to extend even to Paul himself that possibility. We can indeed gauge the measure of his resentment and unbelief by his quizzical, if not cynical remarks when he writes: "Here, Paul gives play to the idea of a *private* 'revelation' by which he means that he is directly in touch with some other revelatory body, presumably 'the Holy Spirit' " (127-8). He goes on, "Paul insists his appointment is direct from Jesus Christ—meaning, *the Supernatural Christ*, to whom in Heaven he has, as it were, a direct line via 'the Holy Spirit.' This is the only certification he needs, which accords with his reason for not discussing with anyone else the Gospel about *Christ Jesus*, as he taught it among the Gentiles.... He only had to discuss it with the Heavenly Jesus through the medium of the Holy Spirit" (146).

Instances in the Old Testament of the Spirit of the Lord coming upon kings, prophets, judges, warriors and even artificers are numerous. The Holy Spirit is recognized as one who teaches God's will to his people and gives direction in the right path (Psalm 143:10); as giving judgment and righteousness (Isaiah 32:15ff.); and the impartation of a new heart and a new spirit as twice over expressed in the Book of the Prophet Ezekiel:

## The Controversy Continues

And I will give them one heart, and put a new spirit within them; I will take the stony heart out of their flesh and give them a heart of flesh, that they may walk in my statutes and keep my ordinances and obey them and they shall be my people and I will be their God (11:19-20).

Cast away from you all the transgressions which you have committed against me, and get yourselves a new heart and a new spirit. Why will you die, O house of Israel? (18:31).

And I will put my spirit within you, and cause you to walk in my statutes and be careful to observe my ordinances (36:26).

Two comments are in place here. These portions in Ezekiel do not mention the *holy Spirit*, as such, but there is the suggestion that a new heart is necessary to create the desire to obey God's ordinances and, we might add, to enjoy a delight in doing His will rather than by acting only out of a sense of discipline and duty. This parallels the concept of the *circumcised heart* alluded to in Jeremiah 9:25, where the prophet warns that God will punish all those who are circumcised "but yet uncircumcised." This same thought is radically developed by Paul when he writes:

> He is a Jew who is one inwardly, and real circumcision is a matter of the heart, spiritual and not literal. His praise is not from men but from God (Romans 2:29).

Secondly, that Ezekiel wants his reader to understand he is writing of the Spirit of the Lord is beyond contradiction, and it is this same *agent*, a term used by Eisenman, as above, which lifts Ezekiel and brings him to the east gate of the house of the Lord (11:1), and then comes upon him to inspire his prophecy (11:5). On this basis, we can argue that Eisenman has no case when he castigates the idea that Philip was caught up by the Spirit following his baptism of the Ethiopian eunuch (Acts 8:39). Nor can it be denied that a clear and strong linkage occurs in these Old Testament passages between the Holy Spirit and a new heart. This reaches its Old Testament consummation in the unforgettable words of David the King after his grievous sin,

> Create in me a clean heart, O God, and put a new and right

spirit within me. Cast me not away from thy presence, and take not thy holy Spirit from me (Psalm 51:10,11).

Clearly he recognized his dependence on the Holy Spirit, not only to activate his conscience, but to make repentance real and genuine, effecting indeed a true reconciliation with God.

If Eisenman takes exception to Paul's claim to guidance by the Spirit, utterance by the Spirit, and power in the Spirit, he is then obligated to clarify his own definitions of the Spirit. Paul's listing of the gifts of the Spirit, as he understood them, is an eloquent testimony to those transforming virtues which can come to someone who is seeking a holy and a righteous life style:

… the fruit of the Spirit is love, joy, peace, patience, kindness, goodness, faithfulness, gentleness, [and] self-control.

It will be worrying indeed if Eisenman's apparently monopolistic view of the Spirit of God implies that the Gentiles are most probably ineligible for the gift. It would seem that exactly the same objections which had been raised by the Circumcision party in the first century C.E. are with us today. Personally, I much prefer, and am profoundly grateful for the more generous view of Pinchas Lapide, who benevolently believes that the Christian Gospel is "a way of salvation which God has opened up in order to bring the Gentile world into community of God's Israel" (see my page 82). And surely this view is a valid interpretation of Joel who foresaw the outpouring of the Spirit, unquestionably on the sons and daughters of Israel, but also "upon all flesh" (2:28).

Paul, in the first half of the first century, fervently believed that the fullness of the times had arrived for the rest of the world to be awakened to the existence and redemptive purpose of the one and only true God. A reading of his sermon given in Athens, and recorded in Acts 17:22-31, makes this abundantly clear. His insistence that the time had come for Israel to share her messianic hope and message of redemption with the Gentiles earned him the opposition of many Jews. Even on the strength of Eisenman's own definition of anti-Semitism, however, Paul could not be so charged.

It is when Eisenman goes farther to make the astonishing allegation

## The Controversy Continues

that the Gospels and parts of the Acts of the Apostles were the product of a later writer, or writers who fraudulently conspired to produce a pro-Roman and possibly an anti-Semitic religion, we simply have to stand up and protest. If the Gospel was seen to be at variance with certain aspects of the Judaism of the day, neither was it in league with Rome. As Paul had declared, it was both foolishness to the Gentiles and a stumblingblock to the Jews.

It is a matter of historical record that Christians would not bow to Caesar and were always under the special scrutiny of emperors. Pliny's letter to Trajan is a proof of this kind of investigation. Domitian called for an examination of leading Christians, but dismissed them as simpletons and ordered the cessation of the Imperial order which had commanded their persecution. From time to time active and sometimes ruthless persecution broke out as under Nero in the mid '60s and by Diocletian as late as 303 C.E. Trajan, though apparently tolerant at first, ordered the execution of Simeon bar Cleophas, 'a cousin of our Lord' as described by Hegesippus.[35] There tended to be a lurking fear of those Jews who were seen as members of the Davidic family. However, well after the crushing of the Second Jewish Revolt led by Simeon bar Kochba, Christians continued to be harassed not by reason of any Jewish connection but, again, on the grounds that they were refusing to worship in the form prescribed by the state. The Decian persecution of 250 C.E. was one of the worst, seeking more to torture than to kill. Origen was one of those who so suffered.

It has to be shown that many things fly in the face of Eisenman's hypothesis of how, why and when our Gospels were compiled. His belief that the Gospel writers were out to please Roman readers receives flat contradiction from history itself, as we have just seen. He fails to give fair and adequate recognition to the highly controversial, if not threatening message of the Kingdom of God which Jesus had clearly articulated. He also fails to admit that sayings of Jesus had existed long before the end of the first century, and to which our Gospel writers were both indebted and have been found to be faithful in their transmission of these sayings. We have already alluded to the significant statement by E. P. Sanders that we have no indication of any Christian writer who wished "to step forward and claim for himself" the writing of the parables of Jesus and their interpretation (p. 128). We have every reason to believe these were original to Jesus and largely Palestinian in genre. In no way can we accept these as deliberately manufactured inventions or distortions, and the products of a clever conspiracy by end-of-century revisionists.

Eisenman is obliged to the Ebionites for confirmation of his thesis that the early Jamesian church was essentially an extension of Judaism, and faithful to the Law of Moses. He must also accept that this same strand of Christianity had sufficient knowledge of the life and teachings of Jesus to accept him as a prophet, one who was anointed by the Holy Spirit at his baptism, acknowledged as Messiah and who, moreover, was the Son of Man destined to return in clouds of glory. To them Jesus was no phantom figure, or whose historical existence was in any doubt. He is careful to point out that the Ebionites came to be regarded as heretical by Gentile Christians and their writings suppressed. At the same time he must be reminded that the same Judaistic Christians, be they Nazarenes (Acts 24:5) or later known as Ebionites, were officially rejected by the Rabbis in 135 C.E., also as heretics, no doubt because of their support of Jesus. On both sides they were considered to be mavericks, but the inescapable point here is that the teachings of the historical Jesus were in circulation from the earliest times of the church. It is nothing short of remarkable how unbelievably little of the teachings of Jesus appear in Eisenman's would-be exhaustive study of *James the Brother of Jesus*.

That these teachings were commonplace among Jewish and Gentile Christians is evidenced by the author of Acts when he describes the circumstantial meeting in Corinth of four persons. Priscilla and Aquila, who had been expelled from Rome because of the Claudian decree against Jews (49 C.E.), first made their acquaintance with Paul in Corinth. He had not yet reached Rome. Here also this couple was in a position to teach Apollos, a Christian Jew from Alexandria, *more precisely* the things concerning Jesus. After this encounter Apollos ventured north into Achaia, the smallest country in the Peloponnesus, once inhabited by the Ionians. This is an interesting insight given by the author of Acts (18:1-4, 24-28) as to the broad stretch of personal evangelism which occurred in the early days of the church. It would be an over-simplification to suggest that Paulinism was the only influence behind the building and the teaching of the early Gentile church

## The Controversy Continues

Indeed, as it was pointed out earlier (p. 131), Paul's letter to the church in Rome was sent to a church which he himself did not establish. There were those segments of the early church which did not owe their origin to Paul, but rather to Thomas and his associates in the east, and to Peter among the diaspora in the north and west, and indeed to a variety of travelling lay people in an empire which, for its time, had advanced communications.

Another lesson to be taken from the foregoing was the Jewishness of the early Gentile church all the way to Rome. This major segment of the church, however, was in full agreement with the lordship of Jesus Christ, and its proclamation of the *kerygma* appeared to be in complete harmony with Paul's message. Certainly, it would be impossible to identify it with the later Ebionites. Rather, the New Testament Epistle to the Hebrews illustrates the desire of these or other Jewish Christians to relate their newfound faith to the doctrines and practices of the Judaism they had known.* This is a masterly work. For a very long time it was thought to have been of Pauline authorship, but most scholars are convinced that it might well be the writing of either Barnabas, the travelling companion who broke with Paul over John Mark, or Apollos of Alexandria. As noted below, the latter is more likely since his style of interpretation is not unlike that of the famous Jewish philosopher, Philo (ca. 30

---

*The epistle is cited by Clement I, Bishop of Rome (ca. 92-97), and it has been suggested by some that he might have been the author. However, the fact that the epistle suggests impending persecution and the defection of some Jews from the faith, with 'present tense' use of Temple procedures, strongly suggests a pre-70 date. Martin Luther thought it might have been Apollos and this has been supported by such scholars as H. Alford, T. Zahn and H. W. Montefiore. Acts 18:24 describes him as an eloquent, or learned man, "well versed in the Scriptures." A. Harnack suggested Priscilla and Aquila. Calvin pointed out that the writer viewed himself [*herself?*] as a disciple of the apostles (Hebrews 2:2). It is true that the author makes full use of the Septuagint, a Greek translation of the Hebrew Bible made for the benefit of Greek speaking Jews of the Dispersion. As Philo, the well known Jewish philosopher of Alexandria, was known for his allegorizing method, so this writer is significantly typological in his treatment of the Old Testament.

B.C.E.–40 C.E.). In any event, the discussion points up the importance of Jewish Christians who had made the significant adjustment to the revelation of our Lord Jesus Christ, his atoning death and resurrection.

## In Conclusion

The motivation, direction of argument, use of relevant materials and the ultimate aim of any writer should be of interest to the reader. Of course this is especially true if one's faith or philosophy of life is being challenged. We began with a deep and genuine concern for Christian pastors whose intelligence, and even integrity, are being questioned, in that they are said to be failing to communicate to their congregations the latest findings of contemporary theological and historical research. The reader may recall the assurance given to us that such writers were not "personally bent on toppling the edifice of Christendom" (p. 2).

In the case of Dr. Robert Eisenman, however, he is open, honest and non-apologetic for his negative disposition towards Christianity as we know it today. In no way does he conceal his antagonism towards Paulinism in particular. He is also radical enough to suggest that the Jesus we honour and worship is not the person we think we know, if indeed he ever existed at all. His book *James the Brother of Jesus* alleges *the possibility* of a masterly and deceitful conspiracy by first century Christian writers to produce fictitious characters to which they attached the names and titles of other people. As we have observed, this book has received considerable acclaim (pp. 218-219), which is not so surprising in an age of crass scepticism and unbelief.

Frequently with justification it is fashionable today to cast doubt on traditions which for centuries have been unquestioningly accepted. Personally I don't condone the type of person who has only a blind faith, within a well protected glass-house mentality, and who is quick to respond to critics with a counter-charge of either heresy or blasphemy. Christians ought to be above this. We are not to have a spirit of fear, but of power, of love and of a sound mind (cf. 2 Timothy 1:7). C. S. Lewis exhibited this even in the process of becoming a Christian. It is said that he had learned from his Scottish atheist teacher at Great

## The Controversy Continues

Bookham in Surrey how to smell out nonsense and fallacies. Chad Walsh writes: "Soon Lewis found himself testing these weapons against various philosophic stances—popular realism, philosophical idealism, pantheism—and discovering deeper logical flaws in these systems than in theism. Theism itself, which stood up well under logical scrutiny, proved for Lewis the anteroom of Christianity."[36]

In this era of so-called 'human rights' Christians must not deny the rights of others to air their views, even if these are so devastatingly negative and seemingly calculated to demolish our faith. Intellectual and religious tolerance in our western world have largely come from both the Reformation and the Renaissance. Two thousand years ago this philosophy was given personal and unforgettable endorsement by Jesus of Nazareth, who when he was reviled did not so respond to those who mocked him. He not only advocated the turning of the other cheek, but acted it out by going to the cross. If, today, in the arena of religious controversy, the gauntlet is thrown and 'the gloves are off', we may just have a fresh glimpse of the nail-pierced hands of Christ. Persecution of Christians occurs on a grand scale in Rwanda, in Sudan, East Timor, occasionally in Hindu India, with heavy restrictions on them in many Muslim countries; and, historically, over the years of Communism in Russia, and in Mao Tse tung's China*

Opposition to Christian morality is now emerging from western secular humanism, and there is a growing impatience with those who wish to preserve a conservative view of human sexuality. Many wish for a completely post-Christian era so that they can assert their demands for moral anarchy. Some elements of Jesus' apocalyptic teaching warn of a catastrophic decline in faith in the end-time. His words that love will grow cold and immorality will abound are found in Matthew 24:12.

It should be no surprise to us that unbelief and ill-will towards the Christian faith will increase. In the opinions of some, Christianity has failed to stop wars, to solve all inequities in the world, while some seg-

---

\* Cf. *Their Blood Cries Out* by Paul Marshall and Lela Gilbert, with Introduction by Michael Horowitz. Dallas: Word Publishing, 1997.

ments of Christian culture failed to resist racism. As yet no system of thought has produced a world utopia, but the global concern on the part of Christians has been well illustrated in their commendable missionary and humanitarian activities worldwide, and by the powerful eloquence against slavery and racism by parliamentarian William Wilberforce, converted slave trader John Newton, and the memorable Martin Luther King, Jr.

However, before dispensing with Christian faith and values, non-religious secularists must admit that their systems, too, can be guilty of hypocrisy, corruption, racism and even holocaust. Communism is a case in point, suitably described by disillusioned one-time advocates as *The God that Failed* (see p. 163). As Christians, we are surely entitled to ask what indeed will replace the Judeo-Christian value system?

More specific to our study, we must enquire of Robert Eisenman what form of Judaism does he envision for the twenty first century. Our guess is that he favours a revival of legalistic Judaism of the kind that the Qumran community represented, as well as great numbers of the fighting Zealots. It seems to be his view that these, and these alone, upheld the true Jewish concepts of holiness, righteousness and justice, and not the Pharisees who compromised with Rome, and certainly not the Herodian/Sadducean priesthood. The Qumranites and the Zealots were the courageous *freedom fighters* in a Roman dominated Jewish society, a conviction shared by Neil Asher Silberman (see my pp. 67-69). As we have seen in this study, some of these same heroes were fanatics who forced circumcision on reluctant converts, and galvanized their fellow Jews into a war which cost a million lives.

They preferred the Law of Moses to the *lex Romana,* much in the same way that many Muslim countries today opt for the Koranic Law rather than a secular system of common law; and religious fanaticism can be the result. They see what they believe is 'the Great Satan of America' a great nation in danger of ultimate collapse from within because of absolute moral corruption. Our dilemma at the turn of this millennium is to have religious fanaticism on one side, and a secular law system which is devoid of religious values to protect and uphold human decency. The situation has some parallels to the first century. Let us then recapitulate.

As the first century entered the 60s, militant forms of Judaism began

## The Controversy Continues

to dominate Judaea It is the view of this writer that James the Just, while seeking to maintain the tenets of primitive Christianity, found himself in an ever tightening vice. He was resented by the Saducean priesthood, but he was also seen by legalistic extremists as a champion of their cause. His death at the hand of Ananus, the High Priest, gave impetus to the Zealots' determination to intensify their warfare against the Romans. The powerful influence of the Circumcision party was already in evidence at the Jerusalem Council, as recorded in Acts 15, along with its insistence that Paul would comply with Jewish customs. At chapter 23, however, the belligerence of extremists is unmistakable. Here we are told that forty men had bound themselves by an oath neither to eat or drink till they had killed him. No doubt a Sicarii style lynching was being planned.

Just imagine the tensions which James must have felt. He faced a double dilemma. Paul, despite their differences, was still a Christian brother, and a notable figure in the expanding growth of the church in the Mediterranean world. Indeed he had been instrumental in collecting offerings from Gentile congregations for the saints at Jerusalem. James must have been acutely aware that Paul was receiving less than saintly treatment! Nevertheless, James remained loyal to the legalists, firm in his challenge to the priesthood, *but also resolute in his condemnation of warring factions.* This quote from James 4:1-3 is pivotal to an understanding of the essential pacifism of James the Just.

> What causes wars, and what causes fightings among you? You desire ... so you kill ... you covet and and cannot obtain; so you fight and wage war.

It has never been anything of a deep dark secret concealed from the public eye by the writers of the New Testament that James and Paul each had a different theological emphasis. The issues are clearly and honestly portrayed, with Paul on one side stressing justification by faith, and James emphasizing faith demonstrated by works.* That these two church

---

*This difference has been greatly exaggerated from time to time. Cf. Paul's letter to the Romans where he himself cites Deuteronomy 30: 12-14, "For it is not the hearers of the law who are righteous before God, but the doers of the law who will be justified." See also Ephesians 2:10.

leaders were absolutely and forever opposed to each other, however, is to paint a false picture. The idea that Paul wished to isolate himself from the church in Jerusalem, and to act in complete independence of the primitive church is patently untrue. On the contrary he testifies in his letter to the Galatians (2:2-10) that he was willing to check with James, Cephas and John, lest his mission to the Gentiles had been in vain. His call for financial help to go to the church in Jerusalem is clear (1 Corinthians 16:1-3). Finally, he himself insists on returning to Jerusalem despite grave warnings as to the dangers involved (Acts 20:16; 21:4,10-14).

As the reader will recognize, I write in favour of Paul, since, as I see it, he has been made the object of unjustified scorn. Though often outspoken, he was not uncharitable (cf. 1 Corinthians 13), though opposed to a spirit of legalism, he was not immoral; and though rightly proud of his Jewish heritage he had a heart for the Gentiles in their lost condition. I, among many, am grateful that Paulinism, if it must be so called, prevailed in first century Christianity.

A major assumption on the part of Eisenman is that the Acts of the Apostles deliberately ignored James, as the first Bishop of Jerusalem, introducing him almost casually at the time of James of Zebedee's death (12:1,2,17). The Pseudoclementine tradition has James being personally ordained by Jesus immediately after his resurrection, but this is not in agreement with Paul's listing of those who first saw the Lord (1 Corinthians 15:1-9). When we recall that James and his brothers had expressed doubt about Jesus' mission during his three year ministry, it should not be surprising to us that it took time for him to gain his place among the Twelve. That he had become a leader of the Jerusalem church by the time of Peter's arrest by Herod is attested in Acts 12, and, further, where he is seen to be the mediator of the situation at the Jerusalem Council in Acts 15. There is no cover-up here, and neither is there any attempt to deny that differences did exist between the Jamesian and Pauline advocates. Subsequently these differences did lead to an inordinate exaltation of James and an outpouring of hostility towards Paul by the later Judaistic Christians and Ebionites. This fact in itself entitles us to question their *post-apostolic* writings as over against the united testimony of the Pauline, Petrine and Johannine traditions which constitute our Bible.

# The Controversy Continues

It would be entirely presumptuous for a Christian writer to speak to the forms of Judaism which may surface in the twenty first century, whether liberal or conservative. In the past, Judaism has demonstrated that it is not limited to any single interpretation of its faith, be it in terms of the application of the Mosaic Law, its views on marriage and divorce, in its eschatological expectations and even in its Messianism. As Christians, however, we can ask ourselves whether a Paulinist or a Jamesian form of Christianity will best serve the new millennium. Will it be necessary to revive a strict legalism, accepting the position that Jesus came not to abolish the Law, but to fulfil it? (Matthew 5:17). That Jesus had the strictest of views about such subjects as marriage, divorce and the inviolability of children is well known. With the current collapse in morality precisely at these levels, it is easy to prove the vital relevance of the Christian faith to our times.

Without any disrespect to the Jewish or Jamesian-Christian emphasis on circumcision and food dietary laws, important as these may be, today's moral crises call for a much broader response. Circumcision and food laws do not keep Arabs and Israelis from fighting each other. Legislators are embattled over life and death issues—abortion, euthanasia, crime and punishment; while the nations are afraid of each other's capability of nuclear and biological warfare. On the domestic front we are witnessing an avalanche of divorces with the consequential custodial dilemmas for children hurting badly from the splitting of families. It is interesting that the Mosaic Law required compensation to a woman hurt during pregnancy, while Jesus serves notice to any who would cause offence to a child. Better, he warned, that such a culprit should have a millstone hung about his neck, and be drowned in the depths of the sea (Matthew 18:6). Yet abuse of children, youth alienation, drug addiction, prostitution, entertainment's exploitation of sex, and society's vulnerability to sex related diseases, cry out for remedy. Can it be achieved by legislation?

Violence among youth in our schools is reaching gross proportions with outbreaks of senseless killings by minors. This is obligating our legislators to consider radical changes to juvenile laws.

Some will say that a speedy return to the moral teachings of the Old and New Testaments is imperative. To be sure these cover a wide range of human behaviour and relationships. Condemnation of the greed of the rich is well stated by the prophet Amos and by Jesus of Nazareth. Here indeed we are in the company both of Jesus and of James his brother, where the latter argues against the preferred seats being given to those who come with fine clothing and gold rings (James 2:1-7). He also refers to the power of money in the taking of the poor to court. Can legislation effectively restrain the propensity of greed in our business world?

Political dictatorships still plague our world, and the principles of the Kingdom of God and of servanthood of leaders must somehow be implemented (see my Chapter 6). Yet a Saddam Hussein can thwart the efforts of the world community, while others of his ilk can make fun of international law. The force of economic sanctions may be applied or resort made to military action, often with inconclusive results.

The point to be made here is that the rule of law, though commendable, cannot answer all of our problems. In fact this was part of the Pauline argument that even though the Mosaic Law was a deterrent to sin, it was not redemptive of those who had broken the Law. Paul was very much aware of the coupling in Jewish theological vocabulary of the words *tsedek* and *chesed*, i.e. righteousness and mercy. John, in the Fourth Gospel, writes about Moses bringing the law and Jesus bringing grace and truth (1:17).

It is our contention that true Christianity has to be inclusive of aspects of both Jamesianism and Paulinism, and that anything less will produce an imperfect, malformed maverick-type faith. To stress only the law and the demand for penalty will often harden the determination of the offender to retaliate. This is to fight fire with fire, be it a tooth for a tooth. Something has to be found to break the cycle of violence and ill-will. This is exactly how Paul saw the work of Christ, who is, as he puts it, the end (*telos*) of the Law (Romans 10:4). Clearly this is not meant to be an abrogation of the Law, but a way of fulfilling the Law even when we have transgressed it. The Law when broken cannot redeem the person who breaks it.

Moses must have known this when he incorporated within the Torah the whole system of sacrifice as we have it in Exodus and Leviticus. Even within Judaism, however, there developed an ongoing struggle between the Law and the Sacrifices, or in practice between the priests and the prophets. It was seen that there could be no absolutism on the part of either one. This was not to say that the Law was not perfect, but for it to be applied to imperfect humanity was the problem, and still is. On the other hand, when Israel chose to freely capitalize on forgiveness on the basis of the sacrifices, prophets like Isaiah felt entitled to remonstrate on God's behalf:

> "What to me is the multitude of your sacrifices?" says the Lord; "I have had enough of burnt offerings of rams and the fat of fed beasts; I do not delight in the blood of bulls, or of lambs, or of he-goats.... I cannot endure iniquity and solemn assembly" (1:11-13).

It is not surprising, therefore, that in the New Testament theology of sacrifice, expiation and atonement, (as evident in the Pauline, Petrine and Johannine epistles as also in the Epistle to the Hebrews), Christ is seen to replace the Temple worship and its sacrifices. His sacrifice is once and for all. It represents a cessation of the old sacrificial system, and, at least in the case of Paul, this prophetic perception had come to him before the destruction of Jerusalem.

I have found Hyam Maccoby's argument to be fascinating, where he tells us that the Pharisees (when they arrived on the scene in the first century B.C.E.) played an important role in the supervising of the high priests lest they should be less than well-taught in the Law. The Pharisees would see to it that the incumbent of that office would operate "with a modicum of efficiency".[37]

Thus he tells us that the work of the high priest in Jerusalem was purely ceremonial. One has to assume, then, that the sacrifices of the Law were dispensable, a fact which became a hard reality after the destruction of the Temple. However, this adds to the legitimacy of the Christian position that a new era had begun, and that Jesus Christ the righteous is seen to be the expiation for our sins and for the sins of the whole world (1 John 2:1,2).

The removal of guilt remains a problem for today's world. Of course it can be suppressed or denied to the worsening of that person's character. Guilt must have been something very troublesome to the apostle

Paul. Among all the criticisms that have been thrown against him, I know of no one who has ever questioned the apostle's claim to have been a persecutor of the church. Whether, prior to his life-changing experience on the Damascus Road, he was a Pharisee, or a Herodian who was the agent of the High Priest, his early opposition to the new sect was unquestionably fanatical. And this zeal was on account of his desire to be known and recognized as a faithful Jew. He testifies to his own strict adherence to his Jewish heritage and customs, even to the point of boasting of his blamelessness before the Law (Philippians 3:3-6). This self-infatuated egotist fervently believed in his own perfection, but after becoming a Christian he turns more human and admits in the same chapter,

> Not that I have already obtained this or am already perfect; but I press on to make it my own.... I press on toward the goal for the prize of the upward call of God in Christ Jesus (3:12-14).

This is an important piece of autobiography of one who was intensely religious, but in the process was unwittingly committing the sin of self-righteousness. And this precisely was one of the complaints Jesus had expressed against the Pharisees. After the stoning of Stephen, Paul realized how wrong he had been in his persecution of the Christians. His teacher, Gamaliel, was surely closer to the heart of God when he asked the community to refrain from violence against the apostles:

> "Men of Israel, take care what you do with these men.... So in the present case I tell you, keep away from these men and let them alone; for if this plan or this undertaking is of men, it will fail; but if it is of God, you will not be able to overthrow them. You might even be found opposing God" (Acts 5:33-39).

Something had happened to Paul. It was dramatically revealed to him that by persecuting the Christians he was actually persecuting Christ. Not only was there a blinding light that shone externally, but the inner light had dawned. In that momentous encounter he met with the Judge of all hearts, thoughts and actions, and an awakened conscience made him realize that his hatred was directed against God. Now he heard words spoken that completely changed his life. Against the blinding light, he cried out "Who are you, Lord?" And back came

# The Controversy Continues

the answer "I am Jesus whom you are persecuting,"

Well do we realize that even good men, religious to the core, have been known to perpetrate atrocities against others. Paul was in this category and he had to come face to face with the hardness of his own heart. He later affirmed that if he were to boast, he would now glory in the cross of Christ. The suffering and sacrifice of Jesus had challenged his false sense of righteousness. It also gave to him a great sense of release from guilt. He discovered for himself that *tsedek* and *chesed* were both in the heart of God, and that one should never be divorced from the other.

Paul must have realized that the obvious conclusion to be drawn from all this was that people under the Law, or without the Law, and people who had transgressed the Law, all were in need of the mercy of God; and that this mercy comes to us through Jesus Christ. In no way did this mean that Christians could go on living pagan lives, and thus to 'trade' on the atonement of Christ on the cross. 'Cheap grace' is totally unacceptable to Paul when he writes:

> What shall we say then? Are we to continue in sin that grace may abound? By no means! How can we who died to sin still live in it? (Romans 6:1-2).

He is cognizant of extremes. On one hand those who justify themselves and their every action by the Law yet conceal their hidden sins of hate, and, on the other hand, those who believe they can go on sinning by 'cashing in' on the sacrifice of Christ. For him the cross stands at the centre, and will not lean in favour of our pride, nor will it excuse our sin. There is mercy here, and there is forgiveness, but there is also the call to holiness. Through the cross, God demands repentance and expects a transformed life.

Any concept of forgiveness as a licence to further sin is not in God's programme of redemption. Certainly the emphasis of the Good News is on God's forgiveness of the sinner. At various places in his work *James the Brother of Jesus*, Robert Eisenman pours contempt on the idea that Jesus would proclaim a kingdom which would welcome harlots, tax gatherers and other rejects of society, while closing its doors to some who were Pharisees and Scribes. It is a shocking idea, but it is nevertheless a fact of the Gospel, yet in no way is it intended to condone an ongoing immorality in the lives of the forgiven. Although a disputed passage (John 7:53-8:11), even an adulteress does not receive condemnation from Jesus, but is clearly commanded to sin no more.

From Paul we return to James who strikes the same note for which the Gospel is famous, namely that of forgiveness:

> My brethren, if any one among you wanders from the truth and some one brings him back, let him know that whoever brings back a sinner from the error of his way will save his soul from death and will cover a multitude of sins (James 5:19-20).

The history of evangelical revivals will attest to the fact that the Gospel of Jesus Christ again and again brings moral and spiritual renewal to our civilisation, and without it our western world is seen to be perfectly capable of unmitigated corruption and degeneration. Revivals like those of Luther, Calvin, Knox, Wesley, Whitfield, Booth, Moody, Finney, the Evangelical Awakening of England and the Welsh Revival of 1904, have recalled entire nations back to God and have transformed whole societies.

This was the battle, as Paul had visualized it, not a warfare against the Jews whom he still regarded as God's covenant people, but against spiritual wickedness manifested in one form or another among both the Gentiles and the Jews:

> For we are not contending against flesh and blood, but against the principalities, against the powers, against the world rulers of this present darkness, against the spiritual hosts of wickedness in the heavenly [or, high] places (Ephesians 6:12).

We just cannot deny that this is the very response needed for our world in its terrible disarray, disillusionment and self-destructiveness. It is fitting to complete our earlier quote from Carl Jung, himself a secular thinker, but one who recognized the values of religious faith:

> The domestication of humanity has cost the greatest sacrifices. We do not realize against what Christianity had to protect us.... We should scarcely know how to appreciate the enormous feeling of redemption which animated the first disciples, for we can

hardly realize in this day the whirlwinds of the unchained libido which roared through ancient Rome of the Caesars. [38]

But then follows a fully justified criticism of what might be seen as a self-satisfied Christianity, and appropriately a reminder of the need for self-searching among us as Christians. How far have we removed ourselves from the life-transforming power of the Gospel? Let this be a recall to revival, and a fresh challenge to shake off mere religiosity:

> In the past two hundred years Christianity has erected barriers of repression which protect it from the sight of its own sinfulness (Carl Jung).

Frequently Israel needed spiritual revivals and reforms, as in the days of Josiah the king. So also does the church need fresh visitations of the Spirit, and in the present time it is a pressing imperative.

## *The Vicissitudes of Religion in History*

That religious faith and experience is dynamic rather than static is undeniable. From an anthropological point of view, it is the story of development from the worship of tribal deities to an enlightened monotheism. Biblically, it is made clear that God chose a nation of people, the children of Abraham, to come out from the Chaldean culture, and later from under the Egyptian tyranny to be given the Law of Moses in their journey through Sinai. Then followed the priests, the judges and the prophets. Ultimately there arose among the people of Israel a hope that one day the entire world would be governed in peace by God's Messiah. In the long intervening intervals of time, however, devastating things happened to the Jews culminating in the terrible holocaust during the second World War. The pendulum of history had swung between extremes of hope and fear, from development and progress to destruction and despair, from nightmares to a renewal of their dreams. The prophet Ezekiel painted a vivid picture of this process when he visualized the death and resurrection of God's people in his chapter 37.

> Then he said to me, "Mortal, these bones are the whole house of Israel. They say, 'Our bones are dried up, and our hope is lost; we are cut off completely.'" Therefore prophesy, and say to them,

Thus says the Lord God: I am going to open your graves and bring you up from your graves. O my people; and I will bring you back to the land of Israel (37:11-12).

Undeniably the Jewish people have had a destiny of suffering but also of success, of oppression yet of miraculous survival, all of which has been well attested in our own generation.

Christians, too, have found that their God-given mission to the Gentiles at large would follow the same pattern of moral achievement and of diabolical opposition. Unfortunately in each of these cases, however, there seemed to be a reluctance to recognize each other's given roles, one for the Jews to constitute a model nation, and the other for the church to be an agent of redemption among the pagan Gentiles. Surely between them there had to be be a common recognition that a perpetual warfare exists between good and evil, justice and injustice, love and hate, and that this extends to all nations, peoples and cultures in greater or lesser degrees.

Humankind has made colossal advances in education, science, technology and the arts, much of which however is bedeviled by an equally powerful potential to make war and to devastate whole areas of our planet. Hegel saw something of the swing of the pendulum between thesis, antithesis and synthesis. This made its impact on Communist thinkers who felt that their system would be the final answer. It proved to be otherwise, and now the Western world hopes for a glorious economic globalism which will diminish the threat of nationalism and its potency for war. It will be an interesting experiment, and we must wait and see.

The essential pragmatism of the biblical view is that everything must be done to advance the cause of righteousness, justice and peace, but simultaneously for us to be constantly aware of the moral shortcomings of humankind and the insidious corruption of power. Both Jewish and Christian eschatologies share an optimism for a future where the wolf will lie down with the lamb, wars will cease, and the nations will worship God. But these same eschatologies give notice of divine intervention to achieve this when everything else has failed. Thus Old and New Testaments together tell of the Day of the Lord, the coming of Messiah and the final establishment of God's kingdom.

## The Controversy Continues

For the Lord of hosts has a day against all that is proud and lofty, against all that is lifted up and high ... and the haughtiness of man shall be humbled and the pride of men shall be brought low; and the Lord alone will be exalted in that day. And men shall enter the caves of the rocks and the holes of the ground, from before the terror of the Lord, and from the glory of his majesty when he rises to terrify the earth (taken from Isaiah 2:12-15).

Then the kings of the earth and the great men and the generals and the rich and the strong, and every one, slave and free, hid in the caves and among the rocks of the mountains, calling to the mountains and rocks, "Fall on us and hide us from the face of him who is seated on the throne, and from the wrath of the Lamb; for the great day of their wrath has come, and who can stand before it?" (Revelation 6:15-17).

But of that day or that hour no one knows, not even the angels in heaven, nor the Son, but only the Father. Take heed, watch, for you do not know when the time will come (Jesus, as recorded in Mark 13:32-33).

The initiative of God must be recognized here. It is our duty as his servants to serve our generation, to do the best we can in the furthering of God's cause throughout the world, but to accept the fact that this constant conflict between good and evil will be resolved finally only by divine intervention. Some very religious autocrats have made the blunder of believing that by their aggressive and militant efforts, they could bring in the reign of righteousness only to commit the very same mistakes of secular powers. The Jewish Zealots of the 60s took up arms in God's name, as the Crusaders in their day, and as Islamic terrorists have done in our time. As Paul rightly declared, the weapons of our spiritual warfare are not worldly (carnal or military), but are mighty in the destruction of arguments and of every proud obstacle to the knowledge of God (cf. 2 Corinthians 10:3-5). Having done all we possibly can to persuade men and women to obey God's commandments, to seek his mercy and forgiveness, and to live lives well pleasing to him and to their fellow human beings, we must await that day when God will pronounce the coming and the reign of his Messiah.

The Lord says to my lord: 'Sit at my right hand, till I make your enemies your footstool.' The Lord is at your right hand; he will shatter kings on the day of his wrath. He will execute judgement among the nations (Psalm 110:1, 5-6).

Both Judaism and Christianity look forward to the consummating reform and ultimate renewal of all nature when the Messiah of God will come as King of Kings and Lord of Lords. The question for both Christian and Jew, and indeed for the entire world, is, "Who is the King of glory?" It seems to me that the writer of Psalm 24 hinted that Jerusalem would not know when this promised One would be at the door of the city, and in typical Hebraic poetic parallelism, her inhabitants had to ask the question twice over. Christians believe that Messiah came first to suffer at the hands of inhumanity, to share in the agonies of the human experience, and to come again to establish his rightful claim to rule the world for which he died. Hence the fulfilment of the Jewish expectation of two messiahs, one a suffering servant and the other a triumphant king. We believe Jesus to be one and the same, the perfect combination of uncompromising righteousness and of unconditional love.

## Notes

[1] Luke Timothy Johnson. *The Real Jesus*. San Francisco: Harper San Francisco, 1996, p. 168.

[2] Ibid. p. 26.

[3] Ibid. p. 26.

[4] Ibid. pp. 81-82.

[5] Ibid. p. 85.

[6] Ibid. pp. 130-131.

[7] *TIME* article by Richard N. Ostling/New York and Lisa H. Towle/Raleigh, April 8, 1996: p. 44.

[8] *The Real Jesus*, p. 133.

[9] Ibid. p. 86.

[10] Ibid. pp. 145-146

[11] Ibid. pp. 118-119.

[12] Ibid. p. 166.
[13] Ibid. p. 89
[14] EH III.
[15] See Index, *Works of Josephus* trans. Wm Whiston. p. 815
[16] Hegesippus: de Excid. Urb. Hierosolym 2:12
[17] *Antiquities* 18.6-10
[18] Eisenman *James the Brother of Jesus*, p. xxxiii, quoting from MMT, DSS.
[19] Jos. War 2.261-3; Ant. 20.169-72.
[20] B.San. 81b-82b; Tos. Kelim 1.6. See also pages 564 and 574 of *James the Brother of Jesus*, for Eisenman's description of execution procedures.
[21] F. F. Bruce, *The New International Commentary on the New Testament*, p. 125
[22] Quoted from T. Zahn in.H.-J. Schoeps, *Paul: Theology of the Apostle in the Light of Jewish Religious History*, Philadelphia, 1961, p. 67
[23] Harold W. Gamble, *Books and Readers in the Early Church: A History of Early Christian Texts*. Newhaven, CT: Yale University Press, p. 64.
[24] John Dominic Crossan, *The Birth of Christianity*, New York: Harper Collins, 1998, p. 268.
[25] John P. Meier, *A Marginal Jew: Rethinking the Historical Jesus*, New York: Doubleday, 1991, p.115.
[26] Ben Witherington III, Commentary: *Acts of the Apostles*, Grand Rapids and Cambridge: 1998, p. 296 See also Barrett, Acts, Vol. 1, p.425.
[27] H. H. Ben-Sasson, ed. *A History of the Jewish People*, Cambridge: Harvard University Press, 1976, p. 332
[28] Paul Johnson, *A History of the Jews*, London: Weidenfeld and Nicolson, 1987, p.107.
[29] Ibid., p. 107.
[30] Jos., *Antiquities* 14.380.
[31] Jos., *War* 1.148-51; *Antiqs.* 14.58-71.
[32] A. M. Hunter, *The Expository Times*, LXXX1, 1959-60, pp. 166,

222.

[33] Simon J. De Vries in *The Interpreters' One Volume Commentary*, Nashville: Abingdon, 1980, p. 494.

[34] Translation of Lawrence Schiffman, *The Eschatological Community of the Dead Sea Scrolls: A Study of the Rule of the Congregation*, SBL Monograph Series 38 (Atlanta: Scholars Press, 1989), p. 67.

[35] EH 3.32.3-8. Eusebius is dependent on Hegesippus who recorded the martyrdom of Simeon, described as one of the persons 'who took the lead of the whole Church as martyrs.'

[36] C. S. Lewis, *A Grief Observed*, London and New York: Bantam 1976, with an Afterword by Chad Walsh, p. 112.

[37] Hyam Maccoby, *Paul the Mythmaker*, London and New York: Harper & Row, 1986, p. 27.

[38] Cited by Arnold Lunn and Garth Lean in *The New Morality*, London: Blandford Press, 1965, pp. 20-21.

# Postscript

We have travelled a long way, and, frankly, some of our journeyings have been in circles. Such can be the way with scholarship. The stated purpose of this book has been to answer those who claim that Christian pastors are failing to communicate to their congregations the latest findings of today's biblical research. The reader may well ask if it has been worth the trouble. In the current controversy we have found that scholars themselves have offered a variety of opinions on identical issues. Indeed we have sensed conflict between authorities on a number of important subjects, and it might be appropriate to apply the proverb "Physician, heal yourself", before finding fault with others. As a pastor, I am strongly tempted to return the challenge, and to direct it particularly to those writers who betray something of a sadistic pleasure in their attempts to discredit the Christian faith. At the very least, some grave inconsistencies must be highlighted so that the reader himself/herself can test the likely veracity and the integrity of scholars in four areas of the preceding discussions, now summarized below.

## 1. The Historicity of Jesus

Dr. Robert Eisenman started out by seriously questioning the very existence of Jesus, and by disputing the identity given to him by later writers, including even his name. Later in his work which we have reviewed with interest and great care, he admits "In Jesus' case, however, the reply probably is in the affirmative, that he *did* exist, most of all because *Paul refers to him in his letters,* though this reticently" (926). It does seem incredible that a scholar can be so nonchalant about such a pivotal person, the denial of whose existence would call for a total rewrite of our entire Western history. That Jesus was as real in the flesh as James, his brother, and known also as Messiah, is obvious if only from the record given to us by the Jewish historian, Josephus. Indeed it is this very same sentence of testimony, both to Jesus and to James, written by Josephus that Eisenman uses as a primary base for his own untenable thesis.

This writer spins a web of mesmerizing arguments obviously calculated to eclipse Jesus as we know him from the Gospels, and to emphasize instead the greater role of James. He notes how Josephus attributes the judgment which fell on Jerusalem to have been divine retribution for the cruel murder of James the Just. We do not dispute this, but we must reject Eisenman's implied corollary that it had little or nothing to do with Jesus. The simple fact of the matter is that James lived another thirty years beyond the crucifixion of Jesus, and his martyr's death in 62 C.E. was chronologically closer to the beginnings of the 66-70 Jewish War. Indeed he also died at the hands of a high priest, paralleling somewhat the fate of Jesus who was first arrested by Caiaphas following his daring cleansing of the Temple. Jesus remonstrated against the priesthood of his day, and he foresaw the coming inevitable catastrophies. We as Christians do not ignore the significant leadership James gave to the Jerusalem church, as Peter also, but in the apostolic tradition he stood firmly for the messiahship of his brother, Jesus. He would never have subscribed to Eisenman's diminutive and distorted picture of Jesus. Of the One he claims to be either non-existent or relatively unknown, or even unknowable, Dr. Eisenman offers this final and significant comment: "Who and whatever James was, so was Jesus" (963). This closing statement actually brings us back to the undeniable historical reality of Jesus.

## 2. The Character of Jesus

Since the time of Hermann Reimarus (1694-1768) there are those who have supported the view that Jesus was a political agitator, likely a Zealot, who incurred the wrath of the Roman authorities, and who was

## Postscript

crucified for no other reason than that of being a revolutionary. As such, however, he is also seen as a Jewish patriot, but in no way as a 'Saviour' who would bring forgiveness and redemption to the world. A strong advocate of this position in our century was S. G. F. Brandon, of the University of Manchester, who later issued a paper in 1971 repudiating the implications of his former argument (see my page 91). Nevertheless the zealot view of Jesus has resurrected again as in the case of Robert Eisenman.

As we have seen, this scholar completely rejects even the possibility of a Jesus who showed love, compassion and forgiveness to the sinners of his day, and who also attacked the religious establishment for its self-righteous hypocrisy. This kind of Jesus, he argues, was the inventive creation of sentimental writers of a later time who had a political agenda to appease the Roman Caesars. The truth is that Jesus' preaching of the *Kingdom of God* was in no way diluted by the Gospel writers, and Christianity continued to be eyed with suspicion and be subjected to fierce outbreaks of persecution until the time of Constantine in the early fourth century. In the year 156 C.E., Polycarp, Bishop of Smyrna, died by burning because he refused to bow to Caesar. His words testify to the clarity of the early Christians' commitment to the kingship of Christ:

> Eighty and six years have I served him, and he hath done me no wrong, how then can I blaspheme my king who saved me?

Theories, however impressive, convincing or beguiling, must square with the known and irrefutable facts.

### 3. The Mythicizing of other New Testament Figures

In our reading of *James, the Brother of Jesus* we have had to cope with the writer's denial of Stephen, the first recorded Christian martyr after the death of Jesus. This figure is described by Robert Eisenman as "a fictitious stand-in" and that the name given to him may have been borrowed from someone who had been a later convert of Paul in far-off Corinth. Or, it is further suggested, the name may have been taken from an unfortunate servant of the Emperor who, on a mission to Jerusalem, had been ambushed and killed by Zealots near to the city.

The historicity of Stephen, however, and of his martyrdom is positively stated by another eminent and critical scholar who is known for his thoroughness of research. Edgar Lundemann has written:

> 'Stephen's criticism of law and cult are to be regarded as historical.' In the same context Lundemann points out that the Acts account of the martyrdom 'is in accordance with Jewish legal ordinances (cf. Lev. 24:14; Num. 15:35; M. Sanh. 6:1), according to which the stoning had to take place outside the camp. Similarly, the stoning of Stephen may not take place in Jerusalem. First, therefore, he has to be dragged out of the city.... Stoning remains possible as the means of his death, as lynch law often made use of it' (cf. Philo, Spec. 1,54-57).[1]

It is not at all unreasonable to ask why Dr. Eisenman chooses to place the martyrdom of Stephen on the shelf of mythology when the entire thesis of his book depends on the undisputed historicity of the murderous death of James the Just. Both events occurred against the background of a hostile religious establishment. Admittedly, Stephen's speech was a trenchant attack on the Jewish elders of the day. Perhaps one facet of Eisenman's *modus operandi* is to create doubt in the minds of his readers as to the actual existence of the one whose arguments he cannot accept. This might also account for his treatment of the report in the Acts of the Apostles of Philip the evangelist and the Ethiopian eunuch, whose Queen Candace he also questions. This story he believes to be a fabrication by Luke, and one calculated to insult the Jewish practice of circumcision. We must let the readers be the jury, and God be the judge (cf. pp. 246-250).

## 4. The Reliability of Scholars

Such absurd occurrences as the John Allegro affair (my pages 48-49), where reliable scholars felt obliged to publicly denounce this Dead Sea Scrolls investigator for his notorious book, *The Sacred Mushroom and the Cross*, must surely compel thinking members of the public to despair of some so-called scholarship.

There were also those who charged the original International Team of Dead Sea Scroll researchers and the Vatican with suppression of information pertinent to the dates and contents of the Scrolls. It was being alleged that disclosures of their findings would be devastating to the Christian faith. For a time there were other scholars who expressed

## Postscript

dissatisfaction over delays in the handling and distribution of Scrolls data, but the idea of a deep, dark conspiracy perpetrated in the self-interests of the church has been utterly dismissed. All of this, however, illustrates the vulnerability even of the academic community to personal biases, political pressures, and certainly to presumed but false conclusions.

If Christian pastors are to be attacked for allegedly having failed to inform their congregations of the results of sometimes seriously doubtful and unattested biblical criticism, a reverse curve will be in order. Perhaps we should invite these same critics to recall the advice given by Jesus:

> Judge not, that you be not judged. For with the judgment you pronounce you will be judged, and the measure you give will be the measure you get. Let him who is without sin be the first to throw a stone" (taken from Matthew 7:1-2 and John 8:7).

In any event, pastors have a multitude of duties to perform, both social and spiritual, but of paramount importance is their sacred obligation to nourish their congregations with the Word of God. Such a role is set out for them in 2 Timothy 2:14-15:

> Remind them of this, and charge them before the Lord to avoid disputing about words, which does no good, but only ruins the hearers. Do your best to present yourself to God as one approved, a workman who has no need to be ashamed, rightly handling the word of truth. Avoid such godless chatter, for it will lead people into more and more ungodliness, and their talk will eat its way like gangrene.

I well remember a moment in my Dogmatics class in New College, Edinburgh, when a student asked the professor what would happen to all the people who never did have, or never would have a chance to hear the Gospel. His reply was more provocative than edifying, yet it was very wise. Dr. Thomas F. Torrance replied to the question which the student had put to him a second time. His response was a challenging reminder that if in the Medical Faculty of the University, a student were to ask what would happen to a patient who did not receive the prescribed treatment to save his life, he would be judged to be wasting the medical professor's valuable time. Admittedly the answer was evasive but it was also existential. The student settled down and accepted the inescapable corollary, namely that just as this teacher's responsibility was to keep to the matter of healing procedures for recovery rather than speculating in pathology, so likewise the Christian pastor has a primary and urgent duty to preach a life-giving faith. This is positive Christianity! Honest and constructive criticism has its place in all academic disciplines, but a chronic disposition to negative speculations can be unhealthy, if not deadly.

There is a saying that it's better to build a fence at the top of the hill than to have to build a hospital at the bottom. In North America today we are faced with many moral precipices in life with unhappy consequences for a lot of people. Religious and moral teachings in our schools are next to zero, and a new generation is rising up devoid of good guidelines for its behaviour in society. This is certainly a time to encourage ministers and pastors, of whatever faith, to offer wise and positive counsel. The Old Testament has several significant references to the removal of landmarks by which men live and without which people are vulnerable to hurt (cf. Deuteronomy19:14; 27:17-18; Proverbs 22:28; 23:10; and Job 24:2). In preparing young Timothy for his future ministry the veteran apostle gave prophetic warning of similar tendencies which would manifest themselves in the church and in society. He issued a clear and conscientious mandate:

> I charge you in the presence of God and of Christ Jesus who is to judge the living and the dead, and by his appearing and his kingdom: preach the word, be urgent in season and out of season, convince, rebuke, and exhort, be unfailing in patience and in teaching.
>
> For the time is coming when people will not endure sound teaching, but having itching ears they will accumulate for themselves teachers to suit their own likings, and will turn away from listening to the truth and wander into myths. As for you, always be steady, endure suffering, do the work of an evangelist, fulfil your ministry (2 Timothy 4:1-5).

And there we rest our case.

## Notes

[1] Lundemann, Edgar, *Early Christianity according to traditions in Acts.* Minneapolis: Fortress, 1989, p. 93.

# Selected Bibliography

Adamson, J. B. *Epistle of James.* The New International Commentary on the New Testament. Grand Rapids: Eerdmans, 1976; reprinted 1989.

Anderson, Norman. *Jesus Christ: The Witness of History.* Leicester: InterVarsity Press, 1985.

Aristotle. *The Generation of Animals,* Loeb Classical Library, trans. A. L. Peck, London: Heineman, 1943.

Baigent, M. and Leigh, R. *The Dead Sea Scrolls Deception.* New York: Summit, 1991.

Baigent, M, Leigh, R. & Lincoln, H. *The Messianic Legacy.* London: Corgi/Transworld, 1987.

Baillie, Donald M. *God Was In Christ: An Essay on Incarnation and Atonement.* London: Faber and Faber, 1948.

Barclay, William. *The Gospel Of Matthew.* Philadelphia: Westminster, 1958.

*The Gospel of Mark* in the Daily Study Bible. Toronto: G. R. Welch, 1975.

*The Letter to the Romans* in the Daily Study Bible. Edinburgh: Saint Andrew Press, 1955.

Barnett, Paul. *Is The New Testament Reliable?—A Look at the Historical Evidence.* Downers Grove, Ill, InterVarsity Press, 1986.

Ben-Chorin, Schalom. *Bruder Jesus: Der Nazarener in Judischer Sicht.* Munich: 1967.

Ben-Sasson, H.H., ed. *A History of the Jewish People.* Cambridge: Harvard University Press, 1976.

Betz, Otto. *Understanding the Dead Sea Scrolls.* ed. Hershel Shanks. New York: Random House, 1992.

*What do we know about Jesus?* E. T. London: SCM, 1968.

*Was John the Baptist an Essene?* Article in *Understanding the Dead Sea Scrolls.* ed. Hershel Shanks. New York: Random House.

Black, D. A. and Dockery, D. S. *New Testament Criticism & Interpretation.* Grand Rapids: Zondervan, 1991.

Blomberg, C. L. *The Dictionary of Jesus and the Gospels.* eds. Joel B. Green, Scot McKnight, I Howard Marshall. Downers Grove, Ill.: InterVarsity Press, 1992.

Borg, M. *Jesus in Contemporary Scholarship.* Valley Forge: Trinity Press, 1994.

Brandon, S.G.F. *Jesus and the Zealots: A Study of the Political Factor in Primitive Christianity.* Manchester: Manchester University Press, 1967.

Brown, Schuyler. *The Origins Of Christianity*—a Historical Introduction to the New Testament. Oxford: University Press, 1984.

Bruce, F.F. *Acts of the Apostles.* The New International Commentary on the New Testament. Grand Rapids: Eerdmans, 1989.

Bultmann, R. *Jesus,* translated by L. P. Smith and E. H. Lantern, *Jesus and the Word.* London: 1958.

*Theology of The New Testament,* transl. K. Grobel; 2 vols., New York: 1951, 1955.

# Bibliography

Burrows, Miller. *The Dead Sea Scrolls.* New York: Viking, 1955.

Cadbury, H.J. *The Book of Acts in History.* New York: Harper and Brothers, 1955.

Cadoux, C. J. *The Early Church And The World,* reprint 1955, Edinburgh : 1925.

Charlesworth, James H. *Jesus Within Judaism.* New York: Doubleday, 1988.

Cook, Edward M. *Solving the Mysteries of the Dead Sea Scrolls.* Grand Rapids: Zondervan, 1994.

Crossan, John Dominic. *The Historical Jesus—The Life of a Mediterranean Jewish Peasant.* San Francisco: Harper & Collins, 1992.

———. *In Parables—the Challenge of the Historical Jesus.* New York: Harper and Row, 1973.

———. *The Birth of Christianity.* San Francisco: Harper San Francisco, 1998.

Crossman, Richard. *The God that Failed.* New York: Harper and Row, 1950.

Danby, H. *The Jew and Christianity.* London: Sheldon, 1927.

Davies, Stevan & Feldman L. *The Gospel of Thomas and Christian Wisdom.* New York: The Seabury Press, 1983.

Driver, G. R. *The Judaean Scrolls.* New York: Schoken, 1966.

Dunn, James D. G. *Jesus, Paul and the Law.* Louisville: John Knox, 1990.

Eisenman, Robert H. *Maccabees, Zadokites, Christians and Qumran.* Leiden: 1983.

———. *James the Brother of Jesus.* London, New York and Toronto: Penguin Books, 1998.

Eisenman, R. and Wise, M. *The Dead Sea Scrolls Uncovered.* New York: Penguin, 1992.

Eusebius. *Ecclesiastical History.*

Feldman, Louis. *Jew and Gentile in the Ancient World.* Princeton: University Press, 1993.

Fitzmyer, J. *The Qumran Scrolls and the New Testament after Forty Years.* Revue de Qumran 13, 1988.

Flusser, David. *Jesus, ET* by R. Walls. New York: Herder and Herder, 1969; quoted by Donald A. Hagner. *The Jewish Reclamation of Jesus.* Grand Rapids: Zondervan, 1984.

Fox, Robin Lane. *The Unauthorized Version: Truth and Fiction in the Bible.* Knopf/Random, 1992.

Frances, R. T. *Matthew,* Tyndale New Testament Commentary, Leicester: IVP.; Grand Rapids: Eerdmans, 1985.

Frazer, James. *The Golden Bough.* London: Macmillan, 1913.

Fredriksen, Paula. *From Jesus To Christ.* Newhaven: Yale University Press, 1988.

Friedlander, G. *The Jewish Sources of the Sermon on the Mount., 1911.* New York: Ktav, 1969.

Funk, Robert W. and Hoover, Roy W. *The Five Gospels.* New York: Poleridge/Macmillan, 1993.

Gamble, Harold, W. *Books and Readers in the Early Church: A History of Early Christian Texts.* Newhaven CT: Yale University Press, 1995.

Geldenhuys, Norval. The New International Commentary on the New Testament, *Luke.* Grand Rapids: Eerdmans, 1977.

Gerhardsson, B. *The Origins Of The Gospel Traditions.* Philadelphia: 1979.

*Memory And Manuscript*—Oral tradition and written transmission in rabbinic Judaism and early Christianity, transl. Eric J. Sharp, Uppsala: 1961.

Golb, Norman. *Who Wrote the Dead Sea Scrolls?* New York and Toronto: Scribners, 1995.

# Bibliography

Gollwitzer, Helmut. *Der Unge Kundigte.* Stuttgart, 1962.

Grant, Michael. *Jesus—An Historian's Review of the Gospels.* New York: Scribner's, 1977.

Green, J. B., McKnight, S., Marshall, I. Howard, editors. *Dictionary Of Jesus And The Gospels.* Downer's Grove, Illinois: InterVarsity Press, 1992.

Griffiths, Michael. *The Example Of Jesus* (The Jesus Library). Downers Grove, Ill.: I.V.P., 1985.

Hagner, Donald A. *The Jewish Reclamation of Jesus.* Grand Rapids: Zondervan, 1984.

Hays, Richard B. *The Corrected Jesus.* A review essay on *The Five Gospels: The Search for the Authentic Words of Jesus,* on pp. 43-48 of *First Things,* No.43, published by The Institute of Religion and Public Life. New York, 1994.

Hengel, M. *Between Jesus And Paul: Studies In The Earliest History Of Christianity,* transl. J. Bowden, London: 1983.

Hennecke, Edgar. *The New Testament Apocrypha* (Vol.I, *"Gospels and Related Writings"*). London: Lutterworth Press, 1963.

Henry, Carl H. *The Identity of Jesus.* Nashville: Broadman Press, 1992.

Hunter, A. M. *The Expository Times,* LXXXI. 1959.

Jaspers, Karl. *Man Alone.* eds. Eric and Mary Josephson, New York: Dell, 1962.

Jeremias, Joachim. *The Parables of Jesus.* ET, S. H. Hooke (New Testament Library) London: 1963.

*Unknown Sayings of Jesus.* Trans. R. H. Fuller, London, 1964.

*Theology of the New Testament,* Vol. 1, *The Proclamation of Jesus* (London: SCM Press, 1971).

Johnson, Luke Timothy. *The Real Jesus: The Misguided Quest for the Historical Jesus and the Truth of the Traditional Gospels.* San Francisco: Harper San Francisco, 1996.

Johnson, Paul. *A History of the Jews.* London: Weidenfeld and Nicolson, 1987.

Jones, E. Stanley. *Abundant Living.* London: Hodder and Stoughton, 1950.

Josephus, Flavius *Antiquities of the Jews* and *The Jewish War.* Grand Rapids: Kregel Publications, 1963.

Kac, Arthur W. *Rebirth of the State of Israel,* 1958; Grand Rapids: Baker, revised 1976.

Kasemann, Ernst. *Essays on New Testament Themes.* London: S.C.M. Press, 1964.

Kerr, H. T. and Mulder, J. M. *Conversions.* 1983; reprinted, Grand Rapids: Eerdmans, 1985.

Klausner, J. *Jesus of Nazareth: His Life, Times and Teaching.* ET by H. Danby, 1925; reprinted, Boston: Beacon, 1964.

Kloppenborg, John. *The Formation of Q: Trajectories in Ancient Wisdom Collections.* Philadelphia: Fortress Press, 1987.

Kohler, K. *Jesus of Nazareth—In Theology.* The Jewish Encyclopedia, ed. I. Singer. New York: 1901-1906.

Kung, Hans. *Signposts for the Future,* trans. by Edward Quinn. New York: Doubleday, 1978.

Lapide, Pinchas. *Israelis, Jews and Jesus,* transl. P. Heinegg. Garden City: Doubleday, 1979.

Lapide, Pinchas and Moltmann, Jurgen. *Jewish Monotheism and Christian Trinitarian Doctrine,* trans. Leonard Swidler. Philadelphia: Fortress Press, 1981.

Lapide, Pinchas & Ulrich Luz. *Jesus in Two Perspectives—A Jewish-Christian Dialog.* Minneapolis: Augsburg, 1985.

Lapide, Pinchas and Stuhlmacher, Peter. *Paul, Rabbi & Apostle.* Minneapolis: Augsburg, 1992.

LaSor, William Sanford. *The Dead Sea Scrolls and the Christian Faith.* Chicago: Moody, 1962; reprint 1972.

# Bibliography

Lewis, C. S. *Surprised by Joy.* London: Geoffrey Bles, 1955; reprinted London: Harper Collins, 1977.

*A Grief Observed.* New York: Bantam/Seabury, 1976.

Lightfoot, R. M. *St. John's Gospel.* Oxford: Clarendon, 1956.

Linnemann, E. *Historical Criticism of The Bible—Methodology Or Ideology?* ET by Robert W. Yarbrough. Grand Rapids: Baker, 1990.

Longenecker, Richard N. *Paul, Apostle of Liberty.* Grand Rapids: Baker, 1964, reprinted 1976.

Lündemann, Gerd. *Early Christianity according to traditions in Acts.* Minneapolis: Fortress, 1989.

Lunn, Arnold and Lean, Garth. *The New Morality,* London: Blandford Press, 1965.

Maccoby, Hyam. *Revolution in Judaea.* 1973; reprinted New York: Taplinger, 1981.

*The Mythmaker—Paul and the Invention of Christianity.* New York: Harper and Row, 1986.

*Paul and Hellenism.* London: SCM., 1991; Philadelphia: Trinity Press.

Mack, Burton L. *The Lost Gospel: The Book of Q and Christian Origins.* San Francisco: Harper Collins, 1993.

Marshall, I. Howard. *I Believe In The Historical Jesus.* Grand Rapids: Eerdmans, 1979.

Marshall, Paul and Lela, Gilbert. *Their Blood Cries Out.* Dallas: Word Publishing, 1997.

Mayor, Joseph B. *The Epistle of James* (Reprint of Macmillan edition, 1913). Grand Rapids: Kregel Publications, 1990.

Meyer, Marvin. New Translation of *The Gospel of Thomas.* San Francisco: HarperSanFransisco, 1992.

McDowell, J. and Wilson, Bill. *He Walked Among Us.* Nashville: Nelson, 1993.

McKnight, Scot. *A Light among the Gentiles: Jewish Missionary Activity in the Second Temple Period.* Minneapolis: Fortress, 1991.

Meier, John P. *A Marginal Jew: Rethinking The Historical Jesus.* New York: Doubleday, 1991.

Montefiore, C. G. *The Old Testament and Its Ethical Teaching.* The Hibbert Journal (1917-18).

*What Jews Think About Jesus.* The Hibbert Journal (1934-5).

Moore, G. F. *Judaism In The First Centuries of The Christian Era: The Age of The Tarraim, Vol. 1,* Cambridge: Harvard University Press, 1962.

Morris, Leon. *The Gospel According to St. John.* The New International Commentary on the New Testament: Grand Rapids: Eerdmans, 1981.

Neill, Stephen. *Jesus Through Many Eyes.* Philadelphia: Fortress, 1976.

Nietzsche, Friedrich. *Assorted Opinions and Maxims,* published in 1879 as the first supplement to *Human, All Too Human,* 2nd edition published in 1886 and quoted in *A Nietzsche Reader,* ed. R. J. Hollingdale Harmondsworth, Eng.: Penguin Books, 1977.

Pascal, Blaise. *Great Shorter Works of Pascal,* transl. Emile Cailliet and John C. Blankenagel. Philadelphia: Westminster Press, 1948.

Peck, Scott M. *People of the Lie: The Hope for Healing Human Evil.* New York: Simon and Schuster, 1981.

Perrin, Norman. *Rediscovering the Teaching of Jesus.* New York: Harper & Row, 1967.

*The New Testament: An Introduction.* Harcourt: 1974.

Phillips, J. B. *Ring Of Truth.* New York: MacMillan, 1967.

Pinnock, Clark H. *Reason Enough,* Burlington: Welch, 1985.

Polkinghorne, John. *Belief in God in an Age of Science.* Newhaven CT., and London: Yale University Press, 1998.

Quast, Kevin. *Reading the Gospel of John.* New York: Paulist Press, 1991.

# Bibliography

Ramsey, Michael. *Jesus And The Living Past:* The Hale Lectures, 1978. New York: Oxford University Press, 1980.

Richardson, Alan. ed. *A Dictionary of Christian Theology.* London: SCM., 1969.

Robinson, J. A. T. *Redating The New Testament.* London: S.C.M., 1976.

*The Priority Of John,* ed. by J. F. Oakley. London: S.C.M., and Philadelphia: Trinity Press, 1985.

Rubenstein, R. L. and Roth, J. K. *Approaches to Auschwitz—The Holocaust and Its Legacy.* Atlanta: John Knox, 1987.

Sanders, E. P. and Davies, Margaret. *Studying The Synoptic Gospels.* London: S.C.M., 1989.

Sandmel, Samuel. *We Jews and Jesus.* New York: Oxford University Press, 1965, 1973.

*Judaism And Christian Beginnings.* New York: Oxford University Press, 1978.

Scott, E. F. *The Validity of The Gospel Record.* London: Nicholson & Watson, 1938.

Schiffman, Lawrence H. *At the Crossroads: Tannaitic Perspectives on Jewish-Christian Schism.* Jewish and Christian Self-Definition. Philadelphia: 1981.

*Understanding The Dead Sea Scrolls.* ed. H. Shanks. New York: Random House, 1992.

Schonfield, H. J. *The Passover Plot: A New Interpretation of the Life and Death of Jesus.* New York: Geis, 1966.

Schürer, Emil. *History of the Jewish People, in the Age of Jesus Christ.* Revised and edited by Geza Vermes, Fergus Miller, and Matthew Black. Edinburgh: T. & T. Clark, 1979.

Schweitzer, A. *The Quest Of The Historical Jesus: A Critical Study Of Its Progress From Reimarus To Wrede,* with a Preface by F. C. Burkitt; transl. W. Montgomery. New York 1910, reprint 1964.

Schweizer, E. *Jesus,* transl. D. E. Green (New Testament Library), London: 1971.

Schillebeeckx, E. *Jesus: An Experiment In Christology,* transl. H. Hoskins. New York: Seabury Press, 1979.

Shanks, Hershel. *Understanding The Dead Sea Scrolls.* New York: Random House, 1992.

Silberman, Neil Asher. *The Hidden Scrolls.* New York: Grosset/Putnam, 1994.

Smith, Morton. *Jesus the Magician.* New York: Harper & Row, 1978.

Singer, I. Ed. *The Jewish Encyclopedia.* New York: 1901—1906.

Sox, David. *The Gospel of Barnabas.* London: 1984.

Spong, John Shelby. *Resurrection: Myth or Reality?* San Franscisco: Harper, 1994.

Stauffer, Ethelbert. *Jesus and the Wilderness Community at Qumran.* Philadelphia: Fortress, 1964.

Stanton, Graham. *Gospel Truth? New Light on Jesus and the Gospels.* Valley Forge: Trinity Press, 1995.

Stendahl, K. *The School Of St. Matthew And Its Use Of The Old Testament.* Philadelphia: Fortress, 1968.

Stewart, James J. S. *The Life And Teaching Of Jesus Christ.* Edinburgh: Church of Scotland, 1933, 1957 and 1981.

Storr, Anthony. *Human Aggression.* Hammondsworth, Eng.: Penguin, 1975.

Stott, John R.W. *Involvement: Social and Sexual Relationships in the Modern World.* Old Tappan: Revell, 1985.

Taylor, Vincent. *The Gospel According to St. Mark.* Macmillan: 1952.

Tacitus. *Annals*

Thiering, Barbara. *Jesus and the Riddle of the Dead Sea Scrolls.* New York: Doubleday, 1992.

# Bibliography

Toombes, Lawrence E. *The Interpreter's Bible,* Nashville: Abingdon, 1971, 1980.

Vanderkam, James C. Articles in *Understanding the Dead Sea Scrolls,* ed. Hershel Shanks; New York: Random House, 1993.

Vermes, Geza. *Jesus The Jew: A Historian's Reading Of The Gospels.* 1973; reprinted New York: Collins, 1977. Vermes, Geza. *Jesus and the World of Judaism,* Philadelphia: Fortress, 1983.

Watson, Francis. *Paul, Judaism and the Gentiles.* Cambridge University Press, London & New York, 1986.

Westerholm, Stephen. *Paul, Judaism and the Gentiles.* Cambridge University Press, London & New York, 1986.

Wilson, A. N. *Jesus.* London: Flamingo Harper Collins, 1993.

Wilson, Edmund. *The Scrolls from the Dead Sea.* London: Collins, 1955.

Witherington III, Ben. *The Jesus Quest: The Third Search for the Jew of Nazareth.* Downers Grove, Illinois: InterVarsity Press, 1995.

*Acts of the Apostles: A Socio-Rhetorical Commentary.* Grand Rapids: Eerdmans, 1998.

Wright, N.T. *Who Was Jesus?* Grand Rapids: Eerdmans, 1992.

Zeitlin, Irving M. *Jesus And The Judaism Of His Time.* Cambridge: Polity Press, 1988.

Zeitlin, Solomon. *The Rise and Fall of the Judaean State.* Philadelphia: 1978.

# Index

Aaron, 45, 89, 159, 220
Abelard, Peter, 76, 80
Abgarus, 233, 246
Abortion, 200, 273
Abraham, 70, 120, 206, 236, 237, 247
   Children of, 118, 122, 279
Abu-Isa, 143
Abulafia of Spain, 143
Achaia, 266
Acts of the Apostles, 30, 31, 32, 34, 39-40, 45, 90, 113, 116, 133, 212, 218, 231, 233, 238, 239, 241, 248, 255, 264, 266, 272, 283
Adam, primal man, 241
Adamson, James, 50
Addai, 245
Agabus, 220, 233, 234
Agrippa I, 233
Agrippa II, 233

Albright, W.F., 92, 219
Alexander the Great, 36
Alexander, Philip, 181
Alexandria, 244, 266, 267
Allegro, John, 47, 48, 49, 96, 288
Amos, 273
Ananias, 246, 247
Ananus, high priest, 26, 65, 229, 232, 236, 243, 270
Angelophanies, 173
Anthony, Mark, 252
Anti-Semitism, 177, 179, 250, 253, 255, 257, 258, 264
Antichrist, 194
Antioch, 116
Antioch of Pisidia, 171
Antiochus Epiphanes, 20, 89, 225, 250
Antiquities: See Josephus, 26,

46, 79, 111, 229, 283
Aphroditus, Temple of, 134
Apocrypha, 103
Apollos, 127, 266, 267
Apostles, 32, 35, 72, 117, 153, 160, 172, 179, 238, 257, 261, 276
Apostles' Creed, 183
Aquila, 130, 266
Areopagus, 173, 214
Aretas, 142, 235
Aristobulus II, 251, 252
Aristotle, 199, 202
Arrian, 36
Asa, king of Judaea, 180
Assagioli, Roberto, 198
Athens, 264
Augustine, 206
Auschwitz, 71, 73, 80
Auswaks, A., 218
Babylon, 190
Bagatti, Bellarino, 92
Baigent, Michael, 9, 12, 13, 30, 48, 49, 92, 93, 94, 143, 218
Baillie, Donald M., 194
Balaam, 29
Balfour Agreement, 77
Baptism, 54, 60, 63, 115, 116, 119, 120, 129, 241, 246, 247, 249, 250, 263, 266
Barclay, William, 36, 41, 136, 138
Barmen, Council of, 75
Barnabas, 34, 116, 233, 267
Barnabas, Gospel of, 104, 112
Barnett, Paul, 41
Bartlett, John, 77
Bathsheba, 97
Beatitudes, the, 149, 150, 226
Beelzebub, 192
Belial, 62, 192, 193
Ben Chorin, 84, 85
Berdyaev, Nicolas, 75
Bernard of Clairvaux, 76, 80, 206
Bethany, 57, 135
Bethlehem, 200
Betz, Otto, 25, 40, 49, 62, 63, 64, 79
Biblical Archaeology Review, 14, 47
Biblical Archaeology Society, 14
Blake, William, 94
Blomberg, C.L., 36, 41, 108, 112
Blood controversy, 260
Bloom, Harold, 106
Bonhoeffer, Dietrich, 75
Booth, William, 162
Borg, Marcus, 20
Branch of David, 55
Brandon, S.G.F., 90, 91, 93, 287

Brothers of Jesus, 179, 244
Brown, Raymond, 92
Brown, Schuyler, 31, 40
Bruce, F.F., 237, 283
Buber, Martin, 84
Bultmann, Rudolf, 18, 23, 103, 212
Burrows, Millar, 48, 78
Caesar's household, 131, 234
Caesarea, 220, 233, 248
Caesars, 27, 139, 157, 278, 287
Caiaphas, 52, 286
Cairo Genizah, 28, 225
Caligula, 34, 35
Calvin, John, 76, 278
Cana, 94, 95
Candace, 248, 288
Capernaum, 122
Celibacy, 13, 67, 135
Cenchreae, harbour town of Corinth, 121
Centurions, 122, 129, 206
Cephas, 90, 117, 127, 172, 175, 178, 271
Chanukkah, 201
Charlesworth, J.H., 38, 41, 87, 94, 104, 111, 112, 153, 168
China, 269
Chrestus, 27, 130, 252
Christ Jesus, 121, 142, 256, 262, 276, 290
Christmas, 201

Christology, 37
Chronicles, First, 141
Chronicles, Second, 180
Church, 11, 12, 13, 16, 29, 32, 34, 35, 37, 39, 40, 51, 52, 55, 57, 58, 60, 62, 66, 69, 70, 72, 73, 74, 75, 78, 80, 84, 86, 91, 92, 99, 101, 104, 106, 113, 116, 117, 121, 125, 127, 129, 130, 133, 134, 135, 136, 142, 144, 146, 153, 155, 156, 157, 160, 161, 170, 172, 173, 177, 180, 181, 183, 199, 206, 215, 217, 218, 222, 223, 230, 231, 233, 234, 235, 236, 238, 239, 240, 241, 243, 244, 249, 252, 256, 257, 258, 259, 260, 261, 266, 267, 271, 272, 275, 279, 280, 283, 284, 286, 289, 290
Church Fathers, 73
Chwolsohn, Daniel, 84
Circumcision, 105, 106, 114, 115, 116, 119, 120, 122, 125, 131, 132, 241, 246, 247, 250, 257, 261, 264, 273, 288
Circumcision of non-Jews, 118, 121, 249, 270
Circumcision Party, 116, 261, 264, 270
Claudian Decree, 252, 266
Claudius, 27, 31, 130

Clement of Alexandria, 244
Clement of Rome, 243, 244
Cleopas, 98
Colossians, Epistle to the, 127, 134, 191, 196, 197
Colson, Charles, 208
Communion of the Lord's Supper, 259
Communism, 207, 269, 270
Constantine, 73, 142, 287
Cook, Edward, M., 56
Corinth, 134, 235, 266
Corinthians, 135
   First Epistle, 30, 35, 54, 69, 96, 113, 117, 119, 127, 129, 130, 133, 134, 135, 136, 147, 151, 157, 172, 173, 174, 175, 182, 191, 206, 214, 216, 235, 259, 260, 271
   Second Epistle, 59, 128, 129, 134, 181, 182, 193, 215, 216, 220, 235, 281
Cornelius, 116, 123
Cromwell, Oliver, 76
Cross, Frank Moore, 44, 45, 78
Crossan, J. Dominic, 92, 101, 107, 108, 145, 147, 148, 242, 243
Crossman, R., 163
Crusades, 76, 142
Cup of the Lord, 259, 260

Cynics, 98, 101, 102, 107, 148
Cyrus, of Persia, 52, 124
Damascus Document, 59, 62, 64, 84, 85, 261
Damascus Road, 117, 170, 216, 228, 275
Daniel, 52, 57, 173, 174, 191
David, king of Israel, 45, 52, 55, 64, 91, 97, 139, 140, 141, 154, 159, 162, 164, 169, 174, 180, 189, 204, 209, 216, 259, 262, 263
Davidic family, 209, 265
Davies, Margaret, 16, 23, 151, 152, 168
Dead Sea Scrolls, 8, 12, 13, 14, 23, 39, 40, 43, 44, 45, 48, 49, 51, 66, 67, 68, 70, 78, 79, 83, 87, 92, 93, 110, 111, 159, 168, 192, 201, 217, 218, 225, 243, 253, 255, 258, 261, 283, 288
Decapolis, 251
Decian persecution, 265
Declaration of Geneva, 200
Declaration of the Rights of a Child, 199
Delp, Alfred, 75
Delphi, 31
Dept. of Antiquities, 47
Desposyni, 155
Deuteronomy, 29, 53, 98, 100, 254
Devil, 64, 122, 183, 188, 190,

306

192, 193, 196, 225
Diaspora, 72, 125, 129, 237, 260, 267
Dio Cassius, 36
Diocletian, 265
Diogenes of Sinope, 107
Dispersion, 267
Disraeli family, 77
Dodd, C.H., 69, 152
Domitian, 26, 37, 234, 252, 265
Driver, Godfrey R., 44, 47
Drummond, Henry, 133
Dunant, Jean Henri, 157
Dunn, James D.G., 115, 117, 137, 138
East Timor, 269
Easter, 82, 171, 172, 176
Ebionites, 114, 130, 239, 240, 241, 245, 266, 267, 272
Ecclesiastes, 151
Ecole Biblique, 47
Edessa, 234, 246
Edessenes, 245
Egypt, 100, 103, 139, 223, 237, 252
Eighteen Benedictions, 40, 73
Einstein, Albert, 20
Eisenman, Robert, 13, 14, 20, 45, 46, 49, 50, 52, 53, 55, 56, 58, 65, 69, 70, 74, 76, 78, 79, 91, 93, 111, 143, 144, 145, 154, 203, 206,

217, 218, 219, 220, 221, 222, 223, 224, 225, 226, 227, 228, 229, 230, 231, 232, 233, 234, 235, 236, 237, 238, 239, 240, 241, 243, 244, 245, 246, 247, 248, 249, 250, 252, 253, 254, 255, 256, 257, 258, 259, 261, 262, 263, 264, 265, 266, 268, 270, 272, 277, 283, 285, 286, 287, 288
Eliezer, Rabbi, 29
Elijah, 87, 174, 228, 230
Elizabeth, mother of John the Baptist, 63
Elymas, the sorcerer, 96
Emmor, 237
Endor, 190
Engels, 165
Epaphroditus, 233, 234, 235
Ephesians, Epistle to, 133, 196, 197, 278
Ephesus, 37
Ephron the Hittite, 237
Epictetus, 148
Epiphanius, 224, 228, 229
Esdraelon, Plain of, 153
Essenes, 49, 54, 63, 86, 87
Esther, Book of, 43
Esther, Queen, 139
Ethiopia, 248
Ethiopian eunuch, 220, 246, 263, 288

Eucharist, 259, 260
Euodia(s), 136
Euphrates, 234
Eusebius, 40, 41, 155, 167, 223, 224, 225, 236, 248, 284
Exodus, 174, 220, 274
Ezekiel, 71, 132, 173, 190, 262, 263, 279
Ezra, 47
Fascism, 197
Feldman, L., 125
Ferdinand, king of Spain, 156
Festival of Tabernacles, 45
Fitzmyer, Joseph, 51, 79
Five Gospels, The, 15, 102, 103, 106
Flusser, David, 52, 82, 86, 99, 110, 111, 203
Food laws, 273
Forgery, 103, 104
Form Criticism, 17
Fourth Gospel, 33, 37, 38, 39, 41, 172, 274
Fourth Philosophy, 231
Fox, Robin Lane, 30, 40, 194, 202, 204, 209
France, R.T., 106
Frazer, James, 25, 40
Fredriksen, Paula, 34, 41, 72, 80, 113
Freud, Sigmund, 197, 198
Friedlander, Gerald, 82, 110

Funk, Robert W., 15, 17, 108
Galatians, Epistle to, 61, 62, 69, 117, 118, 119, 121, 133, 174, 214, 215, 216, 221, 244, 257, 271
Galerius, 145
Galilee, 20, 88, 89, 94, 98, 107, 109, 128, 141, 153, 155, 171, 176, 180, 212, 223, 226, 230, 251, 255
Gallio, 31
Gamaliel, 40, 72, 73, 84, 86, 87, 89, 276
Gamaliel II, 40, 73, 86
Gamble, H., 242, 283
Gandhi, Mahatmi, 148
Geiger, Abraham, 84
Genesis, 189, 194, 195, 247
Geneva Conventions, 157
Gentiles, 53, 72, 116, 118, 120, 121, 122, 123, 124, 125, 126, 131, 132, 137, 146, 147, 158, 159, 160, 166, 175, 206, 225, 240, 246, 248, 253, 255, 256, 261, 262, 264, 271, 272, 278, 279, 280
*Globe and Mail*, Toronto, 218
Gnostic dualism, 106, 107, 128, 192
Gnostics, 31, 49, 103, 193, 242
Golb, Norman, 51, 69, 70
Gollwitzer, Helmut, 119
Gomorrah, 189

Gospels, The, 11, 13, 15, 16, 30, 31, 33, 34, 35, 36, 39, 45, 51, 82, 99, 101, 102, 103, 108, 116, 122, 147, 154, 179, 182, 204, 205, 212, 215, 224, 226, 230, 239, 244, 250, 255, 258, 265
Goulder, Michael, 181
Graetz, Heinrich, 86
Graham, Billy, 149
Grant, Michael, 11, 30, 31, 59, 93
Gruber, Dean Heinrich, 75
Habakkuk Pesher, 257, 258, 259
Hagner, Donald A., 84, 110
Haman of Persia, 252
Hanina ben Dosa, 87, 88
Harnack, Adolf von, 54, 103
Hasidim, 87, 88
Hasmonean dynasty, 44, 45, 60, 251
Hays, Richard B., 15, 23, 102
Hebrews, Epistle to, 19, 40, 46, 89, 117, 119, 159, 169, 196, 267, 275
Hebron, 237
Hegesippus, 224, 225, 226, 229, 265, 282, 284
Helen, Queen of Edessa, 234, 246, 247
Hellenism, 20, 107, 138, 168, 191, 201, 250

Henry, Matthew, 203
Henry, Patrick, 68
Herod Agrippa I, 233
Herod the Great, 70, 226, 252
Herod, Antipas, 65, 95, 107, 142, 148, 153, 219, 272
Hiel (1 Kings 16:34), 44
Hillel, Rabbi, 84, 85, 100, 149
Hippocratic Oath, 200
Hitler, Adolf, 75, 76, 140, 188
Holocaust, 33, 75, 76, 252, 270, 279
Holtzmann, H.J., 103
Holy Spirit, 32, 38, 63, 65, 106, 116, 132, 182, 216, 241, 261, 262, 263, 266
Honi, 88, 228, 230
Honorius, 151
Hoover, Roy W., 15, 102
Horowitz, Michael, 269
Hugenots, 78, 156
Hunter, A. M., 38, 41, 255, 283
Hunter, S. F., 234
Hussein, Saddam, 274
Hyrcanus, John, 251
Idumaeans, 232, 233
Inquisition, the Spanish, 156
Irenaeus, 39, 114
Isaiah, 52, 55, 57, 97, 99, 118, 119, 124, 125, 132, 137, 141, 159, 160, 190, 247, 249, 262, 274, 280

Islam, 68, 104, 166
Israel, 29, 56, 59, 62, 63, 65, 67, 70, 71, 72, 76, 78, 82, 95, 97, 100, 119, 121, 122, 123, 124, 125, 126, 132, 139, 140, 141, 142, 143, 148, 152, 153, 154, 158, 159, 160, 164, 166, 169, 177, 179, 189, 190, 191, 192, 201, 209, 221, 223, 231, 236, 237, 238, 251, 253, 255, 261, 262, 263, 264, 274, 276, 279
Israelites, 89, 91, 140, 220, 254, 257, 260, 273
Izates, 246, 247, 249
Jacob, 126, 206, 237, 238
James the Just, brother of Jesus, 13, 14, 26, 45, 49, 66, 96, 105, 106, 172, 205, 218, 222, 223, 224, 225, 226, 227, 229, 236, 238, 239, 240, 243, 244, 245, 250, 266, 268, 270, 271, 272, 273, 277, 283, 286, 288
  his non-Zealot pacifism, 270
James VI, king of Scotland, 142
James, apostle and son of Zebedee, 37, 146, 199, 205, 232, 259, 272, 288
James, Epistle of, 50, 69, 127, 228, 230, 271, 273, 278
James, son of Judas the Galilean, 231

Jamnia (or Jabney or Yavne), 28
Janneus, Alexander, 45, 86
Jaspers, Karl, 187, 201
Jeremiah, 97, 100, 189, 221, 260, 263
Jeremias, Joachim, 103, 112, 152
Jericho, 43, 44, 227, 228, 238, 254
Jerusalem, 21, 26, 28, 34, 43, 55, 58, 61, 66, 67, 69, 70, 71, 73, 74, 75, 82, 86, 87, 91, 97, 109, 111, 116, 121, 124, 125, 141, 143, 144, 153, 154, 163, 166, 170, 171, 176, 180, 190, 204, 212, 215, 219, 222, 223, 226, 228, 229, 231, 232, 233, 235, 236, 237, 238, 240, 248, 250, 253, 254, 255, 256, 257, 260, 261, 262, 271, 272, 275, 282, 286, 287
Jerusalem Council, 240, 246, 249, 271, 272
Jerusalem Post, 218
Jesus Christ, 12, 17, 22, 45, 50, 113, 118, 127, 129, 130, 162, 166, 169, 179, 183, 185, 195, 206, 207, 212, 215, 221, 223, 262, 267, 275, 277
  His death, 33, 61, 90, 171, 216, 287
  His deity, 38

His name, 14, 45, 46, 47, 50, 54, 57, 129
His resurrection, 169-183
of Nazareth, 11, 28, 32, 46, 82, 86, 109, 113, 127, 141, 176, 203, 205, 208, 215, 230, 269, 273
teachings of, 20, 105, 145, 147, 151, 163, 226, 241, 242
Jesus Party, 231
Jesus Seminar, 15, 16, 18, 20, 33, 102, 106, 108, 144, 152, 211, 212, 213, 215
Jesus, son of Ananias, 47
Jewish War (66-70 C.E.), 25, 56, 144, 217, 222, 231, 250, 286
Jews, 11, 26, 27, 46, 51, 52, 66, 67, 68, 71, 72, 73, 75, 76, 77, 78, 79, 81, 90, 93, 118, 119, 120, 122, 125, 126, 128, 129, 130, 132, 140, 143, 156, 157, 159, 163, 165, 166, 174, 175, 179, 180, 192, 197, 216, 219, 222, 229, 232, 235, 236, 237, 240, 250, 251, 252, 253, 254, 256, 257, 260, 262, 264, 265, 278, 279, 280, 283
Joanna, 172
Job, 173, 190, 290
Joel, 261, 262, 264

John the Baptist, 45, 49, 54, 56, 62, 63, 64, 65, 97, 118, 122, 129, 141, 149, 249, 261
John, the Apostle, 37, 39, 41, 51, 146, 199, 232, 259, 271
the First Epistle, 69, 107, 127, 191, 275
the Gospel of, 11, 33, 34, 35, 38, 39, 40, 41, 61, 69, 88, 90, 91, 96, 98, 106, 109, 122, 137, 147, 148, 151, 152, 153, 155, 161, 164, 175, 179, 180, 192, 206, 221, 224, 231, 241, 253, 254, 255, 259, 274, 277, 289
Johnson, Luke Timothy, 21, 211, 212, 213, 214, 215, 216, 217, 282
Johnson, Paul, 66, 79, 283
Jonah, 97
Jones, Frank, 33
Jones, Jimmy, 58
Jones, Martin Lloyd, 206
Jordan, 141, 144, 232
Joseph (Old Test.), 165, 237
Joseph of Arimathea, 179, 180
Josephus, 25, 26, 27, 46, 49, 63, 73, 79, 80, 82, 89, 92, 107, 111, 142, 222, 223, 225, 229, 231, 232, 234, 235, 236, 237, 239, 246,

250, 251, 252, 253, 256, 258, 282, 286
Joses, brother of Jesus, 155
Joshua, 44, 46, 190, 204, 223, 238, 251, 254
Joshua's speech, 237, 238
Judaea, 27, 34, 41, 43, 44, 45, 52, 56, 59, 63, 67, 80, 86, 94, 107, 109, 110, 111, 115, 124, 128, 137, 141, 144, 167, 180, 212, 222, 223, 234, 237, 252, 256, 270
Judaism, 18, 20, 23, 41, 43, 51, 58, 59, 62, 67, 68, 72, 73, 74, 78, 82, 87, 91, 100, 102, 104, 107, 110, 111, 112, 116, 117, 120, 121, 124, 125, 126, 136, 144, 166, 168, 188, 191, 192, 194, 195, 221, 222, 231, 246, 249, 251, 253, 258, 265, 266, 267, 270, 272, 274, 281
Judaism, conversion to, 120, 234, 237, 247
Judaistic Christians, 73, 114, 266, 272
Judaizers, 118, 131
Judas Iscariot, 53, 91, 104, 107, 177, 178, 179, 180
Judas the Galilean, 89, 230, 231, 236
Judas Thomas the Twin, 105
Judas, brother of Jesus, 179

Jude, 40, 69, 179
Jung, Carl G., 157, 278
Justin Martyr, 114
Kaminka, A., 82
Kandake, 247, 248
Kazantzakis, Nikos, 204
Kenedaeos, 247, 248
Kerygma, Apostolic summary of the Gospel, 131, 170, 267
King, Martin Luther, 148, 269
Kingdom of God, 16, 20, 32, 89, 102, 121, 122, 140, 141, 142, 143, 145, 147, 151, 152, 153, 154, 156, 157, 159, 161, 162, 163, 166, 167, 171, 183, 265, 274, 287
Kingship of Jesus, 160
Kirkegaard, Soren, 186, 187
Klausner, J., 82
Kloppenborg, John, 108
Kohler, K., 86
Kokhba, 44, 70, 74, 119, 143, 144
Koranic Law, 270
Koresh, David, 58, 68
Kung, Hans, 110
Lachmann, Karl, 103
Lapide, 114, 125, 264
Lapide, Pinchas, 82
LaSor, W. Sanford, 79
Last Supper, 36, 53, 101, 152
Law of Moses, 114, 120, 222,

250, 266, 270, 279
Lean, Garth, 168, 284
Leary, Timothy, 188
Leigh, Richard, 12, 13, 30, 48, 49, 74, 76, 92, 93, 94, 143, 154, 204, 218
Lenin, 165
Levinson, Peter, 82
Levites, 61
Levitical Law, 60, 100
Lewis, C.S., 207, 268, 269
Liar, 45, 49, 93, 262
  Man of the Lie, 74, 257
  or 'Spouter', 261
Lichtenberg, Bernard, 75
Licinius, 145
Lightfoot, R.H., 39
Lincoln, Henry, 12, 74, 76, 154, 204
Linnemann, Eta, 18
Logos, 37, 255
Longenecker, Richard, 135
Lord's Supper, 260
Lucian of Samosata, 28
Luke, the Gospel of, 16, 30, 31, 32, 33, 34, 35, 36, 37, 39, 52, 56, 57, 59, 60, 62, 63, 64, 69, 84, 86, 88, 89, 90, 93, 96, 98, 103, 115, 122, 133, 142, 149, 160, 162, 166, 167, 172, 175, 177, 178, 215, 219, 224, 226, 231, 232, 235, 237, 238, 239, 245, 247, 249, 253, 288
Lundemann, E., 288
Lunn, Arnold, 168, 284
Luther, Martin, 76, 142, 278
Luz, U., 110
Maccabean Revolt, 20, 44, 251
Maccabees, 89, 91
Maccabeus, 44
Maccabeus, John & Simon, Judas and Mattathias, 44
Maccoby, Hyam, 84, 113, 114, 116, 117, 119, 120, 159, 191, 192, 275
Mack, Burton L., 18, 20, 101, 102, 103, 105, 107, 108, 144, 148
Magdalene, Mary, 20, 49, 104, 135, 155, 172, 204
Magna Carta, 139
Magus, Simon, 21
Manual of Discipline, 53, 55, 60, 64, 159, 260
Mao Tse Tung, 103, 165, 269
Mark, Gospel of, 12, 16, 33, 34, 35, 36, 37, 39, 40, 63, 64, 69, 88, 90, 95, 96, 97, 103, 106, 107, 115, 119, 123, 133, 135, 141, 146, 148, 152, 154, 155, 162, 167, 172, 178, 179, 180, 192, 215, 224, 226, 227, 241, 244, 253, 254, 267, 281
Marshall, Howard I., 17

Marshall, Paul, 269
Martha and Mary, 135
Marx, Karl, 165, 197, 198
Marxism, 197
Mary, mother of Jesus
    her virginity, 166, 183, 244, 246
Masada, 53, 58, 66, 232, 236
Mattathias, ben Joseph, 25
Matthew, the Gospel of, 16, 33, 34, 35, 36, 37, 39, 51, 54, 56, 59, 60, 62, 63, 64, 69, 83, 84, 85, 86, 88, 90, 97, 99, 100, 101, 103, 113, 122, 124, 129, 134, 135, 141, 149, 150, 151, 153, 154, 160, 162, 166, 167, 172, 177, 178, 189, 194, 198, 208, 213, 215, 222, 224, 226, 245, 250, 253, 254, 269, 273, 289
May, Rollo, 198
McDowell, Josh, 85, 94, 194
McKnight, S., 41
Meier, John P., 26, 92, 103, 213, 245
Melchizedek, 158, 159
Melville, Andrew, 142
Menachem, 236
Mennonites, 78, 151
Messiah, 26, 29, 52, 53, 54, 55, 56, 68, 78, 82, 94, 115, 148, 154, 155, 158, 159, 162, 164, 229, 266, 280, 281, 286
Messiahs, 53, 148, 159
Messiahship, 114, 241, 286
Messianism, 250
Michael, 59, 143, 191
Midrash, 35, 174, 180
Miracles, 39, 95, 192, 227, 228, 229, 230
Mishnah, 236
Mitchell, Stephen, 20
Monobazus, 247
Montefiore, Claude G., 81
Montefiore, H. W., 267
Moses of Crete, 143
Moses, giver of the Law, 82, 84, 96, 118, 149, 174, 204, 220, 223, 240, 241, 274
Mount Gerazim, 251
Muggeridge, Malcolm, 207
Muhammad, the Prophet, 104
Muslims, 76, 143, 156, 166, 220, 248
Nag Hammadi, 103, 242
Nahum, 83
Napoleon Bonaparte, 140
Nathan, 97
Nathanael, 91
Nazarenes, 73, 91, 93, 266
Nazareth, 11, 28, 32, 46, 57, 82, 86, 88, 91, 92, 93, 109, 127, 141, 153, 176, 203, 205, 208, 215, 230, 269, 273

Nazi, 33, 75, 191
Nebuchudnezzar, 139
Nelson, Culver, 33
Nero, 27, 35, 37, 74, 234, 252, 265
Neusner, Jacob, 16, 181
New Covenant, 100, 221, 259, 260
Newton, Isaac, 19, 20
Newton, John, 206
Nicodemus, 180
Niemoller, Martin, 75
Nietzsche, Friedrich, 186, 187, 197
Niger, 232, 233
Nineveh, 97
Noachic covenant, 120
Noah, 189
Nozrim, 28, 91
Oblias, 225
Oedipus, 198
Onias the Righteous, 228, 230
Ophel, 237
Origen, 244, 265
Original Sin, 188
Palestine, 28, 38, 39, 117, 143, 230, 244, 255
Papias, 40, 244
Parables of Jesus, 152, 165, 265
Pascal, Blaise, 206
Passover, 29, 204, 225, 260
Patmos, 37
Paul, the apostle, 13, 21, 30, 31, 34, 35, 46, 49, 51, 59, 61, 62, 68, 69, 72, 73, 84, 93, 96, 113, 115, 117, 118, 119, 121, 125, 127, 128, 129, 130, 131, 132, 133, 134, 135, 136, 144, 147, 151, 160, 169, 171, 172, 173, 174, 175, 181, 182, 190, 191, 192, 196, 203, 205, 214, 216, 220, 221, 222, 232, 233, 234, 235, 240, 241, 243, 244, 245, 246, 249, 250, 252, 256, 257, 258, 259, 260, 262, 263, 264, 266, 271, 272, 274, 275, 276, 277, 278, 281, 286, 287
  the Benjamite, 169, 250
Paulinism, 113, 219, 222, 258, 266, 268, 272, 274
Peck, Scott, 193
Pella, 144
Pentecost, Day of, 35, 123, 154, 170, 176, 256
Perea, 144, 232
Peregrinus, 28
Perrin, Norman, 112
Peter, the apostle, 34, 35, 37, 51, 69, 89, 106, 113, 116, 123, 129, 170, 175, 205, 238, 243, 244, 256, 261, 267, 272, 286
  First Epistle, 21, 69, 119, 129, 260
  Second Epistle, 127, 160,

Pharisees, 46, 54, 57, 60, 73, 82, 83, 84, 86, 97, 99, 100, 102, 107, 115, 123, 126, 173, 225, 238, 251, 253, 254, 270, 275, 277
Pharoahs, 139
Philip, Gospel of, 104
Philip, the evangelist, 232, 233, 247, 248, 249, 263, 288
Philip, the Strategos, 233
Philippians, Epistle of, 50, 69, 127, 129, 136, 171, 216, 234, 276
Phillips, J. B., 7
Phillips, Wendel, 19
Philo, 87, 92, 267, 288
Phinehas, 89
Phoebe, 136
Pilate, Pontius, 11, 26, 27, 90, 127, 147, 160, 164, 176, 183, 254
Piltdown Man, 16
Pinnock, Clark, 197, 198
Pliny the Elder, 63, 67
Pliny the Younger, 27, 145, 265
Polkinghorne, John, 19, 20
Polycarp, 39, 145, 287
Pompey, 88, 237, 251
Pope, Alexander, 186
Poppea, wife of Nero, 252
Priscilla and Aquila, 130, 266
Protoevangelicum Jacobi, 244

Two Apocalypses, 244
Proverbs, 128, 187, 290
Psalms, Book of, 43, 63, 64, 158, 159, 177
Pseudepigrapha, 43
Pseudoclementines, 226, 239, 241, 243
  Homilies, 243
  Recognitions, 220, 227, 228, 238, 241, 243
Ptolemy, son of Abubos, 44
Q (Quelle) document, 33, 102, 103, 108, 152, 241, 243
Qimron, Elisha, 14
Quakers, 78, 151
Quast, Kevin, 38
Quirinius, 231
Qumran, 8, 14, 21, 39, 43, 44, 45, 46, 48, 52, 53, 54, 55, 56, 57, 58, 59, 60, 61, 62, 63, 64, 65, 66, 67, 69, 71, 83, 85, 86, 87, 91, 93, 94, 124, 143, 144, 192, 193, 218, 224, 225, 230, 250, 253, 259, 260, 262, 270
Rabbinic tradition, 151
Rahab, 254
Ramsay, Michael, 199
Red Cross, International, 71, 157
Reformation, 76, 142, 269
Reimarus, Hermann S., 90, 115, 286
Renaissance, 269

Renan, Ernest, 87, 198
Resurrection, 20, 30, 31, 35, 49, 56, 57, 61, 69, 72, 73, 82, 84, 95, 96, 101, 113, 115, 131, 152, 159, 169, 170, 171, 172, 173, 174, 176, 180, 181, 182, 183, 212, 214, 215, 216, 228, 267, 272, 279
Revelation, Book of, 71, 159, 164, 188, 191, 193, 194, 253, 255, 281
Rhode Island, 77, 161
Richardson, Alan, 194
Robinson, J. A. T., 37
Robinson, James, 14
Robinson, John, 221
Roman army, 66, 126
Roman authorities, 90, 122, 144, 147, 286
Romans, Epistle to, 78, 120, 125, 126, 127, 128, 132, 134, 136, 137, 144, 160, 161, 169, 182, 186, 190, 215, 216, 253, 257, 263, 274, 277
Rome, 26, 27, 49, 59, 73, 74, 88, 89, 90, 125, 130, 131, 133, 139, 144, 145, 157, 199, 231, 233, 234, 237, 247, 250, 251, 252, 265, 266, 270, 278
Rosenzweig, Franz, 125
Roth, John K., 73, 74, 76

Rothschild family, 77
Rubenstein, Richard L., 71, 73, 74
Russia, 75
Rwanda, 269
Sabbath, 46, 59, 60, 62, 100, 114, 116
Sacrifices, 157, 260, 274, 275, 278
Sadducees, 57, 73, 83, 84, 115, 238, 254
Safrai, Shmeul, 144
Salome, 172
Salvation Army, 59, 162
Samaria, 124, 251
Samaritan, 53, 61, 135, 192, 199, 232, 251
Samuel, 97, 140, 190
Sanders, E.P., 16, 18, 102, 151, 152, 226, 265
Sanhedrin, 28, 89, 236, 237, 252
Satan, 126, 188, 190, 191, 192, 193, 194, 195, 196, 270
Saul of Tarsus, 169, 205, 228, 238, 239, 247, 250
Saul, king of Israel, 139, 190
Schiffman, Lawrence H., 51, 83, 85, 120, 217, 260
Schoenthal, Rhea, 37
Schonfield, Hugh, 96, 204
Schweitzer, Albert, 17, 25, 122
*Scotsman*, The, 219

Scribes, 97, 99, 129, 192, 225, 254, 277
Scythopolis, 251
Second Revolt, 251, 265
Selma, 148
Sepphoris, 92, 107, 231
Septuagint, 46
Serene of Syria, 143
Sermon on the Mount, 82
Shabbetai Tzevi, 143
Shaftesbury, Lord, 201
Shakespeare, William, 190
Shammai, Rabbi, 85, 100
Shanks, Hershel, 14, 47, 48, 217
Shelley, Percy B., 163
Shemoneh Esreh, 40, 86
Sicarii, 74, 231, 250, 271
Sidon, 123
Silas, 232, 233
Silberman, Neil Asher, 14, 46, 59, 66, 67, 68, 69, 70, 144, 145, 203, 206, 270
Simeon bar Cleophas, 265
Simeon bar Kochba (or Kokhba), 44, 70, 74, 265
Simeon, Niger, 233
Simon Iscariot, 231
Simon Peter, 35, 106, 175, 176
Simon the Cananaean, 90, 231
Simon the magician, 96
Simon the Zealot, 90, 231
Simon, brother of Jesus, 155

Sixtus IV, Pope, 156
Smellie, Alexander, 142
Smith, Morton, 94, 204
Smyrna, 39, 143, 287
Sodom, 189
Solomon, king of Israel, 45, 70, 140, 141, 158, 204
Son
    Son of God, 51, 52, 57, 109, 117, 156, 158, 163, 169, 174, 207, 209
    Son of Man, 52, 102, 108, 146, 154, 165, 167, 208, 215, 225, 226, 227, 266
    Son of the Most High, 51, 52
    Sons of Darkness, 53, 59, 68, 192
    Sons of Light, 51, 68
    Sons of the Devil, 64
Sorcery, 29
Sox, David, 104
Spong, John S., 35, 170, 171, 172, 175, 176, 177, 179, 180, 182
Stalin, Josef, 140
Stanton, Graham, 29
Stephen, martyr, 170, 176, 205, 206, 226, 232, 235, 236, 237, 238, 239, 276, 287, 288
Stewart, James S., 36
Stoics, 148

Stoker, William D., 103
Storr, Anthony, 185
Stott, John, 200
Streeter, B.H., 103
Stuhlmacher, Peter, 137
Sudan, 269
Suetonius, 27, 36, 130
Suffering Servant, 55, 109, 118, 159, 249, 282
Synagogue of Freedmen, 236
Synoptic Gospels, 16, 38, 69, 147, 162, 215, 232, 241, 243
Syntyche, 136
Syria, 251
Syro-Phoenician woman, 123
Tabernacles, Feast of, 176
Tacitus, 27, 36, 125, 252, 256
Tarsus, 137, 169, 238, 245, 247
Taylor, Vincent, 137
Teacher of Righteousness, 13, 45, 49, 62, 64, 65, 225, 230, 243
Teicher, J.L., 14, 49
Temple of Jerusalem, 34, 38, 43, 45, 61, 69, 70, 71, 115, 118, 125, 129, 154, 158, 215, 221, 222, 225, 237, 238, 252, 254, 260, 275, 286
Terrorism, 161, 165
Testimonium Flavianum, 26, 229

Thaddaeus, 245
Theodotus, 237
Theophanies, 173, 174
Theophilus, 30, 32
Theresa, Mother, 161
Thessalonians
    First Epistle, 69, 130, 256
    Second Epistle, 134
Thiering, Barbara, 14, 20, 49, 94, 155, 217
Thomas, Gospel of, 15, 102, 103, 104, 106, 153, 242
Thomas, the Apostle, 35, 96, 136, 245, 267
Tiberias, city of, 107
Tiberias, emperor, 36
Tiberias, governor, 224
Time magazine, 37, 82, 209, 211
Timothy, 121, 290
    First Epistle, 16, 17, 246
    Second Epistle, 162, 198, 203, 268, 289, 290
Titus, 121
Titus, emperor, 26, 66
Toombs, Lawrence E., 168
Torah, 52, 60, 62, 83, 84, 99, 136, 274
*Toronto Star*, The, 33
Torrance, T.F., 289
Trajan, 27, 145, 155, 252, 265
Transfiguration, 174, 212, 228
Twelve Disciples, the, 104, 108,

117, 148, 172, 175, 178, 272
Twelve tribes, 140, 164, 255
Tyre, King of, 190
Ulla, 29
United Nations, 199
Uzziah, King of Israel, 45, 97
Vanderkam, J.C., 14, 48, 159
Vatican, 8, 47, 48, 143, 157, 218, 288
Vaux, Roland, de, Fr., 47, 48
Vermes, Geza, 18, 20, 23, 47, 56, 81, 86, 87, 88, 94, 181, 208
Vespasian, emperor, 26, 66, 253
Victoria, queen, 139, 156
Virgin birth, 114, 171, 194, 200, 241
Virginity
    Mary, mother of Jesus, 244
    See also James, brother of Jesus, 244
Walsh, Chad, 268
War Scroll, 59, 143, 192, 250
Watson, Francis, 131
Watt, Isaac, 157
Weiss, Bernard, 103
Wesley, John, 206, 278
Wicked priest, 45, 49, 65, 243
Wilberforce, William, 148
Wilke, Christian, 103
Williams, Roger, 77, 161
Wilson, A.N., 39, 87, 93, 94, 95, 96, 255

Wilson, Bill, 85, 194
Wilson, Edmund, 47
Winter, Paul, 84
Wise, Michael, 45, 46, 52, 53, 55, 56, 69
Witherington III, Ben, 102, 248
Wordsworth, William, 163
World War II, 75, 77
Women: the views of Jesus and Paul, 135, 136
Wrede, William, 115
Wright brothers, 19
Wright, N.T., 15, 170, 180, 211, 213
Yadin, Yigael, 66
Yesha, Yeshu'a and Yehoshua, 46, 47, 223
Yohanan ben Zacchai, Rabbi, 253
Yom Kippur, 228
Yudghan, Juda, 143
Yutang, Lin, 208
Zachaeus, tax gatherer, 149
Zacharias, father of John the Baptist, 64
Zaddik, 224, 225
Zadokite, Zadokim, 44, 60, 61, 65, 91
Zahn, T., 283
Zakkai, Rabbi Yochanan ben, 73
Zealots, 58, 73, 74, 89, 90, 91,

320

93, 94, 126, 143, 145, 222, 231, 232, 235, 270, 281, 287
Zebedee, sons of, 146, 154, 205, 272, 288
Zechariah, 55, 124, 159, 166, 177, 179, 190, 262
Zedekiah, 258
Zeitlin, Irving, 38, 84, 87, 91
Zeitlin, Solomon, 86, 114
Zion, 76, 126, 158, 164
Zionism, 261